THE HERO'S GUIDE TO Being an Outlaw

THE HERO'S GUIDES

Book 1: The Hero's Guide to Saving Your Kingdom

Book 2: The Hero's Guide to Storming the Castle

Book 3: The Hero's Guide to Being an Outlaw

THE HERO'S GUIDE TO Being AN Outlaw

Written by

CHRISTOPHER HEALY

With drawings by

TODD HARRIS

WALDEN POND PRESS
An Imprint of HarperCollins*Publishers*

Walden Pond Press is an imprint of HarperCollins Publishers.
Walden Pond Press and the skipping stone logo are trademarks and registered trademarks of Walden Media, LLC.

For information address HarperCollins Children's Books, a division of HarperCollins Publishers, 195 Broadway, New York, NY 10007.
www.harpercollinschildrens.com

Library of Congress Cataloging-in-Publication Data
Healy, Christopher, 1972– author.
The hero's guide to being an outlaw / written by Christopher Healy ; with drawings by Todd Harris.
pages cm
Summary: "Posters plastered across the thirteen kingdoms are saying that Briar Rose has been murdered—and the four Princes Charming (Prince Liam, Prince Frederic, Prince Duncan, and Prince Gustav) are the prime suspects. In a desperate attempt to clear their names, they discover that Briar's murder is just one part of a nefarious plot to take control of all thirteen kingdoms—a plot that will lead to the doorstep of an eerily familiar fortress for a final showdown with an eerily familiar enemy"— Publisher's description.
ISBN 978-0-06-211849-3 (pbk.)
1. Characters and characteristics in literature—Juvenile fiction. 2. Heroes—Juvenile fiction. 3. Princes—Juvenile fiction. 4. Fairy tales. 5. Humorous stories. 6. Characters in literature—Fiction. 7. Heroes—Fiction. 8. Princes—Fiction. 9. Fairy tales.
PZ7.H34462 Heb 2014 2013362529
[Fic] CIP
AC

Typography by Amy Ryan
19 20 BRR 10 9 8 7 6 5
❖
First paperback edition, 2015

To Charlotte, Jonah, Jenn, and Stu

TABLE OF CONTENTS

MAP OF THE THIRTEEN KINGDOMS

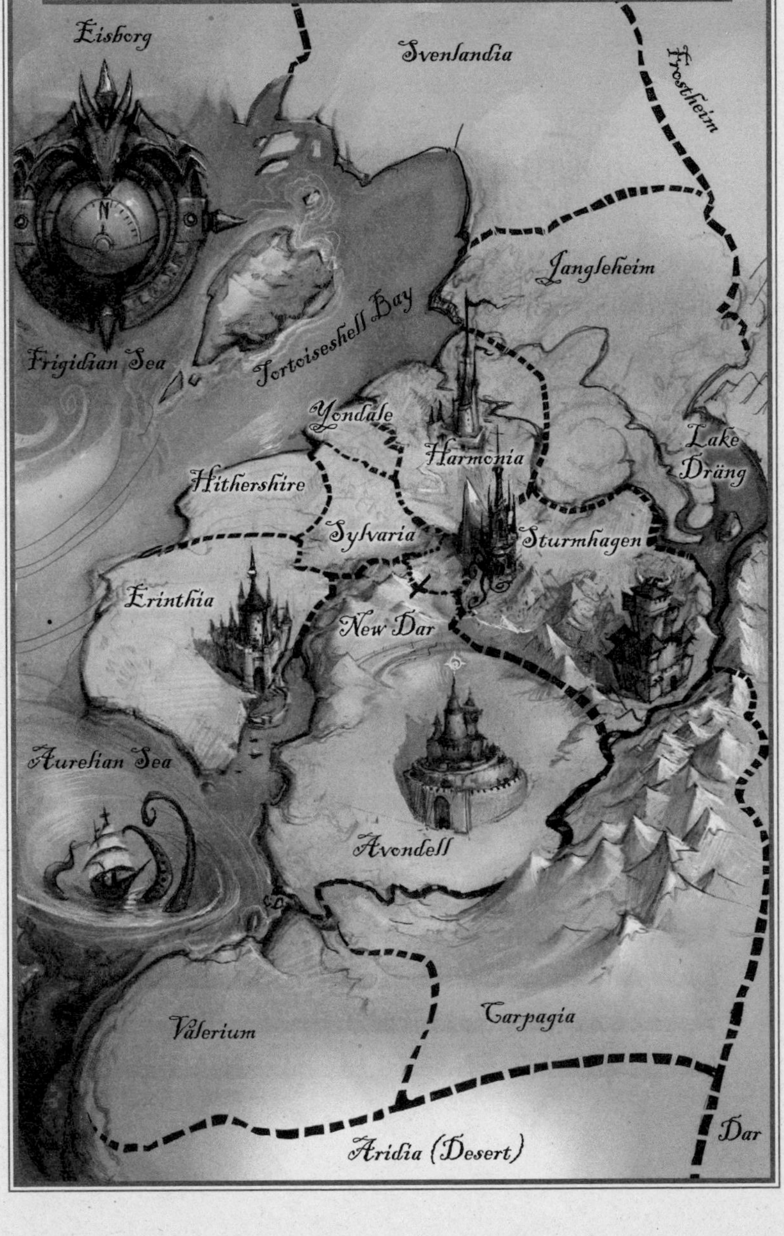

PROLOGUE

THINGS YOU DON'T KNOW ABOUT OUTLAWS

Outlaws have too many feathers in their hats.

Outlaws are allergic to seafood.

Outlaws never forget to floss.

Oh, and outlaws are people who are hunted down because they have been accused of terrible crimes.

Okay, I suppose it's possible you knew that last bit already. But if so, then you may be wondering, "What's with all the outlaw stuff? This is a book about the League of Princes, right? Those guys are *heroes*. Or at least hero-*ish*."

And after reading the first two books of this series (which might be a good idea before you go any further with this one), yes, you'd have every reason to assume that the famed Princes Charming—Liam, Frederic, Duncan, and

Gustav—would always stand firmly on the right side of the law. First they saved their kingdoms from a vengeful witch, and then they stormed a castle to snatch a dangerously powerful magic item out of the hands of the Bandit King. These princes are definitely good guys.

And yet, in this book, they become outlaws. In fact, it was only a few months after the aforementioned castle storming that the entire League found their faces on Wanted posters all across the Thirteen Kingdoms.

Before you start crying "Spoiler!" let me point out that you would have found out about the whole Wanted poster thing in Chapter 4 anyway. And seriously, the title of the book kind of gives it away, doesn't it? If I wanted to give you a real spoiler, I would have mentioned the fiasco that occurs in Chapter 16—Frederic struggling for air beneath pounding ocean waves, Gustav struggling to pry open the powerful jaws of a sea serpent, Liam struggling to locate his friends amid the bobbing wreckage of their ship, and Duncan struggling to remove his head from a bucket of chum.

But let's not get distracted. Because that whole shipwreck nightmare never would have happened if the Princes Charming hadn't managed to get themselves branded as outlaws. And *that* would never have happened if they'd actually managed to succeed in their mission when they stormed the Bandit King's castle. But, no, they'd walked away from that mission without even realizing they'd failed. Come, let's go back to Prince Frederic's kingdom of Harmonia, and I'll show you what I mean.

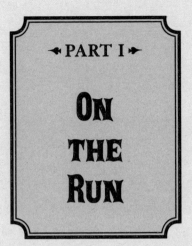

PART I

On the Run

1

AN OUTLAW IS NEVER AROUND WHEN YOU NEED ONE

"Harrumph."

King Wilberforce was in a foul mood, as he had been ever since Prince Frederic had stormed out of the palace months earlier. His son had never lashed out at him like that before. And to think it was simply because he had banished his son's fiancée. What choice did he have? Ella was a bad influence. He couldn't even keep track of how many times she had nearly gotten Frederic killed. Exiling the girl was what any good father would have done.

At least that's what Wilberforce told himself as he sat on his velvet-cushioned throne grumbling in a positively unkingly manner. Apparently forgetting his rule that "a proper man never fidgets," he absentmindedly fiddled with the dozens of glistening medals that adorned his finely tailored purple jacket. His normally stiff, right-angled shoulders began to dip into a position that came dangerously close to resembling a slump.

"Harrumph," the king grunted again.

"Your Highness?" asked the tall, thin, well-mannered man standing before the throne. "I mean no disrespect, but I feel the need to remind you that I am . . . here. Unless, of course, you summoned me only so that you would have someone at whom you could grunt. In which case, by all means, Your Highness—grunt away."

"I don't understand the boy," Wilberforce said, half mumbling. "You're his valet, Reginald. You know him better than anyone. Why would he go? What's wrong with him?"

"Perhaps part of the problem, Your Highness, is that you refer to him as 'the boy,'" Reginald said. "Frederic is a grown man."

"Who acts like a boy," the king responded. "Why would he feel a need to go off in search of *adventure*?" He snarled the word as if it were a curse. Before Reginald could respond, the king rambled on. "Do I not provide enough entertainment here at the palace? We hold royal balls every other week. Banquets! Bard concerts! Frederic never even stopped by the royal art gallery to see the new series of cat portraits

I commissioned for him. One of them shows a kitten in a hammock; Frederic loves that sort of thing."

"Perhaps, sire," Reginald finally interjected, "the prince was looking for more of a challenge."

"Challenge?" The king pshawed. "As if that boy could handle a challenge. He's got no backbone, no determination, no drive. Why, I gave him a custom-made backgammon set last year. After *one try*, he whined that it was too hard to play."

"To be fair, Your Highness, I believe his difficulty with the game was due to the *round dice* you forced him to use. They never stopped rolling."

Wilberforce arched an eyebrow. "You expected me to give my son those pointy-edged, cube-style dice? He'd lose an eye."

"Well, if you are going to be such a stickler for safety, why not give him dice the size of honeydews," Reginald said dryly. While he technically served the king, his loyalty lay with the prince he'd practically raised from birth. "After all, regular-size dice are a dangerous choking hazard."

"You're being cheeky with me, aren't you, Reginald?"

"Cheeky, sire?" the valet replied.

"You're giving me cheek. Sass. Cheeky sass."

"I would never dream of it, Your Highness. Look at all

those medals on your chest: Best Posture, Team Solitaire Champion, Silkiest Mustache. I have nothing but the utmost respect for a monarch with so many . . . *amazing* accomplishments to his credit."

"Cheek!" Wilberforce bellowed. "Cheeeeeek!" He stood and pointed toward the exit, his arm as stiff as a road sign. "I want you out, Reginald. Leave at once."

"The room?" Reginald asked. "Or the palace?"

"Think bigger," the king sneered.

"The kingdom then. As you wish." Reginald bowed his head. "Someday I hope you realize that just because your wife died as an adventurer doesn't mean your son will, too. You need to let Frederic make his own choices. Otherwise you will only drive him further away." He turned and walked out.

Wilberforce leaned forward in his throne. "If you find Frederic out there . . ." But Reginald was already gone. The king slouched back in his seat and added—to no one—"Take care of him."

He unpinned one of the medals from his jacket and took a look at it. WINNER: CRUSTIEST LOAF, HARMONIAN BAKE FAIR. He tossed the award angrily to the floor and went back to brooding. Sometime later, the door opened and Wilberforce quickly straightened up as an attendant stepped in.

"Sorry to disturb you, Your Highness," the attendant said. "But there's someone here to see you."

Frederic! Wilberforce thought. *He's come home.* "Send him in. Right away."

"Your visitor? Um, he's got some friends with him," the attendant began.

"Yes, of course, I should have figured he'd still be traveling with those ne'er-do-wells," the king said hurriedly. "But we'll deal with them later. Just get the boy in here."

"Boy? But—"

"Go! Let him in!"

The attendant scrambled from the throne room. Wilberforce worked his face into a welcoming smile, almost trembling as he waited. But a moment later, he frowned and cocked a quizzical eyebrow as his visitor entered the chamber. It was not Frederic. It was a tall, broad-shouldered, scar-faced man with some sort of monstrous skull sitting on his head like a helmet. And he had ten more equally questionable characters standing behind him, all brandishing nicked, battle-worn swords.

King Wilberforce shrank back. "Who . . . who are you?" he whispered.

"I am Rundark, Warlord of Dar and ruler of New Dar," said the stranger. His thick, braided beard rattled against his armored chest as he spoke. "And I am here to make an offer to the king of Harmonia."

Now, if Frederic had been there, he certainly would have warned his father about Lord Rundark, the vicious and brutal dictator who had nearly destroyed the League of Princes that past summer. Frederic could have told his father about the Jeopardous Jade Djinn Gem, the mystical artifact that gave Rundark the power to control people like human puppets. He might even have mentioned how Rundark—and the Gem along with him—were supposed to have been swallowed by a school of hungry bladejaw eels. But at that moment, when Frederic could have been very, very helpful to his father, he was many miles away, passing out at the sight of a hobgoblin with a splinter in its toe.

2

AN OUTLAW FAINTS AT THE SIGHT OF BLOOD

Frederic wasn't always helpless. Sure, he'd grown up in a palace with spill-proof goblets, padded bathtubs, and servants who wiped his nose for him; but those days were long behind him. Well, okay, a few months behind him. But in that time, Frederic *had* changed. He was now a man who had battled witches, negotiated with giants, and escaped from dungeons. He had proven he could be brave—when he had an ally or three at his side, that is. Working solo was still a challenge for him. And sadly, there was not a friend in sight when the hobgoblin lifted its crusty foot and wiggled its fat, infected toe in his face.

As Frederic's head hit the dirt and consciousness slowly faded away, his mind replayed the events of the previous three months, the pitiful chain of events that had brought him to this point.

It all began when Frederic walked out on his father. He marched out through his palace's arched marble gateway, his head a dizzying swirl of emotions—shame at having let Ella get banished, pride at having finally stood up to his father, anxiety over the prospect of leaving his royal comforts behind forever. But he had a plan: Go see Rapunzel. The long-haired healer from Sturmhagen had an easygoing warmth that made Frederic feel calm and comfortable whenever he saw her. She got his jokes, she made the best turnip soup he'd ever tasted, and she'd saved his life twice. Just thinking of Rapunzel made Frederic feel like everything was going to be all right.

Unfortunately, seeing her didn't have quite the same effect. When Frederic finally reached Rapunzel's cottage in the deep woods of Sturmhagen, he noticed that she was not alone. Through her kitchen window, he spotted the familiar, broad-shouldered silhouette of his friend Prince Gustav. *I shouldn't be surprised,* Frederic thought. *Gustav was* her *Prince Charming, after all.*

"Good for him," Frederic said aloud, trying to convince himself he really felt that way. He turned his horse around, trotted back into the forest, and began . . . wandering.

He spent several days on the shores of Lake Dräng with

Reese the giant—but he didn't like the way Reese's colossal mother, Maude, licked her lips when she looked at him, so he decided to move on. He got a warm welcome at Troll Place, but the "bed" that Mr. Troll constructed for him—a splintery piece of wood precariously balanced between two jagged rocks—didn't even come close to his comfort standards; so he politely told his host that he had an important appointment elsewhere. He tried Duncan and Snow White's estate in Sylvaria, but learned from the dwarfs that the couple had moved out.

"I suppose you'd like to know where they went," Frank the dwarf said, somehow making it sound like an insult.

"Yes, I would," Frederic replied.

"Just what I thought," Frank grumbled. And he walked away.

Frederic had no doubt that if he showed up on the doorsteps of Avondell Palace, Liam would offer him a room. But Liam's wife would be there, also—and Briar Rose was not a person with whom Frederic cherished the thought of being roomies.

After thirteen weeks on the road, and with nowhere else to go, Frederic headed back to Harmonia. He arrived outside the palace at twilight but couldn't bring himself to actually reenter the gates. Instead, he led his horse, Gwendolyn, a few yards away, where he laid out a blanket and sat down against the palace's wrought iron fence, gently caressing the gold-braid tassels that hung from the shoulder pads of his baby-blue suit. Eventually his eyelids drooped. But before he got a chance to dream about warm peach tarts and cardamom ice cream, he was awakened by a strange blue light mere inches from his face.

"Fairy!" he shrieked, before jumping to his feet and attempting—fruitlessly—to climb the fence.

"Wrong thing! Wrong thing!" he heard a twinkly voice call as he slid down the iron bars and landed gracelessly on the grass. He turned around and got a better look at the creature that had terrified him—a tiny woman, bathed in bluish light, hovering three feet off the ground. Frederic began to breathe a little easier.

"I, uh . . . I don't know if you were trying to tell me that I was *doing* the wrong thing or that I had *called* you the wrong thing," Frederic said softly, "but in either case, I think the latter is true. You're *not* a fairy, are you?"

The little blue woman smiled, her silvery antennae twitching. "Wrong thing. Wrongety-wrong."

"If I'm not mistaken, you're a sprite," Frederic said, remembering Rapunzel's description of her otherworldly helpers.

"Right thing!" the sprite squealed, and she flew loops in the air.

Frederic grinned. "Sorry about my initial reaction," he said, his cheeks reddening. "I've never actually met a sprite before. I thought you might be a fairy, and fairies make me nervous. Not that I've ever met a fairy either. But my friend Liam had a run-in with a very nasty one. You know the Sleeping Beauty story? Anyway . . . pleased to make your acquaintance. I am Prince Frederic." He bowed.

"Of coursety you's Frederic," the sprite said with a giggle that sounded like sleigh bells. "Frederic is skinny like candy cane. Frederic wears clothes with golden spaghettis. Frederic never touchety dirt. You's Frederic. Just like Zel say."

Frederic frowned. "Is that really how Rapunzel described me?" Then he perked up. "No, wait. That doesn't matter! Rapunzel described me! She sent you to find me?"

"Right thing!" The sprite mimicked his bow, hovering in midair. "Blink," she said.

"Blink?"

"Blink!"

"Um, okay." Frederic blinked his eyes.

The sprite shook her head and chuckled. She pointed to herself. "This is Blink."

"Ah, your *name* is Blink. Well, Miss Blink, why did Rapunzel send you to me?"

"Zel needs helpety-help. Too many forest peoples been hurt lately. Zel said you help. Comety-come."

"I'm not sure how much help I'll be," Frederic said. "I mean, I'll go, of course. But I'm not exactly a skilled medic. And seeing as Rapunzel has magical healing tears anyway, I just wonder—"

"Comety-come!" Blink squeaked loudly.

"Right away!" Frederic sputtered as he folded his blanket and placed it neatly in Gwendolyn's saddlebag. "Uh, Miss Blink? You wouldn't happen to know if there's *another* man, um . . . helping Rapunzel already? A very large man? With long, blond hair and questionable hygiene?"

"You not understand 'comety-come'?"

Frederic hopped on his horse and followed the sprite all the way back to the cottage in Sturmhagen. He was relieved to see that Gustav was not present. Rapunzel, however, was not there either.

"Is anybody home?" Frederic called out. His answer came in the form of a second blip of blue light zooming up to his face—another sprite, male this time.

"You's Frederic," he said. "Skinny like candy cane."

"Yes, that's me." Frederic sighed. He climbed down from

his horse. "Is Rapunzel about?"

"Zel's in forest. Too many patients. Busety-busy," the sprite rattled off. "You wait here."

"I can do that," Frederic replied. "But, in the meantime, I suppose . . ." And then he realized that both sprites were gone, having already zipped off among the thickly clustered pines that lined the small valley. He took a deep breath. "Well, I suppose I'll make myself comfortable."

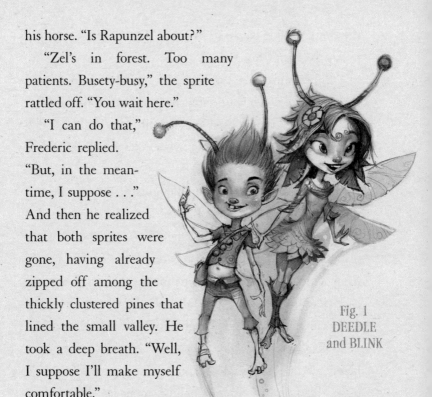

Fig. 1
DEEDLE
and BLINK

That was when the hobgoblin limped out of the woods. Dripping with what was either sweat or slime, the rust-colored creature shambled toward Frederic. It was only half the prince's height; but something about its long, pointed ears, bulbous nose, and jagged teeth told Frederic that this was not a creature to be messed with.

He ran into the cottage and slammed the door. But

the thing outside began to knock. "My toe," the hobgoblin moaned. "Hurts. So. Much."

"Uh, Rapunzel's not in right now," Frederic said. "I'd be happy to take down your name and contact information."

"Help me," the monster sniffled through the door. "The golden lady says all who come to her cottage will be healed. Please."

Frederic's mind turned to thoughts of his favorite fictional hero. He asked himself, *What would Sir Bertram do?* No matter what kind of challenge he faced—be it an orc using uncouth language or a baroness eating her entrée from a dessert plate—Sir Bertram the Dainty remained calm, levelheaded, and, above all, polite. There was no question as to what the dandy knight would do in this situation.

"Okay," Frederic said. "Let's . . . uh, see what we have here." He opened the door and cautiously stepped outside to see the drippy monster wobbling on one leg. "A hobbling hobgoblin. Heh. Try saying that five times fast. Well, I will hazard a guess that there is something wrong with your foot."

"Yes," the hobgoblin said. "Look!" It slapped its damp hands on Frederic's shoulders and raised its bare foot toward the prince's face, flaunting the three-inch-long shard of broken, splintery wood stuck in the fat flesh of its big toe.

That's when Frederic passed out.

3

AN OUTLAW PLAYS DOCTOR

When he opened his eyes, Frederic expected to see the grisly snarl of the hobgoblin. He was pleasantly surprised to be greeted by Rapunzel's smiling face instead, her big eyes bright and her round cheeks dimpled.

"Thank you for coming," she said. "But must you make me think you're dead every time you show up at my house?"

"In my defense," Frederic said, "I looked fine and healthy when I arrived here this time. You just happened to miss it. Lovely new dress, by the way. The blue brings out your eyes."

"It's good to see you, too," she said, blushing slightly. She pulled her waist-length blond hair back and tied it into a massive ponytail. "But this is actually the same old white dress I've always had. I dyed it. Felt like it was time for a change." She helped him up.

"Is someone playing a tambourine?" Frederic asked as he massaged the sore spot on the back of his head where his skull had hit the ground.

"That's just Blink and Deedle," Rapunzel said, nodding toward the two sprites hovering nearby. "They sound like that when they speak their own language. They must not want you to hear what they're saying about you."

"Why?" Frederic asked, trying to smooth the wrinkles out of his clothes. "Is it bad? Do you have a mirror?"

Rapunzel chuckled. "Relax, Frederic. I don't understand a lot of sprite language, but I'm pretty sure they're not mocking your appearance. I think they're laughing at you for fainting."

"Right thing!" Blink shouted gleefully.

Frederic loosened his collar. "How did you know I . . ." And then he noticed the hobgoblin sitting a few feet away on an overturned bucket. The creature waved its now splinter-free foot at him. "Ah, I see," Frederic said. "*He* must have filled you in. Well, you see, it was a very *large* splinter, and—"

"It wasn't just a splinter," Rapunzel said. "It was an arrow. Part of one, anyway. Most of it had broken off when this poor fellow was running for help."

"I was lucky to get away with my life," the hobgoblin said. "They would have killed me for sure."

"Who?" Frederic asked.

"Humans—big, ugly ones," the creature said. "Of course, you *all* look big and ugly to me. No offense. But I didn't do a thing to these guys. I was just out herding cats, minding my own business, when they came by and shot at me."

Frederic turned to Rapunzel and whispered, "Do you think he's telling the truth?"

"Unfortunately, yes," she replied. "I've heard similar stories from other patients. An awful lot of forest dwellers have been attacked these past few weeks. Too many for me to handle on my own, frankly. Which is why I sent for you. I was hoping you'd be willing to assist me."

"Assist how?"

"While I'm healing the more grievous injuries with my tears," she said, "you would be taking care of the patients with, um . . . everyday problems."

"Like splinters?"

"Yes, well . . ." She let out a short, uncomfortable laugh. "If I'd known you would be alone, I would have instructed the sprites to stay with you. I guess I expected you to bring Ella along."

"You did?" Frederic slumped a bit. "Oh, yes, Ella . . .

well, she and I . . . She and I have sort of gone our separate ways."

"Oh!" Rapunzel's eyebrows shot up. "I mean, that's . . . Um, I'm sorry?"

"Oh, no need for condolences," Frederic said. "It was mutual. She and I just weren't right for each other. For example, on our way home from Rauberia, I wanted to stop for the night at an adorable little bed-and-breakfast called Granny Pumpkin's Cozy Cottage—they offer twenty-four-hour scone service. But Ella insisted on an inn we saw named the Battered Kidney. At least that's what I think it was called—there was an unconscious man draped over the sign. I didn't think any place could be worse than the Stumpy Boarhound, but this one was. By the time I'd gotten our horses tied up outside, Ella was already involved in a brawl. I walked in to find her pouncing across the bar with a dagger between her teeth. That was when I started seriously rethinking our relationship.

"Don't get me wrong—Ella and I will always be the best of friends. As long as she forgives me for letting her get banished from Harmonia, that is. But anyway . . . *I* was surprised to see that Gustav wasn't here."

"Gustav?" Rapunzel asked suspiciously. "Why would Gustav be here?"

"I don't know," Frederic blurted. He cleared his throat. "Just because, you know, he lives nearby. If you needed help, I thought maybe you'd ask him first."

"I need a nurse," Rapunzel said. "Someone gentle. With a good bedside manner. Does that sound like Gustav?"

Frederic laughed.

"If you stay, I promise it will get easier," Rapunzel said. "I'll have Blink and Deedle guide you through everything."

"No, no, no! Nixety-nix!" cried Deedle, flying between them. "Our job is lookety for new patients; no time for helpety candy cane princes."

"Where did this candy cane thing come from?" Frederic asked.

"Shushety, Deedle!" Blink squeaked, popping up next to her fellow sprite. "This what Zel needs, this what we do. And if Frederic fall-down-go-boompety again, at least we can finish jobs for him."

"I really don't think I went *boompety*," Frederic mumbled. He turned to Rapunzel. "Couldn't you just leave me with a bucket of your tears? It doesn't sound too difficult if all I need to do is flick a drop at anyone who shows up."

"I'm sorry," she answered, shaking her head. "After we lost track of the vial I gave you in Deeb Rauber's castle, I don't feel comfortable doing that again. I would hate for my tears to be misused. And to be honest, I don't want to waste any. We all assume that my magic will last forever, but what if it doesn't? What if there's only so much of it in me? What if there comes a time when tears I cry are just salty water?"

Frederic was silent.

"So will you do it?" Rapunzel asked, her big, hopeful eyes fixed on Frederic's. "Will you help?"

He took a deep breath. *As if I could say no to you.* He nodded, and Rapunzel threw her arms around him.

"Morning!"

Lying on his cot in the stable, Frederic opened his eyes just in time to see Rapunzel tossing an apple to him. He tried to catch it, but it bounced off his face and landed in his lap.

"Sorry I can't fix a better breakfast today," she said hastily. "I've got an emergency to get to in Fluglesborg. The sprites are waiting. See you tonight."

"Tonight?" he asked, still groggy. But Rapunzel had ridden off on her mare, Pippi. "Okay, then," Frederic said. He rubbed the sleep from his eyes, picked up the apple, and took it outside to wash it (the fruit had touched his pants, after all). On his way to the well, however, he was stopped in his tracks by a streak of blue light.

"New patient!" Deedle cried.

"Already?" Frederic combed his fingers through his sandy-brown hair. "But I must look a fright."

"Right thing!" Blink chirped. She flew in from the forest with a sad-looking dog-man shuffling behind her.

"Can I change, at least?" Frederic asked. He was wearing one of his lavender silk "sleep suits." And cashmere slippers.

"Dog-man. Now," Deedle commanded.

Frederic huffed and turned to the patient. The dog-man nodded his scruffy terrier head toward his rear end and whimpered.

"Brokety tail," Blink explained.

Frederic grimaced. "That looks painful." He poked at the fractured tail, and the dog-man let out an ear-piercing howl.

"Wrong thing! Wrong thing!" the sprites shouted.

"I gathered that," Frederic said. "Apologies, sir. Umm . . ."

"Tail hurts when tail moves," Blink said helpfully.

"Ooh! We need to make a splint!" Frederic said. "Just like Sir Bertram the Dainty did in *The Case of the Overwaxed Dance Floor* when his squire, Niles Tibbets-Wick, stubbed his pinkie finger. Blink, Deedle—can you find me a piece of wood and some string?"

Five minutes later, the dog-man was panting happily

as he trotted back into the woods with his newly splinted tail. And Frederic was feeling pretty darn proud of himself, which helped get him through the next several hours of treating patients, one right after another.

Later that afternoon, when Frederic had just waved good-bye to a squinting gnome for whom he'd sewn a very fashionable eye patch, Rapunzel returned. She rode out from the nearby trees and hopped down from her horse looking exhausted.

"Yay! Zel's back!" Blink shouted.

"We can go now!" Deedle chirped. The sprites sped into the woods.

"So, what was the crisis in Fluglesborg?" Frederic asked.

"Another of these seemingly random attacks by armed men," Rapunzel said. "Whoever they are, they're marching across Sturmhagen from the east, and they'll apparently attack anyone who crosses their path."

"Hmm," Frederic said, sitting down on a short log bench under the eave of the cottage. "I'd think they were Deeb Rauber's guys, but the bandit army is more about stealing stuff than assaulting people. Maybe I should send for Liam."

"Perhaps," Rapunzel said, sitting down next to him even though there wasn't much room on the bench. "How did things go here? I hope you weren't overwhelmed."

"Overwhelmed? Oh, not at all," Frederic said, sitting a bit taller. "Piece of cake, actually. I handled the whole task quite masterfully, if I do say so myself."

"Really?" Rapunzel sounded amused. "You're still in your pajamas."

Frederic looked down at himself. "Well, I didn't say I was *under*whelmed. Not overwhelmed, not underwhelmed—just whelmed. I was whelmed."

Rapunzel shook her head. "Frederic, I hope you realize you can be yourself around me. You don't have to pretend you're anything you're not."

"Oh, I'm not pretending," he said earnestly. "I really am this awkward."

"Good," she said. "Because you and I, we're . . . friends. And friends should feel comfortable with each other."

Fig. 2
FREDERIC, oblivious

"I do feel comfortable. A little too comfortable, perhaps. I'll go change out of my pj's." He started toward the barn when the sprites burst from the trees in a panic.

"Helpety! In the woods!" Blink shouted.

"What is it?" Rapunzel asked, standing up.

"He's hurt!" Blink said.

"Who is?" Rapunzel asked.

"He said not to get Zel," Deedle added, glaring at his partner. "Said he's not hurt bad."

"But it *is* bad!" Blink insisted. "Arrows in his back. Leg in a trap. Can't walkety!"

"*Who?*" Frederic asked.

"Gustav," both sprites said in unison.

4

AN OUTLAW FEELS NO PAIN

Prince Gustav had been in worse predicaments. There was, of course, the time he was thrown from a high tower into a thorny bramble (the incident after which Rapunzel famously healed him). And more recently he nearly had the life choked out of him by a ridiculously oversize dungeon keeper (Rapunzel fixed him up after that one, too). So to the long-haired, big-muscled, well-armored Gustav, having a couple of arrows in his shoulder and one leg caught in a steel-jawed bugbear trap felt like something he could deal with on his own. Sure, it hurt worse than the time his brothers had slipped an angry porcupine into his bed, and yes, he was stuck with no way to reach food or water, but he wasn't *really* worried. Hey, he was in the wilderness; he figured that eventually some impatient buzzard would assume he was dead already, start sniffing around a little too close, and—*boom!*—drumsticks! No, this was a situation Gustav felt pretty certain he could handle.

Until Rapunzel showed up.

He groaned the moment he saw her rosy-cheeked face appear from behind a gnarled fir tree, the sprites orbiting her like miniature moons.

"Aw, for crying out loud," Gustav groused. "I told you little blue traitors not to bring Sister Goldenhair out here."

"The sprites did the right thing," Rapunzel said.

"We *had* to tellety Zel," Blink argued. "You're dying!"

"I am *not* dying!" Gustav snapped. And he immediately winced in pain. "Annoying, know-it-all firefly."

Rapunzel ran over to him and examined his wounded leg, which was crunched at the ankle between the steel teeth of a hunter's trap. "Oh, dear. You look awful."

"I know, I know," Frederic said, panting, as he staggered up and flopped against a tree to catch his breath. "My face always gets red like this when I run. It'll go back to normal in a half hour or so. Oh! You weren't talking to me."

"Tassels? What the heck are *you* doing here?" Gustav cried in bewilderment. "And where are your tassels?"

Frederic joined Rapunzel, crouching down by the fallen prince. “Good day to you, too, Gustav,” he said. “Rapunzel, I assume your tears can take care of this?”

“Heal the wounds, sure,” she said. “But free his leg?”

“Pfft!” Gustav scoffed. “What good are those magical tears of yours if you can’t even cry open a bugbear trap?”

Rapunzel glared at him.

“Relax, Blondie,” Gustav said. “You know I’m just kiddin’ ya. Look, find me a nice, strong piece of metal, and I’ll pry the thing open myself.”

She turned to the sprites flitting beside her head. “There’s a crowbar in the stable by the extra horseshoes. Do you two think you could carry it back here?”

Deedle and Blink bolted away in a blue streak.

“Now, let’s see about those arrows,” Rapunzel said.

“What arrows?” Gustav said coolly. He casually reached over his shoulder and yanked the two barbed shafts from his back. “See . . . I’m . . . fine,” he wheezed between clenched teeth, his face twisted into the kind of expression you’d see on a poorly carved jack-o’-lantern.

Frederic teetered, but righted himself. “Me, too! I’m fine. No fainting here.”

Rapunzel shook her head. “I don’t know which of you is worse.”

"Who did this to you, Gustav?" Frederic asked.

"Bounty hunters," he said. "Tall, homely guy with gnarly teeth, a pointy-eared guy with a bow, a beady-eyed one with giant trained ferrets, couple of others."

"Did you say ferrets?" Frederic asked. "People train giant ferrets?"

"Never mind that," Rapunzel said. "Explain the bounty hunters. What could a bounty hunter hope to get by capturing you?"

"Um, untold riches," Gustav said, looking at them incredulously. "Because I'm one of the most wanted men in the Thirteen Kingdoms."

"Wanted for what?" The idea was so farfetched, Frederic almost laughed.

Gustav paused. "You two really don't know?"

Frederic and Rapunzel shook their heads.

"Here," Gustav said, reaching down into the boot of his free leg and retrieving a rolled-up parchment. "I pulled one of these off the wall of a butcher's shop in Smorgsjürgen. But they're everywhere. I figured you would've seen 'em by now."

He handed the paper to Frederic, who unrolled it and started reading.

WANTED

for the CRIME of MURDER:
the SO-CALLED "LEAGUE of PRINCES,"
the members of which are as follows–
PRINCE LIAM of ERINTHIA;
PRINCE GUSTAV of STURMHAGEN;
PRINCE FREDERIC of HARMONIA;
PRINCE DUNCAN of SYLVARIA;
PRINCESS LILA of ERINTHIA;
PRINCESS SNOW WHITE of SYLVARIA;
the LADY ELLA, swordswoman of HARMONIA;
and the LADY RAPUNZEL,
mystic of STURMHAGEN.

Frederic looked up. "I can't believe what I'm seeing," he gasped.

"I know," Gustav said, sounding offended. "Those girls aren't in the League! It's the League of *Princes*, for Pete's sake!"

"How could I be accused of murder?" Rapunzel snapped. "I've devoted my life to healing people!"

"It doesn't make any sense," Frederic stammered. "And . . . and . . . whose murder?"

"Read on," Gustav said solemnly. Frederic unrolled more of the Wanted poster.

The LEAGUE has been found GUILTY of the MOST CRUEL MURDER of HER MAJESTY BRIAR ROSE, PRINCESS of AVONDELL.

"Oh, no," Frederic gasped. "Briar has been . . . ?"

"Apparently so," Gustav said. "And some blasted bard wrote a song about how *we* did it. It's all anybody's been talking about for the past couple days. I can't believe neither of you has heard it."

"This is beyond horrible," Rapunzel said. "I saved Briar's life just a short while ago. That snakebite almost killed her, but I brought her back. And now . . ."

"It's too awful for words," Frederic said.

"I know," Gustav added. "I mean, she may not have been the friendliest person we've ever met . . . and she *did* force Capey to marry her against his wishes . . . and she *did* throw us all in prison for no good reason . . . and she *did* try to sacrifice all of us so she could steal a magic jewel and take over the world . . ." Gustav paused. "Sheesh, no wonder everybody thinks we did it."

"But there's no evidence," Frederic said, still rattled by the news. "I mean, there can't be, since we didn't do it. Who told the bards we were responsible? Who would set us up like that?"

"And people really believe we're killers?" Rapunzel asked, looking slightly green.

"Based on the things they've thrown at me, yes," Gustav replied. "Axes, bricks, flaming barrels—and those were just random farmers outside my door. The real bounty hunters didn't catch up to me until yesterday."

A terrifying thought crossed Frederic's mind. He read the last lines of the Wanted poster.

ANYONE WHO DELIVERS
the FUGITIVES–ALIVE–
to the ROYAL COURT in AVONDELL,
SHALL RECEIVE, as his REWARD,
UNTOLD RICHES.

"Those bounty hunters are still chasing you, aren't they?" he said. "And now they'll find all three of us?"

"Don't get your pj's in a bunch," Gustav said, waving his hand dismissively. "I ditched those jerks way back by the Carpagian border. It'll be days before they pick up my trail again."

At which point they suddenly found themselves surrounded by bounty hunters. Six men stepped out of the trees, including one who held three pony-size, gray-furred creatures on leashes.

"See, giant ferrets," Gustav said.

"These ain't no giant ferrets. They're giant mongeese," drawled the beady-eyed man who held the leashes. His pets hissed and bared their glistening fangs. "Vicious, cunning, snake-eating mongeese."

"Mongooses," Frederic corrected.

"You can't help yourself, can you?" Rapunzel said to him.

"They're mongeese!" the bounty hunter snapped. "They're

Fig. 3
BOUNTY HUNTERS, assorted

my animals, and I say they're mongeese!"

"You know, I have been telling you for ages that 'mongeese' is incorrect," said another hunter, a slender elf with a longbow slung over his shoulder.

"Look, it's 'goose' and 'geese,' right?" the first replied. "So 'mongoose,' 'mongeese.'"

"You gotta admit, though," added a stout, orange-bearded bounty hunter, "'mongeese' does sound kinda dumb."

"Enough!" A hooded man stepped forward; two curved swords formed an *X* on his back, and his belt was lined with daggers. He pulled back his hood, revealing a creased face and thin lips that curled over a mouthful of misshapen,

discolored teeth. "The next person who argues grammar gets a dagger in his eye."

He sauntered up to Frederic and yanked the Wanted poster from the prince's hand. He pointed to the sketch of Frederic's face. "That you?" he asked.

Frederic took a closer look at the drawing. "Uh, yes, that would be me. No point in denying it. The picture is an unfortunately accurate likeness. It figures, you know. The artist we hire to do our family portraits makes me look like I'm half goblin, the sculptor who crafts the League's victory statue gives me a nose like a toucan, but the guy who draws the Wanted poster? *He* nails it." He sighed and continued, "But now you have us at a disadvantage. You know who I am, but you have yet to introduce yourself."

The leader smiled. "I'm Greenfang," he said. "I like you. You've got moxie. Shame they'll probably kill you when I turn you in." He called to the others, "Take him; the girl, too." A pair of tall, blond twins grabbed Frederic and Rapunzel. While Frederic feared for his life and that of his friends, he couldn't help feeling at least a smidgen of pride—no one had ever told him he had moxie before.

Greenfang, in the meantime, walked over to Gustav, who was still stuck on the ground. The bounty hunter drew one of his long scimitars, jammed the blade between the teeth of the trap, and pried it open, freeing Gustav's leg.

Gustav slapped a hand to his forehead. "Starf it all!" he cursed. "I *have* a sword! I could've done that!" His forgotten weapon was then, of course, quickly taken away.

As the three prisoners were led through the thick woods, Gustav hopping slowly along on one leg, the elven archer kept his bow trained on them.

"Give it a rest, Pointy Ears," Gustav snarked. "It's not like I can run."

"Oh, you wouldn't be able to escape even if you were in prime physical condition," the archer replied coolly. "And since you so callously feel the need to bring it up, there is no race in the Thirteen Kingdoms with more finely crafted ears than us elves."

"Aren't you a little tall to be an elf?" Gustav said. "Shouldn't you be off making toys somewhere?"

The archer sniffed haughtily. "I am an Avondellian elf. You are thinking of those uncultured craftsmen, the Svenlandian elves. Pudgy little cretins, always baking cookies or mending shoes. And those ridiculous, curly-toed slippers they wear! Feh! Those lowly creatures don't deserve to go by the name of Elf. They might as well start posing for lawn ornaments like the gnomes."

"Pete!" Greenfang snapped at him. "I'm gonna shove

your silky ponytail down your throat if you go off on one more rant about the Svenlandian elves. Better yet, I'll cut you out of the reward money."

Pete huffed but kept his mouth shut. They exited the forest, coming out onto a gravelly road, where the prisoners were loaded into a large iron cage that sat on the flat bed of a waiting wagon.

"So, Mr. Greenfang," Frederic said as the cage door was locked. "I assume you're doing this for the gold—am I correct?"

"I see why they call you the smart one," Greenfang replied.

"Do they? I always thought of Liam as the smart one," Frederic said. "Well, anyway, I wanted to remind you that I happen to be a wealthy prince. If you were to let us go, I'd be happy to pay you *more* than Avondell is offering."

Greenfang let out a dry, rasping laugh. "No kingdom's got more money than Avondell," he said. "Enjoy the ride." The orange-bearded hunter took the reins of the wagon, while the others all mounted horses (or in one case, a giant mongoose) and galloped away.

"What now?" Frederic asked, bracing himself as the wagon began to roll. "The bounty hunters are all up ahead of us. If we're going to escape, now is the time."

"First things first," Rapunzel said. She quickly blinked a tear onto Gustav's mangled ankle. Wiping her cheek, she cast a warm smile at him. "Can't save the day if you're not in top form, right?"

Gustav wiggled his foot a few times, a wide grin on his face. "All right," he said. "Let's get outta here." He stood up, swung his newly healed leg, and landed a colossal kick against the cage's iron-bar door. The door didn't budge. Gustav, however, fell onto his back, groaning and clutching his newly rebroken foot. Rapunzel stared at him, incredulous.

"Blink!" Frederic said.

"All right, all right. I'll give him another tear," Rapunzel said. "Just hold on a sec; I'm going to have a hard time working this one up."

"No, Blink and Deedle!" Frederic said. Two blue lights hovered just outside the cage door, keeping up with the rolling wagon. "Did you bring the crowbar?"

"Too heavety," Blink said, shaking her little head.

"You need to go get help then," Frederic whispered to them, glancing around to make sure none of their captors were watching.

"Who?" Rapunzel asked. "None of our friends are within even a day's ride of here."

"Right . . . Aha!" Frederic's eyes lit up. "Go to Castle

Sturmhagen and tell Gustav's brothers we need their assistance."

"No," Gustav said adamantly. "Nuh-uh. Not gonna happen." Gustav's older brothers were bullies, plain and simple. All sixteen of them. They'd tormented their youngest sibling for his entire life: mocking him, pulling pranks on him, and stealing his glory whenever possible. These were the very men who undeservedly took credit for the League's rescue of the kidnapped bards.

"Sixteen strong fighters who can probably catch up to us with just a couple hours of riding," Frederic said. "Sorry, Gustav, they're our best hope. Go, sprites—alert the princes of Sturmhagen! And be speedy about it." Out of the corner of his eye, he noticed the intense way Rapunzel was looking at him. He thought it might be admiration. Either that or he had a piece of apple skin stuck between his front teeth. He shut his mouth, just in case.

The sprites rocketed off.

Still holding his foot in the air, Gustav grumbled, "Just what I was hoping for—a family reunion."

Twenty minutes later, Blink and Deedle arrived at the stark, white-stone walls of Castle Sturmhagen. An hour of searching its antler- and fur-festooned halls, however, proved fruitless. Not one prince was to be found. The sprites hovered under a stuffed caribou head, baffled.

"No biggety princes," Deedle said.

"Impossible," Blink replied impatiently. "Should be so many."

A maid wearing an elk-hide apron stepped out of a nearby bedroom and jumped in terror. "Get away from me, you wee blue demons!" she shouted.

"Wrong thing!" Blink snapped. She crossed her arms and, though she was hovering in midair, she tapped her foot as if there were solid ground beneath her. "Tell us where biggety princes are."

"We havety message for them," Deedle added.

"Message, eh?" The maid squinted skeptically at the creatures floating before her. "Well, you're in the wrong place. Down in the dungeon's where they are."

"Princes guard prisoners?" Deedle asked.

"The princes *are* the prisoners," the maid said. "Quite a shock, I know. All sixteen of 'em turned traitor. King Olaf himself, the lads' own father, had to lock 'em away. All of us around here are takin' the news pretty hard. I don't even know what those boys did to— Wait a minute. Why am I telling this to you? I don't even know what you are. I should— Huh? Where'd you go?"

The sprites had zoomed up to the throne room, where they hid behind a wall-mounted torch spying on King Olaf. The seven-foot-tall monarch sat hunched on his pinewood throne like an old, gray grizzly. The sprites would have flown right up to him and demanded to know why he'd imprisoned his sons, but the king was not alone. The left-hand throne, usually reserved for Queen Berthilda, was filled (or overfilled, actually) by a stranger—a man who was so tremendously muscular that he made Olaf look like a dwarf in comparison. The enormous mountain of a man sat there, breathing heavily, a red-and-black mask tied around the top of his head and an insanely long, ropelike mustache dangling all the way to his belly.

The sprites had never seen Wrathgar before, so they didn't know he was the sadistic dungeon master who'd nearly killed Gustav months earlier. Nor did they know that Wrathgar was one of Lord Rundark's fiercest and most trusted generals. But they knew trouble when they saw it. They fled immediately.

"What now?" Blink asked as they darted out into the cobblestone courtyard.

"Need someone else to helpety Zel," Deedle panted.

"Ooh! Princety Charmings!" Blink yipped with inspiration.

"Two Princety Charmings stuckety with Zel."

"Yes, but there two more. Zel say so. And one is the bestety hero of all."

"Which one?"

Blink squeezed her eyes shut, thought for a moment, then popped them back open. "Duncan! Princety Duncan. He live in Sylvaria."

Deedle shrugged. "Let's go to Sylvaria!"

5

AN OUTLAW LISTENS TO HIS DAD

Castlevaria, the home of Sylvaria's ruling family, was different from the royal palaces of other kingdoms. For one thing, it was bright salmon pink. Most castle makers stick with the raw stone look or, if they're going for something fancier, perhaps polished marble. But Castlevaria was designed by its primary resident, King King—a man who had once instructed his royal scientists to "jazz up the rainbow." "Try sticking a new color between orange and yellow," he'd told them. The scientists all quit after that.

In fact, over the course of their twenty-five years in power, King King and Queen Apricotta had seen virtually everyone who worked for them resign. By this point the castle staff consisted only of three untrained guards, a one-armed chambermaid, and a nine-year-old houseboy named Pip. The royal family had to take care of almost everything themselves. Which is why Snow White, wife to Sylvaria's Prince Duncan, was beginning to regret their decision to leave their woodland estate and move into Castlevaria.

"Dunky, you know I'm never one to shy away from chores—they provide an excellent opportunity for whistling," Snow said while working her way through the washing of a four-foot-high stack of plates (the queen had served blueberries for breakfast and decided it would be fun to put each berry on its own plate). Even while toiling at the sink, the petite princess wore an elaborate dress of her own creation—this one was canary yellow with swirly ribbons dangling from the sleeves. She paused to pull one of the ribbons out of the soapy water. "But living here is exhausting."

Fig. 4
CASTLEVARIA

Duncan, who was sitting at his kitchen "author's desk" (he had one in every room), did not look up from the pages of the book in which he was writing. "I'm sorry, Snowy. But aren't you happy that I've gotten so much closer to my family?" he said. He wore an outfit that was, for Duncan, relatively subdued—a velvet vest, puffy blue pantaloons, and curly-toed shoes. Sitting atop his wavy black hair was a miniature derby that Snow had made for him as a congratulations-on-saving-the-kingdom gift. "And I'm getting a lot of work done on my book here," he continued, tapping the pages of his almost-finished *Hero's Guide to Being a Hero*. "I'm about to start the chapter on the dangers of ill-fitting leggings."

He glanced over at his wife. "But I don't want you to be unhappy," he said. "Do you think we should go back to live with the dwarfs again?"

Snow sighed and adjusted her acorn-encrusted tiara. "No. But are you sure we can't hire some more people to help out around here?"

"No one else will work here," Duncan said with an apologetic shrug. "It's not like we haven't tried to get people. And you should have seen some of the incentives my family has offered to potential servants—unlimited use of the royal toenail clipper, all the asparagus you can eat, a new origami pigeon every Friday . . . although we probably shouldn't have offered that one, since none of us knows how to do origami."

"Pip, what do you like about working here?" Snow asked, turning to the grubby-faced boy who was sweeping one of Castlevaria's fifty-seven fireplaces.

"Well, I like feeling safe," he said. "My last boss was an ogre. Literally. I was always afraid I might end up his next meal."

"That's it," Duncan said cheerily. "I'll make up some new Help Wanted signs: 'Come work for the royal family. We will not eat you.' Figgy Shortshanks!" That last bit was Duncan naming a mouse that skittered out of the cupboard.

Just then, the kitchen door suddenly flew off its hinges. (Don't worry; it had never been attached.) "That is exciting *every* time," King King said, clapping. "I'm going to do it again." The gangly monarch stood the door back up, pushed it down with a crash, and applauded once more. As he bounced, his hair, curling up from beneath his pillow-top crown, flapped like a pair of wings.

"Come along, Son," the king said. "I need to teach you all about ruling a kingdom."

"No, you don't, Dad," Duncan speedily replied. "Anyway, I've got a book to finish. My fans are waiting." He returned to scribbling on a blank page.

Perhaps you can relate. If you have ever been a child (and I'm reasonably sure you have), then you've no doubt experienced the frustration of having a parent pull you away from an enjoyable pastime in order to instruct you on how to reattach loose buttons, clean leaves out of rain gutters, or separate egg yolks—and you have paid little attention because you know in your heart that you will never in your life have cause to do such things. That is exactly how Duncan was feeling at that moment. Even though he was fully grown. Adults don't really like it when their parents tell them how to do something either. And in this case, Duncan was justified, since his father's skills as a ruler were questionable at best.

"Nonsense," King King said, flourishing his red-and-green-checkered robe. "Come with me." He took his son by the hand and pulled him from his seat.

"Have fun," Snow chirped as her husband was yanked out of the room.

"Dad, do we have to do this?" Duncan moaned.

"Yes, yes. Very important business," the king said. He led Duncan down a long, twisting corridor into a large chamber, the walls of which were lined with dried-pasta mosaics. "Ah, here we are," the monarch said. He pointed to a cushiony armchair upholstered with tiger-striped velvet. "That is a throne. That's where the king sits. And if you'll look to the left, you'll see another throne. And that lady in it is a queen."

"Yes, I know," Duncan mumbled, waving to his mother halfheartedly.

"Hello, Duncan," Queen Apricotta said with a smile, her bright-orange pigtails waggling. "Ooh, is it time for you to learn about all your future kingly duties?"

"Apparently so," Duncan said sourly. "Even though I don't think—"

But King King tugged him over to the two inky-haired twins who were standing by the window staring at each other through thick, round goggles. "You probably also know Mavis and Marvella," the king said.

"For sixteen years now," Duncan said with a sigh.

The girls turned to look at their brother. "Duncan, you've turned huge," Marvella gasped.

"No, girls, he's still Duncan size," the queen said from her throne. "You've just got your magnifying goggles on."

The twins lifted their goggles and nodded. "Ah."

"We were playing Shrinky People," Mavis explained. The girls put their goggles back on. "Ahh! We've shrunk again! Everything's giant!"

"Yes, Mavis and Marvella are your sisters," the king said. "But they have official titles as well. Mavis is Royal Treasurer, which means she keeps track of all the kingdom's gold. And Marvella is . . . hmm, I want to say Minister of Poultry. I don't quite remember. But neither job is very important. Being king, however, *is* very important. When you are king, you have a lot to do. You make proclamations—about things like what our national insect will be, or whether a meal can really be called brunch if it's served after noon. As king you decide what color to paint the fence. You look at maps; you organize chickens— No, wait, that's probably Marvella's job. But most importantly, there are people—real people—who live out there in Sylvaria who are called 'subjects.' And occasionally, those subjects *need* something. So they come here to the castle to ask you for it. Which is so nice, because people actually *come here*."

Duncan had missed most of his father's speech; he was watching his sisters and thinking how fun those magnifying goggles looked. When he realized the king had stopped talking, he turned to him and asked, "But why are you telling me all this? You're king, not me."

"For the time being," King King said. "But someday I won't be around anymore, and the kingdom will be passed on to you. Maybe sooner than you think."

Duncan frowned. "That's a bit doom-and-gloomy for you, Dad. You're still young. Well, not *young* young—you have a lot of nose hair, and you smell like old library books. But young for a king. Look at Snow's father, the king of Yondale; he's a hundred and twelve and still has all his original teeth—by which I mean his baby teeth. It's very odd to see an old man with such itty-bitty teeth in his mouth. My point is: You'll be around for years and years yet, so why bother with this?"

King King chuckled. "Don't worry, Son; I'm not foreshadowing my own demise or anything," he said, patting Duncan on the head. "I just want to make sure you're ready to rule the realm someday. Now come along. Let me show you where we keep the royal back scratcher."

But the back scratcher would have to wait. At that very moment, two glowing blue sprites burst into the throne room.

"Visitors!" Queen Apricotta squealed in delight, and began primping her pigtails.

Mavis and Marvella flipped up their goggles and gawked. "*Real* shrinky people," Marvella whispered in awe.

"Are you the ambassadors from Fairyland?" the king asked. "I've been waiting for you. You're seventeen years late. Not that I'm complaining, mind you. How was your trip?"

"We needs Princety Charming!" Deedle cried.

"Princety Duncan!" Blink clarified.

"That's me!" Duncan blurted in surprise. "That's both me! As long as 'princety' and 'prince' mean the same thing."

"Really? You?" Deedle asked skeptically.

Duncan nodded. The sprites looked at each other and shrugged.

"Creepety men took Zel," Blink said.

"Who's Zel?" Duncan asked.

"You sure you right guy?" Deedle asked. "Zel! Goldety hair, fixety people . . ."

"Oh, you mean Punzy," Duncan said.

"No, we mean Zel. Who's Punzy?" Deedle snipped.

"Frederic and Gustav, too," Blink interjected. "Creepety men grabbed all of them."

That was all Duncan needed to hear. He raised his chin and declared, "Duty calls, everyone! I must go!"

He saw his family's faces droop. "Don't worry, though. I'll be back. And I'll bring souvenirs!" Everybody smiled again.

Ten seconds later, after getting as many details as he could from the sprites, Duncan ran back to the kitchen and pushed down the door. "Frederic, Gustav, and Rapunzel have been captured! I've got to go rescue them at once!"

Snow dropped the plate she was washing back into the sink. "I'll grab our things," she said eagerly.

"You want to come with me?" Duncan asked, surprised. "On an adventure?"

"As long as we get to leave the castle, yes."

They dashed off together. Pip looked up mournfully from his soot pile. "There go the only half-sane people in this place," he said. "But then again, who am I to judge? I'm talking to myself."

"Dunky, should we get Liam to help us?" Snow asked as they grabbed their horses from the stable.

Duncan shook his head. "I wouldn't want to bother him on his honeymoon."

6

AN OUTLAW CRIES FOR HELP

Several months earlier, about the same time Frederic left Harmonia, Prince Liam had struck out on his own as well. He didn't know exactly why Briar Rose had decided to annul their marriage, but he didn't want to risk sticking around and giving her the chance to change her mind. He raced out of Avondell, telling himself that the best times of his life were just beginning. He didn't have to be a hero anymore. No one was hounding him with calls for help; no one was begging him to rescue their kidnapped grandmother or to save their farm from invading bandersnatches. He was finally free to live whatever kind of life he wanted. The only problem was, he had no idea what he wanted to do.

He tried his hand at goatherding for a while; but after

several weeks without a single wolf attack, he grew bored and traded his goats for a new cape. He attempted to make a living building log cabins for woodland families, but his very first clients fired him for adding too many escape hatches. He even took a shot at setting up a roadside stand and selling homemade acorn-head figurines—but he had no artistic talent and most passersby assumed his statuettes were clumps of trail mix. On the morning that one of his customers chipped a tooth trying to eat a Prince Gustav figure, Liam knew he'd made a mistake. Being a hero was the only thing he knew how to do.

And it was all he wanted to do.

He just needed to figure out where to do it. He certainly wasn't going to stay in Briar's home kingdom of Avondell, and he had no desire to face his parents back in Erinthia, so he trekked to nearby Hithershire—a land that, as far as he knew, was sorely lacking in big-name national heroes.

Hithershire has bandits and monsters and natural disasters, just like any other kingdom, Liam said to himself as he galloped over the hilly, green countryside of his newly chosen homeland, *but no champion to protect its people. Until now.* Sitting astride his sturdy black stallion, Thunderbreaker, with a gleaming sword at his side and a deep-blue cape fluttering behind him, Liam felt energized and ready for anything. It didn't take him long to come across a situation that was crying out for some heroic intervention.

An apple cart had been overturned on a dirt road, with half a dozen bodies lying unmoving around it. *Bandit attack,* Liam thought. He spurred Thunderbreaker and sped up to the cart, where he leapt down, drawing his sword before his feet hit the ground. Two apple vendors flinched when they saw him.

"Have no fear, citizens," Liam said. "You're safe now."

"Yeah, we know," said the first vendor, a tall, messy-haired young man in a dirty apron. "It's pretty great, isn't it?"

"Who are you anyway?" the second fruit seller asked.

"I'm Prince Liam of Erinthia. I'm here to rescue you."

"A bit late for that, eh?" the man chuckled, elbowing his partner.

Maintaining his battle stance, Liam looked around. Now that he could see them up close, the bodies on the ground all appeared to be bandits—each unconscious, with his hands and feet tied. Liam frowned.

"Did you see the fight?" the tall vendor asked. He had a huge smile on his face and a dreamy look in his eyes. "She was amazing."

"She took 'em all out in about ten seconds flat," the shorter man added.

"Who did?" Liam asked.

"Our new hero," the tall man beamed. "Ella, Mistress of the Sword."

"Ella?" Liam asked skeptically. "Short brown hair? Swishy pants?"

"Oh, you've seen her then?" the tall one asked giddily. "Isn't she incredible?"

"Ella did this? Why is she even in Hithershire?" Liam mused. "And where's Frederic? She wasn't with a very, er, *elegant* man, was she?"

The tall merchant shook his head. "No, just her. *Wonderful* her."

The shorter vendor clutched his hands to his chest. "I can't wait till we get robbed again."

"So, just to be clear, you guys *don't* need any more rescuing?" Liam asked.

"Nope."

Liam sighed and turned back to his waiting horse.

"Hey, wait!" the tall merchant said. "You're, like, a hero, too, right? A hero wouldn't make us clean this all up by ourselves, would he?"

Liam surveyed the four hundred or so apples scattered along the road and sighed again. Ninety minutes later, with the cart righted and all the apples back in place, Liam finally remounted his horse and bade the merchants farewell.

"Don't worry," the tall one said. "We'll tell everyone about you—Prince Liam, Retriever of Fallen Fruits!"

"Oh, please do," Liam droned as he rode off.

Over the next couple of weeks, Liam heard the citizens of Hithershire singing Ella's praises in every village he visited. But Ella herself always seemed one step ahead of him. He would show up mere minutes after she'd chased a gang of thieving goblins from a candy store, pulled frightened toddlers from a burning nursery, or hog-tied a disappointed mugger. *I've got to find her,* Liam thought—and there was only one way he could think of to get her attention.

"Help! Help!" he called. He stood alone by a windmill on the outskirts of the town of Digglesbury. "Help!" he cried again. Then he crossed his arms and waited. As he expected, it wasn't long before Ella appeared, dropping down from the windmill blades with her rapier drawn, ready to strike.

"What seems to be the . . . huh? Liam!" She threw her arms around him in a warm embrace. "It's so good to see you. But what gives? You don't need help."

"I needed help finding you," he said. "So . . . thanks."

Ella crossed her arms and narrowed her eyes. "I don't

appreciate the trickery. And what if there's some poor person who *really* needs my aid out there right now?"

"I wouldn't be too worried," Liam said with a sly grin. "I think you've already taken out every criminal in this kingdom."

Ella couldn't help but grin too. And Liam couldn't help but notice how perfectly she seemed to fit into the role of adventuring hero. She wore a laced green vest over a puffy-sleeved swashbuckler's shirt and a pair of her trademark satiny "fighting pants" tucked into tall black boots. Her hair was cut into a short, asymmetrical bob—a look she'd decided to keep after getting an impromptu restyling by the fangs of a bladejaw eel the previous summer.

"Thank you," she said. "So, what are you doing in these parts anyway?"

"I came here to be the hero of Hithershire."

"Job's already taken." Ella grinned again and performed a fancy flourish with her blade. "Besides, why would you want it? Two kingdoms not enough? You've already got Erinthia *and* Avondell. Speaking of which, I'm surprised Briar let you this far out of her sight." She suddenly hunched up, her eyes darting back and forth. "Wait, she's not lurking under a rock somewhere, is she?"

"No, I haven't seen Briar since our marriage was annulled."

Ella's eyes widened. "Whoa. You really ended it? How in the world did you convince her to agree to that?"

Liam cleared his throat. "I, um, can be very persuasive when I want to be. And I decided I'd finally had enough of her."

"Wow," Ella said, running her fingers through her hair, trying to process the news. "I'm just surprised. I mean, the last time I saw you, you seemed pretty content to head back to Avondell and be Briar's dutiful husband."

Liam bristled. "The same way you went off with Frederic."

"Yeah, well . . . ," she began sheepishly. "That only lasted long enough for us to get back to Harmonia. I haven't seen him since then. I sort of . . . broke up with him."

Both of them were silent for quite some time.

"Well, this is interesting," Liam finally said. "We're both, um, available. I suppose we could—"

"We could be partners," Ella said. "Partners in fighting crime. Let's thwart the evildoers of Hithershire together and . . . see how it goes."

Liam offered his hand, and Ella shook it.

"Partners it is," he said. "Let's show 'em what we've got."

Fig. 5
FORGED
PARTNERSHIP

Liam and Ella's partnership lasted approximately forty-five minutes.

In the next town, they stumbled upon a burglary in progress—thieves ransacking the mayor's house. Ella wanted to swing in through an open window and surprise the robbers;

Liam insisted on a head-on attack through the front door. Neither was willing to compromise. They each did their own things; and by the time it was over, the house was a wreck, Liam was tangled in the living room drapes, Ella had a flour sack over her head, and the crooks were safely back at their hideout with a wheelbarrow full of stolen loot.

"I was better off on my own," Ella huffed.

"Then you should stay on your own," Liam snapped.

"I will!" Ella growled, getting right in his face.

"And so will I!" he snarled back.

"As soon as we clean this place up!"

"Yeah! As soon as . . . oh. Uh, sure, all right." He sheepishly rehung a picture frame that had been knocked down.

Two hours later, when the house was spotless, Ella and Liam stormed out in opposite directions. Neither noticed the sheriff only a few yards away, hanging a Wanted poster on the mayor's fence—a poster with their faces on it.

The following afternoon, while patrolling as a solo hero once again, Liam heard another call for help. *Man,* he thought, *Hithershire is* not *a safe place.* He followed the cries to a secluded field behind a rickety barn, where he saw a white-haired old man dangling upside down from a peach tree.

"Oh, thank goodness," the man croaked. "All the blood is rushing to my head." He pointed up at his right foot, which had a rope looped around the ankle. "It's a trap," he said with an embarrassed shrug.

That was when Liam spotted movement out of the corner of his eye—Ella! She was entering the field from the other side of the barn. As soon as she and Liam made eye contact, they each took off in a mad dash for the tree.

"My rescue!" Ella shouted, running as fast as she could.

"I was here first!" Liam grunted, charging forward.

When they were each within a few yards of the hanging man, they both dove. The old man nimbly pulled himself up and out of the way, letting Liam and Ella crash into each other, forehead to forehead.

"Well, that was easier than I'd hoped," the old man said. With one hand, he gracefully slipped the rope off his ankle and hopped down to the ground. He motioned to an unseen partner in the branches of the tree and stepped back as a weighted net fell onto his would-be saviors. Liam and Ella, still clutching their throbbing heads, looked up in shock at the old man's nearly toothless grin.

"I *did* say it was a trap." He chuckled. "You two have had the pleasure of being captured by Wiley Whitehair, oldest bounty hunter in the Thirteen Kingdoms."

Pinned under the heavy net, Liam and Ella couldn't even think about drawing their swords. Instead they glared at each other.

"This is all your fault," Ella hissed.

"My fault?" Liam scoffed. "You're the one who couldn't stand back and let me make one stinking rescue."

"If you didn't feel such a burning need to out-hero me, we wouldn't be in this mess," Ella said.

"Come on down, boys," Whitehair called up into the tree. Three more bounty hunters leapt down from among the leaves. The first was a rotund man with thick mutton-chop sideburns, the second a wiry teenager in a mask, and the third . . . Well, Liam and Ella recognized the third immediately.

"Ruffian," Liam growled. "I should have known this had something to do with Briar Rose. Fine, take me back to Avondell. But let Ella go."

"Ooh, sounds like a confession," said Whitehair, rubbing his hands together. "But I'm afraid I have to say no to your request. We're gettin' money for both of you. Hey, Ruffian, since you've got a history with this fella, why don't you be the one to tie him up for us. Yellow Tom, you take care of the girl."

Ruffian the Blue, Briar's bounty hunter of choice, stared

at Liam from under his dark hood. But as the stocky Yellow Tom bent to lift the net, Ruffian thumped the man over the head with the handle of his sword, knocking him flat.

"What'd you do that for?" sputtered Whitehair. "We were supposed to split the money four ways. I shoulda known you'd turn on us, you greedy moper." He drew a long dagger from his belt and turned to the masked teenager. "C'mon, kid," he said. "He can't fight both of us at once!"

The ancient bounty hunter started to run at Ruffian. But after only one step, he fell chest-first into the dirt, tripped up by the fast-moving staff of the masked teen. Whitehair rolled over and bounced to his feet. "Traitorous brat! You're teamin' with Ruffian?" the old man snarled. He brought his arm back and prepared to hurl his dagger. "I shoulda known better than to work with a little boy."

"I'm not a boy," the young bounty hunter said, pulling off her mask and releasing a bouncy wave of chestnut curls. Whitehair blinked in confusion before she whomped him over the head with her staff.

"Lila!" Liam and Ella shouted in unison.

"You're getting better with the staff," Ruffian said to Lila, frowning through the compliment. "But pulling off the mask was an unnecessary bit of showboating. The two seconds it took you to do that could have cost you your life."

"Sorry, Ruff," Lila said, looking chastened. "I guess my brother and I inherited the same flair for showmanship."

"Are you saying that because I like to flourish my cape?" Liam asked defensively. "Because I'll have you know that a good cape flourishing can provide a useful— Wait! I don't even know what's going on here! Someone explain."

Lila took a deep breath. "I'd tell you to sit down for this, but you're both already on the ground. You might want to stay there." And as Ruffian hoisted the heavy, weighted net off Ella and Liam, Lila broke the news to them.

"Briar is . . . dead?" Liam asked, staring off at the old barn. He couldn't bring himself to make eye contact with his sister at that moment. "And someone thinks I did it?"

"*Everyone* thinks you did it," Ruffian said flatly.

"They think we *all* did it," Lila clarified. "I'm on the list, too. That's why I've been traveling in disguise."

"I can't believe this," Ella said. "I mean, it's no secret that I wasn't Briar's biggest fan, but this is . . . horrible."

Lila crouched next to her brother and put her arm around his shoulders. "You okay?" she asked.

"If you'd asked me a few months ago," he said softly, "I would have listed Briar as the person I hated most in the world. But ever since the Bandit King's castle, I've been wondering if I'd judged her too harshly. Now I'll never know."

Ruffian harrumphed loudly but didn't elaborate beyond that.

Ella got to her feet. "Sorry to be practical at a time like this, but we can't stay here. Every bounty hunter in the Thirteen Kingdoms will be looking for us. Not to mention every knight, soldier, and village constable. We need to warn Frederic and the others."

Liam stood and cleared his throat. "You're right," he said. "We need to get to Harmonia, Sylvaria, Sturmhagen . . . that's a lot of ground to cover. We should leave right away."

"No, you shouldn't," Ruffian said. His silver goatee was the only part of his face visible under the shadow of his hood. "Since Lila cares about the two of you, I feel the need to point out that you are making a critical mistake."

"Aw, c'mon, Ruff, you care about them, too, don't you?" Lila said, giving the gloomy figure a playful poke in the ribs.

"No," Ruffian said. "And yet I will still inform you that your best course of action is to go into hiding."

"Not going to happen," Ella said.

"Not while our friends are in danger," Liam added.

"To be seen on the open road would be beyond foolhardy," Ruffian insisted.

"We'll make sure we're not seen," Ella said, sounding very sure of herself.

Ruffian glanced into Lila's big, hopeful eyes, then turned back to the others. "Let me try to explain it to you this way: I am the *best* bounty hunter in the land. Whitehair there is the *oldest* bounty hunter in the land. Yellow Tom is the *hungriest*. And there is another man who is the *most dangerous* bounty hunter in the land. His name is Greenfang. And you can guarantee he will be after you as well."

"We'll take our chances," Ella said.

"Sylvaria is just across the border from here," Liam added. "If we head out now, we can make it to Duncan by late afternoon." He turned to his sister. "And you, young lady—"

"Don't call me 'young lady.'"

"She'll be fine," Ruffian interjected.

Liam kissed the top of Lila's head before he and Ella mounted their horses and rode off.

"You're welcome!" Lila yelled bitterly as they galloped out of sight.

"Don't worry," Ruffian said. "Nobody listens to me either."

"So what do you and I do now?" Lila asked.

Ruffian sniffled. "We find the real killer."

7

AN OUTLAW GETS NUTS

Of course, Duncan was not home. He and Snow White had already left to rescue Frederic, Gustav, and Rapunzel. Ella and Liam figured this out . . . eventually.

"I'm sorry, did you say Duncan and Snow went to *rescue* somebody?"

"Yes, you," King King said.

"They went to rescue *me*?" Liam asked, scratching his temple.

"You're Frederic, aren't you?" the king asked.

"No, I'm Liam."

"Wait," Ella interjected. "Are you saying Frederic got captured?"

"We're not saying it," Queen Apricotta said. "The blue

twinkle-bugs said it."

Liam looked to Ella. "I think the bounty hunters already have Frederic."

"Yes," King King confirmed. "Also someone named Punzy. And another one named Zel. Or— Wait, maybe it was Gustav."

"Where are they?" Ella asked.

"The mooooooooooon," Mavis and Marvella chimed in.

"Huh?"

"Twinkle-bugs live on the moon," Marvella explained.

"No," Liam huffed. "I don't care where the twiddle-bugs are—"

"*Twinkle*-bugs," Mavis corrected. "You're dreamy, but you don't listen well."

Liam slapped his hand to his forehead.

"Did the twinkle-bugs say where the bounty hunters were taking Frederic?" Ella asked.

"To Avondell," Queen Apricotta said. "Along Old Pinebrush Road, heading westward out of Sturmhagen."

"See, Mom listens well," Mavis said. Queen Apricotta blushed.

Along Old Pinebrush Road, heading westward out of Sturmhagen, Greenfang and his crew rolled into Avondell, their cage full of prisoners lagging at the tail end of their entourage. Frederic, Rapunzel, and Gustav sat on the cold metal floor, glumly watching the forest pass by. Without warning, a walnut—with a tiny, folded piece of paper tied around it—sailed into the cage and plunked against Gustav's head.

"Hey!" he snapped. "What's the big idea?" He picked up the walnut and went to throw it back into the trees, but Frederic grabbed his arm.

"No!" Frederic blurted.

The orange-bearded bounty hunter, who was driving their prison wagon, turned around. "What's going on back there?"

"Oh, nothing, sir," Frederic said. "A passing bird just dropped a nut on my friend's head."

The man eyed them with suspicion, but his attention was drawn back to the road when the wagon hit a bump, rattling the cage and jingling the brass keys that hung from the side of the driver's bench. Frederic grabbed the walnut and carefully unfolded the attached note. "Can't you see it's a message?" he whispered at Gustav.

"What's it say?" Rapunzel asked softly, leaning closer to see the paper.

Written in itty-bitty letters were the words:

RESCUE TIME! DISTRACT THE DRIVER.

They all looked up. On the side of the road, just beyond the trees, Duncan and Snow were riding their horses, keeping pace with the prison wagon. The couple waved to them giddily.

"Where did *they* come from?" Gustav gasped. Then he shrugged. "At least it's not my brothers."

"What do we do?" Rapunzel asked.

Frederic took a deep breath. "We do what the note says."

He scooted to the back of the cage, behind the driver. "Excuse me, Mr. . . . um."

"Orangebeard," the bounty hunter said.

"Mr. Orangebeard," Frederic said politely. "I wanted to thank you. We may have hit a little bump just now, but on the whole, this ride has been exceptionally smooth. Far more enjoyable than one would expect when traveling by iron cage."

"Well, thank you," said the man, proudly raising his furry orange chin. "You should be glad it's me at the reins and not Norin Black-Ax." He indicated one of the big blond twins, riding up ahead. "That guy can't avoid a pothole for his life."

"Black-ax, huh?" Frederic said. "Do all bounty hunters have a color in their names?"

"It's tradition," the driver said. "You know Greenfang, of

course. The elf over there is Periwinkle Pete. And the fella with the mongooses is Erik the Mauve. Norin's brother is Corin Silversword. Although his sword is black, so that one's a bit confusing."

While the driver was chatting with Frederic, Snow White expertly whipped a peach pit at the wagon and knocked the dangling key ring off its hook. Frederic heard the keys hit the road and pretended to crash against the bars of the cage.

"Whoa," he said. "Must've hit another bump!"

"That was weird," said Orangebeard. "I didn't even feel it."

"My fault, really," Frederic said. "I shouldn't distract you from your driving. Carry on." He turned back to Gustav and Rapunzel.

"Snow's aim is truly amazing," Rapunzel whispered in admiration.

"What's next?" Gustav wondered aloud. The question was soon answered when Duncan's horse, Papa Scoots Jr., darted out of the trees and onto the road behind the wagon. At first they thought the horse had no rider, but they soon noticed Duncan hanging upside down, under the animal's belly.

Rapunzel readied her tears.

With his wavy-haired head dangling inches from the

rocky ground, Duncan scooped up the keys. Placing the brass ring between his teeth, he strenuously pulled himself up the side of his horse and back into the saddle. He took a moment to give his friends a thumbs-up before leaping from his mount and landing on the rear of the prison wagon. He gripped the bars of the cage door to stay upright. Papa Scoots Jr., happy to be free of Duncan, veered off into the trees once again.

"Gustav, you look great," Duncan said as he tried to keep his balance on a narrow lip of wood. "Have you lost weight?"

"Stick the key in the hole," Gustav snarled, "before I squeeze you between these bars and pull you in here with us."

"Oh, right." Duncan unlocked the cage.

Frederic glanced over his shoulder, relieved to see that Orangebeard still had his back to them. "I can't believe this is working," he said.

It *was* working. Almost perfectly. Too bad Duncan's wasn't the only rescue attempt that afternoon on Old Pinebrush Road.

8

AN OUTLAW PUTS HIS RIGHT FOOT IN, PUTS HIS RIGHT FOOT OUT

"This must be them," Liam whispered. He and Ella, on horseback, sat hidden among the evergreens, watching Greenfang and his platoon of bounty hunters come up the road toward them.

"But where are Frederic and the others?" Ella asked. "And *what* are those giant animals?"

"They look like mongooses," said Liam. "Or is it mongeese?" He shrugged. "That'll be the first thing Frederic says to us after we rescue him."

"Look, I see a wagon in the distance!" Ella pointed down the road. "That's got to be where they're being held."

"Perfect," Liam said, pulling a long rope from his

saddlebag. "Once the riders have passed, I'll take out the wagon driver. We can steal the whole thing and be gone before they even notice."

"Won't work," Ella said. "There's no way that wagon can outrun their horses."

"Well, what would you suggest?" Liam asked, sharpness in his voice.

"We stay hidden," she replied. "Take out as many as we can in an ambush."

"Well, the *smart* thing to do would be to take out the driver."

"And alert the more dangerous guys to our presence?"

"That wouldn't— Oh, crud. They're almost here. I've got to get into position." Liam jumped from his horse and shinnied up a nearby tree to set his rope.

"Don't do it, Liam," Ella hissed. "You'll give us away." She pulled out a slingshot, loaded a stone, and took aim at the approaching Greenfang.

"Put that away!" Liam whisper-shouted as he looped his rope over a high branch. "You're going to tip off the wagon driver. We do this my way."

"You're not always right, Liam," Ella snarled, steadying her hand and pulling back on the slingshot.

"I'm not always *wrong* either!"

Neither of them was aware that, at that very moment, Duncan was on the back of the prison wagon, swinging open the cage door to free their friends.

The bounty hunters passed the copse of trees that hid Ella and Liam. Ella clenched her jaw and kept her slingshot trained on Greenfang but didn't fire. Liam wrapped his hands around his rope but didn't jump. Each was waiting for the other to make a move. Until, finally, both lost their patience—at the exact same time. The stone rocketed from Ella's slingshot, straight at Greenfang's head—but before it could hit its mark, a mongoose leapt into the air, blocking the shot. The animal let out a shrill yowl as it was knocked off the road.

"Ambush!" Greenfang shouted.

But Liam was already swinging through the air. Orangebeard looked up just in time to see the bottoms of Liam's boots before they pounded into his whiskery face. The bounty hunter tumbled to the dirt as Liam landed on the driver's bench and yanked on the reins, bringing the horses to a sharp stop.

Duncan, who was already precariously balanced on the back of the wagon, dropped the keys and flew forward *into* the cage, the door of which slammed shut and locked behind him.

"I don't remember planning that part," he said, lying in Gustav's lap.

"Liam?" Frederic asked.

"You can thank me later," Liam said, turning to face the captives. "Right now, we have to get out of here."

This was punctuated by four quick *thwipp*ing sounds as Periwinkle Pete fired a volley of arrows at the wagon. Each hit its mark, pinning the edge of Liam's cape to the wooden driver's bench. Liam struggled, trying to face front again, but he was trapped under his own cape. "Oh, crud."

Ella, in the meantime, had charged out of the woods on her horse and was crossing swords with all the remaining bounty hunters. "Hey, Liam," she yelled, ducking a swipe from Greenfang. "You wanna start the getaway anytime soon?"

"I'm trying," Liam grunted as he thrashed about under the tightly stretched cape. "Anybody back there have something sharp? I can't reach my sword."

Duncan opened his belt pouch and pulled out the small sculpting knife that he carried "just in case I come across some clay." He passed it to Liam, who clasped the little blade awkwardly between two fingers and began hacking away at his collar. "I can't believe I'm losing my cape *this* early," he grumbled.

"Oh, my goodness! Ella's in trouble," Frederic said as his former fiancée simultaneously kicked away a giant mongoose and deflected a battle-ax.

Gustav stared longingly at the battle. "Aw, man. I *so* want in on that."

"Look!" Rapunzel said, pointing behind the wagon.

Snow White had crept out of the forest on foot, her many colored ribbons flapping in the breeze. She picked up the fallen key ring and cautiously approached the prison wagon.

"Yay, Snowy!" Duncan whispered gleefully.

With care, Snow climbed up onto the back of the wagon.

"You can do it, Snow!" Frederic cheered softly.

"Of course I can," Snow said. "Do you know how often Duncan locks himself inside things? All sorts of things, too: trunks, cabinets, lunch boxes—"

"Snow, the *cage*," Rapunzel reminded her.

Snow giggled sheepishly, turned the key, and swung open the door—at precisely the moment that Liam succeeded in cutting free of his cape. "All right," he said. "Let's get out of here!" He cracked the reins and startled the horses into action.

As the wagon took off at top speed, Snow wobbled and began to fall backward. Everybody in the cage dove for her, each grabbing a ribbon. Together, they all yanked her back up—and into the cage with them. The door slammed shut behind her.

"You've got to be kidding me," Gustav grumbled. They'd now increased the number of prisoners from three to five.

"It's okay," Snow said, holding up her arm. "I still have the key— *EEP!*" The wagon hit a bump, and the key ring flew from Snow's hand, landing in the dirt behind them.

"You've got to be kidding me," Gustav repeated.

"Don't worry," Liam said, glancing over his shoulder at them. "As long as I'm in the driver's seat— *Oof!*" Liam was sent flying to the ground as a giant mongoose pounced onto the driver's bench and took his place.

"Jackie Fat-Whiskers!" Duncan shouted.

As the wagon careened along the road, the prisoners looked out the back to see Liam rolling in the dust. "Oh, good!" Snow called to him. "Now you can get the keys!"

The bounty hunters scattered as the wagon hurtled toward them, giving Ella a much-needed break. She spotted Liam lying capeless in the dirt and raced to him. He snatched the keys off the ground and climbed up to sit behind her on her horse.

"Don't say a word," Liam grumped.

"I don't need to," Ella said, allowing herself a slight smirk as they took off in pursuit of the runaway wagon.

Greenfang got a good look at their faces as they sped past him. "This is our lucky day—they've got bounties on their heads, too!" He turned to his men. "Double Trouble, get after that horse! The rest of you, stop the cage!"

As Ella and Liam rode, the twin bounty hunters closed in on either side of them, grinning wickedly. Norin Black-Ax swung his black ax, and Corin Silversword swung his not-silver sword.

"Duck!" Liam and Ella yelled to each other in unison. The brothers' weapons clanged together, and both twins were knocked from their mounts.

"Lummoxes!" Greenfang spat.

Duncan cheered as he and his friends awkwardly bounced against one another in the overcrowded cage. "Huzzah! We're getting away!"

"I hate to be the one to break this to you," Rapunzel said, trying to hold herself in one place, "but I'm pretty sure mongooses can't drive."

The animal turned around, reins in its mouth, and gave them an offended growl.

"Keep your eye on the road, weasel!" Gustav barked. The mongoose looked back to the curvy, downhill mountain path they were now on and whimpered.

Pushing her horse to go as fast as it could, Ella caught

up to the runaway wagon. "Give me the keys," she said to Liam.

"Why?" he asked.

"I'm going to jump onto the wagon."

"No, I'll do it."

"Liam, this is not the time." She snatched the keys from his hand and leapt off the galloping horse, landing on the back edge of the wagon. She gripped the cage bars to steady herself. "Take care of the mongoose," she called back to Liam.

Fig. 6
NOT a WEASEL

Liam grumbled and raced to the front of the wagon, reaching up to snap a twig from a tree branch as he rode. "Hey, mongoose!" he called, waving the stick. "Look what I've got! Look!"

The mongoose dropped the reins from its mouth and turned toward Liam, panting excitedly.

"Fetch!" Liam shouted, hurling the stick deep into the woods. The mongoose leapt from the speeding wagon and disappeared among the trees. Liam carefully hopped back into the driver's seat of the wagon. "Blecch," he groaned when he picked up the soggy, drool-soaked reins.

On the back of the wagon, Ella unlocked and opened the cage door.

"Hold it open! Hold it open!" everyone inside cried. "Don't let it close again!"

"Relax," Ella said, stepping into the cage. "We're home free. Liam, take us out of here!"

"With pleasure," he replied, cracking the reins once more.

This was punctuated by several quick *thwipp*ing sounds. The bounty hunters were right back on their tail, and Periwinkle Pete had launched another volley of arrows. Each hit its mark, and the wagon's team of horses—with their harnesses severed—took off in separate directions. Liam yelped and squeezed the now-useless reins as the wagon plummeted uncontrollably down the winding mountain road.

"Lamebrain!" Greenfang barked at his archer. "We need them alive, fool!"

Pete brought his horse to an abrupt halt, kicking up clouds of dust. "I am an elf," he said, proudly crossing his arms. "I shall continue the chase once I have received a proper apology."

Greenfang fumed. "Why am I working with you again?"

The runaway cage, in the meantime, swayed and rattled—as did its passengers. The road narrowed, and tree limbs cracked against the iron bars.

"I think I liked it better when the big doggie was driving," Snow said as her acorn tiara bounced off her head.

"Don't worry, Snow," Duncan said. "I've got you. Everything will be all right."

"Duncan, that's *my* hand," said Frederic.

"It's so soft," Duncan said with admiration.

"I moisturize."

"Everybody hold on!" Liam shouted as the wagon hit a steeply angled boulder and launched into the air. When the wheels hit the ground again, Frederic and Duncan—still hand in hand—went airborne, sailing toward the open door. Gustav reached out to catch them, tripped over Snow's tiara, and tumbled out of the cage with them. The three men rolled to a painful stop amid the gravel.

"Well, that's one way to get out," Gustav groaned.

Periwinkle Pete, fresh from an apology that he found sorely lacking in sincerity, was once again racing after the wagon on his horse when he saw the pile of princes plop into his path. He whipped his reins to the left and made a sharp turn—directly into Greenfang's horse. The two steeds collided and their riders fell, tumbling into Erik the Mauve and his startled mongoose. All three bounty hunters rolled off the road and down an embankment.

"Get up, get up," Gustav said, dragging Frederic and Duncan to their feet. He took off on foot down the hill, and his fellow princes followed.

The wagon continued to barrel downhill, heading toward a sharp bend in the road. "Brace yourselves," Liam said, his fingers curling around the edge of his seat. Inside, Snow and Rapunzel huddled under Ella's arms. The wagon reached the bend, catapulted over a scattering of large rocks and shrubs, and landed with a splash in a thick and bubbling mud pit. Liam slid off the bench and plunked into the goo; the women all fell toward the front of the cage; the door slammed shut; and the keys slid out and disappeared below the muck.

"We're alive," Rapunzel said, finding it hard to believe.

"I would prefer not to do that again," Snow added.

"Liam, get over here and help find the keys," Ella said as she reached out between the bars and sifted through the brown slime.

Wiping sludge from his eyes, Liam dug around fruitlessly. "I can't find them."

Gustav arrived, with Frederic and Duncan panting behind him.

"Blondie, you're okay," he shouted as he plodded into the mire.

"Sort of," Rapunzel said. "We're still stuck in this cage."

"It's worse than just that," Frederic added, looking up the hill behind them. The bounty hunters were coming. On their mounts again. All of them.

"Hey, that's not fair," said Duncan. "The bad guys got their horses back, and I've lost poor Papa Scoots yet again."

"We've got to get this cage open," Liam said, pulling pointlessly on the locked iron door.

"It's not going to happen," Ella said.

"We'll fight them off," Gustav said, cracking his knuckles.

"No, all of you, listen to me," Ella said. "You need to leave. They have horses and weapons and . . . mongeese. Get away while you can. The only thing worse than some of us getting caught is *all* of us getting caught."

Everyone looked to Liam. He took a deep breath and nodded.

"I'll be back, Snowy," Duncan said with far less than his usual amount of perk.

Frederic and Gustav both flashed reluctant looks at Rapunzel. "Guys, run away," she said. "They're almost here."

The princes sloshed out of the mud and took off down the mountainside. Before they vanished out of sight, Liam turned back and called, "We *will* save you."

"Save yourselves first!" Ella yelled back. And the princes were gone.

Greenfang's gang arrived a few seconds later and dismounted.

"What a mess," Greenfang said, scowling.

"Well, we still got three of 'em," said Orangebeard. "Which is how many we had to start with."

Greenfang leaned over and snarled in his henchman's face. "We could have had *all* of them. I still *want* all of them." He looked at the women in the cage, then walked over to the rugged slope down which the princes had fled. "Pete! Erik! Come with me. We're going after them. On the mongooses."

"Mongeese," Erik said halfheartedly.

"The rest of you," Greenfang said, "haul this wagon out of the muck and take it to the royal court in Avondell. The faster we get these ladies onto Death Row, the faster we get our gold."

"I really hope Death Row isn't what it sounds like," Rapunzel said, growing pale.

"Yeah," said Snow. "Maybe it's not so much a *row* as it is one big room full of prisoners waiting to die."

"That . . . was not my point," Rapunzel said.

Ella put her hands on the shoulders of the other two women. "We will get out of this," she said with reassurance. Then she looked off into the distance. "It's the guys I'm worried about."

9

AN OUTLAW GOES GREEN

The princes were exhausted. They'd been running for three solid days, hiking across miles of rugged terrain, ducking behind trees and sliding down hillsides in order to stay ahead of the bounty hunters who dogged them the entire way. They would have given anything for a bed or a hot meal, but towns and villages needed to be strictly avoided—a sad fact they discovered when they sought refuge at an inn in the tiny hamlet of Tartlesboro and almost lost Duncan to a grieving innkeeper with a hot skillet.

A satin-draped minstrel was in the process of serenading the inn's dining room guests as the princes ducked inside. "He's good and he's kind and he never says curses! / He makes kingdoms better, when they started off worses!" The honey-voiced man sang as he plucked on a mandolin.

"I wonder who he's singing about," Duncan said.

"At least it's not us for once," Frederic said, shutting the door behind them and peeking out a nearby window to check for any signs of bounty hunters.

But that was when the innkeeper, who had been busy at the stove, heard the door slam and turned to see who his new customers were. His face turned instantly red, and his nostrils flared.

"Murderous fiends! You took away our Sleeping Beauty!" the angry man shouted as he leapt over the bar and swung his cast-iron pan straight at Duncan's face. Luckily, Gustav saved the day by throwing his petite friend out of the way—and through a table.

"I'm no murderer," Duncan protested as Liam and Frederic pulled him from the splinters. "The only thing killer about me is my dance moves." But his defense went unheeded—and every customer in the place joined the innkeeper in chasing the princes out of town.

And so it was back into the wilderness, where, within minutes, they heard the slobbery panting of pursuing mongooses. When the princes finally stumbled upon the banks of Rambling River, they were more than just relieved.

"This is the perfect place to lose them," Liam said. "We

won't leave a trail on water."

A fisherman's canoe sat by the riverside. They climbed in and pushed off (leaving a note and a few coins behind for the boat's former owner). Floating downstream, they finally had a chance to catch their breaths—except for Frederic, whose head was planted firmly between his legs.

"Did you drop something?" Duncan asked.

"No," Frederic replied, his voice quivery. "I've just never been in a boat before. And apparently I get seasick."

"Riversick," Duncan corrected, though not unsympathetically.

Gustav shifted uneasily in his seat. "What's the plan now?" he asked. "Straight to Avondell Palace, right? We bust the girls out of jail?"

"Anything to get us back on dry land," Frederic muttered.

Gustav grabbed the oars. "All right, then. Let's hightail it to Avondell Palace."

"No," said Liam forcefully. "We're not doing this again."

The others looked at him askance. "What's the problem?" Gustav asked. "Quitting the hero business just because we're outlaws now?"

"No," Liam said again. "I mean, yes, we have to help our friends, but we're not doing *this* again." He held out his hands to indicate the soiled, tattered state they were in. "Every time one of us gets captured, the others all run off half-cocked on some barely planned rescue mission. And we always manage to foul things up worse than they were when we started. Look at what happened at my wedding. Look at what happened with those bounty hunters!"

"To be fair," Frederic said, "Duncan and Snow were doing pretty well until—"

"That's not the point!" Liam said. "We're going to get Ella, Rapunzel, and Snow free. But we're going to do it *right* this time."

"And how's that exactly?" Gustav asked.

"We're going to prove our innocence," Liam said.

In an unnecessarily dark chamber at the heart of the fortress formerly known as Castle von Deeb, Lord Rundark crossed his arms against his burly chest and watched his army of bandits at work. Scores of grunting, sweaty henchmen tramped past him, lugging taffy machines, Ping-Pong tables, and tubs of raw cookie dough. Once outside, these offending items would be tossed into the moat along with every other reminder of the young Deeb Rauber's reign as Bandit King.

Rauberia was no more. This was New Dar now—a land

in which there was no time or place for trivial things like entertainment or recreation. Lord Rundark made sure of that.

As four bandits worked together to haul out a chocolate-smeared trampoline, one of them made the mistake of whistling. The other three stopped in their tracks, closed their eyes, and braced themselves for what they knew was to come. A second later, the Warlord was looming over the absentminded whistler, snorting like an angry bull. With his bare hands, Rundark folded the trampoline around the man, trapping him like beans in a burrito. "Carry on," the Warlord said.

He stepped back and watched the remaining three carry out the twisted trampoline with its pitiful passenger.

Fig. 7
NEW TENANT

Back during Rauber's rule, one of them might have freed their friend once they were outside, but Rundark had no worries about such a thing happening now. His brutal, iron-fisted ways had earned him the utter loyalty of these men.

A black-clad messenger jogged into the room, an emissary from the League of Evil Couriers. The man's hands trembled, and his breath was short. "Lord Rundark, I bring news from Avondell," he announced in a quivery voice.

Rundark stared at him, waiting.

"Three of the ladies have arrived there as prisoners," the courier said. He swallowed hard. "But I regret to inform you that the young princess from Erinthia and all four of the princes have thus far eluded capture. Bounty hunters are still in pursuit, though, so it's just a matter of time. I'm sure."

The Warlord stroked the long braids of his wild, black beard before he suddenly stepped off into a shadowy corner of the obsidian chamber and began mumbling softly. *He's talking to himself,* the messenger thought. *He's completely insane. And I'm dead.* But then he heard a second voice. Rundark wasn't alone. He was talking to someone hidden in the darkness. No, not just talking—*arguing.* The courier strained to listen, praying that his own doom was not the topic of conversation. ". . . best not to take chances," he thought he heard one of them say. He was just about to attempt a quiet exit when Rundark grabbed something shiny and turned back into the dim lamplight. The Warlord stood before the messenger, holding a large glass-like orb on his palm.

"Take this to our friends by the sea," Rundark said. "They will know what to do with it."

"At once," the courier said, taking the big crystal ball and nearly collapsing with relief. He turned to leave.

"Oh," said Rundark. "And after you've made your delivery, come back here and jump into the moat with the bladejaw eels."

"Yes, sir." The messenger sighed and took off on his trip to Yondale.

10

AN OUTLAW SMELLS SOMETHING FISHY

At night the Twisted Forest of Yondale is the kind of eerie, shadow-bathed, creak-and-groan-filled place that makes you believe its gnarled and drooping trees are going to snap to life and bite your head off. By the light of day it's slightly less intimidating—you may feel like the trees are only going to eat one of your feet or maybe a few fingers. So as Lila rode through the Twisted Forest, she reminded herself that sweet, naive, little Snow White had managed to brave these woods on her own. It had been here in the Twisted Forest that Snow's stepmother, who was queen of Yondale at the time, had abandoned the young princess and left her to die. But Snow had survived and made it into the much happier forest of Sylvaria (which was, coincidentally, called the Much Happier Forest). *And I will survive my trip too*, Lila told herself. *After all, I've got the world's greatest bounty hunter by my side.*

"So why did we come here again?" she asked Ruffian, ducking as she rode under a particularly evil-looking oak.

"Wiley Whitehair is from Yondale," Ruffian said, glancing down at her from his much taller horse. "So is Greenfang. And they were the first hunters to find out about the bounty on the League of Princes. They saw the Wanted posters by Yondale Harbor."

"Of course!" Lila said excitedly. "You'd think posters would have gone up in Avondell first, since that's supposedly where Briar was killed. But we didn't hear about it until days later, when Reynaldo wrote his song. If news of the murder spread from Yondale first, maybe this is where the crime actually took place."

"If you know everything, why do you bother asking questions?"

"Are you smiling under that hood?" Lila asked playfully.

"I assure you I am not," Ruffian said.

"Sometimes I think you're the only one who actually believes in me, Ruff."

"I really do wish you would stop calling me that," the bounty hunter droned.

"You know it's true, Ruff. Even my brother still thinks I'm useless."

"I do not believe that is the case. You need to give Prince Liam some leeway right now. He has suffered a loss, and as I can tell you from personal experience, loss has profound ways of affecting a man."

"You're talking about your daughter, right?"

Ruffian closed his eyes and pictured the girl, barely Lila's age at the time, who had disappeared years earlier—the one person he had never been able to find. "As I said before," he sniffed, "why do you bother asking questions?"

"Sorry," Lila said quickly. They rode in silence until the trees opened up onto bright-green fields, and they could see the rooftops of Yondale City beyond.

"Well, that's a relief," Lila said. She patted her pony on its dappled neck. "I think Radish here was getting a little spooked by that forest."

"I don't understand children," Ruffian grumbled. "Who names a horse Radish?"

Lila cracked up laughing. "*That's* why I did it!" she hooted, practically doubled over in her saddle as they trotted across the sunny meadow. "For *that*! It's a laugh every time someone asks me!" She wiped a tear from her eye. "Oh, that's so worth it. Ask me again!"

"I will not."

Lila and Ruffian made their way along the busy, seashell-paved streets of Yondale City to its bustling harbor, where burly men pushed wheelbarrows full of flopping flounders, and fat seagulls swooped from the sky to snag stray bits of fish guts. They saw wobbly sailors stumbling out of taverns with names like the Mermaid's Spittoon and the Salty Trousers. They saw mangy sea cats chasing after runaway crabs. And they saw League of Princes Wanted posters on every corner. Lila put on a wide-brimmed hat and tucked her hair up under it, hoping it would help disguise her. When the pair hit the docks and began asking questions, the sailors and fishermen were quick to provide answers—they were all familiar with the reputation of Ruffian the Blue.

"Those posters?" one lobster trapper asked as he unloaded buckets of shellfish from his boat. "Yeah, everyone'round here has heard about the 'Horrible Princess Murder.'"

"Wow," said Lila. "Even in Yondale they thought Briar was horrible."

"I was referrin' to the *murder* as horrible," said the lobsterman. "Not the princess. The lady was Sleepin' Beauty! Lovely girl by all accounts."

"Hah!" Lila scoffed.

"We have reason to believe the princess might have met her fate here in Yondale Harbor," the bounty hunter said, eager to change the topic.

"Well, it's not exactly *uncommon* for people to disappear from these wharfs," said a wool-capped shrimp wrangler. "But it's unlikely a princess woulda been wandering around here at night."

"Could ya give us a description of her?" the lobster trapper asked.

"Bony," Lila said. "Big, ridiculous pile of reddish hair. Skin like an albino clam. Face all scrunched up like this. . . ." She pursed her lips and wrinkled her nose as if she smelled

Fig. 8
INVESTIGATION, salty

rotting fish (which she did).

"Sounds an awful lot like that passenger who went out on the *Dreadwind* 'bout ten nights back," said a squid rustler, wiping his ink-stained hands on his apron.

"*Dreadwind?*" asked Ruffian.

"It's a ship," the squid rustler said. "Pirates—nasty ones."

"Wait," said Lila, furrowing her brow. "So Briar was kidnapped by pirates? Is she even dead?"

"The lady you're describin' was certainly alive when she got on that ship," said a nearby krill herder. "I saw 'er, too."

"As did I," added the shrimp wrangler. "Only I wouldn't call it a kidnapping. She just walked aboard like nothing was wrong."

"Yeah, there were two guys in black walking with her," said the squid rustler. "But just walking. Not grabbing or pushing or carrying or anything. They walked her up to the *Dreadwind*, she got on, and they walked away."

"I wonder if they were the same fellas in black who hung up the Wanted signs the next morning," said the lobsterman. "I figured 'em for Avondellian soldiers."

"They couldn't have been," said Lila. "Avondellian soldiers wear blue-and-silver pinstripe. Those thugs you saw were probably Briar's secret henchmen." She tugged at Ruffian's cowl. "Ruff, do you see what this means? Briar faked her own death! And then she framed the League for it."

"We have no proof of that," Ruffian said. "We don't even know for certain that the woman in question *was* Princess Briar."

"You know who could tell you?" the shrimp wrangler said, kicking away a seagull that was nipping at his bait-filled pockets. "King Edwyn."

"Why would the king of Yondale know anything about this?" Lila asked.

"Because before the strange lady got on the *Dreadwind*," he explained, "she was in the royal palace. She came down to the harbor straight from there." He pointed up to a ramshackle old castle sitting atop a nearby cliff, overlooking the harbor. Squawking seagulls circled its crumbling towers.

"Come," Ruffian said to Lila. "We need to have an audience with the king."

The inside of Yondale's royal palace was just as shoddy as its exterior. Grimy footprints dotted once-elegant carpets in hallways where crooked portraits dangled from fraying wires. It had been Yondale's queen who had kept on top of the staff and made sure the castle was spotless, but ever since she got chased off a cliff by some angry dwarfs, the place had fallen into a state of neglect. There was nothing stopping

King Edwyn from having his home fixed up; he just didn't care enough. His daughter had moved away, and his wife turned out to be a homicidal witch. He wanted some time by himself, so he sent all his servants on indefinite vacations.

When Lila and Ruffian found the ancient monarch, he was sitting on a small, dusty stool by a tiny square table where he'd been playing the same game of chess against himself for almost two years. A tarnished crown sat atop his bald head, and his long blue-gray beard was tucked into his pants. With shaky, bent fingers, he slid a pawn one space over on the chessboard. Then he looked up at his guests. There were so many wrinkles on his face, it was hard for Lila to tell where his eyes were.

"Princess Briar Rose of Avondell?" King Edwyn asked in a voice like a rusty hinge. "Yes. Yes, she paid me a visit not too long ago. Sweet girl."

"Your Highness," said Ruffian, "if I might ask the purpose of her visit?"

"She asked permission to use our pier that evening," Edwyn said. "Which was very considerate."

"Asked permission?" Lila said. "Never mind. It wasn't Briar."

"What else did the princess say?" Ruffian inquired.

"She . . ." The elderly king paused and scratched his

liver-spotted head with a chess knight. “I can’t remember. I guess it couldn’t have been too important.”

“Please try, sir,” Lila said. “I mean, you know Briar’s supposed to be dead, right? And that *your daughter* is one of the people being blamed for it?”

The king looked stunned. “Snow White? Oh, that’s ridiculous. Snow would never harm anybody.”

“Of course not,” Lila said. “But half the world thinks she’s a murderer thanks to that awful Briar Rose. She faked her death and wants your daughter to rot for it!”

“We don’t know that,” Ruffian started to say, but Lila spoke right over him.

“Your sweet, gentle daughter is being treated like a criminal! That’s why you have to think back to that night.”

King Edwyn took a deep, rattly breath. “Well, when Princess Briar Rose was here, she asked me about the pier,” he said. “And then she . . .” The old man’s face suddenly froze, and his eyes glazed over.

“Your Highness?” Ruffian prodded.

“I have told you everything I know,” the king suddenly said, his speech stiff and stilted. He was staring straight ahead, at no one in particular. “I think it is best that you two people leave this castle at once.”

“King?” Lila asked.

"You heard my words," the king said. "We are through here. You must go."

Ruffian put his hand on Lila's back and ushered her away from the old man.

"That was really weird, wasn't it?" Lila whispered as they headed for the exit. "It was like we were suddenly talking to a different person, right?"

"Once again you ask questions you know the answers to," Ruffian replied. His eyes darted around the room as they walked. Suddenly he drew his sword, dashed over to a large picture window, and threw aside its moth-eaten drapes to reveal a bald, tattoo-covered man in a vest and kilt. Lila recognized him instantly: Madu, the weresnake from Dar. And between the clenched fingers of his left hand she spotted a glimmer of orange gemstone.

"The Jeopardous Jade Djinn Gem," Lila breathed. "But how?"

Madu drew his broadsword and swung it at Ruffian. With the Darian's concentration broken, King Edwyn snapped back to normal.

"Huh?" the old man muttered, blinking at his chessboard. "Ooh, I see a good move!"

"Get the king out of here!" Ruffian called to Lila as he clashed blades with Madu. She ran back to King Edwyn.

"You're in danger, sir," she said, holding out her hand to him. "Come with me."

But her view of the elderly figure was blocked as a big, stocky man covered from head to toe in spiked armor stepped in between them. "Sorry, but we need the old guy here," said Jezek. He held up his arm and called to Madu, "Throw it here!"

Madu backed away from Ruffian, flicked his arm, and sent a flash of orange sailing through the air. Jezek caught it.

Lila turned and fled, but halfway to the door she felt a jolt as her muscles suddenly tensed up. She wanted desperately to keep running, but her limbs felt like they'd been encased in concrete. A voice echoed inside her skull: *Come back here.* And then she was turning and slowly walking back across the room, straight to the spike-covered brute. She knew Jezek was controlling her with the Djinn Gem, but she was powerless to stop it. She tried to stay focused but found her mind and her vision growing hazier by the second.

Ruffian noticed Lila's zombie-like stare and snapped into a frenzy. He elbowed Madu in the face, wrapped the long curtain around him, and ran for Jezek. Chess pieces flew as the bounty hunter snatched up the king's game board and swung it at the only part of Jezek not covered in spikes—his face. The board broke across the Darian's nose and sent him stumbling backward.

Lila heard Ruffian yell "Run!"—and she was overjoyed to realize that she *could*. As she scrambled for the exit, Lila saw Madu writhing on the ground, his body twisting and contorting as he transformed into a thirty-foot-long sand snake.

Lila could hear the crinkling paper sound of the giant serpent slithering behind her as she and Ruffian raced down the hall to the palace entryway. Just before they reached the doors, Ruffian let out a pained groan. "Hnnh!"

The snake's jaws were clamped over his shoulder, its fangs sunk deep into his flesh. Lila pulled her quarterstaff out of its holster and, with all her might, whacked the snake across the nose. The creature winced, released Ruffian, and swished back down the hall. Ruffian slumped against the wall and slid to the floor.

"You okay, Ruff?" Lila crouched beside her mentor.

"No," he said bluntly. "The venom is in my veins. You have to go on alone."

"Like that's gonna happen," Lila scoffed, putting her arm around his shoulder and trying to stand him up.

"Stop it, Lila," he wheezed. "They'll be back any second. You need to go."

"Not without you."

Ruffian removed his hood. His skin looked waxy. "I'll be fine, Lila," he said. "This isn't the first snakebite I've ever had. My blood is resistant to most venoms."

"You don't look very resistant," she said. "Your face is all veiny."

"Look me in the eye, Lila," he said. "I need to know you will stay alive. I cannot lose another one."

Footsteps sounded from down the hall. The Darians were coming. More than just two of them. Using the doorframe, Ruffian dragged himself to his feet. "I'll hold them off. Please go. Tell your brother what we've learned."

Two black-clad Darian thugs burst into the entryway, striking at Ruffian with their swords. Ailing though he was, the bounty hunter deflected their blows. "Run," he wheezed at Lila. "Now. Go."

Lila fled. *He said he'd be fine*, she told herself. *He said he could resist the venom*. But she was smart enough to know that sometimes when an adult doesn't want to frighten a child, he will tell the child what she wants to hear, whether it is true or not. Tears flowed down her cheeks as she ran along the cliffside path.

Moments later, inside Yondale Castle, Madu and Jezek stood in a small stone alcove with high stained glass windows, a hazy-eyed King Edwyn at their side. Sitting on a pedestal before them was a glowing crystal orb that appeared to be filled with swirling green mist. The mist parted, revealing the scarred face of Lord Rundark.

"It is done, Warlord," Jezek said.

"The girl?" Rundark asked.

"She got away," Jezek reported. "Just like you wanted."

11

AN OUTLAW SQUATS WHERE HE SHOULDN'T

"Are you certain nothing lives here?" Frederic asked of the dirt-walled burrow in which he and the other princes crouched, ducking to avoid the dangling roots overhead. He glanced around at the many shadow-black recesses that were not illuminated by Liam's small torch. "I'm pretty sure those are bones over there."

"They are. Very *old* bones," Liam said.

"Ooh, a puzzle," Duncan said, scooting over to the pile of tooth-marked remains. He started rearranging the bones. "Let's see what they make."

"My point is that whatever creature dug this hole is long gone," Liam said. "So let's brainstorm; you know it won't be long before we have to run again. Greenfang's been breathing down our necks for days."

"Yeah, so much for the river throwing him off our trail," Gustav said.

"The thornbushes didn't exactly work either," Frederic added. "Nor the swamp. Or the waterfall."

"Don't forget the corn maze," Duncan added.

"Yes," Liam grumbled. "How could any of us forget the corn maze?"

"I'm still picking loose kernels out of my slippers," Frederic griped.

"Focus, people," Liam snapped. "We've got a mystery to solve."

"Oh, yes. Well, let's see," said Frederic. "Who were Briar's enemies?"

"You mean besides us?" Gustav asked.

"Honestly, no one was very happy with her after she annulled our marriage," Liam said,

Fig. 9
PREVIOUS TENANT

staring into the flickering flame of his torch. "But who would be the most upset?" His eyes went wide with horror. "My parents."

"You really think your mother and father had Briar killed?" Frederic asked.

"And then blamed me for it?" Liam wondered aloud. "I don't want it to be true, but I can't rule it out. No one wanted this royal marriage more than they did."

"Then I guess we should head to Erinthia," Frederic said.

"Perfect timing," Duncan said. "Because I just finished putting these bones together. And now we know what kind of creature died here in this cave." With a flourish of his hands, he presented his work. "It was . . . a *skeleton*!"

"Brilliant," Gustav mumbled.

"Hmm, those remains are human," Liam said, inspecting the bones. "Maybe we shouldn't be in this burrow after all."

"And that's my cue to leave," Frederic said, crawling between Liam and Gustav to the root-tangled cave opening. Just as he reached the exit, a figure appeared in front of him. Greenfang grabbed him by the collar of his filthy pajama shirt and dragged him out into the open. The bounty hunter tossed Frederic over to Erik the Mauve, then bent down and called into the burrow, "The rest of you can come out now.

None of you better make a run for it, unless you want Pete to use your friend here for target practice."

The princes crawled out of the hole, one by one, to face the three bounty hunters—and the three giant mongooses.

"I give you credit for trying," Greenfang said, squinting at them. "Most folks can't evade me for even one day, let alone a week. But in the end, all you've done is get yourselves tired and me angry. Do you know why they call me the most dangerous bounty hunter in the land? Because I never give up on a quarry. Never." He squinted even harder. "I once chased a man into a volcano."

"Well, you've never faced men like us before," Liam said, staring him down.

"You mean an overconfident braggart, a muscle-bound doofus, a tiny weirdo, and a beanpole in silk pajamas?" Greenfang said. "Yeah, I'll give you that. It's a new combination for me. Now let's get you to Avondell."

"I have a question," Duncan said, raising his hand. "What do mongooses eat?"

"It's mon*geese*," Erik corrected.

"No, really, it's *not*," Pete huffed. "It's mongooses."

"EITHER IS ACCEPTABLE!" Greenfang shouted at them.

Erik cleared his throat and began tying Frederic's wrists.

"Anyway, they eat snakes mostly," he said. Then he narrowed his eyes at Duncan. "But they'd tear into you if I told 'em to."

"Oh, I'm not worried about that," Duncan said. "I was just wondering if maybe it was a mongoose that lived in that cave. But it can't be. Whatever lives in there doesn't eat snakes—it eats skeletons."

Pete sighed. "Don't you people know a bugbear den when you see one?"

"Bugbear?" Frederic said nervously. "What's that?"

"Ghastly creatures," Pete said. "Thick fur like a troll, but also shelled like a beetle. They've large pincer claws and eight eyes like a spider."

"Sort of like that thing in the tree above us?" Duncan asked, pointing upward. With a loud hiss, a hideous, ogre-size bugbear leapt down among them. Startled, Pete loosed an arrow at the attacking creature, hitting it in the chest—but that only made it angrier. The monster snapped its lobster-like claws at Greenfang, who drew his dual swords to defend himself. At Erik's command, the mongooses began clawing at the raging bugbear, but their fangs were of little use against the monster's hard shell.

Not caring to stick around and congratulate whoever won this particular fight, the princes fled into the dense forest. They climbed hills, waded across creeks, trudged through bogs, traipsed through meadows (the only part Frederic liked), and slunk through caverns, looking over their shoulders the entire way. After a week of paranoid hiking, they finally crested a rocky tor and spied the Palace of Erinthia on the horizon.

12

AN OUTLAW NEVER FORGETS MOM AND DAD

Getting to the gaudy, gold-trimmed palace was a daunting task in its own right, considering how every man, woman, and child on the thriving streets of Erinthiopolis seemed to be on the lookout for Public Enemy Number One: their own Prince Liam. But thanks to some well-chosen disguises (hooded robes emblazoned with the crest of the Royal Foot Massagers' Society), the fugitives managed to sneak along the city's back streets and into the palace through a kitchen storage entrance.

"Can I get this thing off now?" Gustav grumbled, pulling down his hood as soon as they stepped into the large pantry. Standing among the jar- and crate-lined shelves, he began to untie his robe as well. "It feels too much like a cape."

"How can it feel like a cape?" Frederic retorted. "It has sleeves!"

"Would you two please keep it down?" Liam snapped. "We're *sneaking* here, people. I can't believe I'm saying this, but why can't you be more like Duncan?"

Fig. 10
ROYAL FOOT
MASSAGERS SOCIETY, fake

Gustav frowned. "The only reason Prince Pipsqueak isn't talking is because his mouth is full of peanut butter."

They all turned to Duncan, who was four fingers deep into a jar he'd just swiped off the shelf. "Cashew butter, actually," he said sheepishly, offering a gunky, brown-toothed smile.

Liam slapped his hand to his forehead and sighed. "Gustav, keep your robe on," he said flatly. "Let's go find my parents." He opened the door to the palace's inner corridors and found himself face-to-face with a startled servant.

"What are you doing in here?" the short, apron-wearing man blurted as Liam quickly turned his back and pulled his hood tight. "I'll call the— Oh, I'm sorry. You're the foot massagers. It must be time for the king's weekly treatment."

"Yes, that's right," said Liam, deepening his voice.

"But why are you in the pantry?" the servant asked, trying to peer around and get a look at Liam's face.

Frederic snatched the jar out of Duncan's hands. "Cashew butter!" he said. "It's full of skin-softening oils. His Majesty likes it when we rub it between his toes."

"And it's delicious," Duncan added.

The man shrugged. "Whatever makes the king happy." He let the princes pass. "You should hurry, though," he added. "It's almost His Majesty's bedtime."

As fast as he dared move without arousing suspicion, Liam led the others up to the third floor, flashing his Massagers' Society emblem at anyone who gave them a second look. When they reached his parents' private chambers, Liam put his hand on the doorknob, ready to burst in and surprise them—but before he could, Duncan knocked.

Liam shot him a look of death.

Duncan shrugged. "It's the polite thing to do," he said apologetically.

Liam and the other princes stampeded into the bedroom, locking the door behind them, just as the round-bellied King Gareth, in his nightclothes, was shutting his wardrobe. Leaving the wardrobe doors slightly ajar, the king spun to face his visitors. The princes removed their hoods.

"Oh-ho! It is you," Gareth said. "This visit, it is unexpected."

"Yes, Father, it's me," Liam said. "I've come for answers. Where is Mother?"

"Your mother," the king repeated, staring at his son. "She is traveling, no? On a faraway journey. She will be so sad to have missed you. You know how the lady is—always crying, 'Why does not my son visit his poor mother?'"

Liam furrowed his brow. "Is something wrong with you? You're acting odd."

"Odd? Me? No, never. This thing you suggest, it is so silly." Gareth crossed his legs and leaned casually against the wardrobe, stroking his heavy, walrus-like mustache. "This . . . oddness you hear in my voice, it is merely joy upon seeing my beautiful son and his friends, yes? Please, tell me about your day."

"Well, we slept in a hollow log last night," Duncan began. "And when I woke this morning, I discovered that a family of lizards had moved into my pants. Then—"

"You're hiding something, Father," Liam said forcefully. He took a step closer to the king. "Tell me the truth about Briar."

"Briar? Oh, the Sleeping Beauty, yes?" Gareth said. "What happened to this girl, it is, as we say in my country, *very sad.*"

Frederic's eyes went wide. "Vero," he sputtered.

Liam shoved his father aside and flung open the wardrobe. Staring out at them from amid a rack of gold lamé cloaks was Vero, the dapper Carpagian swordsman who had served as right-hand man to Deeb Rauber.

"Good evening," the bandit said. With a flick of his long ponytail, he stepped out into the room, looking as dashing as ever in his tall black boots and puffy-sleeved shirt. He seemed unfazed, not even reaching for the sleek rapier that hung at his side. "You think you have gotten the better of me," Vero continued. "But I trust you know what I hold in my hand here, yes?" He raised a fist and separated his fingers just enough to let an eerie orange glow escape from between them.

"The Jeopardous Jade Djinn Gem," Frederic whispered.

"But we saw it destroyed," Liam said.

"The things you see, maybe you cannot believe them all," Vero said. He motioned to King Gareth, who was standing statue still in the corner.

"It is true," the king suddenly said. "I am, as they say in his country, *under his control.* Watch me tug my silly mustache." He yanked on his own mustache.

"You see?" Vero said with a smile. "This gem, it works well, no?"

"So Deeb Rauber is behind all this?" Liam asked, incredulous.

"Huh. I can't stand the brat, but I never took him for a murderer," Gustav said.

"I assure you, Deeb Rauber no longer sits on the throne of Rauberia," Vero said.

"You overthrew him?" Frederic asked. "You're in charge now?"

"If only it were so," Vero said wistfully. "But, no, I serve a man greater than I."

"Hey, not that this isn't a fascinating conversation and all," Gustav said, "but we're gonna fight, right?"

"We are at a stalemate, no?" Vero said. "There are four of you and one of me. But I have the Gem. I would say the odds are evened out."

"Can *odds* be *evened*?" Duncan asked. "That just sounds wrong."

"I have a proposal for you," Vero continued. "I remember you, Prince Liam. The lady who was your student—Ella—*her* I got to duel; I was quite impressed. But you and I, we have never had the opportunity. I propose that you and I duel right now. One-on-one. If I win, you four men go to the dungeon; if you win—something I am not concerned about—I give you the Gem."

"I, uh, don't have a sword," Liam said, his cheeks flushing.

"Here, take one of mine," Vero said, plucking an extra rapier out of the wardrobe and tossing it to Liam. "And you have my word as a Carpagian that I will not use the Gem on you. But in return, I want your three friends to give their word that they will not interfere."

Frederic and Gustav nodded.

"I'm not sure which word I should give," said Duncan. "Maybe 'collywobbles'—that's one I don't use very often."

"They give their word," Liam said. "Guys, step back."

The other three princes shuffled across the room and

gathered by the queen's fully stocked wig tree to watch the fight.

"Ready?" Vero asked.

Liam took a fencing stance and raised his blade. Vero popped the Gem into his vest pocket and flashed an empty palm. "Promise kept. As you know, the Gem cannot work without direct contact."

This was true, which is why King Gareth, who was still standing in the corner, suddenly regained control of himself. The king blinked a few times and started hollering. "Liam! What are you doing here? I can't believe you have the nerve to show your face in this kingdom after what you've done! And *you*—evil ponytail man! You've been torturing my brain with your stilted speech and odd phrasings. Guards! Guards! Get in here now! Guards!"

"Sorry, Vero. Duel's going to have to wait," Liam said. "But thanks for the sword. Quick, guys, out the window. There's a drainpipe we can slide down."

"But we still don't know what's going on," Frederic said.

"And something tells me we're not going to get much cooperation from my dad," Liam insisted. "The window—*now*!"

As Vero began fumbling around in his pocket for the Gem, Duncan rushed to the open window and peered out.

"Hey, I know those guys," Duncan said. Gustav yanked him away, a split second before an arrow zipped in and impaled one of the queen's beehive wigs.

"It's Snaggletooth and his buddies," Gustav said. "They've found us again."

"Remember back when I was a little impressed by you guys?" they heard Greenfang shout from outside. "Now I'm just annoyed."

"And I'm not so happy either," Erik the Mauve added. "I lost two mongeese in that bugbear fight."

"So escaping through the window is out," Frederic announced.

Two guards kicked the door open. "Your Highness! What's the emergency?"

"That man with the ponytail is a . . ." Gareth began to shout. Then a glazed look came over his eyes. ". . . a . . . a trusted friend of mine. And quite handsome, no? He is no bother. But the four in the robes, they are not genuine foot rubbers. Arrest them."

Vero had his hand in his vest pocket and a sly smile on his face.

"Liam, tell them who you really are," Frederic said.

"That's not going to help," Liam replied. They were in a bad situation, and he could think of only one way out.

"Gustav, do what you do best."

Gustav grinned. "Sturrrrrm-hayyyyyy-gennnn!" he shouted, and charged headfirst at the guards. The two men were so taken aback, they didn't even raise their swords; they just yelped as the brawny prince plowed into them and blasted them out into the hallway. Liam, Frederic, and Duncan followed.

More guards were rushing up the corridor as the princes fled down a spiral staircase to the ground level. They dashed along a seemingly endless hallway, in which everything from baseboards to wastebaskets was lined with gold, until they finally saw an open window, its curtains fluttering in the breeze as if beckoning them. But just as they prepared to leap *out* that window, somebody else climbed *in*.

"Sis?" Liam gasped.

Lila was startled at first, but as soon as she realized who was standing before her, she threw her arms around her brother and buried her face in his chest. "Oh, Liam, it's terrible," she said. "The Djinn Gem—"

"We know," Liam said, spinning her around and nudging her back out the window. "We don't know how Rauber's men managed to get it back, but we'll discuss that later. Right now we need to flee before Dad's guards catch up."

"Dad's guards?" Lila asked.

"And Greenfang," Frederic added, following her out.

"Greenfang?" Lila asked, even more baffled.

Once outside, the five of them ran. They ran as fast and as far as they could, until, somewhere in a dark, garbage-strewn back alley of Erinthiopolis, Frederic saw a chair—an old, termite-ravaged chair that someone had tossed out with the trash—and sat down on it.

"I'm sorry," he said, panting. "But do you know how long it's been since I've sat on anything other than a rock?"

Seeing no sign of their pursuers, the others paused to catch their breaths as well. "Ooh, check it out," Duncan said, rooting through a random rubbish bin. "Someone tossed out this perfectly good cap." He pulled a purple tricornered hat from the trash and placed it directly on his head.

"I'm so glad I ran into you guys," Lila said, leaning on her quarterstaff while she removed her left boot and shook pebbles from it.

"Where's Ruffian?" Frederic asked, fanning himself with someone's discarded spatula.

Lila closed her eyes and shook her head.

"Oh," Frederic said softly, lowering his eyes. "I'm sorry."

"How?" Liam asked, putting his arm around her.

"The Darians," she said bitterly. "He made sure I got

away, though. Oh, I wish we'd seen you there, Liam. How did we manage to miss each other in Yondale?"

"Yondale?" Liam asked. "We were never in Yondale."

"But how do you know about the Gem then?" Lila asked. "The Darians are using the Gem to control King Edwyn in Yondale."

"Snow's dad!" Duncan said. "We haven't seen him in so long. Does he still have that piece of tomato in his beard?"

"Wait, Lila, what are you talking about?" Liam asked. "The Darians can't be using the Gem in Yondale. Vero is using the Gem on Dad—*here*!"

"Impossible," Lila said. "The Djinn Gem is in Yondale. Trust me—I saw it."

"So did we, kid," Gustav said.

"Well, the Gem can't be in two places at once," Frederic said.

Lila's nose twitched in frustration. "Look, all I know is that that freaky snake guy and a bunch of other Darians used the Gem on King Edwyn in Yondale. And it seems like they probably also used it on Briar to make her get on that ship."

"Briar?" Liam burst.

"Oh, yeah!" Lila shouted, jumping up and grabbing

Liam by the collar. "You got me so flustered I didn't even tell you: Briar is alive!"

All four princes—even Duncan—were shocked into silence. After a moment Liam threw his arms around his sister and hugged her tightly.

"That's the best news we've heard in ages," Frederic said. "Briar is alive."

"I still have a chance to thank her," Liam said softly.

"And we can prove we didn't kill her," Gustav said.

"And I can finally get back that pencil she borrowed," Duncan added.

Everybody stared at him.

"It was a really good pencil," he said.

Gustav shoved him into a garbage can.

Liam cleared his throat. "Listen up, people. This is serious. The Darians have taken over two kingdoms already. And we have no reason to believe they'll stop there."

Frederic's eyebrows shot up. "*That's* who was causing all that turmoil in the woods of Sturmhagen," he said. "Darians—marching through on their way to conquer these other kingdoms."

"And we have to stop them before they take control of *everything*," said Liam. "Which they could do, since they have apparently retrieved the Djinn Gem. Let's not forget what happened when Ella was under the spell of that accursed jewel."

"She almost killed you," said Duncan proudly. "See? I remember some stuff."

"And, um, sorry to point out the obvious, but it seems like they've got at least two of these Gems," said Lila. "How do we know there aren't even more?"

"We don't," said Liam. "The future of all the Thirteen Kingdoms is at stake. Which is why the League of Princes needs to stop running. We need to take the fight to the Darians."

"How?" Frederic asked. "We can't even show our faces in public without greedy mobs chasing us."

"That's why our first priority is still clearing our names," Liam said.

"Which we do by finding Briar," Lila chimed in.

"Exactly," Liam said.

"She got loaded onto a ship called the *Dreadwind*," Lila said.

"Funny," Duncan chuckled. "Dreadwind is Frank's nickname for my flute."

"We'll have to be super careful going back into Yondale Harbor, though," Lila continued. "The place is crawling with Darians."

"Thanks for the heads-up," Liam said. "But you're not coming with us."

"Seriously?" Lila huffed, balling her hands into fists.

"Calm down, Sis. You can't come because I need you to warn everybody about the Darians. At least two monarchs have already fallen to their scheme. You need to warn the rulers of the other eleven kingdoms."

She eyed her brother skeptically. "That's an awful lot of traveling you expect me to do."

"Actually, you only need to go to Harmonia," Frederic said. "Find Smimf. With his Seven-League Boots, he can probably hit eleven kingdoms in one afternoon."

"Will you do this for us?" Liam asked, looking his sister in the eye.

"Yeah," she said grudgingly.

"Thank you," Liam said. "Gustav will go with you."

"He will?" said Gustav. "I mean, yeah, I will. I've got your back, kid."

"Thanks, but no," Lila said, holding up her hand. "I can handle the messenger bit on my own. You guys stick together and find Briar."

"Fine," Gustav said knowingly. "You go alone. I'll stay *right here* with the other guys." He gave Liam a not-so-subtle wink.

"Gustav," Lila said with a sigh, "don't waste your time trying to follow me. You know I'll lose you in three seconds."

The big prince's shoulders slumped. "Yeah, I know," he grumbled.

"All right, Sis," Liam said. "You can do this. But please take care of yourself."

"I will," she replied, hugging her brother. She wondered briefly if she and the princes should swap jobs, but she knew they'd never go for it. "Just make sure you find Briar."

"I promise," Liam said.

Duncan began strutting around, modeling his new tricornered cap. "Well, this hat was an even luckier find than I'd thought," he said. "I'm all ready for some seafaring!"

"Seafaring?" Frederic asked, turning a bit green at the thought.

"Were you even listening?" Lila asked. "The *Dreadwind* is a ship. If you guys are going to find it, you need to head out to sea yourselves."

Liam nodded. "And I know just the pirate to ask for a ride."

PART II

Out to Sea

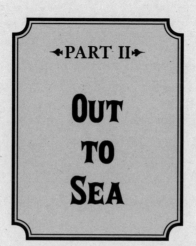

13

AN OUTLAW NEVER GOES HUNGRY

Not all of Flargstagg smelled like an old sock stuffed with rancid pumpkin rinds. On their way through the sunny side of town, the princes passed a few cottages that carried the distinctly pleasant scent of lemon zest and one where they took in a glorious whiff of nutmeg. But as soon as they crossed into the less-desirable half of the village, they were stopped in their tracks by the odor of the Stumpy Boarhound.

"We're here," Duncan announced. "That is a stink you don't forget."

At the sewage-spattered dead end of a bleak and damp cobblestone street stood the battered old tavern at which the four princes had first officially formed their team. From behind the Stumpy Boarhound's blade-scarred doors came the raucous sounds of what was either a party or a fight.

"Are you sure this is the best idea?" Frederic asked as Liam placed his hand on the bent dagger that served as a door handle. "The clientele here are not exactly model citizens. Need I remind you that the last time we recruited one of them, it didn't turn out very well?"

"Believe me, I remember," Liam said soberly. "But I have a good feeling."

"Ha!" Gustav chuckled. "Look who's suddenly trusting his gut."

Liam threw open the door, and the princes stepped into a scene of utter chaos. Black-eyed thieves emptied their mugs into the faces of swearing barbarians. Goblins swung from the tusks of mounted mammoth heads. Cackling assassins broke plates over the heads of torch-waving burglars. It was still anybody's guess whether this was a fight or a party.

But as soon as everybody saw the princes, the commotion abruptly stopped. An enormous, bald barbarian separated himself from the crowd—Two-Clubs, the bare-bellied brute known for using his pig-size fists to pound his enemies into the ground. "You four are the most wanted criminals in the Thirteen Kingdoms," he said.

The princes braced themselves.

"Congratulations!" Two-Clubs yelled cheerfully. "That's great!" He shook each prince's hand as the crowd around him applauded and burst into loud hoots and howls. Boniface K. Ripsnard, the bent-nosed, stubble-faced owner of the tavern, rushed up to make sure his favorite celebrities weren't overwhelmed.

"Give 'em space, give 'em space," Ripsnard shouted, shoving aside a grubby bandit who was waving his autograph book in Gustav's face. "Welcome back, princes! Follow me. I'll get you set up with some proper food and drink. Or at least some improper food and drink . . . I don't wanna make promises I can't keep."

The bartender led the princes to the Official League Founding Table in the back of the tavern. Customers continued to gawk.

"I think our outlaw status has made us more popular than ever at the Boarhound," Frederic said.

"Oh, without doubt," Ripsnard said, grinning. "We even framed one o' yer Wanted posters." He pointed over the bar, where the poster hung between one of Duncan's old shoes (which had been mounted on a board like a hunting trophy) and a ball of discolored string that was labeled PRINCE FREDERIC'S USED FLOSS.

"My used *what*?" Frederic asked, aghast. "Where did you get that?"

"Outhouse trash bin," Ripsnard said. "Knew it had to be yers 'cause there ain't a single one o' our regulars ever practiced dental hygiene."

"I'm . . . honored?" Frederic said, grimacing.

"Mr. Ripsnard," Liam said, "we need to see Captain Gabberman. Is he here?"

The bartender raised an eyebrow.

"Pirate?" Frederic tried. "Long coat, scraggly black beard?"

"Bunch of missing teeth," Gustav said, and then slyly added, "thanks to me."

"He preordered my book," Duncan threw in cheerfully.

"Oh, you mean *Cap'n* Gabberman," Ripsnard said, nodding. "Sure, I'll send 'im over."

A few minutes later, the grizzled Cap'n Gabberman trotted to the princes' table with a giddy grin on his face.

"What can I be doin' for you fellers?" he asked in a gruff-yet-cheerful voice. His eyes lit up when he noticed Duncan's tricornered cap. "Ah! I'm guessin' ye came to get me opinion on the hat. Two thumbs up, I say! Gives ye a nice bit o' swagger. Could use a feather or two, though, to really spiff it up."

"Feathers, eh?" Duncan muttered, fingering his hat's undecorated brim.

"Cap'n Gabberman, we're here on urgent business," Liam interrupted. "You said if we were ever in need of a fast ship, we should see you. That time has come."

"Aye," the pirate mumbled, scratching his crooked ear. "I did say that, didn't I?"

"Does the offer still hold?" Liam asked. "Is your ship for hire?"

"Might I ask what ye be needin' her fer?" Gabberman asked tentatively.

"We need to track down another ship," Liam said. "The *Dreadwind*."

"The *Dreadwind*?" Gabberman gasped. "But they're pirates!"

"*You're* a pirate," Gustav said, furrowing his brow.

"O' course I am," Gabberman said. "One o' the best. I'm just sayin' the *Dreadwind*'s crew are, ye know, a different *kind* o' pirate."

"Are you afraid of them?" Frederic asked. "Because I'm afraid of *you*. So if you're afraid of *them*—"

"Afraid? Not likely." The bearded buccaneer stood up and forced a laugh. "But even if I was—which I'm not—I ain't passing up a chance to work with the League o' Princes just 'cause of a little fear. Which I do not have."

"So you'll take us?" Liam asked. "The *Dreadwind* left out of Yondale Harbor a little over three weeks ago."

"That's perfect," Gabberman said, nodding vigorously. "That's exactly where me ship is docked."

"Kinda faraway place to keep your ship, isn't it?" Gustav asked.

"Nah," Gabberman scoffed. "That's where all the best pirates be stowin' their ships these days. I'm gonna head up there and get 'er ready. Why don't you fellers relax here for a spell, have a nice meal, and meet up with me later at . . . um . . ."

"Yondale Harbor?" Liam said.

"Aye, that's the place. See ye there. Gotta go." The pirate hurried off.

"Did that seem odd to you at all?" Frederic asked.

"A bit," said Liam. "But we need a ship. Do you know another sea captain who we can trust not to turn us in for the reward?"

"I suppose you're right," Frederic said, standing up. "Shall we go?"

"What about dinner?" Duncan asked, rubbing his tummy. "I'm famished."

"Pipsqueak's right—it's been days since we've had a real

meal," Gustav said. He turned and yelled, "Hey, barkeep! Whaddaya got to eat in this place?"

Frederic crossed his arms. "I would like to point out that the *Dreadwind* has nearly a month's head start on us."

"And *I* would like to point out that you're still in your pajamas." Gustav smirked.

"Zing!" chirped Duncan. He and Gustav high-fived.

Glowering, Frederic looked to Liam for support. "We *are* a bit short on energy," Liam said apologetically.

Ripsnard the bartender appeared. "You want eatings, eh? All righty, lemme see," he said, pulling a scrap of paper from his apron pocket and straining to read it. "Today's specials are pickled gator toes, ground teeth, cream of something-or-other, and . . . um, oatmeal."

"I'll have the oatmeal," Frederic said, pleasantly surprised.

"Ah, no, I misread that," Ripsnard said, squinting closer at the paper. "It's actually oat-*meat*."

Frederic sighed.

"Give me one of everything," said Gustav.

14

AN OUTLAW LEARNS THE ROPES

"How do we know which ship we're looking for?" Frederic asked, trying to suppress a yawn. After a week of hiking—and sleeping in leaf piles—the princes had finally arrived at Yondale Harbor.

"Just keep your eyes peeled for Gabberman," Liam said. He held his hand to his brow, shielding his eyes from the midday sun as he peered onto the deck of every massive galleon and sleek schooner they passed.

Duncan gaped at the forest of tall masts swaying just beyond the piers and the throngs of sailors hauling crates of cannonballs and casks of grog. Flags from each of the Thirteen Kingdoms—as well as banners from strange, unknown lands beyond—whipped in the blustery winds along the pier as gulls squawked loudly overhead. "This is so exciting," he said. "My hat can barely wait to get out to sea!"

Aside from Duncan's tricorne—which, courtesy of one very startled rooster, now had three long red feathers jutting from its brim—the princes had changed into entirely new clothes. Before they'd left the Boarhound, Ripsnard had been kind enough to supply them with unassuming sailors' outfits (and they'd been polite enough not to ask why all the shirts had knife holes in them). But Frederic still felt conspicuous. "You don't think Captain Gabberman's going to stand us up, do you?" he asked, ducking his head from the glance of a passing fisherman.

"No, I think he'd do just about *anything* to work with us," Liam said.

"Probably. It's just that this is a very public place," Frederic said, flipping up his collar. "I hope we find Gabberman before someone else finds *us*."

"You mean those three angry guys on the giant mongoose?" Duncan asked.

"Yes, them," Frederic said. "I'd hate to see them again."

"Then you'd better not look left," Duncan warned.

They all looked left.

A massive mongoose was sniffing its way down the boardwalk with Greenfang, Erik the Mauve, and Periwinkle

Pete all astride its shaggy back.

"They haven't spotted us yet," Liam whispered. "Walk casually and don't make any sudden moves."

There was a sudden rush of wind, and Duncan shrieked. "Whew," he then said calmly. "Almost lost my hat there."

A second later, the mongoose was charging down the pier at them.

"Run!" Liam yelled. The princes took off, tearing through the harbor's open-air market. Gustav shoved aside unsuspecting sailors and sardine salesmen, but it was impossible to move through the thick crowds with any real speed.

"There's Gabby Capperman!" Duncan cried, jumping and pointing to a small ship just past the market area. "I see him!"

"That can't be his ship," Liam said, frowning. "It's so . . . so . . ."

"Keep moving, Mr. Complainy Pants," Gustav barked. But the snarling mongoose plowed down several screaming shoppers and slid its long, hairy body directly into the fugitives' path. Greenfang and Pete hopped down. The four princes clustered together, while the sailors and merchants around them stepped back, whispering to one another in cautious awe.

"Thought you could get away, huh?" Greenfang snarled.

"Yes," Liam retorted. "That would be why we ran."

"Well," the bounty hunter quipped, drawing his twin swords. "I hope you've finally figured out that's never gonna happen."

"Fat chance," Gustav snapped back. "We don't figure out anything."

"Guys," Frederic whispered as the bounty hunters inched closer. "There's an opening between the crab shack and the squid-on-a-stick kiosk over there. Get ready to sprint for it. I know the perfect distraction."

"You're going to tell them all who we really are, aren't you?" Liam whispered.

"Am I that predictable?" Frederic asked. Then he shoved his way to the front of their little huddle and stood tall. "Attention, harbor people!" he shouted. "Do you know why these bounty hunters are after us? We're the League of Princes! From all those Wanted posters! Whoever turns us in gets untold riches!"

Realizing what Frederic was up to, Greenfang dove for him. But the bounty hunter was caught by two quick-acting shark wrestlers. "Hands off," one of the men barked. "That reward is mine!" Suddenly the crowd swarmed. Greedy seafarers and fishmongers pushed and elbowed in an attempt to get their salty paws on the valuable fugitives. As the bounty hunters were swallowed by the chaos, the princes darted behind the crab shack.

"Cap'n Gabberman!" Liam cried out as they ran for the pirate's small, single-masted boat. It was barely a quarter of the size of the large galleons they'd passed earlier and had loose planks of wood dangling from various spots on its barnacle-covered hull. The name painted on its bow read *Wet Walnut*.

"What a piece of junk," Liam muttered.

"I suppose this is what we get for hiring a sea captain out of a landlocked city," Frederic noted.

Gabberman, standing at the ship's rail, waved down to them. "Ah, there ye are! Come on aboard, fellers!"

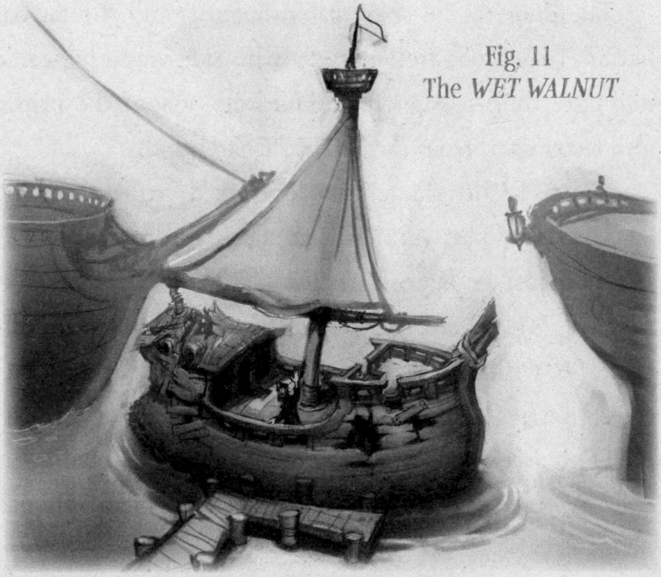

Fig. 11
The *WET WALNUT*

"Lower the ramp," Liam called up to him, casting a concerned glance over his shoulder.

Gabberman scratched his head. "Yeah, I don't think we've got one of those. Try this here rope. That's how I got meself aboard."

The princes scrambled up the rope, shouting, "Go! Go!"

"Go," Gabberman echoed. "Yeah. Hmm. Let's see about that now." He scanned the deck, biting his lower lip.

"What are you doing?" Liam screamed. "Where's your crew?"

"Ah, the crew," Gabberman said. "Yeah, I've got one of those. Crew!"

The door to the ship's cabin opened, and the fat barbarian Two-Clubs trotted out. At his side was a big-eared, half-ogre thug—Daggomire Hardrot—whom the princes also recognized from the Stumpy Boarhound.

"That's it? Just them?" Frederic asked, panicky.

"Pleasure to be working with you," Hardrot rasped.

"Let's just get out of here," Liam said.

"Aye," said Gabberman. "Well, we're still moored to the dock. So, we'll first be needin' to untie them big ropes. If I could just figger out where they're attached . . ."

"This is not your ship, is it?" Liam asked him pointedly. "You've never been on it before today, have you? You probably stole it last night."

"Just twenty minutes ago, actually," Gabberman said. "But, hey, stealin' a ship—that make me a right impressive pirate, don't it?"

"Uh, a little help over here?" Gustav, standing by the rail, was struggling to hold back the mob of greedy fishermen scaling the side of the ship.

"I'm on it," said Two-Clubs. As each invader's head popped up past the railing, the barbarian slammed his hefty fist down onto it, as if he were playing a game of human Whack-a-Mole. Gustav, not to be outdone, began running along the rail, punting reward seekers into the water. Duncan joined them as well, stealing feathers out of the attackers' hats and adding them to his own.

"We need to leave—now!" Liam barked. "Hardrot, you've got a sword—go cut every rope tied to the stern of this ship."

Hardrot stood and stared.

"The back," Liam clarified. "The stern is the back of the ship." He shook his head sadly as the half-ogre ran off. "Gabberman," Liam continued, "do you at least know where the ship's wheel is?"

"Aye!" the pirate said, beaming. "It's up on that upper-deck thingy."

"Go there and get ready while I get these sails up." Liam fiddled with the intricately knotted ropes that held the sail rolled against the mast's long, horizontal yardarm. "Crud," he groaned. "I'll never get these untied in time."

"Pipsqueak can do it," Gustav shouted as he kicked an attacking sailor in the face. "He's good with knots."

Duncan's eyes lit up. "You remembered!"

Duncan ran to the mast and attacked the tangled rope with glee. He quickly loosed it, and—with Liam's help—pulled it to hoist up the big, triangular mainsail. The canvas was frayed and stain spattered, but it quickly caught a big gust of wind and billowed outward. "Woo-hoo!" Duncan crowed as the *Wet Walnut* surged forward into the churning waters of Tortoiseshell Bay.

"Arr! Look at me!" Gabberman cried gleefully. "I'm pilotin' a real live pirate ship!"

"And it looks like we've finally ditched all our unwanted passengers," Gustav said, brushing his hands together. But as he has been known to do, Gustav had spoken too soon. After a running leap from the end of the pier, the mongoose landed, growling, on the ship's deck. Greenfang, Periwinkle Pete, and Erik the Mauve all slid off the animal's back.

"I got these guys," Two-Clubs said, stepping toward them. He raised one of his huge fists—and was promptly rewarded with one of Pete's arrows through his palm. "Yow!" the barbarian cried, falling to his knees and cradling his injured hand. "Oh, man, they're going to start calling me One-Club now!"

Gustav hunkered down for a charge at the archer, but he reluctantly held back when he saw Liam shaking his head.

"Turn this ship around," Greenfang ordered.

"Er, I'm afraid I can't be doing that," Gabberman said.

Pete nocked another arrow and aimed it at the pirate.

"No, he's serious," Frederic said. "He doesn't know how to do it."

Greenfang huffed. "I am less and less impressed by you guys every time we meet. Hey, Pete, take the wheel and steer us back to the dock."

The elf clenched his jaw but did not move.

"Pete!" Greenfang barked. "Go steer. You wanna collect this reward or not?"

"What I want," Pete said, "is a little respect."

"Aw, this ain't gonna end well," Erik mumbled to himself.

"Can you once," Pete continued, "just *once* refer to me by my full and proper Elvish name?"

"No," Greenfang said bluntly. "I am not going to call you Petalblossombreezesong. It's a ridiculous name."

"Not among the elves it isn't!" Pete snapped, his eyebrows

rising so high, they nearly hovered over his head.

Liam looked to Gustav—who was bobbing from side to side like a puppy desperately trying to behave long enough to earn a treat—and gave him a silent nod. The big prince kicked hard against the sail's yardarm, sending the heavy wooden beam swinging in an arc across the deck. It smashed into Periwinkle Pete, sending the elf backward over the rails. He landed in the sea with a splash.

Everyone on deck staggered as the ship made a sharp and sudden turn. A stiff wind kicked up, filled the newly angled sail, and started the *Walnut* moving forward at a faster clip. Gabberman spun the wheel wildly, trying to get back on course, and everybody—except Greenfang, who jammed one of his swords into the deck to steady himself—slid to one side of the ship.

"And I thought the canoe was bad!" Frederic cried.

As bodies piled up along the railing, Hardrot let out a joyous whoop. "A brawl!" the half-ogre howled. "Now this I understand!" He bit down hard on the mongoose's long tail. The animal yipped and leapt into the air, at which point Hardrot rammed his shoulder into the beast and sent it flailing into the surf.

"My mongoose!" Erik the Mauve scrambled to the edge of the deck, looking for his animal. A belt from Two-Clubs's one good fist sent him in for a dip.

"All righty," Cap'n Gabberman said as the swaying and dipping of the deck finally calmed. "I think I'm gettin' the hang of 'er."

The princes and their allies chased Greenfang to the pointed bow of the boat. "Aha!" said Duncan. "Looks like the bounty hunter has become the bounty hunted."

Up against the front rail, Greenfang turned and faced his pursuers, brandishing his remaining sword. Liam drew his rapier and stepped up to meet him.

"Go home, Greenfang," Liam said. "This hunt is over."

"I *never* give up," Greenfang said with a sneer. Then he hopped overboard.

They were several miles from shore, and by the looks of it, the mob at the docks had been too frenzied to launch any ships in pursuit of them.

"We did it," Liam said. "We're on our way. Now we just need to find Briar."

"And hope that Lila gets her message safely to Harmonia," Frederic added.

So the girl's in Harmonia, eh? thought Greenfang as he clung, unseen, to the side of the ship. He let go, splashed into the water, and began swimming back to shore as a new plan formulated in his mind.

15

AN OUTLAW DOES SOMETHING RASH

The *Wet Walnut* bobbed among the waves of Tortoiseshell Bay, heading westward into the sunset. By morning they would reach the open ocean, and they'd be forced to make a decision: Turn northward into the Frigidian Sea, a body of water known for its icebergs, frost dragons, and snow shrimp (which are, admittedly, the least impressive of the three)—or southward toward the warm, crystalline blue waters of the Aurelian Sea. The princes all hoped they'd be turning south (except Gustav, who had no sense of geography).

"I'm almost afraid to ask, but do you know where we're going?" Liam asked Cap'n Gabberman.

"That way," Gabberman said, pointing toward the front of the ship.

"Thanks," Liam said. "But what is it that's out that way?"

"Nothin', far as I know," Gabberman said. "Just miles and miles o' briny blue, far as the eye can see."

"How are we going to find the *Dreadwind*?" Liam asked.

"Oh, we won't need to," Gabberman stated with certainty. "They'll find *us*. Like I was tryin' to tell ye back at the Boarhound, them *Dreadwind* pirates are a mean lot. There's no ship that comes into or outta Tortoiseshell Bay without them scallywags stakin' their claim to it. If we just float around out there long enough, the *Dreadwind*'ll come to us."

Liam didn't like that plan, but he didn't have much choice in the matter. The only way to find Briar Rose was to find the *Dreadwind*. So when they got far enough west that they could no longer see even a trace of the far-off shore, they lowered the sails and simply floated.

Life at sea was a bit of an adjustment for the passengers (and "crew") of the *Wet Walnut*. Frederic's face was a ghostly shade of green for the first several days until his body finally, slowly began to adjust to the constant rocking motion. Hardrot, the half-ogre, on the other hand, had quite the opposite problem—he found the swaying of the waves a tad too soothing and was asleep for approximately twenty-one hours a day. Once Frederic felt well enough to stagger away from the rail, he called upon his sprite-taught first aid skills and bandaged Two-Clubs's injured hand. Which was a good thing, since the barbarian turned out to be a decent fisherman and began providing hefty meals of halibut, sea bass, and skunkflounder.

Gustav was the only one who still went hungry. After his first bite of fish, his skin broke out into itchy, red blotches.

"Don't eat the fish!" he yelled. "It's poison!"

"Mine's delicious," said Duncan, licking flaky white pieces of mahimahi from his lips.

"I've got to say, mine's a right tasty bit o' business, too," added Gabberman.

"Starf it all!" Gustav yelled, throwing his plate to the deck. While he scratched at his back with one hand, he pointed accusingly at Two-Clubs with the other. "You did this to me, Chef Roundbelly! You put some kind of barbarian curse on my fish! You're jealous of my hair, aren't you?"

"Gustav, I think you might be allergic to seafood," Liam said, trying to calm him down.

"I'm not allergic to things," Gustav growled. "Things are allergic to me!" He kicked over a bucket full of fish scraps and stomped off. Frederic scrambled after him and found him alone on the moonlit rear deck, angrily scratching at his elbows.

"Is everything okay, Gustav? You seem agitated," he said

gingerly. "Well, more agitated than usual."

"Yeah, what of it?" Gustav barked. Then, more softly, he added, "Does agitated mean itchy?"

"It doesn't," Frederic said. "It means upset . . . or irritated—and it's not surprising that you would be either of those things right now: You have a horrible rash, we're stuck at sea *waiting* for dangerous pirates to find us, our kingdoms might be under attack as we speak, and our loved ones have been locked away."

"Loved ones, eh?" Gustav said, loosening the collar of his shirt to reach in and scratch at his chest. "Blondie's gotten to you that much, huh?"

"What? Rapunzel? No. I mean, yes, of course. But I care about Ella and Snow, too," Frederic blurted. Then he paused and let out a long, slow breath. "But yes, I do care about Rapunzel deeply. Is that what this is all about? Are you upset with me because—"

"Because Lady Longhair likes you better?" Gustav interrupted. "C'mon, give me more credit than that. I'm irrigated because I'm tired of being on the run."

"Agitated," Frederic corrected. "Or irritated. I'm not sure which one you meant."

"Either," Gustav continued. "Look, you know me—I'm itching to take the fight to the Darians. I wanna knock some heads, kick some behinds—I don't wanna sit on a boat all day, catching seagulls so Pipsqueak can put their feathers in his hat."

"So that's where those feathers have been coming from," Frederic mumbled.

"Yeah, so, it's the boredom that's getting to me," Gustav continued. "My mood has nothing to do with me being the only one of us who doesn't have a 'loved one' to save. I could care less about that."

Frederic desperately wanted to tell him that the phrase was "*couldn't* care less," but he held back, feeling that a grammar lesson might seem insensitive at the moment. "Gustav, you're a great guy," he said instead. "A little rough around the edges, perhaps, but loyal, and protective—"

"Don't forget strong," Gustav added.

"And strong. Plus, you're a prince—and that never hurts. There's a girl out there for whom you will be the perfect man. Maybe you just haven't met her yet. In the meantime, you have us."

"And a rash," Gustav grunted.

Duncan walked up, carrying an armful of what appeared to be crumbling bricks.

"Hey, Gustav," he said. "Since you can't eat the fish, maybe you can try these. They're a special kind of sailor's biscuit called hardtack—which I know doesn't sound very appealing, but I assume the sailors just call it that because it's so tasty they don't want us landfolk stealing it. Anyway, the whole area downstairs is stacked with them. So, *bon appétit*!" He dropped the pile of hardtack biscuits, which clattered loudly on the deck next to Gustav.

"Don't you two have a handkerchief to fold or something?" Gustav said. "Let me grumble in peace."

Frederic and Duncan nodded and walked away. Gustav tried some of the hardtack and discovered that the name actually made it sound better than it was. It was like chewing a brick of salt sprinkled with sand and broken glass. But at least it didn't make him break out in hives.

"Yes, sir, Your Highness, sir."

"You really need to stop that," Lila said.

"Sorry, sir, Your H— I mean, sorry. Just sorry."

"It's okay," the young princess replied. She looked, with a mixture of sympathy and uncertainty, upon the flush-faced teenage messenger standing before her, the boy—only a few months older than herself—who was clad in an unseasonably thick wool sweater and unseasonably short, above-the-knee pants. "Are you sure you can handle this, Smimf? You look a little strung out."

It wasn't the messenger's odd attire that gave her pause (Smimf always dressed that way). Nor was it his penchant for calling everybody "sir" (although she did grow somewhat tired of it after the thirty-fifth time). Nor even that the boy apparently lived in his tiny messenger shop (there was a wadded-up blanket in the corner, dirty plates on the floor, and several worn-out pairs of shorts draped over the counter). It was Smimf's behavior—the entire time she'd been speaking to him, he'd been shifting his weight from one foot to the other, wringing his scarf in his hands, and nodding almost nonstop. His obvious anxiety was rubbing off.

"Is this job too much for you?" she asked.

"No, no, not at all," Smimf said. He tossed the end of his scarf and let it dangle loosely over his shoulder. "I can deliver all those messages—Sylvaria, Hithershire, Sturmhagen, Frostheim, Jangleheim, Svenlandia, Carpagia, Valerium, and Avondell.

Fig. 12
SMIMF, recruited

Shouldn't take me more than two or three days. I'm your man. Well, not *your* man, but, well . . . heh . . . ah, you know."

You're blowing it, Smimf, he said to himself. For half a year he'd dreamed of the chance to see Princess Lila again, and now that he was with her, he was bungling it big-time.

"You sure?" Lila asked. "Because without those boots of yours . . ."

Thanks to his Seven-League Boots—the shiny, red, flame-emblazoned footwear that allowed him to magically travel great distances in seconds—Smimf had been an incredibly useful ally during the League's assault on the Bandit King's castle. And it was those amazing boots that would give him the power to quickly spread word of Dar's invasion.

"Don't worry, I can do it," Smimf said. "If I seem a little . . . off, it's only because it's never easy to deliver bad news. You know? It's like that time I had to tell my grandmother that I'd accidentally fed her wig to a goat."

Lila stared at him.

"But you probably don't need to hear about that," he continued. "I should get going, seeing as you need me to help you save the world. Not that you *need* me. In fact, I'm sure you *don't* need me. Not that I'm not going to do the job! Of course, I'm going to do the job. I know you need me for *that*. I just mean you probably don't need *anyone*—generally speaking. You're a very capable girl—*woman*!"

Lila grinned. "Yes," she said, amused. "I'm a very capable girl-woman."

"I'm going to stop talking now," said Smimf, his face redder than his scarlet knit cap. "Good-bye, sir, Your Highness, sir!"

With a muffled *whoosh*, the messenger vanished, and Lila felt a rush of wind as the shop door flew open. "Well, that was . . . interesting," she said aloud to herself. She headed for the door. It was only a couple of miles to the Harmonian royal palace, and she planned to personally warn Frederic's father of the Darian threat.

But the moment she stepped outside, she found herself face-to-chest with Greenfang. She stumbled back a few feet and glared up at his crooked-toothed grin.

"Princess Lila," Greenfang said. "The little girl who fancies herself a bounty hunter."

Lila's eyes widened.

"Word travels fast," he said. "We all know you were old Ruffian's apprentice. And I know what happened to the mopy mumbler, too. I guess I'm now the most dangerous bounty hunter in the world—*and* the best."

"Ruffian was better than you'll ever be," Lila spat. She

tried to dart away, but Greenfang caught her by the wrist and twisted it enough to make her wince.

"Unh-uh, little lady," he sneered. "You're coming with me. Your brother may have slipped away for the moment. But you'll make a nice consolation prize."

16

AN OUTLAW ROCKS THE BOAT

"What are you doing with those chum buckets?" Liam asked Cap'n Gabberman as the old pirate tipped two wooden pails over the side of the boat, spilling out loads of rotting fish heads, bones, tails, and other assorted uneaten chunks. He stopped midpour.

"Chum buckets?" he said, looking suddenly delighted by the slop he carried. "Is that what these are? I've heard of those. We're supposed to use 'em somehow to catch us some king-size sea beasties."

"You mean there's a reason we've kept all those scraps?" Frederic asked. "I thought it was just because sailors are disgusting."

"The chum buckets are bait, Frederic," Liam said.

"Bait for what?" Frederic asked.

"Sharks," Gabberman said with a wicked gleam in his eye. "Or as we old salts like to call 'em, tooth barrels."

"Ooh, I'd like to make a tooth barrel soufflé," said Duncan. "How do we use these chump buckets?"

"I think we just lower the buckets over the side—"

There was a loud splash as Gabberman dropped both buckets into the water.

"—*after* we've spotted sharks nearby," Liam finished, shaking his head.

"Ah, I know what yer thinkin'," the grizzled pirate said. "Ol' Cap'n Gabberman just wasted our shark bait. And more'n likely, yer right. But—"

"Maybe we'll get lucky," Frederic interjected. "Let's take a look."

Everybody ran to the rail to stare down at the fish guts bobbing on the foamy swells.

"I think I just saw one fishtail wiggle a bit," Frederic noted hopefully.

Suddenly there was a loud bang, and the whole ship shook. People gripped the railing to remain upright.

"Did a shark do that?" Gustav asked. "Because if so, sharks are even more awesome than I thought."

Another bang and crash, and the *Wet Walnut* was rocked

hard for a second time. Everybody turned around.

"No shark," said Gabberman. "Those would be cannonballs rockin' us. And that would be the *Dreadwind* firin' 'em."

An enormous wooden galleon floated not half a mile to the west. It was easily six times the size of the *Wet Walnut*, practically a floating castle. Its four tall masts seemed ready to scrape the bottoms of the clouds, and twelve portholes along the ship's starboard side were open to reveal the tips of smoking cannons. Fluttering from a pole, just above the *Dreadwind*'s sky-high crow's nest, was a bloodred flag with a laughing, jewel-eyed skull at its center.

"How did it get so close without us noticing?" Liam asked.

"I've no idea," Gabberman said. "Hardrot's on lookout." He gestured toward the *Walnut*'s bow, where the half-ogre was snoring loudly in a laundry basket.

"Let's not give him that job again," Liam said.

"And let's get out of here!" Frederic cried. "Raise the sails, everybody! Captain Mr. Gabberman, please hurry to the wheel!"

"But wait!" Liam said. "We can't just run! This is the day we've been waiting for. We've finally found the *Dreadwind*!"

"Yes, and they're shooting deadly balls of iron at us,"

said Frederic. A whistling sound filled the air, followed by a thunderous crash as a third cannonball slammed into the *Walnut*, this one cracking straight through the center of the deck, mere feet from where Liam and Frederic were standing.

"Okay, I see your point," Liam said. The crew rushed to unfurl the sails (they'd gotten much better at it after weeks at sea), and Gabberman hustled off to the ship's wheel. Minutes later, the *Walnut* was moving—just in time for five more shots from the *Dreadwind* to splash harmlessly into the water behind them.

"Woo-hoo!" Duncan cheered as the *Dreadwind* became nothing more than a speck on the horizon. "We're outrunning them!"

"I guess we finally have reason to be happy for the tiny size of this ship," Frederic said.

"I told ye she was a fast ship," Gabberman said.

"No, you didn't," Gustav retorted.

"It doesn't matter," Liam said with a sigh. "I'm not exactly in the mood for celebrating. After all this time, we finally found what we were looking for, and it almost killed us."

"I guess this is what they mean when they say 'Be careful what you wish for,'" Frederic added.

"Yes. A few days ago, I wished we had a swimming

pool," Duncan announced, peering down into the *Walnut*'s hold through the hole in the deck. "And now the inside of the boat is turning into one."

"I don't know much about ships," Gustav added. "But I'm pretty sure the water's supposed to stay on the outside."

"We've got to plug that hole or we'll sink! Duncan, head down into the hold and find a way to stop the leak," Liam ordered. "The rest of you, start tossing things overboard! With all the excess water we've taken on, we'll need to lighten the ship's load in order to keep up our speed. If you see anything heavy, toss it."

Heads turned to Two-Clubs.

"What are you looking at me for?" the barbarian whined.

"Any*thing*, not any*one*!" Liam clarified, rolling his eyes. He added softly, "Two-Clubs, why don't you go down and help Duncan. Just in case."

The big barbarian rushed downstairs to find Duncan already waist deep in the flood, struggling against the foamy seawater that was gushing in at an alarming rate. "It's like the ocean is spitting at us," Duncan said, gripping his hat tightly.

"What do we stuff it with?" Two-Clubs asked, pondering the gaping hole in the *Walnut*'s hull. "There's nothing down here but hardtack."

Duncan snatched one of the rocklike biscuits and jammed it into the hole. It was immediately washed back at him.

"Hmm," Duncan mused. And then, "Aha!"

He tried again with two pieces of hardtack. Equally useless.

"Heh-heh," Two-Clubs chuckled. "The only place those biscuits will do any good is in my belly."

Duncan's face lit up. "Mr. Clubs! You've given me the perfect idea!"

"Snack break?" The barbarian shrugged his big, bare shoulders. "Okay."

"No, your belly!" Duncan chirped. "Stick it in the hole! It's just about the right size!"

Two-Clubs pouted. "But I'd have to stay down here for the rest of the trip."

"You'll be a hero," Duncan said, patting the barbarian's hairy back.

Two-Clubs rubbed his belly, pondering the idea. "All right," he said. "But only if you promise to bring snacks down to me. I'll need a bite every ten minutes."

"Hmm, that'll be a lot of going up and down for me," Duncan minced. "I wouldn't want to miss anything exciting upstairs. How about every *fifteen* minutes?"

"Twelve."

"It's a deal!" Duncan said as he helped Two-Clubs jam his colossal gut into the opening and cut off the inrush of water.

"Ooooh, I think I got a splinter!" the barbarian wheezed. "Or thirty."

Up on deck, Liam, Gustav, and Frederic ran about, tossing overboard anything that wasn't nailed down (and in Gustav's case, some things that were). Old barrels, broken lanterns, spools of rope, and crates of hardtack splashed into the sea. Gustav ran to the rail with an armload of long, steel-tipped harpoons.

"Hey, Gustav," Frederic said. "Maybe we should hold on to a few of those."

Gustav chucked the harpoons into the waves. "Capey said toss, I toss."

"Problem solved!" Duncan popped up from belowdecks and took a bow.

"Where's Two-Clubs?" Liam asked.

"In the hole," Duncan said. "Speaking of which, what can I give him for a snack? He's going to need something in about eleven minutes."

"This might not be the best situation, but at least we seem to have stopped sinking," Liam noted.

And then the whole ship shuddered.

"Oh, no," Frederic moaned. "Cannonballs again?"

But the *Dreadwind* was nowhere to be seen.

"Hey, guys," Two-Clubs called up through the hole in the deck. "Something's tickling my belly. Something *outside* the boat."

"Eh . . . ye all might want to be holdin' on to something," Gabberman said. "If the stories I've heard are true . . . er, I mean, if I remember correctly from the last time I was sailin' these waters, there are things nastier than pirates swimmin' out there."

An enormous silver-white head burst from beneath the sea foam looking like a cross between a python and a barracuda (with maybe a touch of vampire porcupine thrown in). The serpentine creature spouted a fog of salty mist from between its knifelike teeth before wrapping its long, scaly body around the *Wet Walnut* and beginning to squeeze.

"Cecil!" Duncan shouted.

Gustav looked at him askance. "Seriously? You're naming it?"

"Brace yerselves!" Gabberman cried. "We've got a sea dragon on top o' us!"

Liam took a swipe at the monster with his sword—promptly snapping the rapier's blade in half. "Drat!" Liam spat. "If only we had some harpoons!"

Gustav shrugged sheepishly and began pounding his bare fists against the beast's metallic scales, snarling, "Let go of our boat, you big, fat eel! I hate eels!"

A series of terrifying crunches sounded as the sea serpent tightened its coiled grip on the ship. The *Walnut*'s bow and its stern both rose as its center crumbled into an avalanche of splintered boards.

"Arrgh! Me ship!" Gabberman screamed. "Or, well . . . *somebody's* ship!"

"Look, I found another chum bucket!" Duncan cried, running at the sea serpent. "Maybe we can use it to lure the—" Slip, trip, tumble. And the bucket was firmly lodged over Duncan's head. "Don't worry about me!" he announced, standing back up. "I'll be—" And then he stepped through the hole in the deck.

The dragon thrashed its silvery tail, toppling the mast like a lumberjack felling an oak. It crashed down, shattering deck planks and cracking the rail.

"Huh? Whuzzat?" Hardrot said, popping upright in his laundry basket. And then the basket slid off the shattered deck into the ocean below.

As Gustav continued to beat fruitlessly against the sea monster's side, the floor fell out from beneath him, and he splashed into the darkness belowdecks.

Clinging to the rear railing, Frederic was wild-eyed with terror. "Have I mentioned that I can't swim?"

"You'll be all right, Frederic," Liam said. "Just try to keep your head above—"

The dragon's tail thwapped down between them, practically disintegrating the chunk of boat on which they'd been trying to stay afloat. Suddenly, Frederic found himself surrounded by water. It was above him, below him, left and right; in his mouth and in his nose. *What would Sir Bertram do? What would Sir Bertram do?* he thought, before concluding sadly, *Sir Bertram would drown*.

Then he felt strong hands grab onto his wrist, and soon he was being dragged upward, the sea rushing past him, until finally his head broke through to the surface. He coughed and sputtered as Gustav shoved him up onto a floating door.

"You alive?" Gustav asked, treading water a few feet away.

Frederic nodded, still dazed. The *Wet Walnut* was gone, reduced to nothing more than a scattering of cracked planks and broken beams bobbing among heavy waves. He hoped the others had managed to find their way onto makeshift rafts as well; but between the wind, the choppy seas, and his foggy head, he couldn't spot any of them. Happily, there was

no sign of the sea serpent either. Frederic did, however, see what appeared to be a turkey swimming toward him.

"Oh, no," Frederic whispered. The "turkey" was actually Duncan's many-feathered cap. He snatched it out of the water as it drifted by.

"Stay here," Gustav said. "I'll go find him."

But as soon as Gustav turned, the dragon's spiny, shimmering head burst out of the water in front of him. Frederic screamed as the huge creature opened its mouth wide and, in a split second, snapped its jaws closed again, enveloping Gustav. But an instant later, the frustrated dragon's mouth began to slowly reopen. Gustav was standing on the beast's tongue, forcing its jaws apart with brute strength.

"No way," the brawny prince grunted. "If I can't eat seafood, seafood's not gonna eat me." But Frederic could see that his friend was struggling. The dragon's teeth began to close down on him again.

Then—*BOOM!* A cannonball smacked into the side of the dragon's head. Gustav catapulted from between the creature's scaly lips and plunked into the water yards away. Frederic watched the dragon sway dizzily as its eyes slowly closed and it slipped beneath the surface. *What just happened?* he thought.

It grew suddenly dark as a vast shadow fell over the area. A rope appeared, dangling inches from Frederic's face. He craned his neck back, his eyes following the rope upward for what seemed like miles, all the way to the rail of the hulking *Dreadwind*.

"Coming aboard?" a scar-faced pirate called to him. "Or would you rather we leave you down there until the sea dragon comes back? I'm happy either way."

Frederic grabbed the rope.

17

AN OUTLAW SPEAKS POLITELY TO A LADY

Too afraid to move or speak, Frederic simply sat, dripping and shivering, as he watched brawny pirates haul the other shipwreck victims up onto the deck of the *Dreadwind*. Duncan immediately grabbed his hat back, hugged it, and put it on, its dozen wet feathers dangling limply.

Sopping, Gustav struggled to his feet. "I had that oversize worm right where I wanted it, you know." He swept his wet, drooping hair out of his eyes, revealing a face newly covered in bright-red blotches.

"He's got the pox!" one of the pirates shouted, and they all backed away.

"Don't worry, he's just allergic to seafood," Duncan offered.

The scar-faced pirate chuckled. "So . . . you *bit* the dragon?"

Gustav glared at him. "What of it?"

Don't you dare start a brawl, Gustav, Liam thought. There were twenty armed buccaneers surrounding them, and probably more working in other, unseen areas of the enormous vessel. There was no way he and the other princes would win in an open fight. And if it came to that, he wasn't a hundred percent sure whose side Gabberman, Two-Clubs, and Hardrot would take. But he had to do something. Briar could be on that ship with them. They needed the opportunity to search for her—and that would require a little diplomacy. "We appreciate you not leaving us to drown, Captain," he said as he and the other refugees—except Hardrot, who was already snoozing again—rose to their feet. "But I must ask what you plan to do with us now."

The scar-faced pirate chuckled. "Oh, I'm not the captain of the *Dreadwind*," he said. "Though I see how you could make such a mistake on account of the fine tailoring of my coat. Not to mention my nineteen golden earrings and my handsomely rugged jawline. People say it's my best feature."

"If only I had me a jaw like that," Gabberman said, nodding with admiration.

"I am the first mate of this glorious vessel," the pirate

went on. "Key's the name—Roderick Key. As for what's to be done with you, that will be—"

"That will be up to me," said a tall woman who appeared at the top of a short flight of steps behind the first mate. She stood nearly as high as Gustav, with broad shoulders, a steely gaze, and frizzy black hair that was tied back in a loose ponytail. She wore a long coat similar to Gabberman's (though much fancier, with swirling gold embroidery on the cuffs and lapels) and a tricornered hat similar to Duncan's (though with a more reasonable number of feathers). A gleaming, curved cutlass hung at her belt, and countless jeweled rings adorned her rough-skinned fingers.

"Captain Jerica," Key said, stepping respectfully to the side.

The pirate commander looked her prisoners up and down, frowning. She turned to her first mate. "This can't be them, Mr. Key," she said. "They're pitiful, for Triton's sake. Did you see the little one with the drowned bird on his head?"

"Actually," Duncan began—and Liam's hand clamped over his mouth.

Fig. 14
Captain JERICA

"We do not want them to find out who we are," Liam whispered.

"I know that," Duncan whispered back. "And anyway, it's usually Gustav who blows our cover."

"You two make a great team for that," Liam replied.

Duncan spun around and hugged Gustav. "Did you hear that? We make a great team!"

Gustav pushed him off. "I miss the troll," he said.

For several minutes, Captain Jerica huddled with Mr. Key and her crew members. Then she turned to address the prisoners again. "Well, fellas," she said, her fists resting on her hips. "It seems we've got a bit of a disagreement here as to what should be done with the lot of you. Mr. Key thinks you may be important types, worthy of a hefty ransom. But Mr. Flint over here thinks you're just bumbling tradesmen who were stupid enough to pass through our territory."

"Bumblers! Bumblers!" squawked a rainbow-hued parrot that sat on the shoulder of a slouchy, gray-haired pirate.

"*I'm* Mr. Flint, by the way," the old pirate said, pointing to himself. "Not the bird. Just to be clear about that."

"Sadie Squawkins has beautiful feathers," Duncan called out.

"Why, thank you," Flint said. Then he blinked. "Wait, her name isn't—"

"*Ahem!* Mr. Flint," Captain Jerica said sternly.

"Oh, aye," said Flint. "Anyway, Sadie Squawkins and I reckon these men are just a bunch of bumblers. They're no princes, anyhow."

"Well, uh, which do *you* think, Captain?" Frederic asked, forcing a smile.

Jerica stepped closer. "I think they might both be right," she said coolly. She stared down at her prisoners once again, her eyes lingering on Gustav the longest. "But I've got to be sure, right? So I'm going to ask you fellows a few questions."

"Ooh, I love trivia games!" Duncan shouted, stepping forward. "If the category is 'Awesome Pirate Hats,' I know the answer: Mine, yours, and the striped one on that guy with the curly mustache over there."

Liam grabbed the hem of Duncan's jacket and yanked him back. "What do you want to know?" he asked Jerica.

"Based on the lack of flotsam out there," she began, "your ship was basically empty. If you weren't transporting cargo, what was the purpose of your voyage?"

Frederic thought fast. "We are scientists. Ours was a research vessel."

"Without equipment?" Jerica asked.

"Our equipment sank," Liam said. "I'm sure an experienced seafarer like yourself understands that heavy machinery doesn't float."

"And what, pray tell, were you trying to do with these great machines?" she asked.

Liam and Frederic both opened their mouths to answer, but Jerica raised a hand to shush them. "I've heard enough from you two." She pivoted and locked her green eyes on Gustav. "I want to hear from him."

"Why me?" Gustav asked. He felt strangely flustered, but shook it off. "I'm not scared of you, you know."

"I would be sorely disappointed if you were," the pirate captain said.

"Then why are you picking on me—I mean, picking me?" Gustav asked. "Why not just let, um, those two guys answer the questions?"

"Because they're lying to me," Jerica said. "And I believe I can get the truth out of you. I know your type."

"Ha! Good luck, lady!" Gustav laughed and tapped his thick index finger against his temple. "No one knows what goes on inside this head. Not even me."

Jerica grinned slyly. "Let's see, shall we?"

"Yes, let's," Gustav replied. He flexed his shoulders, that old, fired-up feeling rising in his gut.

Frederic and Liam exchanged worried glances (while Duncan stared enviously at Mr. Flint's parrot.)

"So do you still contend that you and your friends were on a research vessel?" Jerica asked.

"No," Gustav said firmly. "We were on a research *ship*." He crossed his arms and gave a decisive nod, as if he'd just won the argument.

"And what does a research ship do?"

Gustav cleared his throat.

"Did you swallow a jellyfish out there?" Jerica asked, smirking.

Gustav locked eyes with Jerica. "You want to know what a research ship does? We research," he said. "When you search for something and you can't find it, you call us. And we *re*-search for it."

"And, um, what were you re-searching for?" As several of her men snickered, Jerica tried to stifle a laugh. Gustav watched the corners of her lips turn upward, and he was filled with anger. At least he assumed it was anger—that was the main thing he was used to feeling. And he was pretty sure that that's what Jerica's smile made him feel, too. Pretty sure.

"You!" he barked. "We were searching for you!"

"Gustav, don't—" Liam started.

"Shut up, Capey!" Gustav snapped.

"He's not wearing a cape," Jerica said.

"No, really, Gustav—" Frederic sputtered.

"Not now, Tassels!"

"And *he's* not wearing tassels," Jerica mused.

"But wait, Gustav," said Duncan. "I think—"

"Pipe down, Pipsqueak!"

"Okay, that one I get," said Jerica, nodding.

Gustav focused his fury on the pirate captain. "Yeah, you were right," he said. "We're not really a re-search crew. We were after *you*. We're pirate hunters!"

"Fascinating," Jerica said. "Pirate hunters with no cannons. No weapons of any kind, apparently."

"It's called being undercover," Gustav snarked. "Look it up."

A tall, bandanna-wearing pirate whistled to get their attention. "Captain, we actually did find *this* jammed into a hunk of wood that was floating out there." He tossed a gleaming, curved sword to Jerica—one of Greenfang's blades. She caught the weapon and examined it.

"Yeah, that's mine," Gustav said. "That's my pirate-hunting sword. 'Cause I'm a pirate hunter. And I finally tracked down the notorious *Deadwind*."

"*Dreadwind*," Jerica corrected. "But okay, let's go with this story. You lot are big, bad pirate hunters. And now you've caught up to *us*—your ultimate quarry. What are you going to do about it?"

Please don't yell "Sturmhagen" and charge at them, Liam repeated over and over in his head. *Please don't yell "Sturmhagen" and charge at them.*

And to Gustav's credit, he did not. He yelled, "Piiiiraaaate hunnnn-terrrrs!" and charged at them. He managed to bowl over seven buccaneers who were taken by surprise. However, that still left another fourteen or so.

Liam turned to Frederic and Duncan. "We're going to lose this fight," he said quickly. "So don't even try to win—try to find you-know-who." They nodded and darted off in different directions, narrowly avoiding the grabbing hands of pirates who tried to stop them. Liam kicked a short pirate in the gut and stole his sword before dodging blows from two others. "Are you with us?" he called over to Gabberman and Two-Clubs (Hardrot was lying across their laps, fast asleep).

"Aye!" yelled Gabberman, jumping up and smacking one of his captors across the face with a mackerel that had stowed away in the cuff of his coat sleeve.

Two-Clubs shook his half-ogre friend. "Wakey-wakey, Daggomire—it's a fight."

Hardrot's eyes popped open, wide and eager. "Did you say '*fight*'?" Two-Clubs threw him like a missile into a crowd of attacking pirates.

While Liam, Gustav, and Gabberman's gang brawled with the *Dreadwind*ers, Frederic and Duncan skittered around the vast deck, trying to evade pursuing pirates while searching for Briar Rose. Duncan looked under wash buckets, inside coils of rope, and down the barrels of cannons, while Frederic checked *sensible* places. He shouted a curt "Hello?" or "Yoo-hoo!" into every doorway he passed. He darted for the ship's wheelhouse, but before he could even get to the door, it flew open and a broad-chested buccaneer bounded out. Frederic bounced face-first off the stone-hard chest of the oncoming muscleman and flopped backward into the waiting arms of his pursuers.

"So much for that," Frederic muttered. But at that moment a high-pitched shriek sounded from the other side of the wheelhouse, followed by Duncan's shout of "Aha! There you are!"

He found Briar! Frederic thought—until he saw Duncan trot around the corner, proudly clutching Sadie Squawkins and shoving a handful of her scarlet feathers into the brim of his hat. A second later, the bird's gray-bearded owner tackled him. "Get your itty-bitty fingers off my bird!" he growled as the two wrestled and the parrot flew away.

In the meantime, Liam clashed swords with Mr. Key,

who, based on the merry tune he was whistling, seemed to enjoy the duel thoroughly. Two-Clubs tried his best to flatten foes one-handed, while Hardrot crawled along the deck biting ankles, and Gabberman faced off in a slap-fight against Scotty, the feisty cabin boy.

Among all the combatants, though, Gustav was the true powerhouse. He bashed and walloped every pirate who came at him, hardly even bothering to look at his attackers. Even as his fists slammed into his enemies, his eyes scanned the crowd, hoping to spot Jerica among the fray. Finally he saw her, standing atop the raised foredeck by the bow of the ship.

"You're mine, Pirate Lady!" he shouted.

She sliced the air before her with Greenfang's scimitar. "You're as good a brawler as I expected. But do you really think you have a shot when I've got this lovely sword here? Two, actually." With her left hand, she drew her own cutlass.

Gustav climbed onto the raised deck to face her. "My bare hands are good enough to win any fight," he bragged, cracking his knuckles.

"Be that as it may, let's do this fairly." She tossed the cutlass to him. On a typical day, as soon as Gustav caught that sword, he would have begun lashing out at his enemy, slashing and slicing with wild abandon. But on this day he paused. He stood there holding the big, curved cutlass and staring quizzically at Jerica.

What is her mouth doing? he thought. *Why does it keep curving up like that? She's got so many teeth.*

"Hello? I'm getting bored," Jerica said.

Gustav snapped out of his reverie and took a swing at her. She deflected it and advanced on him. Their swords clanged together until Gustav found himself backed up to the edge of the deck. "You're only winning because you've forced me to fight with a girly weapon," he complained.

"The man I defeated to win that sword would be offended," Jerica said. "But fine. Let's switch." Before Gustav even knew what was happening, she yanked the cutlass from his hand and replaced it with Greenfang's scimitar.

"What the—?" Gustav sputtered.

Jerica backed off, giving him a chance to step away from the edge. "Come at me," she said. And Gustav complied, more worked up than ever. Once again she parried each of his blows, only this time she managed to spin him around and back him up to the front rail of the ship, only a half inch away from another dip into the crashing blue waves.

Gustav refused to be cowed. "Ha! You think you're so tough. You're just—"

"Just what? A girl?" Jerica asked, her sword pressed against his.

Gustav snorted. "No girl's ever gotten the better of me."

"Not even Rapunzel?"

Gustav's face went red. "I would've been fine without her help!" he shouted.

"Aha! So you *are* Prince Gustav," Jerica said as she pulled him to safety.

"No! Um, no!" Gustav stammered. "That's not what I said. Don't listen to me! I don't know what— I'm— I'm— Aargh! You tricked me! Now, I'm really going to—"

"To what?" Jerica said. "Please, I'm dying to hear."

But before Gustav got a chance to give an answer (which is good, because he didn't have one), a loud whistle sounded from middeck. The big strongman of a pirate who had captured Frederic was now holding him over the side of the ship, dangling by his ankle. "I think you fellas might want to stop the rumble," the big pirate said. "From what I hear, the skinny guy doesn't swim too well."

Behind him, Mr. Flint held Duncan, who was trying to shield his head from the parrot that was angrily pecking at him.

"Stand down, men," Liam said. "This fight is over." He laid down his sword, and as soon as he did, Key socked him in the chin.

"That's for nicking my coat," the first mate said,

examining a tear in his sleeve. "Do you know how difficult it is to find a good tailor on the high seas?"

Jerica stepped to the lip of the foredeck to address her crew. She didn't seem the slightest bit worried that Gustav stood right beside her with a sword in his hand.

"I have happily confirmed that, as we suspected, these men are indeed the League of Princes," the pirate captain said. "Well, four of them, at least. The grubby one, the hairy one, and the half-naked one must be hired help."

Gabberman nudged Two-Clubs with his ragged elbow. "She's talkin' 'bout us."

Cheers sounded among the crew. Several shouted gleefully about gold and untold riches. Liam looked up at Gustav, half expecting him to head-butt Jerica from behind, but the big prince just stood silently staring at her hair. Suddenly, Frederic's voice was heard over all the cheering.

"Excuse me, Miss Captain?"

"Captain will do," Jerica replied, and she shushed her men. "What is it?"

"Well, based on the ecstatic hooting of your crew, I assume you're planning to . . . Um, I'm sorry, could we possibly have this conversation with me right side up?"

"Go ahead, Tauro," Jerica said. The enormous pirate set Frederic down on the deck.

"Thank you." Frederic continued. "So, as I was saying, I assume you're planning to turn us in for that reward from the kingdom of Avondell."

"You assume correctly," Jerica said.

"Well, I think your information may be outdated," Frederic said. "How long have you been at sea?"

"Near two months, I'd say," said Key.

"Ah, well, that explains it," Frederic said. "You simply haven't heard: The bounty on our heads has been called off. We presented the Avondellians with proof that Princess Briar Rose was, in fact, not murdered, but merely kidnapped by the Darians. Our names were cleared immediately."

Gasps and grumbles sounded from among the pirates.

"Could this be true?" Jerica asked Mr. Key. The first mate shrugged. "Well, even if it is," the captain continued, "you men are still very valuable prisoners."

"Sure, I can't argue that," Frederic said, leaning casually against the foremast. "But wouldn't you rather try for the new reward?"

"What new reward?" Key asked.

"Oh, that's right—you've been out at sea, you don't know," Frederic said. "The bounty that the Avondellians were offering for us—'*untold riches*'—they're now offering the same as a reward to whoever brings Briar Rose home safely. You wouldn't happen to have any idea where the princess is, would you?"

Jerica casually spun her sword in her hand. "There's no need to play coy, Prince Frederic," she said. "Yes, we're the ship that the Darians hired to take the princess out to sea. But you already knew that. The only question left is what we'll do with this new information."

The crew murmured anxiously, while Jerica rubbed the tips of her fingers together, mulling her choices. "Pirates of the *Dreadwind*," she finally announced. "Reverse course! We're going to rescue a princess." She turned to Gustav. "Looks like you and I are going to be spending a lot more time together." Gustav gulped.

Roderick Key nimbly hopped up to the ship's wheel, flipping over a railing rather than using the steps. "Back to the island then, Captain?" he asked Jerica.

"That's right, Mr. Key," she replied.

"Briar is on an island?" Liam asked.

"No," Jerica said. "We're taking a detour into the tropics because I have a craving for coconut juice."

"Seriously?" Liam asked.

Jerica rolled her eyes. "You just told me that a reward awaits me if I find your missing princess," she continued. "You think I'd waste time hunting down a refreshing beverage?"

Liam's face turned red. "No, of course not," he muttered.

"See, there's your mistake," Jerica said, wagging a sassy finger at him. "You shouldn't trust me. I'm entirely capable of doing something like that."

Gustav couldn't help but snicker. Liam's temples throbbed visibly.

"So, Briar really *is* on an island?" Liam asked.

Jerica shot Gustav a "Can you believe this guy?" look, and they both burst into loud laughter.

"Fine," Liam growled. "Mock me all you want—"

"I've been waiting years to hear you say that!" Gustav blurted with glee. "Your hair looks like limp swamp grass, and your eyes are too small for your head. And when you get angry, you make a face like a horse with bad gas."

Liam huffed and gnashed his teeth.

"Just like that," Gustav added, pointing.

Liam folded his arms and said nothing.

"Okayyyy," Jerica said slowly to Liam. "You are obviously not the fun one."

"No, that would be me," Duncan chirped. He leapt onto the portside rail, did a series of squealing pirouettes, and promptly fell overboard. Luckily he landed in a net full of squid that was in the process of being hauled in.

"Meh," said Jerica. "I've seen funner." She turned to the

rest of the princes. "If you'll excuse me, I've got a ship to captain. Explore all you want—just stay out of my cabin. That's off limits. You'd do well to get yourselves acquainted with the *Dreadwind*; she's going to be your home for quite a while. It's at least three weeks' journey to the island where we dropped off your whiny princess."

"Three weeks," Frederic echoed sadly.

"You'd better get ready for some hard work," Jerica said. "As long as you're on board this ship, you're crew. Noseless Joe! Pegbeard! Show the newbies the ropes."

Gabberman clapped his hands. "Huzzah! I get to be on the crew o' the *Dreadwind*! That's even more excitin' than havin' me own ship!"

"This is going to be a very interesting three weeks," Frederic said as they followed their pirate tutors along the deck. "Isn't it, Gustav? Gustav?"

But Gustav wasn't paying attention. He was staring back over his shoulder at Jerica.

18

AN OUTLAW HAS NO WORDS

"If I'd known sailing was this much fun, I would've gotten kidnapped by pirates ages ago," Duncan sang out as he swung through the rigging along the redwood-like masts of the *Dreadwind*. With its enormous sails unfurled, the massive galleon cut through the waves at a speedy clip, spraying salt and foam up along the rails, and dousing the crewmen who were busy hauling in nets—Liam and Gustav among them. The princes plopped their heavy load of flopping fish onto the deck, and Frederic began to sort them—holding each fish at arm's length with a delicate, two-fingered pinch. Gustav's shoulder rose and fell as he chuckled to himself.

"Well, if they'd given me the apron I asked for, I wouldn't have to be so cautious," Frederic said defensively.

"Huh?" Gustav said. "Oh, I'm not laughing at you, Tassels. I was just thinking . . . 'Mock me all you want.' Heh. Priceless."

Liam huffed and shook his head. "That was three days ago. You're never going to let me live that down, are you?"

"Nope," Gustav said, still laughing.

Duncan slid down a rope and landed among his friends. "Ooh, is that a flying fish?" he asked eagerly.

"It doesn't have feathers, if that's what you were hoping," Frederic said, gingerly dropping the fish into its proper bin. "Oh, *now* you look upset? Bounty hunters, shipwrecks, your wife in prison—all of that you laugh through. But you're suddenly glum because a fish doesn't have feathers?"

Duncan sat on the ship's rail and shrugged. "Sometimes laughing helps me forget I'm scared," he said. "And sometimes it's just because something is fun. I mean, this has been one of our more exciting adventures: pirates, sea monsters, this awesome hat . . . But with Snow in danger, there will always be a little part of me that is very, very worried. I think it's my left elbow."

"Duncan's got a point," Liam said seriously. "We can't forget that the women are in grave danger. They're relying on us to come through for them. This is terribly serious business. Not all of us seem to be aware of that." He glared at Gustav.

"What?" Gustav blurted.

"Oh, don't be too hard on Gustav," Duncan said. "You can't blame him for sharing a couple of laughs with the pirate lady when he's in love with her."

"In lo— What? You're mad!" Gustav sputtered. "I am not in anything! Except maybe a mood to head butt you."

"Love may be putting it a bit strongly at this stage," Frederic said as he neatly arranged some herring by size. "But it's pretty clear you're interested in Jerica."

Gustav began to sweat. And blush. He looked like a melting tomato. "It's not— Agh! It's not, you know, *that* kind of interest. I'm just, you know . . . She does that thing with her mouth."

"You mean smiling?" Frederic asked.

"No," Gustav said. "Not regular smiling. Regular smiling is what you do after you've beaten someone up or just finished a good steak. What she does is . . . it's . . ." He huffed and shook his head. "She's the *enemy*, for crying out loud!"

There was an awkward pause as Gustav panted, catching his breath.

"I don't think she's as bad as she makes herself out to be," Duncan finally said.

"And for what it's worth," Frederic added gently, "I think she's got a little crush on you, too."

Gustav's eyes widened. "Really?"

His three friends all nodded.

"Well, okay then," he said. He brushed his long blond hair back with his fingers and started feeling at his face. "Am I still all blotchy?"

"What are you planning to do?" Frederic asked.

"I'm gonna talk to her," Gustav replied. He cleared his throat, cracked his neck, and started toward the captain's quarters.

"I thought *talking* was the only thing you were afraid of," Liam said.

"I'm Gustav the Mighty. I'm not afraid of anything."

Mavis and Marvella gawked at each other, convinced that the imaginary elephant they'd been grooming had just blasted them with a powerful gust of air from its invisible trunk. In reality, it was Smimf, who whizzed past them on his way into the throne room at Castlevaria. He was virtually impossible to see while running at his top speeds, so the entire Sylvarian royal family got quite a surprise when the young messenger appeared to pop out of thin air. Queen Apricotta, who'd been busy drawing faces on fruit, was so shocked that she tossed her bowl of smiling plums up in the air. Only King King seemed unmoved, barely shifting in his seat.

"Good day, sirs, Your Highnesses, sirs. I apologize for the startling entrance, but the news I am delivering is of a rather urgent variety."

The king cocked his head like a curious puppy.

"I come bearing a message from the League of Princes," Smimf rattled off. "Well, technically it was Princess Lila who sent me, but she works with the League. So does your son. Which I'm sure you know, so I probably didn't need to mention that. But anyway, you need to be on the lookout for the Darians."

"Who's Darren?" Queen Apricotta asked.

"Darians, sir, Your Highness, sir. They've got a magical gem, and they're on the march across the Thirteen Kingdoms, intending to take over everything. It'll be a bad scene, sir. Worse than that time my grandmother's wooden foot caught fire."

The king became suddenly active. He waved his arms, waggled his fingers, and pumped his fist—but his eyes remained blank.

"Are you all right, sir, Your Highness, sir?" Smimf asked, growing concerned. "You've got a . . . strange look in your eyes."

"Don't mind Daddy," Marvella said. "He's *always* a bit strange."

"I don't mean normal strange," Smimf said. "I mean *strange* strange. Like the way my grandmother looked after she drank that gallon of paint."

King King opened his mouth as if to scream, but no sound came out.

Smimf furrowed his brow. "Okay, sir, I guess I'll be leaving," he said. "But I hope you'll heed Princess Lila's advice and get Sylvaria's army ready."

"Sylvaria doesn't have an army, young man," the queen said. "Perhaps she said we should get our *arms* ready?" She began flapping like a bird.

"No army?" asked Smimf. "Then who were all those armed men outside?"

At that moment, a head poked out from an alcove in the back of the room—a bald head, with pale, almost bluish skin and teeth that had been filed into sharp triangles. This human barracuda briefly locked eyes with Smimf and began pounding a nearby gong. A horde of Darian soldiers rushed into the throne room, swords and spears at the ready. Smimf gasped when he saw them and zipped off instantly. The warriors froze in their tracks, baffled by the messenger's disappearance.

Queen Apricotta looked back toward the nightmarish-looking bald man and asked, "Are you Darren?"

Frustrated, the man waved off the other Darians and ducked back inside his hideaway—a dusty old storage area filled with empty shelves. A sign above the alcove read A PLACE FOR THINGS WE FORGET TO PUT AWAY.

In the darkness, the pale Darian lifted a glowing crystal orb. He rubbed it, and the swirling green mists within the glass parted, revealing the face of his master.

"What is it, Falco?" Lord Rundark asked.

The mute Darian made a series of rapid hand gestures, and Rundark nodded in understanding. (Yes, Falco could not speak—but that had not stopped the Warlord from positioning him as the puppet controller of Sylvaria, a kingdom where he rightly figured that any odd behavior would go unnoticed.)

"Continue as you were told, Falco," Rundark replied. "Worry not. Our forces are in place. And the princes are en route to their final destination."

Falco put away the orb and checked on the royal family. The twins were shuffling around the room, feeling the air with outstretched hands, hoping to find the messenger, whom they assumed to be invisible. Their mother had gone back to dotting cartoon eyes onto lemons. All was back to normal.

Fig. 15
VISION ORB

But one kingdom over, in a barely lit basement chamber, Lord Rundark was troubled. He turned away from the king-size crystal orb that sat on a chest-high pedestal constructed of human bones. "I should kill the princes now and be done with it," he said into the shadows.

"Patience," a thin voice replied. "It'll be much better this way. Unforgettable."

"I don't care," Rundark said.

"You will soon have everything you want," the voice said. It sounded irritated. "Now it's my turn. And remember that without me, you couldn't have any of this—not without years of war and hardship. Who showed you how to split the Gem? Who amplified its power? Who gave you the orbs?"

"Enough," Rundark said. "I will hold to our bargain." He sauntered over to a large map that was nailed to the wall below two drippy, wax-caked candle sconces. It was a map of the Thirteen Kingdoms, not that you could easily tell, thanks to all the thick red Xs scratched across it. "After all, you are right: This bargain of ours *has* given me the world."

19

AN OUTLAW BOATS TO THE ROCK

It was a little awkward when Gustav first attempted to "talk" to Jerica. His icebreaker was "Hey, Pirate Lady! So what's up with this seafaring stuff?"

To which Jerica responded, "I would appreciate it if you call me Captain. Or, at the very least, call me Jerica."

To which Gustav responded, "I'm gonna call you Pirate Lady."

To which Jerica responded by calling him Goldilocks.

To which Gustav responded by kicking a barrel overboard.

To which Mr. Flint responded by yelling, "Hey, those were my parrot treats!"

But things went much smoother the second time

around. And in the ensuing weeks at sea, the two spent most of their days together (Gustav and Jerica, that is—not Mr. Flint). They told crude jokes and tall tales, they dueled, they went shark fishing. They had mast-climbing contests, barrel-chucking contests, and even eating contests (the *Dreadwind*, to Gustav's relief, had a full stock of fruits, grains, and dried meats). They played pranks on each other (it took Gustav days to get the squid ink out of his hair) and took every possible opportunity to make fun of Liam together.

"He's certainly having a good time," Frederic said to Liam one afternoon as they watched Gustav and Jerica guffawing up in the crow's nest.

"I wish I could say the same," Liam replied sourly, pulling a DUNK ME sign off his back.

"Believe me, fun is the furthest thing from *my* mind," Frederic said. "I worry about Rapunzel and Ella and Snow every day. Not to mention that this ship does not have so much as a single bar of soap on it. Or a pair of tweezers. And have you seen what the salt air is doing to my skin? Look at my hands! It's like I have mummified iguanas sticking out of my sleeves! But, um, mostly I'm concerned about the ladies. And I know that Gustav is, too. But in the midst of all this hardship and horror, he's managed to find a little oasis of happiness. And seeing him smile has been the only thing that's made my time on this ship tolerable."

Liam nodded. "No, you're right. It is heartening so see any light in this time of darkness." And then, with a thump and a squirt, a rotten grapefruit splattered on his head, while yards above, Gustav and Jerica high-fived.

And on they sailed, through calm seas and rough, through blinding sun and pelting rain, through days of solemn silence and nights of raucous singing. All the while, First Mate Key stayed at the wheel, guiding the ship southward and doing his best to handle Duncan's constant onslaught of questions.

"What's a mizzenmast?" Duncan lay on the deck, staring up at him.

"It's the one toward the rear," Key replied, keeping his eyes on the sea ahead.

"How'd you get the scar on your face?"

"Shaving accident."

"Oh, not a duel?"

Key smirked. "I don't get hurt in duels. The other guy does."

"Touché," said Duncan. He was now swinging from a beam overhead. "Why don't you talk like a pirate?"

"I do talk like a pirate."

"You don't talk like Cap'n Gabberman."

"Gabberman talks like an idiot."

"Who would win: a pirate or a ninja?"

"You've got a lot of energy, don't you? You know, the foredecks are great for running laps, if you need to burn some of it off."

Duncan balanced on a barrel. "What's that shiny thing out in the water?"

"I think that's enough questions for today."

"No, really, what's that—"

"Enough!"

Duncan yelped and dashed off.

Gustav, meanwhile, prepared a surprise for Jerica. He planned to get her back for the squid ink trick by ambushing her with a barrage of hardtack. His arms loaded, he tiptoed up to the captain's cabin, flung open the door, and began hurling flavorless biscuits. Jerica was not amused.

"Get out!" she barked, quickly stashing a glassy, shimmering *something* under her desk. Gustav immediately stopped tossing hardtack and gave an innocent shrug.

"What did I—"

"There was *one place*!" Jerica screamed as she jumped up, knocking over her chair. "*One place* I said not to go! Now, get out!"

She slammed the door in his dumbstruck face.

"But . . ." He dropped the rest of his bread-bombs and shuffled off. In earlier days, when Gustav was upset, he would often climb into a tree and sit there until he felt like talking to human beings again. Stuck on a ship, he did the next best thing.

Jerica found him ten minutes later, sitting on the topmost crossbeam of the ship's mainmast. "You look pathetic," she said as she hauled herself up and scooted out to sit next to him. He offered her nothing but a sullen frown.

"I though Liam was the mopey one," she tried.

Gustav let out a tiny snuffle of a chuckle. "I should toss you in the ocean just for making a comparison like that," he said.

"I'd like to see you try," Jerica replied, and waited a second to see if he actually would. "Look, we've had some good times together on this voyage, I'll admit. But that doesn't mean you can barge into my private quarters like that. I gave you an order, and you disobeyed it. Am I not supposed to get angry about that?"

"I thought we were—"

"We were nothing," she said. "We *are* nothing—other than shipmates who've had a few laughs together."

Gustav looked her in the eye. "That's not true," he said,

with more conviction than he expected. "It's different, and you know it."

"All right, fine. Yes, it is different. Because you were my *prisoner*. And I'm not exactly known for getting along swimmingly with my captives. But, hey, for whatever reason, you and I hit it off. And that's exactly why this needs to stop. You're getting too close, and we can't have that. I'm a sea captain; you're allergic to fish. It would never work."

Gustav grumbled. "I shoulda known better than to trust a girl."

"I'm a woman," Jerica said.

"Yeah, first woman I ever had fun with," he muttered. "Fine, Pirate Lady. Just tell me one thing. What were you messing around with when I busted in on you? It looked kinda like a—"

Jerica leaned forward and kissed him. Gustav's eyes went wide. "What . . ." he stammered. "What was . . . for . . . that for . . . what . . . ?"

Jerica was about to answer when there was a thunderous thud, and the entire ship rocked violently from side to side. Gustav lost his balance and slipped from the beam, but Jerica caught his hand as he fell. The big prince was twice her weight, and she struggled to hold on to him as, below them, the whole crew began to scramble.

"Sea dragon!" shouted Mr. Key.

"The shiny thing in the water! That's what I was trying to tell you," Duncan said, popping up from behind a crate of empty crab shells.

The serpentine beast raised its head up from the waves and snorted hot, briny mist onto the scattering pirates. It was covered everywhere in glinting silver-white scales, save for one dark, bruised circle on its left cheek.

"Well, I'll be pickled in prawn juice," Key said, straining to hold the wheel steady. "It's the same beastie that sank your old ship. He must've been tracking us for weeks. Cannons, men! The only thing worse than a sea dragon is a *vengeful* sea dragon!"

The *Dreadwind* was too large for the monster to wrap itself around as it had done with the *Wet Walnut*, but the creature was fully capable of bashing a hole through the massive galleon's side planks—and that is exactly what it tried to do. The hissing dragon rammed its crested skull against the ship's starboard side, each blow sending those on board for a painful tumble across the deck. One particularly powerful jolt sent Frederic flipping through the air, heading straight for the rail. Tauro, the crew's musclebound bruiser, caught the prince in his arms like a baby.

"We've got to stop meeting like this," the big pirate

quipped. He set Frederic down and rushed to a nearby cannon. Tauro reached into a slatted crate for ammunition. But before he could retrieve any, the dragon's tail—thick as an elephant—crashed through the rail and smacked him unconscious. Frederic yelped and ducked behind a cask of grog.

Where are all the cannon blasts? Frederic thought. He looked around; the dragon was thrashing with maniacal fury, and the *Dreadwind* was in complete chaos. Sails were torn, and the mizzenmast was cracked in two. Several people had gone overboard. Of the three cannons on deck, one was now lying on its side, and a second was missing entirely, having vanished through a section of splintered rail. And the stairwell to the cannons belowdecks was blocked—jammed by a huge section of fallen mast. That left only the gun right in front of Frederic.

"I suppose it can't be too difficult to use," he said. "Put the cannonball in the cannon, light the fuse—*boom*. Yes, I can do that." He reached down and attempted to lift a cannonball. It was the heaviest thing he'd ever tried to pick up. It might as well have been glued to the deck. "Well, that's just ridiculous," he said, flopping onto his rear. "Where is Gustav when I need him?"

And then he looked up. Sixty feet above, Gustav was

flapping like laundry on a clothesline, while Jerica lay flattened out on the mast's crossbeam, holding on to his arm as tightly as she could. Had Frederic been able to hear them, he would have heard Gustav say, "Just drop me into the thing's mouth. We all know I'm the reason it came after us. It got a taste of me before, and now it wants more. I'm delicious."

And then he would have heard Jerica reply, "Shut up, Goldilocks."

But instead, all Frederic heard was "Why do they get to swing on the masts while we have to fight the dragon?"

"Duncan!" Frederic cried. "Where'd you come from?"

Liam stumbled up behind him. "We were trapped by a fallen Two-Clubs," he panted. "Took a while to get out from under him."

"We need to—" Frederic was cut off by another booming crash that nearly knocked them all off their feet.

"—stop that dragon," Liam finished.

"We should use the shooty-thingy," Duncan said, very proud of the idea.

"Indeed," Frederic replied, bracing himself on the teetering deck. "But I need a little help loading it."

"I've got it," Liam said. He squatted and, with a pained grunt, hoisted one of the cannonballs a few inches off the floor. "Holy cow. Why do they make these things so heavy?"

Frederic gasped. The dragon had stopped thrashing, but it now had its eyes set on Gustav, who was wriggling like a worm before its eyes.

"Teamwork, people!" Liam shouted. "Lift! Lift!" Frederic and Duncan crouched down with him, and together the trio lugged the weighty iron ball to the end of the cannon barrel and shoved it inside.

"Duncan, give me a match," Liam said urgently.

"What makes you think I've got a match?" Duncan asked.

"Because you're you."

Duncan felt inside his pocket and pulled out a match. Liam took it and lit the cannon's fuse. "Everybody get back!" he yelled. They darted away from the powerful weapon and its dwindling fuse, gathering behind a supply bin to watch from a safe distance.

"I have a question," Duncan said.

"Not now," Liam said.

"That's just what the scar-faced pirate said when I tried to tell him about the dragon," Duncan said. "I think people need to stop asking me to stop asking things."

"Fine, Duncan," Liam said. "What?"

"Shouldn't we have aimed the shooty-thingy at the dragon?"

"Oh, crud." The cannon was about to fire its load at nothing but seawater. And the sea serpent was flicking its forked tongue at Gustav's dangling toes.

Fig. 16
SEA DRAGON,
vengeful

"Make a lot of noise!" Liam shouted. He, Frederic, and Duncan ran back out into the open. They jumped and shouted and waved their arms like crazy.

"Hey, Cecil!" Duncan cried. "Over here, Cecil!"

The sea dragon's head darted in their direction. It opened its jaws wide enough to swallow all three of them in one gulp, and lunged. Liam dove back, pulling the others away with him, and the dragon's teeth chomped down into the deck. The beast bit off a huge hunk of ship—deck, rail, and cannon included.

The princes huddled as the sinewy creature raised itself up above them once more, baring its rapier-like fangs in what seemed like a smile. And then they heard the muffled boom of the cannon going off deep inside the dragon's gut. The beast went cross-eyed as black smoke leaked from between its teeth, and it slowly sank to the bottom of the sea.

Mr. Key, who'd been straining at the wheel the entire time, let out a long victory hoot. "Not the most orthodox use of a cannon I've ever seen," he said. "But it got the job done."

Up on the mainmast, Jerica was relieved that the ship had finally stopped swaying. She took a deep breath and hauled Gustav back up. He lay there on the beam and looked at her. Her sleeves were torn, her hair in tangles. She was a sweaty, disheveled, red-faced mess. *She's magnificent,* he thought.

"Hey, Pirate Lady," he began to say, but she quickly cut him off.

"Not now, Goldilocks," she said. She was staring off at the southern horizon. "There's the island."

20

AN OUTLAW FORGETS TO PACK A CHANGE OF CLOTHES

The island loomed on the horizon, a squat, brown lump of earth marring the sleek beauty of a sea that was as blue as the clear sky above it. Honestly, to call it an "island" was generous. It was more like a floating dirt pile. Other than a few runty, gray bushes and one jutting, rocky hill, it appeared completely flat. And empty. From several miles away, on the bow of the *Dreadwind*, the princes took turns peering at it through a spyglass.

"You sure that's where you dropped Briar?" Liam asked skeptically. "Because it looks to me like nobody's home."

"There isn't another island for miles in any direction," said Jerica, while her crewmen lowered the ship's anchor. "That little hill you see has a cave in it. She's probably inside.

Unless you think she was stupid enough to try to swim for it."

"Briar swim?" Liam said, half chuckling. "No, if that's where you put her, I'm sure she's still there."

"Well, this is it then," Jerica said. "You guys should probably get going." She began to walk away.

"Whoa, Pirate Lady," Gustav said, catching her arm. "Aren't you coming?"

"No," she said. She looked him in the eye, but only for a second before she turned away again. "In case you didn't notice, your scaly friend did a number on my ship. I've got repairs to oversee."

"What's-his-name can do it," Gustav said. "And the other guy."

"I'm captain of this ship. I have responsibilities," she said. "Deal with it." And she marched over to some pirates who were hammering away at a broken rail.

"What's up with her?" Gustav wondered aloud.

"The captain is always going to do what's right by her crew," said Mr. Key. He paused and took a deep breath. "Even if it means abandoning the fellows who just saved her ship."

"Well, 'abandoning' is a harsh word for it," Liam said.

Key nodded. "Anyway, like the captain said, you'd best be off."

"Aren't we going to get any closer?" Frederic asked, looking at the miles of blue between them and the island.

"The reefs would tear apart the hull of a ship this size," said Key. "You'll have to take a dinghy."

"I'll row you there," Tauro said, climbing into a smallish wooden boat that was suspended just off the portside rail. The princes followed, and two large crewmen spun wooden cranks to lower the dinghy into the water. Tauro untied the ropes and paddled toward the tiny island.

As the dinghy approached that brown and desolate shore, Frederic couldn't shake the creeping feeling that something was wrong. He didn't like that they hadn't seen Briar yet. As soon as the water was wading depth, Liam, Duncan, and Gustav bounced from the boat like coiled springs and splashed onto the shore, shouting Briar's name. But Frederic couldn't quite bring himself to leave the dinghy.

"Go with your friends," said Tauro. "I'll take care of the boat."

Frederic took a deep breath, stepped out into the knee-deep water, and sloshed after the others. His heart was thumping wildly. In fact, it felt like every organ in his body was thumping wildly—even the ones that didn't normally thump.

But then, from behind the rocky hill, there appeared a lopsided pile of dirty auburn hair. And it was slumped on the head of Princess Briar Rose. She was pale and bony (more so than usual), and her once-elegant gown had been reduced to sparkling tatters. She was grime smeared and barefoot. But she was alive.

She craned her head around, confused at first to be hearing her name—or any human voice, for that matter. But as soon as she saw the princes, her eyes went wide. She waved her arms wildly and ran toward them.

"Liam!" she shouted.

"Briar!" Liam threw his arms open and sped up his run.

"Liam!" she cried again, this time sounding oddly angry.

"Briar?" Liam said as he reached her and threw his arms around her.

"Liam, you idiot!" Briar growled, shoving him aside and running by. "You complete and total idiots!" she hollered as she darted past the other princes.

"What? What?" Frederic sputtered.

"You let them get away!" Briar railed, gesturing madly toward the shore. They all stared. Tauro was well on his way back to the *Dreadwind*.

"Wait! Wait!" Frederic called, stumbling back into the water. "Mr. Tauro! Come back!"

Liam and Duncan joined in, jumping and waving. But to no avail.

Briar slapped her hand to her forehead. "They're not going to come back, morons," she said. "They haven't *forgotten* you. This was their plan. To maroon you here. To dump you on this dirt patch to rot away with me."

"No," Liam muttered, the horror of their situation dawning on him. "No, no, no, no, no."

"I don't understand," Frederic said sadly.

"Of course you don't." Briar rolled her eyes. "If you'd understood anything, you wouldn't have fallen into the trap."

"Trap?"

"Yes, Rundark's trap," she huffed. "Almost three months ago he kidnapped me and had those pirates drop me on this ungodly pile of rock. My only hope was that you geniuses wouldn't let him do the exact same thing to you. So, thank you once again for being total losers."

"Wait, did you say Rundark?" Liam asked. "Rundark's dead."

"Guess again, Professor," Briar snarked. "Follow me."

She shuffled back to the other side of the hill, and the men reluctantly followed. "When your pirate buddies abandoned me here to die, they left me with only one thing . . . *this*." She ducked and led them through a chiseled opening in the rocky surface, into a moist and gloomy cave. At its center stood a stone pedestal, on which sat a smooth crystal sphere.

"Are we going bowling?" Duncan asked.

"Just shut up and wait," Briar said. "I'm sure the pirates are delivering the message as we speak. It should . . . *turn on* any minute now."

As if on cue, the orb began to glow. Green mists swirled under the surface of the glass, then parted, revealing a face. The princes knew those dark eyes, those shaggy eyebrows, and that coarse, braided beard all too well. Lord Rundark.

As shocked as the princes were to see the Warlord's face in the orb, they were even more surprised to hear his voice. "Ah, I see my agents on the *Dreadwind* were correct—you've finally made it," he said. "I suppose I should thank you. It was so helpful of you to remain engaged in your little game of tag with the bounty hunters while I began my takeover of the Thirteen Kingdoms. And then you so cooperatively followed all the clues I intentionally laid out for you—and even went so far as to *seek out* the agents I had hired to kidnap you. Quite nice, really."

"Why do we always end up doing that?" Liam moaned, pulling at his hair.

"And now I bid you farewell," Rundark continued.

"Enjoy your time on the island. It will be your final resting place." The mists grew thicker and enveloped the Warlord's grinning head.

"Rundark!" Liam called. But the glow rapidly dimmed until the orb was dark and dead again. Liam began pacing. "This can't all be true," he mumbled. "Jerica was working with Rundark the whole time?"

"Well, she did tell us not to trust her," Duncan said helpfully.

"Something doesn't add up," Liam insisted. There was panic in his voice. This would be his worst failure yet. Not only would the Thirteen Kingdoms all fall to the forces of Dar, but Ella, Rapunzel, and Snow would never be proven innocent. They could be executed. He didn't want to believe it. "We need to signal the *Dreadwind*," he said. "Rundark was lying. There's no way he could have been communicating with Jerica from wherever he is."

Gustav let out a long, horribly pained moan. "She had one of these crystal balls in her cabin," he said. "Everything Rundark said was true. And everything Jerica said was a lie." He left the cave, walked back to the shore, and watched as the *Dreadwind* dwindled down to nothing more than a tiny speck on the horizon. Even when the ship was completely gone from view, he refused to come back inside. He sat on the dark sand, rested his elbows on his knees, and dropped his head into his hands. Despite all the bruisings, beatings, and burnings he'd received over the years, he couldn't remember anything ever hurting so much.

Back in the cave, the others were also distraught.

"So we're stranded on this island forever?" Liam said. "Left to rot and die?"

"Oh, no," Briar said. "It was *me* they left to rot and die. Although I *haven't* yet! Because I'm not afraid to eat tadpoles and algae!" She stuck her tongue out at the orb. "Anyway, *you four* don't get the pleasure of rotting. Rundark plans to destroy you in some spectacular fashion and let the whole world see it through these crystal balls."

"How do you know all this?" Liam asked.

"He likes to fire up the magic orb in the middle of the night and ramble on and on just to torture me while I'm trying to sleep."

Everyone was silent for a moment, until Frederic said, "That plan doesn't sound like Rundark. I thought of him as a very straightforward, crush-your-enemies type of villain. This all seems a bit elaborate for him."

"And since when did he become a magic-user?" Liam added. "Yes, something doesn't add up. Maybe Rundark's not working alone."

"There are three things I don't understand," said Duncan, and he began counting them off on his fingers: "How Rundark came back from the dead . . . how he's still using the Djinn Gem . . . and how people fit model ships into those tiny bottles."

"You know, guys," Briar said wearily, "playing whodunit is all well and good, but shouldn't we be trying to think up a way off this rock?"

"She's right," said Liam, standing tall and snapping into his Brave Leader voice. "It's not just our friends and loved ones who are in danger, but the entire world as we know it. We need to save the day. But we can't do it from this little patch of earth in the middle of the sea. So what is priority number one?"

"Escape!" shouted Frederic.

"Escape!" shouted Duncan. "And then model ships!"

"Let's put our heads together, people," Liam said. "We can do this!"

The three princes cheered and embraced one another, feeling at that moment like they could accomplish anything. Which was nice, even though, in reality, it was far from the truth. In fact, they never did think up a way to get off that island.

PART III

In the Slammer

21

AN OUTLAW ENJOYS COZY ACCOMMODATIONS

The Avondellians weren't just rich—they were classy. They prized beauty beyond almost all else. From palace to tool shed, nearly every building in the capital city was adorned with stunning mosaics, vibrantly painted murals, or elegant, gold-laced engravings. Pay a visit to the most meager peasant home and you would find a government-mandated stained glass coffee table and hand-carved ivory doorknobs. In the minds of Avondell's elite, there was no greater punishment than to be deprived of style. Which is why the royal dungeon—housed in subterranean levels below the palace—was specially designed to be bleak and ugly. Its cells were grim cubicles of stone littered with straw and often crawling with vermin. Worse yet, they were intentionally painted with clashing colors. And they were decorated with artwork deemed too distasteful to hang in the homes of law-abiding citizens: velvet portraits of crying clowns, for instance, or glow-in-the-dark unicorn collages.

It was among these hideously tacky cells that Ella, Snow, and Rapunzel prepared to spend the remaining days of their lives—which, if the Avondellian authorities had their way, would not be many. But rather than jumping in, right at that moment of sorrow and despair, let's step back a full two months, long before all that business with the princes on the island, to a day that was filled with *slightly less* sorrow and despair—the day the fugitive women were delivered to Avondell's dungeon by Orangebeard and the Twins. They had been made to wear drab beige prison frocks and pin their hair up into decidedly un-fancy buns (and given that Rapunzel's voluminous hair was knee-length to begin with, she looked like she had a second head). Many a sad, fallen face stared out at them from behind bars as they passed. Quite a few snarling, angry faces as well.

"These are real criminals," Rapunzel said with a shudder. "We're innocent. We don't belong here."

"I hope you don't think you're the first person to ever say such a thing," replied one of the guards. He and his partner wore neatly pressed blue suits with silver pinstripes and carnations tacked onto the lapels. But they also had razor-keen swords hanging from their suede belts.

"But in our case it's true," Snow said. "We never did a thing to hurt Briar. Except for when I knocked her down at the circus. And that time I shut her fingers in the wagon door. And when I bumped her into that table of deviled eggs at the ball. But some of those were accidents! Well, one was. Okay, none."

"Snow, you're not helping," Ella said bluntly.

The guards stopped them at the end of a long, dim hallway. "In you go," said one as he ushered Ella and Snow into a gaudy, pink-and-teal cell. "Sorry, but you're going to have to double up. We're full at the moment. It's been a busy couple of weeks for the royal sheriff and his men." He locked the iron-bar door behind them.

"What about me?" Rapunzel asked, wringing her hands.

"You'll be right across the way." The guards unlocked a cell across the hall and gave Rapunzel a gentle shove to get her inside. The door locked with a clang, and the guards disappeared down the corridor.

"I didn't ask for a roommate," said a voice from behind Rapunzel. She spun to see a woman, six and a half feet tall, with stiff, broad shoulders and arms like stone columns. The stranger's wide, ruddy face was surrounded by loose, flyaway strands of red hair that had escaped from her tight bun, giving her a Medusa-like look.

Rapunzel backed up against the bars. "I can't say I ever did either," she stammered as the larger woman glowered at her.

"Back away from her," Ella growled from across the corridor. "Or else."

"Or else what?" the tall woman asked smugly. "What are you going to do from all the way over there?"

Snow whipped a pistachio, which smacked the woman right between the eyes. "Gah!" she yelped, waving her hands in surrender. "Okay, calm down. I wasn't going to hurt anybody. It's just, you know, this is a *prison*. I was trying to act tough."

"*Act* tough?" Rapunzel asked, still tensed. "So you're not *really* tough?"

"No, I am," the tall woman replied. "I'm as tough as they come. Bunch of bandits tried to steal my cow once. Big mistake. You ever see a guy get bashed by a swinging cow?" She paused to smile wistfully. "But I'm not a criminal or anything. Most of the poor folks locked in here right now aren't; just unlucky so-and-sos who happened to break one of the king's crazy new laws." She held out her hand, and Rapunzel reluctantly shook it. "Name's Val," the cellmate continued. "Val Jeanval."

"What did you do to get tossed in here, Val?" Ella asked.

"I stole a loaf of bread," she answered. "And beat twelve of the king's soldiers with it. It was a *really* stale baguette—made for a pretty nice weapon."

They all stared at her. "So you *are* a criminal," said Rapunzel.

"I am *not*," Val insisted. "I'm a freedom fighter! Part of the Resistance! Or at least I would be if there was a Resistance. The king's gotta go. He's become nothing more than a bully. He's forcing poor families to spend their only gold on stuff like ruby chandeliers. He's outlawed any music that wasn't written by his own pompous bard, Reynaldo, Duke of Rhyme. And he's put these harsh 'style laws' into place. I saw a man get hauled away just because he was wearing socks with sandals. Admittedly, that's not a great look, but—come on!"

Fig. 17
VAL JEANVAL

"Wow," Ella mused. "I thought *Briar* was the tyrant in the family. Her parents always seemed like decent rulers."

"Things changed after they lost their precious princess," Val said soberly. "Look, I'm not unsympathetic, but whatever the reason for the king's left turn into Loonytown, the way he's been abusing his power is wrong." She shrugged. "Well, that's my story. What are you ladies in for?"

Ella let out an uncomfortable chuckle and said, "We've sort of been blamed for *causing* your king to lose his precious princess."

"But we didn't do it!" Rapunzel added quickly.

"Whoa. So you're . . ." Val tapped her long index finger against her lips. "Neat. Famous cellmates. Don't worry, I believe you. But, dang—of all the things to be falsely accused of . . . Frankly, I'm surprised they put you down here in the regular cells. I'd expect you guys to get the Chiller."

Snow clapped her hands. "Frozen desserts!"

"No, the Chiller's where they send the . . . troublesome prisoners," Val explained. "It's a special cell upstairs somewhere. Folks around here are really careful about not getting sent to the Chiller, so I can't tell you much more than that. But I'd be careful if I were you. With the king in dictator mode, you can expect him to be especially hard on you three."

"That's right! His Majesty *will* make you pay dearly for your crimes!" The harshly spat comment came from a man who turned around the corner at just that moment: a waxy-faced fellow with unnaturally yellow hair. He wore a uniform similar to that of the prison guards, but with epaulets at his shoulders and a bright-blue ascot around his neck. "And if you want your last two months on Earth to be even slightly tolerable, you had best refrain from referring to His Majesty by words such as 'dictator.'"

"Last two months?" Ella asked.

"I am here to inform you that your execution has been set for Midwinter's Eve," he said, eyeing the women with disgust. "Were it up to me, you would already be at the gallows. But considering the horrific nature of your crimes, His Majesty has decided Avondell's revenge should be the centerpiece of our holiday celebration."

"I don't suppose there will be a trial?" Rapunzel asked hopefully.

The officer let out a cold, fake-sounding laugh. "Ha. Ha. Ha. His Majesty has already found you guilty."

"On what evidence?" Ella snapped.

"Word of your guilt has been reported in the songs of the bard," he replied. "What more evidence is needed?"

"Excuse me, Mr. Prison Guard," Snow said, squeezing

her head between the bars to get a better look at the man. "But there's something maybe you should explain to your king. As someone who has been the subject of a few bards' songs herself, I can tell you that those fellows are not always—"

"I am no mere prison guard!" the man barked. "I am the *Captain* of the Guard. Captain Euphustus Bailywimple. And you will address me as such."

"Okay, Mr. Such," Snow said.

"No!" the officer barked. "Address me as Captain Euphustsus Bailywimple."

"I have to say the whole thing every time?" Snow asked, pained at the thought.

"Yes," Bailywimple said, looking down his stubby, upturned nose at her. "And what's more, you will refer to the king of Avondell only as His Majesty, the Most Right and Honorable King Basil the First, long may he reign."

"Excuse me again, Captain Festivus Dailywindow," Snow said, raising her hand. "But is the 'long may he reign' *part* of his name? Or was that just a bit of fancy business you added at the end?"

The captain huffed. "It is not *part* of His Majesty's name. But you still have to say it. And *my* name is Captain *Euphustus Bailywimple*. Now get your head back inside the cell!"

"I'd like to, Captain Fungus Bullwinkle," Snow said sheepishly. "But it seems to be stuck."

With a grunt of frustration, Bailywimple plopped his palm onto Snow's forehead and began trying to shove her head back between the bars. Snow winced.

"Don't touch her," Ella said coldly as she reached out and clamped her own hand around the captain's wrist. Across the hall, Rapunzel hid her face, while Val's eyes lit up in amazement.

Bailywimple turned his head slowly to look Ella in the eye. "Remove your hand at once," he said, barely above a whisper.

"You remove yours," Ella replied, without so much as a blink.

"It's okay," said Snow, wiggling her head back into the cell. "See, I'm free."

But Ella continued to stare icily at the officer and kept a firm grip on him.

"Let go," Bailywimple said. "Or you will pay the consequences."

"What are you going to do?" Ella asked. "Put me in *more* jail?"

"Release me," Bailywimple said through clenched teeth. "Or so help me, you'll spend a *week* in the Chiller."

Ella let him go—but not before making him slap himself in the face.

"The Chiller it is," he said.

"I'm so sorry," Snow said to Ella as Bailywimple stomped down the hall screaming for more guards. "I didn't mean to get you in trouble."

"You didn't; I did it on purpose," Ella whispered to her. "I've got to find us an escape route, and this may be my best shot at scoping one out."

Bailywimple charged back down the corridor with two guards in tow. They unlocked Ella's cell and pulled her out.

"See you in a week," she said cheerily as the guards marched her away. Bailywimple sneered at the other prisoners and followed.

"Well, that was exciting," said Val.

Rapunzel began pacing rapidly. "How did I get myself into this?" she muttered. "Where did I go wrong? I was a humanitarian. A healer! I had a nice place in a woods, a few tiny blue friends, plenty of turnips. What was so wrong with that? Nothing! It was great! I was doing great! But could I leave well enough alone? Oh, no! I had to say, *Wait, Frederic! I'll come storm a bandit's castle with you! I'll get involved with the kind of people who . . . who . . . wear capes! And tick off bounty hunters! And slap prison guards!* I mean, why not?

That sounds like me, right? Did I lose my mind?"

"I'm gonna go with yes," Val said, eyeing her cautiously.

As soon as Snow was sure that no one was listening, she told them what Ella had whispered to her. Rapunzel sat down on her threadbare cot and rested her head in her hands. "I suppose I should be heartened by that," she said. "But I'm not. We're on Death Row, Snow. With no chance of proving our innocence. And the only one of us who has any real heroing experience just got hauled off to some mysterious torture chamber. It's hard not to feel the weight hanging over my head."

"That's just your hair," Snow replied. She plopped herself cross-legged on the floor. "Look, it's like Frank the dwarf always says: When life gives you lemons, throw them at Duncan. By which I believe he means: When you're in a bad spot, trust in your friends to help you out."

"I don't think that's what he means," Rapunzel said. "But I don't think we have a choice in the matter either. We have to wait to see what happens when Ella comes back. *If* she comes back."

22

AN OUTLAW DOESN'T KNOW WHAT KIND OF BIRD SHE IS

Ella did not come back. At least, not when she was supposed to. That long, stressful week of waiting turned into an even longer, more stressful month of despair for Rapunzel and Snow. By their fifth week of imprisonment, it seemed they'd given up hope. They must have, because they resorted to an activity that people only engage in when they know with certainty that they will be trapped someplace for a long, long time: They played Twenty Questions.

"Are you an animal?" Val asked, sitting on the floor, chewing a piece of straw.

"Yes," said Rapunzel, flopped on her cot. "Sixteen left."

"Are you a kind of bird?" Val asked.

"Yes. Fifteen."

"Ooh!" yipped Snow, bouncing on the small "chair" she'd managed to weave together using loose straw gathered from her cell floor. "Are you Mimpy?"

"Snow," Rapunzel said gently, "I keep telling you—I don't know the names of the animals that wander through your backyard."

"Mimpy is a duck," Snow said helpfully.

"I am not . . . Mimpy," Rapunzel said. "Fourteen."

"Could I crush you with one hand?" Val asked.

Rapunzel cringed. "Is there anything less . . . *disturbing* you could ask?"

"I'm just trying to narrow it down," Val said. "There are some birds I could crush with one hand and others I'd need two hands for."

"I suppose so," Rapunzel said. "But, I mean . . . couldn't you ask, 'Are you *bigger* than my hand?' That wouldn't have worked?"

"There are birds that are bigger than my hand that I could still crush with one hand," Val said.

Rapunzel buried her face in her pillow. She looked up again when she heard footsteps coming down the corridor. "Ella! Thank goodness!" She jumped up and ran to the bars, as did Val. A guard tossed Ella into the cell with Snow and tromped back off the way he'd come.

"Are you okay?" Rapunzel sputtered.

"What was it like?" Val burst.

"I made a straw chair," Snow said proudly.

"Whoa, one at a time, people," Ella said, holding up her hands. "Rapunzel, no worries—I'm doing pretty great. Val, the Chiller isn't half as bad as you think. And Snow, that's . . . pretty impressive, actually."

"Why were you gone so long?" Rapunzel asked.

"I made the mistake of calling Bailywimple's ascot a tie." Ella rolled her eyes at the memory. "Sorry if I scared you ladies. But, listen. The Chiller is way up at the tippy-top of the palace's highest tower. Inside, though, it's not much different from the cells down here. Except the art is *way* worse."

"Worse than *this*?" Val asked, pointing at a framed paint-by-number of frolicking saucer-eyed babies that read I WUV OO.

Ella nodded and Val shuddered. "But on the whole, the Chiller is . . . nothing," Ella continued. "I think they call it the Chiller because it's drafty."

"Well, sleeping in a draft *is* bad for you," Rapunzel said.

"Granted," Ella replied. "But here's the thing: It's drafty because there's a window. An *open* window!"

"You mean no bars or nothing?" Val asked. Everyone perked up.

"Nope," Ella said. "My guess is they figure they don't

need bars because it's so high up. There's at least a sixty-foot drop to the palace roof. And then another three stories to the ground after that."

"Oh, so you *didn't* find an escape route," Rapunzel said, her face falling.

"No, I did," Ella snapped. "I'm convinced the Chiller is our way out. We just don't know how to use it yet. There's still, what . . . nearly a month left for us figure it out?"

"Hush up," Val warned. "We've got visitors."

Footsteps echoed down the hall, and soon the frowning face of Captain Bailywimple appeared around the corner. He was shoving along a new prisoner, whose hands were bound behind her back—a young girl with a big pouf of curly hair tied at the back her head.

"Lila!" Ella shouted, both furious and worried.

"Ella!" Lila called. She tried to run ahead, but Bailywimple yanked her back.

"Not so fast, brat," he hissed. "You won't get away from me again."

"Please, Mr. Captain of the Guard," Lila begged.

"His name is Captain Eucalyptus Bellybutton," Snow said helpfully.

"I've been telling you," Lila continued, "I wasn't trying to escape. I was trying to get to the king."

"Yes," Bailywimple sneered. "And thank heavens I was able to foil your assassination plot."

"I don't want to hurt the king," Lila insisted. "I just need to speak to him. It's urgent! I promise. You can keep me tied up. I just need to talk to him."

"Come on," Ella urged. "Hear her out, Bailywimple."

The officer's waxy complexion turned a fiery red. "What could this urchin possibly say that would be of any interest to King Basil?"

"How about that his daughter is alive!" The corridor was suddenly filled with the sounds of gasps and rattling metal as all the prisoners gripped the bars of their cell doors. "And I also need to warn him that his kingdom is in danger," Lila continued. "The Darians have the Jade Djinn Gem, and they've already used it to take over Erinthia. Yondale, too. Sorry, Snow, they've got your dad. Ruffian and I found them there and . . . Anyway, it's only a matter of time before they reach Avondell."

The prisoners couldn't believe what they were hearing, but they trusted Lila. Not so for Bailywimple. "You have quite an imagination, child," he scoffed as he unlocked a cell door and nudged her in with Rapunzel and Val.

"What if it's true?" Ella said. "Think of the mistake you'd be making."

Bailywimple raised his chin. "In the history of the Avondellian Royal Guard, no man has received more honors than I. Every medal, plaque, and statuette handed out by His Majesty in the past ten years has ended up in my personal trophy case. To put it plainly, I don't make mistakes."

"You don't need to tell us how dedicated you are to this kingdom, Captain Euphustus Bailywimple," Ella said, recalling the diplomacy she'd used long ago to escape when she was held hostage by a giant. "But everybody makes a mistake sometime. And if this were your first, it would be a doozy. Think of what the consequences would be for His Majesty, the Most Right and Honorable King Basil the First, long may he reign."

Bailywimple paused. He furrowed his neon-yellow brow as he mulled over his options. He took a deep breath, but before he could utter a word, Lila jumped in.

"Fine, keep being a loser, Bailypimple!" she barked furiously. "We'll see how smug and self-righteous you are when the Darians come trampling over all your fancy-pantsed army guys! Hope they don't muss up your spiffy little neckbow!"

"It's an ascot," Bailywimple huffed. "To think I almost gave credence to the tall tales of a known murderer." He marched away.

"The kid's got spunk," Val said.

But Ella threw her head back in frustration. "Lila, why? He was so close . . ."

"I'm sorry," Lila said. She plopped onto a cot and put her head in her hands. A tear ran down her cheek. "I'm messing everything up lately. Liam gave me one stupid task—one! And Greenfang caught me so easily. He's a jerk, but he's right—I'm a princess, not a bounty hunter. It was probably my fault that Ruff . . ." She looked up at Rapunzel. "Remember when that giant snake guy bit Briar? Do you think she would've survived if you hadn't healed her?"

"I don't know," Rapunzel replied, gently stroking the younger girl's hair. "Is that what happened to Ruffian?"

Lila nodded. "I never should've left him."

"Lila, I'm sorry I snapped at you," Ella said. "I didn't realize . . ."

"You've got to go easier on yourself," Rapunzel said. "You're only thirteen."

"Thirteen?" Val blurted. "Aw, jeez. So, in addition to giant snakes and Darians, you're also battling the worst enemy of all—puberty!"

Lila chuckled. "Thanks, um . . . whoever you are."

"I'm Val. I beat twelve people with a baguette."

"Sweet," Lila said.

Just then, foosteps. The fluorescent-lemon head of Captain Bailywimple reappeared from down the hall. "The young lady has an audience with His Majesty," he said, his voice clipped and tight.

Ella jumped up. "Great. Let's go."

"*Just* the young princess," Bailywimple said as he unlocked Lila's cell.

"You told them about Briar and the Darians?" Lila asked as she stepped out.

Bailywimple gave her a scornful look. "You are a fool if you think *I* would risk wasting my king's time with the obviously imaginary fantasies of an imprisoned hooligan," he said snidely. "You can tell your tall tales yourself—and *you* can suffer whatever consequences come of doing so."

"Thank you all the same," she said. "I knew you would come around."

The Captain of the Guard gave a haughty snort and led Lila down the hall. He would never admit it, but Ella was right. Bailywimple was a dutiful servant of the crown; the possibility that he could harm his kingdom by withholding information was too much for him to bear. *But if it turns out that these women have made a fool of me,* he thought, *they will regret ever stepping foot on Avondellian soil.*

23

AN OUTLAW TALKS ALL PROPER-LIKE

Have your parents ever dragged you into one of those stores that sell very tiny, super-expensive knick-knacks? Stuff like swan-shaped porcelain pepper shakers, and miniature saucers painted with the faces of famous people you don't recognize? You're not sure exactly *why* any of these things are so valuable, but all you can think about is how much trouble you'd be in if you accidentally broke one of them? That's how Lila felt when she stepped into the throne room of King Basil and Queen Petunia. She'd been in Briar's throne room before—which was plenty fancy itself—but it paled in comparison to the royal couple's reception chamber.

Between the crystal vases that lined her path, the tinted

glass mobiles that dangled from the arched ceiling, and the bejeweled masks that adorned the walls, Lila was afraid to even hiccup. She looked down as she walked, hoping that her dirt-caked feet weren't leaving stains on the painstakingly hand-stitched carpet beneath her. When she heard Bailywimple clear his throat behind her, she looked up.

King Basil, clean shaven and clad in a neatly tailored royal-blue suit, looked younger than his years. Auburn hair rolled in waves down to his shoulders from under a glistening platinum crown. His face, however, was hard to read—neither menacing or friendly. The queen was noticeably absent; but Reynaldo, the bard, sat at the king's side on a plush velvet stool, his floppy, oversize cap surrounding his wavy-haired head like a halo. He strummed his lute lazily, barely paying attention to the young princess as she entered.

Lila wasn't sure if she was supposed to start talking, but King Basil solved that riddle for her. "Ah, my ex-son-in-law's sister," he said flatly. "If you have news, speak. My time is valuable."

"Well," she started, "the, um, good news, Your Highness, is that your daughter is alive! But the bad news . . ." From there the words just spilled out. She filled them in on every detail of the League's adventure thus far, both the bits she'd experienced firsthand and the parts she'd learned about from her fellow heroes. The king, the bard, and Bailywimple seemed to hang on every word. Out of breath, she finished: "So, you need to bulk up Avondell's defenses immediately. Tell that General Kuffin guy to get his catapults ready. And if I were you—"

"You most certainly are not me," Basil said sharply. "If you were me, you would not be foolish enough to try to fool the King of Avondell. Who is me. Although, in this scenario, you are me. So you'd be the king, trying to fool yourself. Which is doubly foolish."

"Sir?" Lila didn't know where this was going, but it didn't sound good.

"What I am saying is: no more fibs!" Basil turned to the bard. "Reynaldo, my most talented friend, compose us a new tune: 'The Tragedy of Lila the Liar.'"

The bard flicked his long hair, smoothed out his mustache, and began singing:

"Listen, dear hearts, to a tale most improper—
A prissy young princess who told a big whopper.
The great, wise King Basil she thought she could trick,
But her skills of deception, they proved not so slick."

Lila's survival instinct clicked in. She stomped on Bailywimple's foot and ran.

"Gah! Stop her!" the Captain of the Guard cried out. And Lila quickly found two brawny pin-striped figures blocking her path.

"Crud," she muttered as Bailywimple limped over and grabbed her arm.

"Foolish child," he said under his breath. "Or should I say, foolish *me*. I should have known better."

"Captain Bailywimple, I understand how badly you miss our poor Briar Rose, so I can forgive you for being manipulated by the treachery of these prisoners," King Basil said. "However, we can't afford to have them spreading false hope among the citizens of our good kingdom. We have no choice but to move up the execution. Prepare the gallows for tomorrow morning."

Lila sputtered, but couldn't think of another word to say as Bailywimple dragged her from the throne room.

24

AN OUTLAW NEEDS A GOOD STYLIST

"Tomorrow?" Snow yelped in horror. "There's *no way* I'll finish weaving this throw pillow by then!"

Lila was back in her cell and had just tearfully broken the news to the others. "I'm so sorry, guys," she said. "I should've left well enough alone."

"I'm gonna miss you, roomie," Val said to Rapunzel. "I never even got to find out what kind of bird you were."

"They're going to *hang* us," Rapunzel muttered as she paced frantically. "I don't even like to hang laundry. The poor clothes look so helpless up there."

"People!" Ella barked. "No one is getting hanged. The only thing that has changed is our time frame. We make our escape today."

"As opposed to tomorrow, *after* we've been hanged?" Rapunzel deadpanned.

"Since when did you become so sarcastic?" Ella asked.

Rapunzel shrugged. "Prison changes a woman."

"Darn straight," Lila said with conviction. "And I'm not going to let it beat me down." She stood, rolled up her sleeves, and nodded to Ella. "What's the plan?"

"The four of us are getting out of this palace tonight, through the window in the Chiller tower," Ella said. "Then we go find the guys. And if we can't find them . . . we stop the Darians ourselves."

Blank stares.

"Are we or are we not heroes?" Ella asked.

More stares.

"Snow, who saved my life when I was under the spell of the Gem?" Ella said. There was passion in her voice and an excited gleam in her eyes. "Rapunzel, who tracked a dangerous bounty hunter into the woods all by herself? Lila, who crossed a moat full of bladejaw eels, squeezed down a pitch-black snake hole, and went toe-to-toe with the Bandit King? In case you're having trouble following me, the answers are you! You three! We can do this. We have to do this! Maybe the guys will pull through and save the day in the end, but maybe they won't. And if that's the case . . . who will?"

Snow raised her hand. "Us?"

Ella nodded.

"Yes!" Snow jumped and pumped her fist in the air. "I'll show Dunky he's not the only one in the family who can rush foolishly into danger!"

"Not exactly what I was going for, but I'll take it," Ella said. She looked across the hall. "Lila, you're the bravest person I've ever met. You will make Ruffian proud."

"You're right," the young girl replied with a wink. "I totally will."

Rapunzel, however, was silent, lost in thought. *Can't win 'em all,* Ella thought.

"So, how you planning on getting down from the Chiller?" Val asked. She'd been standing by, watching the proceedings. "You said it's a sixty-foot drop, right?"

"Yeah . . ." Ella furrowed her brow in thought. "Snow, can you take apart all this little furniture and weave the straw into a rope?"

"Sure," Snow said, and immediately went to work. Her hands moving with hummingbird speed (she'd learned from the dwarfs, who were *expert* weavers), she disassembled her mini-chairs and mini-sofas and began winding the strands of straw into a thick rope. Five minutes later—with a proud "Ta-da!"—she held up her finished product. It was a rope.

But it didn't even reach the floor.

"I guess there was less straw than I realized," Ella said with a sigh.

"It makes a nice belt, though," Snow said, tying the rope around her waist. "Consolation prize!"

"Maybe we can steal some rope from somewhere," Lila suggested.

Fig. 18
RAPUNZEL,
imprisoned

"Or tear up the sheets," Ella suggested, trying to add up their lengths in her head.

"Ooh! I've got it!" Snow squealed. "Giant eagles!"

"Um, ladies?" It was Rapunzel. She reached up and laboriously unpinned her bun. Golden hair washed down over her shoulders like a waterfall, cascading all the way to the floor, where it gathered in shimmery piles at her feet.

"I do not remember your hair being *that* long," Ella said, gaping.

"It wasn't," Rapunzel said. "But we've been here for a over a month."

"Well, sure, my hair's grown, too," Ella said. "Like an *inch*."

"Mine's magic," Rapunzel said. "Normally, I cut it every couple of days, just to keep it from dragging on the ground. But as kind as our hosts have been here, they didn't provide me with scissors. So it's been growing. I just keep tightening the bun."

The other women marveled. Rapunzel's cell was practically flooded with golden-blond hair.

"How much do you think there is right now?" Ella asked.

Rapunzel wasn't sure, so Lila took one strand and followed its winding, weaving, overlapping line, all the way from her scalp to its eventual end, somewhere under Val's cot. They estimated it at just over forty-five feet long.

"A fifteen foot drop we can handle," Ella said, as Lila and Val giddily helped Rapunzel wrap her voluminous hair back up into a giant bun (which was not easy). "So the only thing left for us to do is get up to the Chiller."

"And how are we going to manage that?" Rapunzel asked.

"We're going to misbehave."

25

AN OUTLAW USES HER HEAD

Ella was the first to go.

Just a few minutes after they'd gotten Rapunzel's hair wrapped back up, the ladies were paid a visit by the same two bored (but nattily dressed) guardsmen who regularly delivered their meals.

"Guess what we have to give these ladies for lunch today, Simpson?" droned one of the guards.

"I don't know, Wilford," mumbled the other. "Could it be more gruel?"

"How did you ever guess?" Wilford said flatly.

When they opened the door to Ella's cell, she zipped out past them. The guards dropped their trays with a clang and took off in pursuit. They caught her only a few yards down the hall, after Ella conveniently stumbled. "Didn't really think you could get away, did you?" Simpson said as the men grabbed her arms.

"No cage can hold me!" Ella snarled (a bit overdramatically).

"Is that right?" said Wilford. "Let us see how you like the Chiller."

Four hours later, when it was time for tea (yes, the Avondellians made sure their prisoners never missed teatime), Lila took her turn. When Simpson handed her a cup, she casually emptied it over his head.

"What did you go and do that for?" the guard said, more confused than angry.

"I'm an evil, wicked criminal, remember?" said Lila. She tweaked his nose.

"That's it! To the Chiller with you!" Simpson barked.

"Can you do that?" Wilford asked. "There's already one up there."

"I don't see how that makes a difference," Simpson grumbled. "Let them *both* catch a cold from that horrible draft." And off they went.

At dinnertime, Snow made her move. "King Bagel is a stinky old ninnyhammer," she announced loudly as the guards set down her bowl of gruel.

"That's rather salty language for a lady like yourself," said Wilford, eyeing her distastefully.

"Who's this King Bagel, anyway?" Simpson asked. "The one from Svenlandia?"

Snow blinked. "He's your king," Snow said.

Simpson pursed his lips. "Now you're just being sassy. You know very well what our king's name is."

"I assure you I do not," Snow said honestly.

The guards exchanged glances. "You know the penalty for sass," Wilford said.

Simpson nodded. "Chiller."

When it came time for dessert, the guards complimented Rapunzel. "After the dreadful behavior exhibited today, we'd like to thank you for being a model prisoner. It's nice to see a convict who remembers her manners."

"Thank you," Rapunzel replied instinctively. "Um, I mean . . ." She frantically scanned her cell, desperately seeking out some mischief to make. Val looked on with bemused curiosity.

"Guards, watch this," Rapunzel finally said. She grabbed a painting off the wall—a portrait of puppies in tutus—and punched her fist through the canvas.

The guards gasped. "You can't treat a work of art that way," said Wilford. "Even a lackluster piece like that."

Val flashed a thumbs-up, and Rapunzel couldn't help grinning.

Rapunzel watched as the guards locked the door of the Chiller and headed down the first of many flights of stairs. "Okay, they're gone," she said to the others. Then she rubbed her hands along her goose pimply upper arms. "You know, it really is chilly up here."

Ella, Lila, and Snow waited at the open window, their thin prison dresses serving as poor protection from the nippy autumn wind. A hundred feet in the air, they had a clear view not only of the palace grounds, but of miles of rolling green countryside in all directions, though the setting sun was quickly casting most of that grand vista into shadow.

"It's getting dark, people. Time to move," Ella said. "Rapunzel, do you need help with your hair?"

"I've got it," she replied, letting her mega-bun unroll and fill the room. Ella and Lila helped her feed her lengthy tresses over the windowsill. Just as Rapunzel's hair was dangling outside at its full length, Snow squeaked out a warning.

Fig. 19
The CHILLER

"Someone's coming!"

"What? Who?" Ella asked, annoyed.

"I don't know." Snow shrugged. "But I hear a tippy-tap. And a pitter-patter. Also, a thumpety-thump. And those things usually mean feet. They're almost here."

All four women scrambled, gathering around Rapunzel and trying to act as if they were all casually sitting on the windowsill together. When the door swung open, they saw Wilford, covered in some sort of green slime. Next to him was Simpson, his clothing shredded as if he'd been attacked by an angry wolverine. Both men were fuming. They shoved Val into the Chiller, grumbled a few impolite words, slammed the door, and tromped back downstairs.

"You didn't think I was going to let you ladies escape without me, did you?" said Val.

"You almost ruined everything," Ella said sharply.

"But I didn't," Val said cheerily. "So let's get on with the breakout, eh?"

Rapunzel looked askance at Val. "I don't even want to ask what you did to those guards."

"You sure?" said Val. "'Cause it was pretty amazing."

"Ooh, I'd like to hear—" Lila began.

"Later," Ella said forcefully. "Val, if you're coming, help. If not, stay out of our way."

"How heavy of a load can your hair handle?" Ella asked Rapunzel.

"I was able to bear Gustav's weight," she answered. "So I can probably hold two of you ladies at once. Though maybe not Val. No offense."

"I'll go first," Ella said. "I'll make sure there's no trouble afoot on the roof, then signal for Lila and Snow to come down together. Then Val." She snatched the sheet off the Chiller's sole cot. "Then Rapunzel jumps, and we catch her in this sheet."

Rapunzel went white. "On second thought, I'll just spend the night here. Like you said, the Chiller's really not so bad. You can come back and rescue me in the morning."

"Let's go," said Ella. "Oh, and if we do happen to run into any guards—"

"I'll take care of 'em," Val said, pounding her fist into her palm.

"You will not," Ella said adamantly.

"Ooh! I can take care of them," said Snow. "I'm very good at taking care of people. I take care of Duncan all the time after he slips on a banana peel or burns his nose in the oven or gets his hand stuck in a pickle jar."

"I don't think that's the kind of 'taking care' she means," Rapunzel said.

"Oh, I see," Snow said snippily. "I suppose *you* want the job. Just because you're a magical healer."

"Don't look at me," Rapunzel scoffed. "I'm not 'taking care' of anybody."

"Why not?" Snow asked, aghast. "You're a magical healer!"

"I ought to *take care* of the both of you," Val laughed.

"Wait, now you're even confusing me," Lila said. "Are you talking about the good 'taking care of' or the bad 'taking care of'?"

Ella suddenly had much more respect for Liam. *This is what he deals with all the time*, she said to herself. *It's a miracle the League has ever gotten* anything *done.*

"I'm heading out, people," she said as she climbed through the window. "Just please don't do anything stupid." In the moonlight, she slid down to the dangling ends of Rapunzel's hair and let herself drop the final fifteen feet to the roof. She landed safely and, balancing carefully on the sloped green tiles, circled the tower, pleased to find no guards stationed on or near the rooftop. She waved up to the others. Lila and Snow rappelled down the side of the tower and dropped, one by one, into Ella's waiting arms. *So far, so good.*

Val swung one leg over the window but paused.

"Eh, maybe I shouldn't do this," Val said. "I'm probably

heavier than those three combined. I don't wanna be responsible for your doom or anything."

Rapunzel was surprised to find herself offended by the remark. "Look, I chose to be here," she said. "All this adventure business may be somewhat foreign to me. And deep down, I may wish we were able to settle this whole thing by sitting down and chatting with the Darians over a nice salad. Something with croutons would be nice. But I'm *in* this just as much as Ella, Snow, and Lila. Well, maybe not as much as Ella. Nobody's in it as much as Ella. But, anyway, um . . . shut your mouth and climb down my hair."

"Consider it shut," Val said. And out she went.

Several stories below, Simpson and Wilford tidied themselves up in the washroom. Simpson frowned into a mirror as he tried to smooth out his ravaged coat. Wilford stood over a basin of water, splashing slime off his face. It just so happened that the guards' washroom had a window that looked out on the Chiller tower. And as Wilford grabbed a cloth to dry his face, his eyes caught movement outside.

"Simpson, look!" he said, pointing.

"Well, I'll be . . . ," his partner gasped. "Escaping out of a tower on Rapunzel's hair! Who could've expected that?"

They sounded the alarm.

26

AN OUTLAW HEARS BELLS

Lila gripped Ella's arm in a panic. "Why is there a bell ringing?" she asked. "A very loud bell?"

"We've been spotted," Ella said anxiously. She called up to Val, "Hurry!"

Val was halfway down the tower when she suddenly felt herself being reeled back upward. *Uh-oh,* she thought. *Still thirty feet up. I can jump that. But, Rapunzel . . .* She held tight and rode the slowly disappearing train of hair back up the tower.

Inside the Chiller, three guards surrounded Rapunzel. One held his sword up menacingly, while the others struggled to haul in the makeshift "escape ladder." They could tell from the weight that they were reeling in more than just hair. Still, they were not expecting Val to suddenly appear at the window, roar like a bear that had just learned of a worldwide honey shortage, and launch herself at them. She grabbed the two hair-pullers by the arms and slammed them against opposite walls.

"I'll get you," the third guard shouted, running for Val with his sword held high. But all he got was a face full of floor, thanks to Rapunzel sticking out her leg to trip him. Val caught the guard's sword as it flew from his hand. She then scooped Rapunzel up under her left arm and ran back to the window.

"Get that sheet ready!" she shouted, and leapt out.

Ella and the others stretched the sheet taut, but Val and Rapunzel never reached it. Halfway down, their descent abruptly stopped. They were stuck, swinging like a pendulum a good twenty feet from the palace roof.

"Huh?" Val looked up to see the three guards piled in the window, gripping the ends of Rapunzel's hair. Grunting, the guards began hauling them up once again.

"Does this look painful?" Rapunzel whimpered. "Because it is."

"You said your hair grows back quick, right?" Val asked. She raised her stolen sword and, with one swift swipe, chopped through Rapunzel's golden locks. The pair plopped down into the waiting sheet, and the others set them down gently. As Rapunzel stood up wincing, she felt her head. Her hair was now even shorter than Ella's—and standing straight up.

"Well, that's different," she said. The women speedily sidestepped to the edge of the roof.

"Pretty quick thinking there, eh?" Val said proudly.

"Yeah, it was great. Except now we have a new problem," Ella said, peering over the eaves to the ground below. "We're still three stories up."

"You know, I *did* suggest giant eagles," Snow chided.

The alarm bell rang on, and they could hear muffled shouts below.

"Guys, follow me!" Lila said. "You know how many times I've climbed up and down these palace walls?"

The group followed her along the rain gutters to the eastern edge of the roof. Below them were dozens upon dozens of topiaries—bushes and hedges carved into the shapes of various animals. Lila leapt onto the long, curved neck of a shrubbery dragon, climbed down to its leafy back, hopped over to the thick green neck of a topiary grizzly, and then flipped down to the grass. Snow, Ella, and even Rapunzel followed quickly behind her, the not-too-distant shouts and footsteps of angry soldiers spurring them on. When Val attempted the same course, however, the neck of the ersatz dragon snapped and fell. The toppled dragon neck flattened a gnu bush and an echidna shrub, and Val found herself caught up in the branches of a rather thorny gerbil. As the others pulled her free, they all glanced up at the roof they'd just leapt from. Seven frustrated guardsmen were cursing and stomping their feet, having just lost their ability to follow the women to the ground.

"Yeah, that's right," Val shouted up at them. "I did that on purpose!"

The women sped off as cries of "Halt!" and "Get them!" filled the night air.

"And now the wall," Ella said as they moved. A high stone wall—which was painted quite beautifully in sweeping pastel swirls—encircled the entire palace and its lush gardens. "Let's head for that pear tree behind the animal bushes. I think we can reach the top of the wall if we climb it."

"Wait—the gate!" Lila whisper-shouted.

Ella froze in her tracks. The ornate wrought iron rear gate, which was only fifty yards off down a flower-lined cobblestone path, was sitting just slightly ajar. "There's no way they'd leave the gate open," she said. "It's got to be a trap."

"But it's a whole lot closer," Rapunzel said. She had a point. They could see the silhouettes of spear-wielding guards rounding the corner of the palace behind them. They changed course and headed for the gate.

"I can't believe it's going to be this easy," Lila said.

Rapunzel frowned. "Have you ever heard of jinxing?"

"That's the dance where you squat and kick your legs, right?" Snow asked.

"No," said Captain Euphustus Bailywimple, stepping out of the shadows to block the gateway. His rapier was in his hand. "Jinxing is when you create your own bad luck."

Val ran at him with her sword, but after one quick-as-a-blink slash from Bailywimple's blade, she was disarmed. Ella stretched her arms out to either side and stood protectively in front of the others. She glared at the Captain of the Guard, waiting for him to make

Fig. 20
CAPTAIN EUPHUSTUS
BAILYWIMPLE

his move. The three seconds of silence that followed seemed to last a month.

"Is it true?" Bailywimple finally said.

"Is what true?" Ella asked.

"Everything Princess Lila said—about Briar Rose being alive and the Darians on the attack. Is it true?"

Lila nodded vehemently. "I swear on my life."

Bailywimple stepped aside. The women stared in confusion.

"What are you waiting for?" he snapped. "I won't be able to keep them busy forever."

They didn't need to be told twice. With the stomps and grunts of approaching soldiers behind them, they dashed out past Bailywimple, who clicked the gate shut behind them. A few seconds later, they could hear him barking at his men: "Why are you wasting your time back here? This gate is locked! They must be hiding among the topiary! Start searching! A reward to the man who captures the fugitives!"

In the gathering darkness, the escapees fled across the open Avondellian countryside.

PART IV

After the Truth

27

AN OUTLAW HITS THE BOOKS

Few beings the size of Wrathgar could call themselves "human." Which is probably why few people who knew Wrathgar ever used that word to describe him. His gargantuan frame, combined with his penchant for grunting and his habit of swallowing whole roasted turkeys, made most of the people around Castle Sturmhagen think of him as more beast than man. (Or perhaps more *mustache* than man, thanks to the two coarse, whiplike braids of facial hair that ran from his upper lip down to his belt.) No one could quite understand why King Olaf had appointed this brooding mountain of muscle as his number one adviser, but no one dared question the matter either.

"We are hungry," Wrathgar made the thick-bearded

king of Sturmhagen say. "Bring us a new cartload of turkeys." All the servants rapidly exited the throne room, leaving their monarch and his massive Darian "sage" alone. Wrathgar then let Olaf stare into space as he walked behind the thrones and removed a shimmering crystal orb from a hidden chest. Wrathgar rubbed the orb in the manner he'd been taught, and watched as eddies of green mist began to swirl within it. The vapors soon parted, and the tattooed face of Madu, the Snake Man, appeared. "You finished construction yet?" Wrathgar rumbled.

"Yeah, we're all good here in Yondale," Madu replied. "You?"

"Ours is all set up," Wrathgar said. "So are the ones in Svenlandia, Jangleheim, and Carpagia, from what I hear."

"So now these princes, they will be done away with, yes?" added a third voice.

"Vero, is that you?" Madu asked with a hiss. "Are you eavesdropping on us?"

The dapper, ponytailed head of Vero appeared next to Madu's in the orb. "Apologies, my Darian friends," he said in his thick Carpagian accent. "It was not my intention to, as we say in my country, *listen in*. I only meant to contact Wrathgar, but when I fire up the orb—*poof*—there you both are. Interesting, yes?"

"Vero's got a point," Wrathgar said.

"Yes, this three-way chatting, it is quite convenient, no?"

"Not *that*," Wrathgar grumbled. "The princes. We've got our men in place, the Mega-orbs have been erected, and the princes are trapped on the island, completely at our mercy. Surely we can kill them *now*. I tire of playing puppeteer with this fat old honey badger of a king."

"I agree," said Madu. "It is time for Dar to step out of the shadows. We shall reveal ourselves to be what we truly are—the rulers of a new empire! Plus, this castle in Yondale is starting to reek of rotten potatoes. And I don't understand how. There are no potatoes here. I think it's the old man. I made him bathe, but the odor still . . . Hold on, there's someone else coming through."

Another face, pale and sinister, began to materialize in the orb.

"Oh, no. It is Falco," Vero said, rolling his eyes. "I swear to you, I can never understand anything this squinty little man is trying to tell us."

Falco snarled and pointed at his ear to clearly indicate *I can hear you!*

"You see what I am saying?" Vero went on. "Impossible."

"Welcome, Falco," Madu said. "Is your Mega-orb set up?"

"Yes, we are ready to wreak chaos and destruction!"

"Wait—who said that?" asked Madu.

"It's me—Princeslayer," said a pointy-bearded face that appeared.

"This orb, it is getting somewhat crowded, no?" said Vero.

"We have a general named Princeslayer?" Madu asked.

"No," Wrathgar said. "That's just Randy."

"I'm not Randy anymore, man! I changed it to Princeslayer. It's a lot more villain-y, right? And now it sounds like I'll finally get to kill some princes!"

"You will not," a new voice intoned. It was Lord Rundark. And in each of their separate throne rooms, in each of their separate kingdoms, each of the five generals almost dropped his orb.

"I see now there is a down side to this group chatting, no?" Vero muttered.

"If you are all so eager for us to move on with our plan," Rundark said, "why haven't you put a stop to the attacks of these so-called freedom fighters. Over the past two months, they've ambushed my men in four different kingdoms!"

"But the damage they have done, it is very small, no?" Vero said defensively. "They have stolen but a handful of weapons and horses. It is, as they say in my country, *not so much*."

Falco raised a hand and wiggled five fingers.

"Falco is right," said Wrathgar. "I hear there are only five of them."

"And *I've* heard they're all girls," Madu said, snickering. "Which can't be true, of course."

"Do not jump to this conclusion so quickly, my slithery friend," Vero said. "I once had the pleasure of dueling the Lady Ella, and I must say, her skill with the sword was—*mwah!*" He made a kissing sound.

"Yeah, well we don't have to worry about her," Madu said. "Since she and her gal pals got hanged in Avondell back on Midwinter's Eve."

The generals began to chatter away, until a harsh bark from Rundark silenced them. "I care not how many of these accursed rebels there are!" The words burst from his mouth like fire from the jaws of a dragon. "Nor do I care whether they wear pants or hoop skirts! They are a distraction. And we will not make our final move against the kingdoms until I am assured that they are out of the picture." He paused, breathing heavily for a second, then continued at a more reasonable volume. "I understand your impatience," he said. "No one wants to see the League of Princes destroyed more than I. No one is more eager to fly the flag of Dar above the royal palaces of all Thirteen Kingdoms. But as I have told you before, we will do this right. We will do this in a way that will ensure Dar's dominion over the world *for all time*."

Suddenly, a seventh voice joined the conversation, though no new face appeared. It was a voice the generals had all heard before, though none knew to whom it belonged. "These princes are men of legend," the mysterious voice said. "Their deaths need to be *legendary*."

"My . . . ally is correct," Rundark said, but there was a glare of frustration in his eyes as he glanced back over his armored shoulder. "The princes will be eliminated in a spectacular fashion before the eyes of the entire world. After that, no one will dare resist us. Rundark out." His image fizzled away.

The generals each stowed their orbs and went back to puppeteering their captive monarchs. Though as Madu closed the curtain to his hidden alcove in the throne room of Yondale Castle, his ears suddenly perked up. "Huh?" He spun his tattooed head to glance at the chamber's dirt-smudged windows. All were shut to keep out the winter cold. "Weird," he mumbled. "Could have sworn I felt a breeze."

Now, these five "freedom fighters" the Warlord mentioned were, of course, Ella, Lila, Snow, Rapunzel, and Val, who were most decidedly not dead. After their escape from

Avondell's prison, they had trekked north and crossed into Sylvaria to warn Duncan's family of the looming threat. But as soon as they saw ax-wielding Darians patrolling the now ironically named Much Happier Forest, they knew that Sylvaria, too, must have fallen.

Disguising themselves under heavy, hooded winter cloaks, they fled to Harmonia and then on to Jangleheim, but—

What's that? You were expecting us to check back in with the Princes Charming? Seriously, nothing has happened with those guys. They've been stuck on a deserted island, bored out of their minds. Gustav splashed around in the surf a lot, claiming to be "punching the ocean," while Frederic moaned about getting sand in his shoes and having to eat cave fungus, and Duncan spent much of his time either naming sand mites or grooming his hat. Liam and Briar threw insults at each other for the first few weeks, but eventually began talking about other things—like unfulfilled ambitions, feeling misunderstood, and how they both thought they'd be a better ruler than their parents. But other than that, nothing very exciting happened. Like I said, they never figured out how to get off that island.

So, back to our resistance fighters, who had *a lot* going on at that point.

The fugitive women had one big point in their favor—most of the world believed they were dead. The morning after their escape, King Basil had publicly announced that his daughter's killers had been recaptured (even though the only person actually thrown behind bars that night was Captain Euphustus Bailywimple). Then, on Midwinter's Eve, Basil told his people that, fearing another escape attempt, he had to cancel the public execution and hang the murderers within the safe confines of his dungeon. (In reality, the only things hung in the dungeon that night were some portraits of monkeys in party hats.)

Ella and the others could only guess as to why the king had carried out this deception—embarrassment, they figured—but they didn't really care. They were free. Although it was now more important than ever that they keep their identities hidden. So they bounced from kingdom to kingdom, seeking a safe haven, but they ran into Darians everywhere they turned. And they received no aid from the citizens of these kingdoms, all of whom had heard their monarchs welcome the Darians as "friends and allies from across the mountains," and who would have been quick to notify the authorities of any rebellious talk. So the Ferocious Female Freedom Fighters (or *"ffff!"* as Snow called them) were born. And they never stopped moving. They ran a zigzag course across the map, from the ice-covered lakes of Jangleheim, across the snowy mountains of Carpagia, and into the bucolic village streets of Valerium, ambushing squads of roving Darians along the way. Using Lila's stealth, Ella's leadership, Snow's marksmanship, and Val's brute strength—with Rapunzel's healing abilities as a nice bit of insurance—they'd managed not only to keep themselves well stocked on supplies, but to seriously annoy the Darian army.

Fig. 21
FFFF!

They were camped in a sparse forest on the western edge of Valerium, enjoying some sandwiches they'd "liberated" from the Darians, when they were startled by a sudden clatter. Smimf popped out of thin air and skidded to a crashing halt amid their bundles of pots, spoons, and cooking supplies. The red-faced, out-of-breath messenger looked sheepishly at Lila as he desperately tried to tidy the mess.

"Hello, sir, Your Highness, sir," he panted. "I was hoping to run into you."

Lila burst out laughing. It was the first real laugh she'd had in months, and it felt good. Smimf had no idea what he'd said to make Princess Lila laugh so much, but whatever it was, it made her smile, so he wasn't going to question it.

Ella stepped in. "Smimf, how did you know where to find us?"

"I didn't, sir, Your Highness, sir," he replied, loosening his scarf. "I had something really important to tell Princess Lila, but I had no idea where she was, so I just ran around looking."

"Randomly?" Lila asked.

"I figured if I ran *everywhere*, I'd eventually find you," Smimf said. "So I did. And it only took two and a half months."

"What did you need to tell her?" Ella asked. The women

all leaned in to listen.

"Well, sir, Your Highness, sir," Smimf began, "I delivered your message to all the kings and queens you asked me to. But I'm pretty sure all of them are having their minds controlled by that Djinn Gem thingamabob."

"All of them?" Ella asked.

"Mr. Smimf, did you happen to see my father, King Edwyn of Yondale?" Snow asked in a voice even more slight and soft than usual. "How did he look?"

Smimf lowered his eyes as he delivered the news. "He was very thin, sir, and very pale. He sat slumped so low in his throne that his chin almost touched the ground. His eyelids drooped, and his body rattled with every breath."

"Oh, thank goodness he's okay!" Snow said with relief. "He's just the way he was when I last saw him."

"Smimf, is there anyplace the Darians haven't gotten hold of?" Ella asked.

The messenger sucked air through his teeth and shook his head. "Only Avondell, as far as I can tell."

"And we can't go back there," Lila said soberly.

"Smimf, would you like a sandwich?" Rapunzel said, looking rather pale. "I think I've lost my appetite."

"Oh, thank you, sir, Your Highness, sir," Smimf said, joining the women on logs around the campfire. "I don't think I've eaten since . . . November."

The sun sank below the horizon, and the trees around them turned into black silhouettes against the clear indigo sky. It was nearly January, and even this far south, a thin blanket of snow covered the ground. The women were snug enough in their fur-lined cloaks, but Smimf's chapped knees knocked together.

"Is there anything else you can tell us that might be helpful?" Ella asked. "Anything unusual that you saw in your travels?"

"Would giant crystal balls count?" Smimf asked. "Because there's one sitting just outside every royal palace."

"Giant crystal balls?" Rapunzel echoed.

"I don't know what else to call them, sir. They've been set on top of enormous wooden stands, so everyone can see them—huge, round, shiny balls. They look kind of like my grandmother's glass eye, only a lot bigger."

"What do you think those are for?" Lila wondered.

"Snow globes!" Snow said gleefully. The others shook their heads.

"Oh, and there are some smaller crystal balls, too," Smimf added.

"Snow globes!" Snow cheered again.

"Do you remember that man from the Bandit King's

castle, the rather—pardon my language—unappealing one with the tattoos? He had a small crystal ball with him in Yondale Castle. And he was talking to it. And it talked back. I heard everything they said."

The women all leaned in closer. Smimf took a bite of his sandwich.

"What did they say?" the women snapped in unison.

"Oh! Sorry," Smimf mumbled through a full mouth. He wiped his lips and went on. "The good news is—your prince friends are still alive."

The women whooped with joy.

"The bad news is that Lord Rundark's going to kill them," Smimf added.

"Lord Rundark! I remember him," Snow said, wrinkling her nose. "I didn't like him."

"But Rundark is dead," Ella said. "We all saw him get pulled underwater by those bladejaw eels."

"You didn't stick around to see those eels cough up a skeleton, though, right?" Val ventured. "Maybe his men fished him out after you ditched the place."

"I was in that moat for all of three seconds, and those eels almost killed me," Ella said. "Rundark was down there for way longer. Even if he crawled out afterward, there's no way he could've survived the injuries. I mean, it's not like

Rapunzel hung around to heal him or anything." She turned to Rapunzel and narrowed her eyes. "You didn't, did you?"

"Of course not!" Rapunzel protested. But then, suddenly, her eyes got very wide and her cheeks went pale. "Oh, dear. My tears. I'd been worried about Frederic, so I gave him a vial of my tears. But the bad guys took it away from him before he got to use it. Oh, no. This is all my fault. My tears healed Lord Rundark."

"We don't know that for sure," Lila said.

"How else do you explain it?" Rapunzel began breathing in short, gasping spurts. "What have I done?"

"Hey, it's okay," Ella said.

"You don't understand," Rapunzel said, walking circles around the fire. "I've devoted my life to healing the sick and maimed. And I have to be honest—if someone had brought Rundark to me and asked me to heal him, I would have."

"What?" Val snapped.

"I can't turn my back on anyone," Rapunzel continued. "It's not in my nature. Do you know how many of these Darian soldiers we've ambushed that I've snuck back and cried on? I even helped Orangebeard fix the big toe he broke during the wagon chase. So, yes, if asked at the time, I would have healed Rundark. And I apparently did. But now that I see what he's done since then, I can't help but feel responsible for all the lives he's ruined and the damage he's caused."

"Go easy on her, Val," Ella said. She put her arm around Rapunzel. "Look, you're not the fiercest warrior here, but you may be the best *human being*."

"Were we having a contest for that?" Snow asked. "Because I would've entered. I'm very good at being a human."

"Look," said Ella. "It's possible that Rapunzel is partly to blame for Rundark's rise to power, but no more so than the rest of us. All of us stormed that castle—and unwittingly put the Djinn Gem right into the Warlord's hands."

"I didn't," Val said.

Ella huffed. "Must you people always be so literal? Never mind. It doesn't matter who created the problem; we're going to fix it. Smimf, tell us everything you witnessed in Yondale."

Smimf recounted every detail of the conversation he'd overheard between Rundark and his generals. When he was done, Ella stood up and rubbed her hands together as the others sat in a small semicircle on snow-dusted logs and listened.

"So Rundark is apparently working with at least one other mystery villain," Ella said, slipping into her hard-boiled-military-commander voice. "My guess is Deeb

Rauber. That cousin of mine has a soft spot for big, showy criminal acts."

"But Mr. Rundark and the Rauber boy didn't seem to be on very friendly terms the last time we saw them," Snow said.

"That was half a year ago," Ella said. "Villains have been known to team up with people they hate if it will help them achieve their diabolical goals. At least that's what happens in a lot of the stories I've read."

Somewhere among the trees, a twig snapped. Lila took note of the sound.

"Anyway," Ella continued, "thanks to Smimf's intelligence—"

"Thank you, sir," Smimf said, raising his head proudly.

Ella went on, not bothering to tell him she was referring to a different kind of intelligence. "—our new top priority is clear: We need to stop Rundark before he executes the princes. Which he apparently won't do until his men have captured the Ferocious Female Freedom Fighters."

"But that's us," said Snow. "We're *ffff!*"

"Except Rundark doesn't know that," Ella went on. "He thinks we're dead. This gives us the perfect chance to take him by surprise."

"Just leave it to me," Val said, admiring her fist. "*Bam!* Sock to the jaw."

"Actually, Val, I don't think you could get close enough to him for that," Ella said. "Our big obstacle will be the Djinn Gem. Rundark can use it to turn us against one another. The last time we faced him, he almost made me kill Liam."

"I still think I could take him," Val said. "But assuming what you say about this gem is true, what do we do about it?"

"We need to fight fire with fire," Ella replied.

"The Gem can make fire, too?" Snow asked, worried.

"Just an expression, Snow," Ella said.

"The Gem can make an expression?" Snow asked. "Does it even have a face?"

"It has lots of faces—it's a *gem*!" Lila quipped, snickering.

"People!" Ella snapped. "Fate of the world in the balance here! Pay attention!" Everyone hushed. "To defeat the Gem, we need something just as powerful."

"A sock to the jaw!" Val said triumphantly.

"No!" Ella howled. She paused for a deep breath. "You know, we work pretty well as the team, but there are times . . ."

"Hey, I got a question," Val said. "What's a djinn?"

"A genie," Lila replied. "A magical being that grants wishes. It was a djinn that made the Gem."

"So why don't we just tell this genie to make a weapon for us?" Val said plainly. "One that could beat the Gem."

"That's brilliant!" Lila chimed. "If we find the djinn's bottle, he has to grant us a wish!"

"Whoa," said Rapunzel. "According to the story, the djinn was somewhere in the middle of the Aridian desert. We can't possibly hope to find one random bottle among acres and acres of empty sand."

"But it's not just a random bottle," Ella said, with that familiar daredevil gleam in her eyes. "In the story, the bottle was found amid sand-covered ruins—and the thief who stole the Gem wandered back out into the desert and died among those same ruins. And that's where Liam's great-great-great-great-great-great-great-grandfather, Prince Dorun, found the Gem."

"And Briar's book will tell us how to get there!" Lila shouted excitedly.

"I really missed a lot by not being on your last adventure, didn't I?" Val said.

"Briar Rose had a book called *Remembrance of Kings Past*," Lila explained. "A history of the Erinthian royal family. There's a whole chapter about the Gem, including excerpts from the diary of Prince Dorun, who found the Gem at the ruins ages ago. Hey, Smimf, I hate to ask this, but—"

Smimf put down his sandwich. "Where is it?" he asked with a sigh.

"Top drawer of the vanity table in Briar's bedroom."

Smimf vanished in a mini-tornado of snowflakes. Before the last flake settled back to the ground, he reappeared with an ancient, leather-bound book in his hands.

"You're the best," Lila said. And Smimf was glad that the cold had already turned his cheeks red, because he could feel himself blushing.

Lila and Ella pored over the book, reading Dorun's diary entries carefully for clues to his route. Nothing was spelled out as clearly as they had hoped, but there were plenty of directions and landmarks noted: "started out south-southwest from the coconut grove," "passed a rock formation shaped like a chicken leg," "turned northward at a giant cactus full of berries," "went through a red stone arch that looked like a bent stick of cherry licorice" (Dorun was rather obsessed with food).

"So we're off to the desert," Lila said.

"Yep," said Ella. "We just need to stock up on supplies and—"

There was a blast of wind as Smimf suddenly returned with armfuls of water casks and baskets of bread and dried meats. They hadn't even noticed him leaving.

"Thank you," Ella said. "And I've got one more task for you. It's a big one."

"Name it, sir, Your Highness, sir."

"From what you've told us about their conversation, it sounds like Rundark will execute the princes if our attacks on his patrols stop," Ella said. "Can you pretend to be the Ferocious Female Freedom Fighters while we're gone? Keep messing with the Darian troops?"

"I can do that, sir," Smimf said, saluting.

"It could be a while," Ella said. "We're going to have to owe you until this is all over."

"Oh, no charge, sir, Your Highness, sir," Smimf said. "I'm always happy to help the League of Princes."

"We're not the League of Princes," Snow said. "We're *ffff*! And we're going to *save* the League of Princes."

28

AN OUTLAW CAN'T TAKE THE HEAT

"I thought I might like the desert," said Snow. "But I do not. It's very . . . beige."

"You just noticed that now?" Val said, taking a swig from her canteen.

"No, I noticed on the first day, but I didn't want to be too hasty in my judgment of the place," Snow replied.

The Ferocious Female Freedom Fighters had been tromping through the searing sand dunes of the Aridian Desert for seven days, and between its blinding light and blaring heat, the sun had become their worst enemy. The women wore damp cloths tied around their woozy heads—except Snow, who wore a floppy, wide-brimmed sunhat, and Rapunzel, whose hair had already grown long enough to fashion into a blond turban.

They had traded their horses for camels—Cammy, Camella, Cameron, Campbell, and Camembert, as Snow named them—at a small merchant's outpost in the coconut groves of southern Valerium, so their feet, at least, were saved from hardship. Even so, it was grueling travel. In addition to the overwhelming heat, Aridia was also deathly boring. There was less to do here than there was back in their Avondellian jail cells.

With the exception of a few random cacti, the camel merchant was the last living thing they'd seen since entering the desert—though he gave them a vague warning about "things that move beneath the grains." And every so often, Lila would turn and glance behind the party, as if she were looking for something. But whenever she was asked, her answer was always a mumbled "Nothing."

Ella carefully matched their route to Dorun's hints in the book, and thus far they'd hit every one of his noted landmarks—though the distance between landmarks was much farther than expected. The diary entries claimed, for instance, that Dorun's party traveled from the "jelly bean–shaped oasis" to the "ice cream scoop rocks" in little more than a day, but it took the women three days to cover that distance. When they reached those round, semispherical boulders, they stopped for a break, hopping down from their camels to cool off in the shade provided by the big stones.

"The timing is all off," Ella groused.

"The book was written hundreds of years ago," Rapunzel said. "Maybe the landscape has shifted over the ages."

"Or Dorun was just really bad at telling time," Lila said.

"Whatever the reason, the situation is . . . not ideal," Ella said. She was kicking herself mentally, feeling like a fool for relying on the word of a centuries-old prince who might very well have been delusional. "The book made us think the trip would take ten days, but we're a week in, and we're not even halfway there."

"So we're running a little behind," Val said casually, shoving a handful of crackers into her mouth and washing it down with another big gulp from her canteen. "Isn't that what we packed extra food and water for?"

"Yes, Val," Ella said solemnly. "We packed twenty-three days' worth of supplies, so—"

"So even if it takes us two weeks to get there," Val began, "we still—"

"We still have to get back," Ella finished. "I don't know about the rest of you, but I'd like this to be a two-way trip."

Val quickly closed the cap on her canteen.

"Maybe we should turn back now," Rapunzel reluctantly

suggested. "At least we know we'd have enough food and water to get back to civilization."

"But the djinn," Ella said. "We can't defeat Rundark without him."

"I'm not usually a turn-back kind of girl," Lila said, somewhat apologetically, "but Rapunzel might be right. Maybe we need to go home, restock, and try again."

Ella sucked on her teeth. There were no good choices here. "We have rations to last us sixteen more days," she said. "Let's ride on for another five days. And if we haven't found the ruins by then, we'll turn back. At that point, we should still have enough food and water to get the five of us home safely."

Lila glanced over her shoulder. "What if we have to split the water *six* ways?"

Everyone looked at her oddly.

"Come out, Deeb," Lila called.

A messy-haired boy about Lila's age crawled out from behind a not-too-distant dune and trudged over to them. His eyes were sunken, his lips chapped, and his cheeks sunburned. Grains of sand fell from the shredded rags he wore and dotted the corners of his mouth. The travelers gaped at him in astonishment and confusion.

"You only saw me because I let you see me," the boy said in a dry, raspy voice.

Lila rolled her eyes. "I've been on to you since Sturmhagen," she said.

"Whatever," he replied. He held out his empty hands. "C'mon, ladies, make with the snacks. I ran out of food three days ago."

"Where did you come from?" Ella snapped. "You've been following us, Deeb? For what? Some kind of sick revenge?"

"Ha! Think about how many nights you ladies have been camping out in the open," he said. "Did any of you ever wake up with a mustache painted on your face? That's right—*no.* So obviously, I'm not out for revenge. Because that woulda been pretty sweet, and I totally coulda done it."

"Ooh, now I recognize you!" Snow said, pointing at him and hopping. "You're that bandit boy!"

"Bandit *King*," he said, reeking of bravado. "Deeb Rauber, the Bandit King. Tyrant Ruler of the Sovereign Nation of Rauberia. Scourge of the Universe and Enemy to All That Is Noble and Good. Feared by All and Equaled by None. And did you not hear me say I was starving?"

"Is he serious?" Val asked. "You're not getting any of our— *Hey*!"

Rapunzel tossed him a canteen and a biscuit, which he quickly tore into.

"Well, we're not going to let him die," she said.

"He's probably lying!" Ella snapped. "You can't trust this kid—"

"Watch who you're calling a kid," Rauber mumbled with a spray of crumbs.

"You expect us to believe you're not spying for Rundark?" Ella asked.

"Rundark?" he scoffed. "Oh, jeez. Wow. The sun really has melted your brains. Let me ask you a question: Last time you saw me, what was I doing?"

"Crawling out from behind that dune back there," Snow said.

"The time *before* that," Rauber droned.

"You were kicking Rundark into a moat full of carnivorous eels," Lila said.

"Ding-ding-ding!" Rauber blared, tapping the tip of his nose. "Yeah, that guy and I are *not friends.* And when his buddies revived him with a vial of magic tears"—Rapunzel pulled her hair in front of her face—"he declared himself king and tried to have me arrested. But that wasn't gonna happen. I'm too smart and too fast."

"Like the tortoise and the hare all rolled into one," Snow said.

"Darn tootin'," Rauber said. "So one night I'm in my hideout, plotting my comeback, when suddenly I hear voices from right below my tree house. You know, you ladies don't talk nearly as quietly as you should when you're on the run from the law. But when I listened in, I realized we're all after the same goal—taking down Rundork. So I followed you. And I have to say—your idea to find that genie is pretty good. In fact, it's exactly what I was gonna do on my own."

"*Pfft!* You didn't know even what the Djinn Gem was when you first saw it," Lila snarked.

"It doesn't matter," Val said bitterly. "The little snot made a big mistake, and now he's gonna die in the desert."

"No, he's not," Rapunzel insisted. "At least not while we have food and water to share. I won't let it happen."

"I'm with Rapunzel," Lila said. She cast a scornful glance at Rauber. "Make no mistake, I hate this kid. But look at him—he won't last another day on his own."

"Hey, I hate you, too," Rauber said cheerfully. "All of you. I'm not gonna pretend I don't. Especially you, Little Miss Erinthia—I owe you for tossing me down the Snake Hole. And Ella, cuz, our hatred for each other goes way back to childhood."

"You're still a child," Ella said flatly.

"My point is that one doesn't rise to the rank of Evil Genius without realizing that sometimes compromise is necessary," Rauber said. "You may not love your choice of partners, but you need to get the job done. So you hold your nose and work with them anyway. And I mean that literally, because have you ladies smelled yourselves lately? *Phew!*"

"I don't know," Ella said, eyeing her young cousin sternly. "You've caused a lot of grief in twelve short years. And not just for us. A big part of me feels like you deserve to rot in the wastes of Aridia. But . . . well, we've got two definite votes for helping Deeb out. And one pretty firmly against. Snow, where do you stand?"

"Over here, by this rock," Snow answered.

"No, I mean—" Ella stopped in midsentence when she saw Deeb dart to the nearest camel, snatch a supply pack from its back, and dash over a nearby dune.

"That little brat!" Val howled and started after him.

"Wait," Lila said, grabbing Val by the arm to stop her. "Maybe we should just let him go. He's not going to last long out there anyway."

"That was the pack with the book in it," Ella said in horror.

"Crud," said Lila. "Let's get him!"

"Stay here," Ella said to Snow and Rapunzel as she, Lila, and Val took off after the fleeing Bandit King.

"At least he won't be hard to follow," Val said, pointing

to the long line of footprints that ran across the sand before them. The women ran, tracing the trail up and over a series of tall, windswept sand hills. As they rounded the crest of their sixth dune, they were knocked onto their backsides by Rauber bursting up the other side of the hill, running in the opposite direction. All four rolled to the bottom, where Val grabbed Deeb's ankle before he could flee again.

"Not so fast," she said with a grin. "If you think you're—"

"You can hold me here and lecture me if you'd like," Rauber said. "But I'm guessing you'd rather run away from *that*." He pointed back up to the top of the dune. An enormous armor-plated insect scrabbled over the edge on long, hairy, segmented legs and clicked its jagged jaws at them. The thing looked like a cross between a rhino, a tarantula, and an angry fork.

"That's a brain-melter beetle!" Lila shouted as she struggled to run in the loose, deep sand. "Don't let it near your head!"

"I wouldn't really let it near *any* part of you," Rauber added.

Val let go of him and drew her sword to face the giant bug. But she wasn't expecting the creature to leap from the top of the dune and land right on top of her.

"No!" Ella cried. She attacked the beast with her sword,

but the blade simply clanged against the monster's armored shells. It turned and flicked Ella aside with one of its spear-like legs.

Fig. 22
BRAIN-MELTER beetle

While its attention was on Ella, Lila tried to drag Val out from under it, but to no avail. Suddenly, the beetle spun its grotesque head back to Lila. Its jaws snapped open, just inches from her face, a long strand of yellow saliva dangling from its mouth. Lila barely had time to be horrified before she heard a sizzle and noticed a stream of smoke rising from the monster's right eye. The beetle hissed, jumped off of Val, and quickly burrowed into the sand, fleeing.

Deeb Rauber stood one dune over, holding a magnifying glass high over his head. He slid down to join the women. "See, I can be useful," he said.

"How did you know to do that?" Ella asked.

"Well, first of all, I'm awesome," he said, puffing out his

scrawny chest. "Secondly, frying bugs with a magnifying glass is practically a second career for me."

While he was busy preening, Ella yanked the pack away from him. "I'll take this, thank you," she said. "And you can come with us. But *I* will ration out your food. And you will only take what I give you."

"Yes, ma'am," he said, giving her a sarcastic salute.

They followed their own tracks back to the boulders, where they found Snow and Rapunzel cowering together between two ice cream scoop stones. And only one camel.

"Thank goodness you're back," Rapunzel cried.

"It was awful," Snow said. "Four giant crickets burst out of the ground and took our camels."

"I'm pretty sure they were beetles," Rapunzel said.

"No, they were definitely camels," Snow said.

"Our rides are gone?" Val said despairingly.

"And all our stuff," Lila added.

"You're welcome!" Rauber said loudly, with a satisfied look on his face. "If I hadn't *saved* the pack with the book in it, you'd be lost out here forever."

Ella rifled through their two remaining packs. "With the, uh, *six* of us, we've barely got enough food and water left to last five days."

"So even if we turn back now, we won't make it all the

way to Valerium," Rapunzel said. She felt like she was about to cry, but didn't want to waste her tears.

"Whoa, hold on!" Rauber said. "What's all this talk about going back? We're halfway there! We've still got the goofy old prince's diary—thanks to me—so we continue to follow it. And we just hope we find those ruins in five days."

"What about the trip home?" Rapunzel asked.

"Duh!" he cried. "We're going there to talk to a *genie*! We'll just wish ourselves home."

"That is surprisingly logical," Ella said.

"But according to the old story, the djinn will only grant the possessor of the bottle one wish," said Lila.

"Yeah, one wish *per person*," Rauber said. "Unless I've counted incorrectly—which I may have, 'cause I never took math—there's more than one of us here."

"Ooh, if we each get a wish, I know what I want to ask for," said Snow. "A sandwich. I'm famished."

Ella looked at her askance. "But what about Duncan?" she asked.

"He'd probably wish for a sandwich, too," Snow answered.

"Yeah, that's not what I meant, but . . . never mind. Let's start moving."

As the sun began to set, filling the sky with streaks of

luminous pink and orange, the Furious Female Freedom Fighters—and the Bandit King—began their long march, keeping their eyes and ears open for shifting sands and clicking sounds. Luckily, they didn't see any more brain-melter beetles. Unluckily, their food ran out on day four. And their water by the end of day five. And by the morning of day six, they still hadn't found the ruins.

29

AN OUTLAW SPINS THE BOTTLE

"I don't understand," Ella muttered, her voice hoarse. "We passed the glazed-ham mesa yesterday morning. That was the last landmark Dorun mentioned. And he said it was only a three-hour march due east from there before he found the ruins."

"I've decided that this Dorun was an idiot," said Val. She and Ella dragged themselves along on foot, while Lila, Snow, and Rapunzel crowded on top of the very unhappy Camella. Rauber plodded several yards behind them.

"Hey, Rapunzel," the Bandit King called out. "If I'm about to die of thirst, can your tears help me?"

"Not unless you plan to drink them," she replied.

Rauber shrugged. "Whatever works."

"Wait, look!" Lila suddenly shouted, pointing to a rise in the east. "Is that a mirage, or am I seeing stone pillars?" She jumped down from the camel and ran. "It's here!" she cried a few second later. "We found it!"

All around her, cracked and broken stone columns jutted from the sand. Beneath a thin covering of gritty grains, she could see glimpses of a white marble floor. And, at the center of it all, a carved pedestal, over which was draped a human skeleton, small bits of lavender silk flapping against its bones in the faint breeze.

"It's the thief from the story," she said, awestruck.

"Wow," Ella muttered as she and the others gazed all around.

"Hurray!" Snow hooted. "Now we can finally eat!"

"Well, not quite yet," Rapunzel said. "We have to find the—"

"Bottle!" Lila cried. She dove to her knees and started brushing sand from something shimmering and green that was wedged in a crack in the marble floor. As soon as she could get her fingers around the long-lost object, she pried it loose. It *could* have been a bottle, but she wasn't exactly sure. It was bottle-ish. Sort of. It was most certainly a container of some type, made of deep-green glass, but its shape was vaguely eggplant-like. If skulls were shaped like eggplants.

Because it was also rather skull-like, with indentations where eyes, nose, and mouth would have been.

"Whoa, that's creepy," Lila said, suddenly wishing this eerie artifact was not sitting in her hands.

"Do you want me to open it?" Ella said.

"No," Lila replied, considering the kind of power she was about to be given if this was indeed the legendary bottle of the djinn. "I've got this." There was a small silver plug, with a tiny metal hoop, sticking out from between the eyes of the eggplant skull. Lila hooked her finger through the hoop and pulled. The plug popped out surprisingly easily. And then there was the boom.

It sounded like all the wind on the planet had suddenly gusted at once. Lila's hair blew back, and she almost dropped the bottle. But thankfully, she held on as from the vessel a form emerged. It was humanoid in shape—at least from the torso up—with muscular arms, a thick neck, and a sharp, angular face. Its shimmering, mist-like "skin" was a deep crimson, and fire seemed to flicker about its head like the world's most unruly hairdo. From the waist down, the djinn was nothing more than a wavering wisp of red smoke that appeared to remain tethered to something inside the bottle.

Everybody froze, paralyzed by fear and awe. Until the djinn spoke.

"Congratulations!" it shouted in a far cheerier-sounding voice than anyone expected. It looked down at Lila. "You are the possessor of the fabled Bottle of *Baribunda*, gateway to the realm of *Baribunda*, home of the Djinni of *Baribunda*. By opening the passageway between our worlds, you, the possessor of the Bottle of *Baribunda*, shall receive as a reward . . . one wish, granted by me, a humble djinn of *Baribunda*. I like saying *Baribunda*. And I hardly ever get a chance to. Back in *Baribunda*, we djinni just communicate with our minds. Sometimes I'm, like, why do I even have a mouth? Just so I can wait around for, like, eight hundred years at a stretch until some human uncorks the stupid bottle? What a boring job! But then someone actually opens the bottle, and I get to pop out and go *Baribunda, Baribunda, Baribunda*—and I'm, like, Oh, yeah, that's totally worth it."

Lila closed her eyes.

"Don't be afraid, Lila," Ella said to her. "Go ahead and wish for a way for us to destroy the Gem."

"No, sorry, too late," said the djinn. "Only one wish. She already made hers."

"What?!" Ella gasped.

Lila opened her eyes—wide. "I . . . I only *thought* something!" she said defensively.

"Still counts," said the djinn.

"But, wait," said Lila. "So did it come true? Did it happen?"

"Good-bye from *Baribunda*!" shouted the djinn. And with a loud suction sound, he whooshed back into the bottle.

Everyone started yammering at once. "What did you wish for?" someone asked—Lila wasn't even sure who.

"It doesn't matter," she answered, angrily dropping the bottle.

Snow dove and caught it before it hit the stone floor. It was still uncorked. *Boom!* Out popped the djinn.

"Congratulations!" the fiery figure shouted. "You are the possessor of the fabled Bottle of *Baribunda*, gateway to the realm of *Baribunda*, home—"

"I wish for a jelly, jelly, dragonfruit, and ginger sandwich," Snow blurted.

"You only let me say two *Baribunda*s," the djinn said, scowling. "But fine. Here!"

A sandwich appeared in Snow's hand. She eagerly bit into it as the djinn shouted, "Good-bye from *Baribunda*!" and swooshed back into the bottle.

Snow swallowed her second big bite before looking up to notice everybody gaping at her. "Do I have jelly on my face?"

"What were you thinking?" Ella asked.

"I told you all I was going to wish for a sandwich," she said.

"But nobody thought you were serious!" Val hollered.

"Well, that was your first mistake," Snow said. "I've never made a joke in my life. But calm down, everyone. We still have . . . one, two, three, *four* wishes left. There's nothing to worry about. And I'll share my sandwich."

"Give that thing to me," Val said, grabbing the bottle out of Snow's hand. "I'll take care of our Rundark problem."

Boom! The djinn appeared. "Congratulations! You are the—"

"I wish I could give that Lord Rundark guy a good sock in the jaw," Val loudly declared.

"Again? Again you cut me off?" the djinn huffed. "Whatever. Wish granted." He zipped back into the bottle.

Val looked around. "So where's Rundark?" she asked with a snarl.

"Maybe your wish will just give you the *chance* to sock him in the jaw," Snow said, and took another bite of her sandwich.

"I can live with that," Val said, smiling as she imagined the scenario.

"No!" Ella shrieked. "No, no, no, no, no!" She marched over to Val, her jaw—and her fists—clenched. "It is *my* turn! *My* turn! I am going to take that bottle now. And I am going to make the wish we came here to make." She grabbed the odd glass vessel from Val. *Boom.*

"Baribunda!" the djinn yelled. *"Baribunda, Baribunda, Baribunda, Baribunda!* Ha! I said it!"

Ella ignored the huge, flaming mist-man. "We are trying to save the world here!" she barked at her teammates. "Not to have lunch!"

Snow wiped a blob of jelly from her lips and looked down at her feet.

"Or to show off how tough and macho we are," Ella continued.

Val scratched her head and winced.

"Or to do secret things we're not going to tell the rest of the group about."

Lila looked sheepish. "I'm afraid that if I tell, it won't come true."

"It's not your *birthday*, Lila," Ella said. "It's— Never mind. Jeez. You people drive me crazy sometimes."

"I haven't done anything wrong," Rapunzel tossed in.

"Why do you need to point that out?!" Ella cried. "You're just like Frederic—you can't let anything go. Sheesh. Most of the time I can handle the craziness I get from you all. Most of the time we make a great team. And it works really well.

But sometimes . . . and I hate that I'm even saying this . . . sometimes you make me wish Liam were here."

"Wish granted," the djinn said.

"What?" Ella sputtered.

A puff of pineapple-scented smoke suddenly appeared a few feet away. And when it cleared, there was Liam, standing in the ruined temple with them, a look of utter bafflement on his face. He was thinner than usual, with a stubbly beard covering his sunken cheeks. His hair hung lank and knotty, and he appeared to be wearing an old pirate costume that someone had thrown in the trash after it had been ravaged by hungry moths and dirty-footed mice.

"Liam!" Lila shouted, unable to believe her eyes. Others joined in, calling his name.

"Where did you come from?" Liam muttered. "And where did the ocean go?"

Ella's frustration over her misinterpreted wish quickly faded. "You're here," she said softly. "I guess I brought you here."

As more of the smoke cleared, though, they realized that Liam wasn't alone. Briar Rose was with him. And she looked terrible. Her skin was almost bone white, and her bounteous auburn hair, which was usually piled high on her head in an intimidatingly regal up-do, instead hung down to her waist in fat, twisted tangles. Her gown had been reduced to something that looked like the toga stolen off an ancient corpse.

"What the heck is she doing here?" Ella asked, a lot less softly.

"Don't ask me," Briar said, her eyes darting. "Where exactly is *here* anyway?"

"Well, look at that," said the djinn. "Got an extra one. He must have been holding her hand when I teleported him."

Liam and Briar quickly dropped each other's hands.

"Hey, the important thing is that you're alive, right?" Ella said with a wavering smile. She gave stiff, awkward hugs to both of them. She was grateful when Lila shoved her way in between them to wrap herself around her brother. The djinn, still out in the open, watched the proceedings with a strange curiosity—until Rapunzel suddenly grabbed hold of the bottle.

"You can teleport people?" she asked.

"Hello? I just did," the supernatural being replied.

"I wish for the rest of the League of Princes to be here with us, too," she said.

"Granted," the djinn said. *Poof!* More pineapple smoke. Gustav appeared, his skin tanner, his hair lighter, and his face covered by a full blond beard. Frederic was beside him, scratching at his own shadowy stubble. And then there was

Duncan, whose cheeks were as smooth as a Granny Smith apple. Duncan could go without shaving for half a century and still not sprout a single whisker.

The ruins erupted into a chaos of welcomings and cursing, embraces and quarrels. The djinn didn't know what to make of it all.

"What the heck just happened?"

"You're back!"

"I'm alive!"

"Where have you been?"

"How could you leave us like that?"

"Why are *you* here?"

"Something's eating your head!"

"That's just my amazing hat."

"Who are you?"

"Get off my foot!"

"Holy cow! Have you noticed the giant red guy floating there?"

Fig. 23
CASTAWAYS

"Do you know what we've been through?"

"Do not hug me."

"I missed you."

"We did fine on our own."

"You are all losers."

In the chaos, Deeb Rauber inched his way over to Rapunzel and wrenched the bottle from her hands. Ella noticed and called out to Gustav, who was nearest to the boy, "Gustav! Stop Deeb! Don't let him make a wish on the genie!"

"Rauber's here?" Gustav sputtered.

"Congratulations!" the djinn said to Rauber. "You are the possessor of the fabled Bottle of *Baribunda*!"

Gustav placed his hand over the top of Rauber's head and lifted him off the ground. He yanked the bottle from his hands and threw him into a pile of sand.

"Congratulations!" the djinn said to Gustav. "*You* are the possessor of the fabled Bottle of *Baribunda*!"

"Ow, man," Rauber moaned from the ground, rubbing his lower back. "We're on the same side, idiot."

"Since when?" Liam asked.

"For almost a week now," Ella said. "Pay attention, and I'll try to make this as brief as possible. Rundark has used the Gem to take over all of the Thirteen Kingdoms except Avondell. He's unbeatable unless we get a weapon that's even more powerful than the Gem. Which is why we're here, in Aridia, with the djinn from the Gem story—that's the spooky red guy."

"I'm from the realm of *Baribunda*," the djinn said. *"Baribunda!"*

"Rauber's not really working with us," Ella went on. "But he's here because he wants to get rid of Rundark, too."

"And I am therefore your partner," Rauber said, standing up slowly.

"Now, Gustav," Ella said. "You are currently the possessor of the bottle. The djinn owes you one wish. Only one. Think carefully about what you're going to say."

"Don't worry," Gustav said. "I get everything you're saying. I'll save the world for you." Holding the bottle under his right arm, he glanced around at the crowd. "But first, I wanna know who Madame Broadshoulders is over there and where she came from."

"That is Val Jeanval—a former rebel from Avondell who was jailed for assaulting a dozen royal soldiers with a stale baguette but who later escaped with the help of your female friends," said the djinn. "Wish granted."

"What? Wait! No!" Gustav cursed and screamed and stomped. "Stupid silent-D thing," he grumbled. He drew back his foot, ready to kick the bottle off into the oblivion of the desert sands.

"Gustav, no!" Rapunzel cried out. "We *each* get a wish!"

Liam snatched the bottle. "I'll take it from here," he said.

"Congratulations!" said the djinn—and Liam let it prattle through its entire *Baribunda* speech, which made it very happy.

"Okay," said Liam. "I've got to be very careful about my wording. We know how tricky the djinn can be. No offense."

"I take it as a compliment," said the djinn.

"And watch what you think," Lila warned. "If you think a wish, it counts!"

"Good to know," said Liam.

"Just say, 'I wish for something that can destroy the Gem,'" suggested Frederic.

"Or say, 'I wish for the Gem to stop working,'" Rapunzel threw in.

"Try 'I wish the Gem never existed,'" tried Ella.

"No," said Gustav. "Destroy the Gem! Or, you know, wish to destroy the Gem."

"Wish that the Gem would stop being mean and just be pretty," said Snow.

"Wish for there to be no such thing as gems," Duncan offered.

"I wish I was back on the deserted island," Briar groaned.

"Quiet!" Liam shouted. "I need to concentrate."

Everybody hushed up.

"Wow," Liam said with a smirk. "I wish it were always that easy to get you guys to shut up."

"Wish granted," said the djinn.

"NOOOOOOOOOOOOOOOO!" Liam howled. It was a howl so long, and so loud, that mountain climbers in Carpagia reported hearing it carried on the wind.

"My turn," Rauber said, and dove for the bottle. Liam tried to yank it away, but Deeb's hands smacked into it and sent it flying through the air. The djinn howled as he was whipped around in circles by the spinning bottle. Everybody panicked, not knowing what would happen if the bottle shattered.

"Duncan, it's coming at you!" Frederic shouted.

Duncan looked up and saw the bottle sailing overhead. He ran, dove, and caught it as he skidded across the ground.

"Nice one, Pipsqueak!" Gustav cheered.

But Rauber was racing toward him.

"Wish, Duncan! Wish!" Snow shouted to him.

Duncan looked up at the djinn, which was wobbling dizzily in the air. "Um," he muttered. "Uh . . . ."

"Quick, Duncan!"

"I wish for a sandwich!" Duncan blurted.

Ten people simultaneously slapped their hands to their foreheads.

"Sorry," Duncan said as a sandwich appeared in his hand. "It was too much pressure. A sandwich was the first thing that came into my head. But since it's here . . ." He peeled back the top layer of bread. "Oh, drat. It's liverwurst." He threw the sandwich into the sand.

"I would've eaten that!" griped Gustav.

Rauber walked up to Duncan, who curled up, guarding the bottle with his body. "Duncan, old buddy," Deeb said, giving the prince a slap on the back. "Gimme a shot at it, man. C'mon, please. What have I ever done to hurt you?"

"You tied me to a tree once," Duncan said. "You stole my stuff a bunch of times. And you tried to chop off my feet."

"In the past six months," Rauber said. "What have I done to hurt you in the past six months?"

"Nothing."

"People change," Rauber said. He addressed the group. "We're all after the same thing here. We want Rundark gone. I give you my word that if you let me get my hands on that bottle, I will wish for something that can help us meet that goal."

Liam looked to Ella. "Who hasn't used their wish yet?" he asked.

"Um, just Frederic and Briar, I think."

"You ladies blew all your wishes before we even showed up?" Liam scoffed.

"Oh, and you men have done such a great job with yours since you've arrived," Ella returned with equal bite.

"Well, hey," Duncan said, sitting upright and holding out the bottle. "Why don't I give Frederic a—"

"Ha!" Rauber squealed as he swiped the bottle from Duncan's hand.

"Congratulations!" the djinn bellowed.

"Mine, mine, mine!" Rauber clucked. "Step back, ladies and jerks—it's time to watch what the Bandit King does when he's got one wish and he needs to make it count. Genie, I wish to be the most powerful being on the planet!"

"Good choice," said the djinn.

Thunder cracked overhead and lightning bolts streaked across the sky. Wind whipped. Sand swirled. And Deeb Rauber grew. He grew and grew until he was towering over them, taller than any creature that had ever lived. And then he began to float, levitating several yards off the ground. Rauber cackled maniacally as he shot flames from his fingers, incinerating brain-melter beetles that were miles away. He wiggled his gargantuan fingers and grinned as, with only the power of his mind, he ripped several of the temple's ancient stone columns out of the ground. The columns floated upward until he shot beams out of his eyes and obliterated them, sending chunks of ten-thousand-year-old architecture raining down. For those on the ground, the ruins quickly became a very dangerous place.

"Is he trying to kill us or just showing off?" Ella cried out.

"If we end up dead, who cares?" Briar yelled back.

As Rauber's laughter echoed across the wastes, Frederic noticed Rapunzel running toward him. It was the only thing in the world that could have made him even temporarily forget the danger he was in. "I'm glad I got to see you again before we were all exterminated by a giant tween," he said as she threw her arms around him. He returned the embrace—until he realized that she was trying to pull him out of the way of a tree-size hunk of marble that was plummeting toward them. They crashed into the sand together, only inches from the killer slab's point of impact.

"Oh," Frederic muttered. "I thought you were just hugging me."

"Maybe later," Rapunzel replied. She gazed up in horror at the still-growing Bandit King. The djinn bottle was no more than a grain of rice between his colossal fingers. And soon he was too big to hold it at all. But he never even noticed when he dropped it. The bottle plummeted down to earth, straight toward Frederic—who was horrible at catching things, so he missed it. Luckily Rapunzel caught it and handed it to him.

"Congratulations!" the djinn proclaimed as it emerged from the eggplanty vessel. He started into his regular speech, but Frederic could barely hear it over all the noise from Rauber destroying the temple around them.

"I wish for Deeb Rauber to return to normal," Frederic said. The noise suddenly stopped, as if someone had flicked a switch and turned down the volume on the world. Rauber, back in his regular twelve-year-old form, lay dazed in a pile of sand and rubble. Within seconds, his confusion gave way to fury. He leapt to his feet.

"What have you done?" he cried. "You fools! Don't you see? That would have worked! With that power I could have destroyed Rundark! And his stupid Gem!"

"And the rest of the world along with it, I'm sure," Liam said.

"Man, you people are *no fun*," Rauber huffed, and he sat in a corner to mope.

"Why did I say 'back to *normal*'?" Frederic muttered. "I should have thrown in some positive adjectives. Courteous, maybe. Polite. *Something*."

He walked over to Briar and handed her the bottle. The djinn was still floating outside it, waiting to see what would happen next. "It's all in your hands, Briar," Frederic said. "I trust you'll do the right thing."

"She will," Liam said, as much to reassure himself as to give a show of support for his ex-wife. Ella bit her lip.

"Well, well, well," said Briar as she strolled casually around a crumbled pillar, petting the odd bottle in her arms. "Look who needs my help now. The very people who, less than a year ago, refused to believe I was anything but pure evil."

"That's not fair, Briar," Liam said. "We were getting along fine on the island."

"Shush, I'm making a speech," Briar hissed. "Now, where was I? Ah, yes . . . Here you are, the very people who—"

"Is this really the best time for speeches, Briar?" Ella asked.

"I am a princess," Briar snapped. "I need my drama! But fine. The point I was trying to make is that you all hated me and I hated all of you, but we went through something together—something scary and difficult and . . . well, even if we'll never love one another, I'd like to think that we all at least have a little respect for one another. Obviously, I'm not including the Rauber kid in this—we all still hate him. And this little speech right here is without doubt the cheesiest thing to ever come out of my mouth, so I hope you losers appreciate it." She paused. "I wish for a way to destroy the Jeopardous Jade Djinn Gem."

The djinn winced. "Eww. Is that really what you people call it? That's a *terrible* name. But . . . wish granted."

A tiny corked jar appeared in Briar's free hand. "What is it?" she asked.

"A magical acid," replied the djinn. "Three drops on the glowing heart of the Gem will remove all its power."

"Wow, that's what you gave us?" Briar snipped. "I was hoping for something that would, I don't know . . . blow it up or something. At the very least, something that wouldn't require so much *precision*."

"Be more specific next time," said the djinn, smirking. "Oh, that's right—there is no next time." And the spirit creature whiffed back into his bottle.

Everyone groaned. Scowling, Briar tossed the bottle to Gustav. "Here," she said. "Go ahead and kick it into oblivion now. Have fun."

"I hope old Flamehead gets the mother of all headaches when I shatter his little house," Gustav growled as he caught the bottle and once again drew back his foot for a big kick. But a second after the vessel was in Gustav's hands, the djinn burst back out. Its eyes showed a glimpse of nervousness. "What are you doing out here, Bottle Boy?" Gustav snarled. "Wanna go for a ride?"

"Hold on! Don't kick it!" Frederic shouted. "I know why

the djinn emerged again—Gustav is the possessor of the bottle again. And he's still owed a wish."

"He is not," the djinn said defensively. "He wished for information about Miss Jeanval, and I provided it. End of story."

"He didn't *wish*," Frederic said. "He said, 'I *want* to know. . . .' 'Want,' not 'wish.'"

The djinn huffed pink smoke from its nostrils. "Well, if you want to be persnickety, he actually said 'wanna.' Which isn't even a word," it grumbled. "But you're technically correct. Still not a wish. Oh, well . . . Congratulations, Prince Gustav. You are the possessor of the fabled Bottle of *Baribunda*. Make a wish."

"Now, be very careful about this, Gustav," Liam said. "Watch your wording."

"Yes, be superspecific," Ella said. "Ask for the Gem to implode or melt or—"

"No, we've only got one wish left," Lila said. "We have to use it to get home."

"But stopping Rundark—" Liam began.

"Is something that will never happen if we're all dead," Ella said. "Lila's right."

Liam nodded. "Wish us back to Avondell, Gustav."

"No, not Avondell!" Rapunzel blurted. "Bad idea! Tell you why later."

"All right then, just wish us home," Frederic suggested.

"No," said Lila. "If you just say 'home,' we'll probably all get zapped back to our own individual homes. We'd be separated."

"And that would be a bad thing, why?" Briar asked.

"Wish us all to Happy Land," Duncan said. "I don't know where that is, but it can't be bad, right?"

"Calm down, everybody. I've got this," said Gustav. He looked the djinn in the eye. "I wish for all of us . . . all of us *here* . . . every human that's currently in this place . . ."

"And one camel," added Snow.

"And one camel," said Gustav. "I wish for all of us to be magically transported to the Stumpy Boarhound."

"Wish granted," said the djinn. *"Baribunda!"* The word faded as if its speaker were being rapidly pulled away down a long tunnel. And then, with a flash of bright light and a blast of fruity wind, eleven famous fugitives—and one camel—suddenly materialized miles and miles away in northwestern Sturmhagen, in the town of Flargstagg, inside the Stumpy Boarhound.

As you might guess, the place went bananas.

30

AN OUTLAW CLEANS HIS PLATE

The League of Princes and the Ferocious Female Freedom Fighters sat around two big tables that had been shoved together in the back corner of the Stumpy Boarhound—and they ate. And they drank. And they ate and drank some more. None of them cared if they found something floating in their water glass or if they bit down on something disturbingly crunchy in their pudding. Every single one of them was hungrier and thirstier than he or she had ever been before. Frederic even partook of a dish that was described as "boiled mammal"—though he did ask for a proper utensil after Ripsnard mistakenly served it to him with a salad fork.

Duncan looked uncharacteristically glum throughout the meal. "I was hoping we'd see Cap'n What's-his-name or Two-Hands here. Or even the sleepy guy," he said. "But I guess they never came back."

"More traitors," Gustav grumbled, and took a swig of lumpy, gray "juice."

"I'm sorry to hear about what happened with that lady pirate," Rapunzel said to him, patting him gently on the shoulder.

"I'm over it," he said brusquely, brushing away her hand. "I'm over women. For good."

As the members of the company finished lunch and began to feel the life energy flooding back into their bodies, they took to talking about the trials and tribulations of the past few months. And it soon became clear that not one of them knew entirely what was going on. So, bit by bit, with different people jumping in at different points, they pieced it all together.

"So are things bad right now, or are they good?" Snow asked, cocking her head like a curious spaniel.

"Well, certainly not good," Ella said. "But . . ."

"They could be worse," Liam agreed.

"They're bad," said Briar, narrowing her eyes at them. "Can we please just call it like it is? Things are awful. Abysmal. Dreadful. Have you gotten the idea yet?" She daintily brushed aside a gnawed possum bone that Gustav had carelessly tossed next to her plate. "The badness of the situation is the only reason I'm here," she continued. "Do you understand the significance of me, Briar Rose, sitting here? In a place like this? With the likes of you? The mere fact that I have deigned to enter this so-called 'eatery' should be proof of how important this mission is. I've probably contracted seven different diseases just from sitting in this chair. So let's drop the pointless optimism and come up with a plan."

For a few seconds no one spoke.

"Briar's right," Liam said.

"Of course she is," Ella mumbled.

"No, really," Liam went on. "Things *are* bad. But that's all the more reason why we *have* to succeed."

"Well, we have a bottle of acid that we can use to destroy Rundark's Gem—*if* we can get close enough to it," said Ella. "So what do we do?"

"The one thing we shouldn't do is stay here much longer," Frederic said, dabbing his lips with a napkin. "Sooner or later, one of these Boarhound fellows will brag about seeing us, and the wrong person will hear it."

Liam grabbed two forks, a butter knife, and a saltshaker, and began shifting them around on the table. "Hmm," he muttered. "Drat, no." He switched the saltshaker with one of the forks. "Hmmm . . . no. Not that either."

"What are you doing?" asked Ella.

"I'm having a hard time figuring it out," Liam said, sliding a spoon between the two forks and turning the knife at an angle.

"That's because you're doing it all wrong, sweetie," Briar cooed. "You stick your fork into the meat and then move your knife back and forth to cut it, like this." She demonstrated, her lips curved downward in mock pity.

Liam furrowed his brow. "Briar, are you the one who just said how important it was for us to start planning?"

"I know, dearest," she replied. "Carry on. Finish figuring out how to raid Rundark's silverware drawer."

"You want to explain it to me?" Ella asked him.

"Well, the salt is the castle and the forks are the . . . never mind," he said. "I can't figure out how we get close enough to Rundark to snatch the Gem from him."

"We've broken into that castle before," Gustav said.

"It wasn't exactly *easy* the first time," Liam replied.

"And there's no way the same tricks will work twice," Ella added. "Still, there's got to be a way."

"A way past the Wall of Secrecy and the Moat of a Thousand Fangs and the hundreds of big, scary Darian guards?" Frederic asked.

"That's where I come in," said Deeb Rauber. Everybody at the table flinched.

"You're still here?" Liam asked, cocking an eyebrow.

"Of course I'm still here." Rauber pulled up a chair and squeezed between Liam and Ella. "You guys have the only real means of fighting Rundark."

"You mean that little jar of acid," said Duncan.

"No, I mean your amazing warrior skills," Rauber said, and he burst out laughing. "*Of course* I mean the jar of acid. But you'll need to get into Castle von Deeb to use it. And that's where I can help. I'm the one who built that place, you know—long before Dumb-dark and his pals moved in. And they don't know about my super-secret hidden entrance. It's a tunnel that goes from the foot of Mount Batwing straight into the central dungeon of the castle."

"And you're willing to show us where this secret entrance is?" Liam asked skeptically.

"On one condition," Rauber said.

"I figured as much," said Ella. "What do you want?"

"You pay no attention whatsoever, do you? I want my kingdom back!" the boy said, squinting devilishly at everyone around the table. "I'll get you in the door, but only if you promise that once Rundark is gone, you guys will skedaddle and let me retake my throne as rightful ruler of

Fig. 24
DEEB RAUBER,
strategist

Rauberia. That's my offer." He sat back and plunked his feet up on the table. "Plus, if you say no," he added, "I will egg all your houses."

Nobody said a word.

"You guys forget your lines?" Rauber scoffed, tipping his chair onto its rear legs. "Let me show you how it goes." He pointed at Frederic and in a whiny voice said, "Rauber's so mean and scary. I don't think we should trust him." He then pointed at Gustav and said in a deep, gruff voice, "I say we just attack Rundark ourselves 'cause I'm a big, strong lummox, and I like to bash my head into anything that moves! Grrr, grrr, grrr!" He switched to Liam, put his hands on his hips, and said in a melodramatic tone, "I think I'm smarter than everyone, so you should all listen to me, and I say the Bandit King is our only hope." Enjoying his own performance, he then looked at Duncan, raised his arms, and flapped his hands in the air, yelling, "I'll do anything! 'Cause I'm a total goofnoodle! Flippy Whizz-pimples!" Then he pointed at Ella and singsonged in a high falsetto, "It doesn't matter what I think, 'cause I'm a girl! Blah, blah, blaAAAAAGGH!"

Lila kicked his chair out from under him. Rauber lay on his back in a sticky pool of crumbs, fruit rinds, and sour milk.

"Too much?" he asked.

31

AN OUTLAW TAKES THE LOW ROAD

The tunnel's entrance sat amid a scattering of bent pine trees and loose boulders in the shadow of the tall, curved peak of Mount Batwing on the border between Sturmhagen and New Dar. It was hidden under a big, hollow rock that rolled easily out of the way with a single shove from Rauber's foot.

"You don't keep it locked?" Frederic asked.

"Don't need to," Rauber said. "No one's going to lay a finger on that rock. Check it out." He gestured down at a skull and crossbones that were painted on the face of the fake stone. Below the image were the words HE WHO TOUCHETH THIS STONE, HIS FACE SHALL MELTETH. SO SAYS THE EVIL SPIRIT OF MOUNT BATWING. He smiled slyly. "There is no evil spirit. *I* wrote that."

"Never would've guessed," Liam said.

Rauber lit a torch and slipped into the dim, damp tunnel, followed by Liam, Frederic, Ella, and Val, who ducked to avoid the low ceiling. As this particular mission called for stealth, the group had decided they should pare down their numbers. Before leaving the tavern, all eleven had stocked up on new weapons and more seasonally appropriate clothing: thick woolen pants, fur-lined coats, heavy boots, and ear-flapped caps. (Thanks to the Boarhound's burglary-prone clientele, there was always plenty of new merchandise coming in.) From Flargstagg, the whole company had trekked through the snowy forests of Sturmhagen to Deeb's astonishingly well-built tree house. It had a sturdy, smooth-sanded floor, casement windows, two chandeliers, and a foosball table. ("The trolls could learn a lot from you," Frederic had mused upon seeing it.) From there, the four-person strike team—plus Gustav and Rapunzel—had journeyed with Rauber to Mount Batwing. Rapunzel and Gustav were along to stand guard at the entrance—not Gustav's first choice of assignment, as you might guess, but one he agreed to after Frederic promised him all the leftover "boiled mammal."

"Don't take too long," Gustav called to the others as they

disappeared into the tunnel. "It's cold out here. You know, for Rapunzel."

Smirking, Rapunzel offered him her cloak.

The passage beneath the dusty wastelands of New Dar was long and dark—but it was paved, so moving along it took no more out of them than walking down a typical cobblestone street. "It would have helped a lot if we'd known about this tunnel last June," Frederic said.

"Another new rule," Rauber hissed. "No one mentions last June."

They felt like they'd been walking for hours, but eventually they reached a door—or rather a flat stone wall with a door-shaped line cut into it. Rauber pulled a lever, and with a faint rumble and a sprinkling of dust, the wall slid to the side. There was a small cellblock before them, with three empty cells on either side. The floor of one was littered with scraps of canary-yellow fabric. Frederic gaped.

"Is this the very cellblock that Liam and I were held in?" he asked.

"Ironic, huh?" Rauber said with a chuckle.

"Go ahead, lead the way," Liam said to the boy.

"Nope, you're on your own from here," Rauber replied. "I said I'd get you in. Nothing more. I'll be waiting right here until you're done."

Annoyed but unsurprised, the others stepped out into the cellblock. As soon as they did, Rauber dashed back the way they'd come. From somewhere farther down the tunnel came the low rumble of another stone door sliding open.

"There was a second tunnel," Ella snarled. "Why did we trust him?"

"Do you think Rauber really *is* Rundark's secret accomplice?" Frederic asked.

Liam huffed. "No, I think the one thing he wasn't lying about was his hatred for the Warlord. But he's obviously got some other plans of his own. And whatever he's run off to do, he's doing it. So let's move fast."

They started down the corridor. Frederic shuddered as they passed one crumbly brick wall that had a huge hole bashed through it and a spool of thread sitting among the debris at its base.

At that moment, two Darian guards burst through a doorway down an adjacent corridor, shouting, "Yes, Lord Rundark! Right away, Lord Rundark!" Liam and the others ducked into an alcove and the guards ran past them, hustling to the dungeon exit and up the stairs. The heroes tiptoed down to a door that stood slightly ajar, and Liam peeked inside. The room was very dimly lit, but he could see that it was one of Rauber's old torture chambers. The Bandit King's instruments of terror—a mechanical hair-puller, a man-shaped box filled with itching powder, and a mechanism bearing the label SPIT-DRIBBLER—had all been demolished and shoved to the walls in broken heaps. Four stone pillars formed a square in the center of the room, and at the heart of that square stood a pedestal formed from dozens of stacked skulls. The top of the pedestal was a stone hand—or possibly a real hand, they couldn't quite tell—clenched into a fist. An eerie orange light pulsed from between the hand's long, clawed fingers: the Jeopardous Jade Djinn Gem.

On the far side of the room stood the familiar, broad-shouldered silhouette of Lord Rundark. He had his back to them as he mumbled into the glowing crystal orb that sat on a small table before him. Liam held a finger to his lips as they slipped carefully into the chamber—Liam and Ella scuttling behind one wide pillar, Frederic and Val behind another. Ella mouthed, "I'm going for it." Liam shook his head adamantly, but Ella was already on her way. She spider-walked out to the middle of the room,

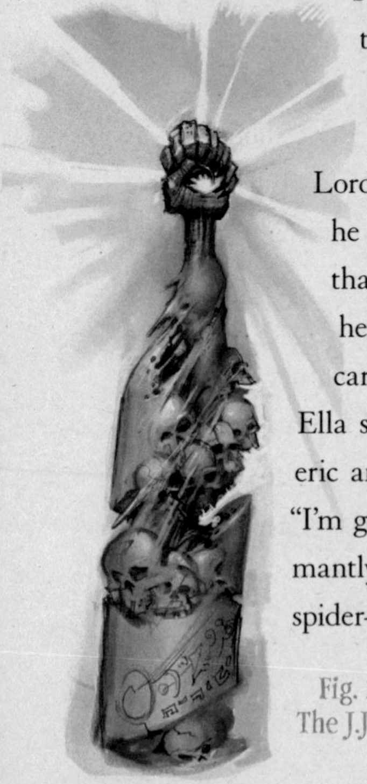

Fig. 25
The J.J.D.G

crouched by the pedestal, and began to pry back the claws of the hand (which was most definitely real—though what kind of creature it once belonged to was anybody's guess).

It took some effort to wrench up the stiff, mummified fingers, but she was getting the job done. One, two, three claws out of the way. Rundark was still occupied with his orb. Four, five, six.

Boy, that thing had a lot of fingers, Frederic thought as he held his breath. Val stood behind him, clutching his shoulders (and squeezing quite a bit too hard for Frederic's tastes).

Seven, eight. Ella bit her lip. She was almost there.

Liam's eyes darted back and forth. To Ella, to Rundark. To Ella, to Rundark. The Warlord scratched an itch behind his ear. *She's going to be caught!* Liam thought.

Nine! Ella pulled back the last of the monstrous claws. The Gem was free. But before she could snatch it, Liam darted from behind his pillar and grabbed her by the arm. He tried to pull her back behind the column. But she planted her feet.

Let go of me, she mouthed at him furiously.

He's going to see you, he mouthed back.

The two were locked in a tug of war. Val and Frederic watched in shock.

"You're going to ruin everything," Ella hissed.

"*You're* going to ruin everything," Liam hissed back.

And then they ruined everything. Ella yanked her hand from his grip, and Liam stumbled backward, crashing into the ruins of the Spit-Dribbler.

The Warlord spun around, beard-braids flailing. His eyebrows rose when he spotted Ella. "You, my dear," he said, "are supposed to be dead."

"I could say the same thing about you," Ella retorted.

"I suppose I was foolish to put my trust in that Avondellian fop," Rundark said. "But I can remedy his mistakes." The chamber door slammed shut—all by itself.

Ella stood and snatched the Gem, but with remarkable speed, Rundark bounded toward her and grabbed her by the wrist. The Gem flew from her hand; Liam scrambled across the floor and caught it.

"Aha!" he cried. "We have the Gem, Rundark!"

"And from what I recall, *you* cannot use it," the Darian said coolly.

"We're not here to use it," Frederic said, stepping out from behind his pillar. "We're here to destroy it."

"And how, pray tell, do you plan to do that?" Rundark asked as he spun Ella around and bent her arm painfully behind her back.

"With a jar of magical acid," said Liam.

"Which *I* have in my pocket, Liam," Ella groaned. She struggled, but Rundark had her trapped firmly in his grasp.

Until Val made her move, that is. She pounced out from behind her pillar, shouting, "Sock to the jaw!" and planted her powerful fist squarely into the side of the Warlord's face. Rundark staggered, released Ella, and crashed backward into a broken hair-pulling machine.

"Wish fulfilled!" Val cheered, raising her arms in triumph.

"You're beaten, Rundark," Liam said as the Warlord climbed back to his feet. "It's four to one."

Rundark laughed. He glanced at Frederic, who quickly tried to pretend he hadn't just been biting his thumbnail. "Three. I'll give you three," the Warlord said. "And three to one might still seem like good odds for you. But I am not exactly *one*."

He thrust his hand forward and sent a stream of mystical blue energy sailing forth, like lightning bursting from his fingertips. The blast hit Val square in the chest. She landed in a heap at Frederic's feet.

"Those blue bolts," Ella muttered.

"They're just like . . . ," Liam began.

Everyone was suddenly aware of a strange, greenish aura that surrounded Rundark. The sickly green vapor slowly peeled itself away from the Warlord's body and re-formed as a second, completely separate figure. It had the shape of a scrawny old woman clad in a gown of flowing rags. She had a pointed nose and even pointier fingers. Random sprouts of hair shot from her scalp in various directions.

"Ooh, I can't tell you how happy I am to see the looks of sheer horror on your pathetic little faces," the spirit crooned in a voice like broken bagpipes. "I was beginning to think you'd forgotten about me."

"Zaubera," said Frederic (because he was the only one who remembered the old witch's name).

32

AN OUTLAW MELTS HEARTS

Frederic, Ella, and Liam were stunned—standing, or rather hovering, before them was the very witch from whom they'd saved their kingdoms nearly two years earlier. (Val was stunned, too, but in a more literal sense, since she'd gotten blasted by Zaubera's magical lightning and couldn't move.)

"Can it really be you?" Liam muttered.

"Of course it's me, you lollygagging dunderhead," the vapor-witch screeched. "Has anyone else ever had hair like this?"

"But you died," Frederic said.

"Ooh, very observant," Zaubera cooed. "You get bonus points for paying attention."

"But you died," Frederic said again.

"I'M A GHOST, PORRIDGE-BRAIN!"

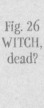

Fig. 26
WITCH,
dead?

The heroes shrank back. As creepy and frightening as Zaubera was in life, she was even more so in death.

"How?" Ella managed to ask.

"How am I a ghost?" the phantom witch echoed. "I died! Isn't that where this conversation started?"

"Allow me to explain," Rundark said, stepping in front of the floating spirit. "Once I'd removed that joke of a Bandit King, my first order of business was to clean up his castle, to remake it in my own fashion. The childish toys with which he'd filled these halls had to go. I was personally smashing the offensive contraptions in this torture chamber when I felt a strange presence. I had felt it several times since arriving at this fortress, but at that instant, the sensation was particularly intense. I recognized it at once as an unrestful spirit—someone who had died in this very castle."

"It was me!" Zaubera interjected, zipping in front of the Warlord and flashing a wide grin full of translucent teeth. "Apparently I didn't make the cut to get into the afterlife. The Beings in charge fed me some gobbledygook about 'not enough good deeds' and yadda, yadda, yadda. So, ever since you and your buddies fed me to that dragon, I've been stuck here, left to haunt the place forever as a floating phantom. I still have all my awesome magical power—but I can't use it! Because, it so happens, you need a *body* for that. These wispy mist-hands aren't enough to shoot a good magic missile out of. It kills me. Figuratively, of course.

"And what made my situation even worse was having to sit by and watch as that little brat, the Bandit King, came in and took over my fortress. All the cheesy decorations he hung up. And the sticky fingerprints on everything. But even that didn't incense me as much as when *you* walking pigeon-droppings showed up here again! I did everything I could to help thwart you."

"I thought you said you had no powers as a ghost," Ella said.

"No witch powers," Zaubera continued. "But I still have ghost powers! Granted they pale in comparison. Mostly little things—moving stuff with my mind and whatnot. But, hey, I managed a few good blows against you guys! I was happy, for instance, to open a certain closet door and make sure the bandits found my old crate of sleeping potions when they needed it. And I helped untie that stupid snake-man when he was knotted around the fence on the roof. But perhaps most fun of all was when I cut the rope in the dumbwaiter. In the end, I must say I rather enjoyed watching your laughable attempt at burglary fail so miserably."

"Hey, we succeeded on that mission!" Liam said, thoroughly offended.

"Did you?" Rundark chimed in. He waved his arms, temporarily scattering Zaubera's misty figure and causing her to reconstitute a few feet away, scowling. "The way I see it," the Warlord continued, "all you did was aid me in taking over the world. Before you arrived, I had no idea that the legendary Jade Djinn Gem was within these walls. You practically placed the thing in my hands."

"But he couldn't do anything with it!" Zaubera added.

"Nothing stylish, at least."

"Who's telling this story?" Rundark snapped, glowering at her. He returned his attention to the heroes. "It's true. The Gem gave me the power to take over any monarch's mind—and thereby his kingdom. But I wanted all Thirteen Kingdoms. And conquering them one by one would have taken decades."

"That's why I revealed myself to the Warlord and offered him a deal," said Zaubera, swishing to Rundark's side. "Here I was—a magic-user with no body. There he was—a body with no magic. So I told him that if he let me borrow his physical form from time to time, I would teach him the mystical skills he needed for his little take-over-the-world spree. He agreed! It was a match made in . . . well, *here*. It was a match made here."

"It was the witch who showed me how to amplify the power of the Gem," Rundark said. "Following her instructions, I chipped thirteen small shards off the gem and gave one to each of my generals. With the right spells cast upon it, the pedestal you see before you turns the Gem into an energy source, beaming its power out to all the individual shards."

"That's why it seemed like the Gem was in so many places at once," Liam said.

"Each of my generals commanded a king," said Rundark. "And I commanded my generals—without ever having to leave this chamber. You have no doubt already experienced the wondrous power of my vision orbs." He gestured to the glowing crystal sphere that sat on the table behind him.

"Another creation of yours truly—thank you very much!" Zaubera beamed. She flitted in front of Rundark and snarled at the heroes. "I'm also the one who designed the grand scheme for your demise. I had powerful magic bombs planted all over that island—each with enough explosive energy to level a small city. I was going to set them off and let them spew their flesh-charring, bone-melting power all over you. And through my colossal Mega-orbs, the whole world would have witnessed your doom as it happened. It would have been glorious! If you hadn't somehow vanished off the island and forced us to change our plans!"

"If you hadn't insisted on such a grandiose plot to begin with," said Rundark, "my men would have put the princes in their graves months ago."

"And what good would that have done?" Zaubera snapped.

"It would have saved us from this time-wasting conversation, for one thing," the Warlord barked back.

"Ruling isn't enough," the witch said. "You need to rule

with pizzazz! If you want your reign of terror to be remembered for eons, you have to start it off right—by making an impression."

"The only impression I need to make is the impression of my fist on my enemies' foreheads," Rundark growled.

"Unimaginative brute!"

"Wasteful wisp!"

As the two villains bickered, Ella motioned to Liam. "Now's our chance," she whispered. She pulled the jar of acid from her pocket and tossed it to him. Liam reached out to catch it. But it never reached his hand. The jar froze in midair.

"You've apparently forgotten how difficult it is to distract me," Zaubera said. She held her ghostly fingers to her temples and flared her see-through nostrils as the jar floated toward her and set itself down on the table.

"Crud," said Liam.

Then Zaubera rubbed her temples some more. The Gem popped out of Liam's hand like a slippery bar of soap and floated over to the table to sit beside the acid jar.

"Double crud," said Liam.

"So this was your secret weapon, eh?" the witch said coyly.

"Another ludicrous attempt at thwarting the unstoppable

power of Dar," Rundark said dismissively. "Doomed to failure from the very start. Because you're far too late."

"Yes, far too late," Zaubera echoed. She turned to Rundark. "Too late for what?"

"We don't need the Gem anymore," the Warlord said. "We've already won."

At that moment, the vision orb lit up, and the mustachioed face of Wrathgar appeared within it. "Lord Rundark, are you there?" the huge Darian called out. "Something's wrong with the Gem. It's stopped working. I had to beat down the fat old king to stop him from running away."

The mists in the orb flickered, and Vero's face appeared as well. "Hello?" he called. "Pardon the interruption, Warlord, but the little baby Gem you have given me, it seems to be, as we say in my country, *malfunctioning*."

"The heart of the Gem has been removed from its transmitter," Rundark said in response. "But it matters not. Throw away your useless shards of orange rock," Ten more distressed faces had appeared in the orb. "The time has come for us to reveal ourselves," the Warlord continued. "Jail the monarchs and introduce yourselves to your people. For now they truly are *your* people. You men are the new kings of the Thirteen Kingdoms. And I am the emperor of all." He picked up the jar of acid and slowly spilled its contents onto the Jeopardous Jade Djinn Gem. The amber-colored acid splashed over the jewel, smoking and hissing. In a matter of seconds, nothing was left but a steaming wet spot on the table.

The heroes exchanged shocked glances.

"You fool!" Zaubera spat at the Warlord. "You can't begin an empire just like that! Without any pomp! Without any glitz! Without any sparzle!"

"But I just have," Rundark said. "My generals—excuse me, my *kings* are addressing their people as we speak." The vision orb had gone dark.

"And you expect those people to welcome their Darian overlords with open arms?" Zaubera asked.

"It's not often I agree with a dead witch, but she's right," Val wheezed from the floor. "The people will rebel."

"Oh, but they won't," Rundark said slyly. "Because I have used the one power that is even more persuasive than the Jade Djinn Gem. I have used *the bards*!"

"I hate bards!" Zaubera shrieked. "I told you not to use them! You used to say you hated them, too!"

"I did," he said. "But I realized the error of my ways. I used to puzzle over how the laughable Rauber boy could have earned such a terrifying reputation—and then it hit me. The bards. Without bards telling the world how clever and fearsome he supposedly was, Rauber would have been nothing. People believe anything they hear in a song. So I kidnapped all the bards and forced them to write a few epic melodies in praise of Dar. Songs that told of the kind, benevolent, and wise rule of Lord Rundark. For months now, those songs have been taking hold. People are already under their sway."

"You've denied me my glorious revenge upon these princes!" Zaubera growled, whirling impatient circles around the Warlord. "In case you haven't figured it out, that's the only reason I'm in this partnership. What do I care if *you* rule the world? I'm a ghost! If I have to spend eternity floating around this castle, I at least want to do so with a smile on my face!"

"Are you so easily defeated, my phantom friend?" Rundark asked. "Do we not have three of your archenemies right here? And some other random woman as well? Activate the orbs. Let us give the people a show. Right now."

Snarling, Zaubera's ghost flew into Rundark's body and merged with it.

"Ahh," the Warlord said, once again surrounded by a pale-green aura. "There's the power." He raised his arms, flexed his fingers, and cooked up two extra-large balls of crackling blue energy.

Val scrambled to protect Ella, but Ella yelled, "Get Frederic!"

Frederic tried to object, but Val tossed him over her shoulder and ran for the door. Liam and Ella were right behind them. None of them made it.

ZAP! SMASH!

Ella and Liam were each blasted between the shoulder blades. They hurtled forward, plowing into Val and knocking her over. Frederic spilled from her arms and skidded into the door with a thud. On his knees, he reached for the handle.

"Always the coward," Rundark spat. "Your fleeing days are over." His glowing fingers popped and fizzed as he worked up another ball of energy. But before he loosed his magical bolt, he paused. There was a sound. They all heard it. It was faint at first but quickly grew louder, until the source of the cry was directly outside the room: "Stuuuuurrrm-haaaaayyyyy-geeeennnnnnn!"

With a crunch and a roar, Gustav ripped the door from its hinges and hurled it at Rundark. The startled warlord was smacked backward into the table and knocked the vision orb loose from its small ebony stand. The crystal ball began to roll away, and Rundark moved quickly to protect it. That moment of distraction was enough for the heroes to make their escape.

"Grab them and run," Frederic sputtered, motioning to the groaning Liam and Ella. "No time to explain."

Gustav hoisted up his injured friends and tore out. Frederic then threw himself back over Val's shoulder, and she ran, too.

As they hurried down the dungeon corridors, they could hear Rundark and Zaubera bickering. "You blew it! You let them get away!" "No, you are *letting* them get away! As we speak! Merge with me again!" "Bah! Your clumsy fingers can't handle my magic!" "Merge with me!" "Fine!"

Gustav slowed for a second. "That sounded like—"

"It is! Go!" Frederic snapped.

They reached the cellblock and darted into the open tunnel, where Rauber was waiting for them. They dashed past the boy as he yanked the lever and slid the false wall back into place. Inside the dungeon, Rundark—glowing with the power of Zaubera's spirit—barreled around the corner to find nothing but an empty cellblock. He cursed through clenched teeth and punched the brick wall.

A short time later, in the white-frosted woods at the base of Mount Batwing, Rapunzel leapt to her feet as her companions burst from the tunnel. Gustav dropped Liam and Ella into the snow, and Rapunzel immediately dashed to their sides and squeezed out tears to heal them.

"Somebody want to tell me what is going on?" Gustav finally said. "I coulda sworn I heard Old Lady Dragonbait back there. I wouldn't even have gone in if I hadn't caught the Bandit Runt strolling out all by himself, whistling like a happy clown."

"You didn't *catch* me." Rauber stood a few feet away, juggling snowballs. "You can't catch someone who isn't running away."

Liam hurled the boy into a snowdrift and pinned him down.

"What did you do in there?" Liam snarled. "You snuck off by yourself. What did you do?"

"Nothing! I swear!" There was a quiveriness in Rauber's voice that none of the princes had ever heard before. And it was there because the Bandit King saw a fierceness in Liam's eyes that *he'd* never seen before. "Nothing big, anyway."

"I swear to you," Liam said darkly, "if this was all some sort of elaborate double cross . . ."

"I never lied," Rauber said as falling snowflakes gathered on his face. "I just figured there was a good chance you guys would mess this up, the way you mess everything up, so I snuck off to put my backup revenge plan into play."

"What backup plan?" Liam barked.

"It's nothing," Rauber said. Gustav kicked a huge pile of snow onto the boy's face. Rauber spat out wads of cold, wet slush. "I put a tack on his chair, all right? I snuck into my old reception chamber and put a tack on the throne. Are you happy now?"

Liam let him go and stood up, shaking his head. "I think I hate that kid more than Rundark and Zaubera combined," he muttered.

"Which reminds me," Frederic said urgently. He grabbed Rapunzel's hand and started back toward Sturmhagen. "Let's finish running away, shall we?"

33

AN OUTLAW HAS EXCELLENT PEOPLE SKILLS

Throughout the forests of Sturmhagen, foxes perked up their pointed ears and owls cocked their feathery heads. The animals weren't used to hearing so many simultaneous gasps echoing through the evergreens.

"Zaubera?" Lila asked. "*The* Zaubera?"

"It's crazy," Gustav said. "Doesn't *anybody* stay dead around here?"

"Well, there is Little Taylor," Frederic said wincingly.

"I know it's hard to believe," said Liam. "But we saw what we saw. Zaubera."

"That woman held me captive for years," Rapunzel said with a shudder. Frederic took her hand.

"She sounds awful," Duncan said. "I'm sure glad I

haven't had any run-ins with her."

"You're . . . kind of the one who did her in," Liam said. "Your dragon did, anyway."

"Oh, *her*!" Duncan said, nodding with sudden enlightenment. "For some reason I had it in my head her name was Wendy. But you're right—I did not care for her. And what ever happened to that dragon?"

"Well, Liam," Frederic said. "Plan of attack?"

"Even without the Gem, Rundark is still pulling the strings in all Thirteen Kingdoms," Liam said. "It's pretty clear that until he and Zaubera are out the picture, we won't get anywhere. So I guess it's back to Castle von Deeb. Rauber, can you tell us anything else about Rundark's defenses? Anything at all?" He glanced around the small-yet-lavish tree house. He saw beanbag chairs, bowls of lemon drops, dartboards with his portrait on them, but no Rauber. The Bandit King had vanished again. "Man, I hate that kid." Liam sighed. "Well, I think this situation has officially become more than the ten of us can handle. We need to do this the old-fashioned way—we need an army."

"Done," Briar said proudly. She may have been perched atop a popcorn maker, but her regal pose made it seem almost throne-like. "Avondell's army is the best in the world."

"Didn't you hear me say your father is working with

Rundark?" Liam asked.

"I have a much easier time believing some cranky old witch rose from the grave than I do believing Daddy is working with the Darians." Briar tapped her fingers agitatedly on the metal lid of the corn popper.

"I'm sorry, Briar," Liam replied. "But Rundark said he'd trusted his man in Avondell to execute Ella and the others."

"Which your father was about to do before we escaped," Ella added.

"He was obviously being controlled by the Gem," Briar snipped.

"But who had the Gem then?" Lila asked. "There've been no signs of Darians anywhere in Avondell."

Briar pursed her lips. "Look, my father was tricked into thinking you losers had murdered me," she said bitterly. "Of course he locked you up. Can you blame him? Right now, *I'd* like to throw you all back in jail." She scanned the faces before her. "Not really." Pause. "Well, maybe a few of you." Pause. "No, none." Pause. "Maybe one. The point is: My father didn't voluntarily team up with a maniacal tyrant just to get ahead in the world. That's not the kind of thing Daddy would do. That's the kind of thing *I* would do. Or would have done. You know, a few months ago."

"We've been in Avondell more recently than you have,

Briar," Ella said soberly. "Your dad has passed all sorts of strict, oppressive laws; and he's locking up anyone who dares to speak out against his maniacal whims. He's not just working with a tyrant—he's *become* one."

Briar went red. "You don't know what you're talking about," she snarled. She stood tall and announced, "I'm going back to Avondell. Who's coming with me?"

No one moved.

"*You're* coming with me, at least—right, Liam?" Briar said, setting her steely-eyed focus on him.

"Look, Briar, I understand why you don't want to believe your father's betrayal," Liam said. "But Ella said—"

"Oh, I see," Briar huffed. "I'm good enough to listen to when you're trapped on a desert island. But as soon as Cinderella's back in the picture—"

"That's not what—"

"Later, losers! Maybe I'll send Avondell's army to rescue you all after you've been captured by the Darians!" She dramatically tossed the rope ladder down from the tree house doorway. "Or maybe I won't." And she was gone.

Liam broke the awkward silence that followed: "Did I say something wrong?"

"Not from where I'm standing," Ella said.

"Technically, you're sitting," Duncan and Snow said in

unison. They smiled at each other and embraced.

Ella went on, gazing into Liam's green eyes. "You know, after the way you interfered with my plan back in Rundark's dungeon, I was *this close* to walking away from the team myself. I kept thinking, 'After everything we've been through, he still doesn't trust me.'"

"I've always trusted you, Ella," he said, taking her by the hand. "I only stopped you from going for the Gem because I didn't want you to get hurt. It's because I care. *I'm* the one who should be risking himself to—"

"Wait. You're the one?" Ella yanked her hand from his. "So you *do* still think you're better than me. At everything."

"Ella, no. You're taking this all too personally." Liam was flustered. "This is just what I do. It's just the way I react in dangerous situations—I jump to help whoever's around me. Just like out at the ruins when I shielded Briar—"

"Ah, yes—Briar," Ella said, rolling her eyes. "I get it. It's perfectly clear now, the problem between you and me. You can't handle being around a woman who can take care of herself." She stood up angrily. "Fine. Let me get out of your way then. I'll do things on my own. Good luck, guys." And she disappeared down the ladder.

"Hold up! I'm going wherever you're going," said Val, scrambling after Ella.

"Don't leave *me* just because my brother's being a jerk!" Lila jumped up and darted for the exit. She pointed at Liam and said, "You did this to yourself," before sliding down the ladder.

"What the heck just happened?" Liam sputtered. He felt like he'd been trampled by a herd of griffins.

"Girls happened, Capey," Gustav grunted. "Girls."

"No, *you* happened, Liam," Frederic said. He walked over, placed his hands on Liam's shoulder, and looked him in the eye. "And I hope you will listen to me, as a friend, when I tell you this: You sounded like my father just now."

Liam cringed.

Duncan looked anxiously to his wife. "You're not going, too, are you, Snowy?"

"No," Snow said in a bittersweet tone. "I liked being part of *ffff!* But I missed you too much to leave you again so soon."

"Part of *what*?" Gustav asked.

Rapunzel stared out through the open doorway, then turned back and gave Frederic a wincing look.

"You're torn, aren't you?" he asked her. "You and Ella have been through a lot together. I'd understand if you wanted to stick with her more than you wanted to stick with Liam."

Rapunzel gently touched his cheek. "You really can be dense sometimes," she said lovingly. "I want to stick with *you.*"

Half a mile away, Ella, Val, and Lila tromped through snowdrifts, zigzagging among the tall pines as they followed a trail of petite footprints.

"So when we find Sleeping Beauty, what do you want me to do to her?" Val asked.

"Oh, these aren't Briar's tracks—hers went due west, home to Avondell, I'm sure," Lila explained. "We're following Rauber's prints. I understand your confusion, though; they've got pretty much the same size feet."

"Yeah, I couldn't care less what that snotty princess does," Ella scoffed. "Liam's the fool who'll end up following her, I'm sure. In fact, I bet you twenty silver pieces he ignores everything we said and goes back to Avondell. We're going to have to end up rescuing him again before this is all over, you know. Probably from Briar. The woman's a snake, right, Lila?"

Lila paused and stared at the footprints.

"Right, Lila?" Ella tried again.

"Huh?" Lila said. "Uh, yeah, a snake." They started walking again.

"But while Liam is running around on wild diva chases, the three of us are going to stop Rundark," Ella said, snapping a branch off a tree as she passed. "We just need to figure out the Warlord's weak spot. And that is why we're going to pry as much information as we can out of my cousin."

"Brilliant plan," Val said, and then added sheepishly, "even if it's sorta the same thing Liam first suggested. Are you sure we shouldn't all work together?"

"Hey, if you want to go back—" Ella began.

"No! No, I'm with you all the way," Val said.

"Thanks," Ella replied. "Out of everyone who was in that tree house, you had the least reason for loyalty, and I want you to know I appreciate your help."

Val blushed. "This may come as a shock," she said, "but historically speaking, I haven't had the easiest time making friends. Especially with other girls. Too much punching, I think. I know I kinda forced my way into your group, but I've been real happy you let me stay."

Ella patted Val on the back. She turned to Lila, who seemed strangely silent. The young girl's mind was obviously elsewhere. "You okay, Lila?" she asked.

"Um, actually, I feel kinda bad saying this—especially right now, considering the whole loyalty speech and everything," Lila said, stopping by a tree and brushing snowflakes from her eyes. "But I think I need to leave. I love that you acknowledged my skills and asked me to track down Rauber for you; but honestly, in this snow, he won't be too hard for you to follow on your own."

"You need to support your brother," Ella said earnestly, but not without disappointment. "I understand."

"No, Liam's being a jerk," Lila replied with a dismissive huff. "I need to go to Yondale. I've . . . I've got to check on something."

"Why don't you just wait till after we've caught up with the punk kid?" Val suggested. "Then Ella and I will go with you."

"No, you two go ahead and find Rauber," Lila said. "That's important. And my business in Yondale . . . it's something I feel like I need to do alone."

Ella looked at Lila with uneasy eyes. *She is exactly how I would have been,* she thought, *if I'd had freedom at her age.* "Be careful out there," she said.

Lila embraced them both and headed northward on her own.

Liam, in the meantime, had developed a plan. "We all know how destructive bard songs can be, but the citizens of this kingdom aren't stupid," he said, slipping into his fur-lined coat. "Our best shot is to rouse the people—incite them to revolt. If we work up a people's army, I have no doubt we can retake Castle Sturmhagen."

And so they struck out on Operation: Rebellion. And by "struck out," I mean failed miserably. In every town they visited, they did indeed rouse the people. Unfortunately, they roused them against the League. In the village of Schnitzelplatz, for instance, they found Darian slavers forcing people to dredge for gold in an icy river. But none of those wet, shivering people wanted to stop, because a bard song had told them Rundark would autograph the battle-ax of whoever panned the most precious nuggets. The soggy citizens refused to listen to a word the princes had to say. They turned on the heroes, calling them traitors, and chased them away, singing a song that sounded vaguely familiar to them: "Listen, dear hearts, to a tale from afar, / of a long-bearded hero from the great land of Dar! / He's good and he's kind and he never says curses! / He makes kingdoms better, when they started off worses!"

To complicate matters further, these bard songs, it seemed, not only had gulled the people into loving Rundark, but had poisoned them again their rightful rulers with a series of terrible lies. ("Listen, dear hearts, to a tale most dismaying / Of greedy King Olaf and the scams he was playing. / While his people all slept, old Olaf schemed / To steal their pet reindeer and eat them all steamed.")

So the heroes fared no better in the town of Moominkugel, where locals notified their Darian overlords the moment the League approached. Or in Björkbjörk, where the villagers actually volunteered to let themselves be thrown at the princes. On the edge of the tiny burg of Lingonblintz, running from their fifth angry mob in as many days, the Leaguers all squeezed into a dirty pigeon coop to avoid capture. It was cramped, crowded, and covered with sticky smatterings of birdseed. They couldn't take a breath without

Fig. 27
MOB, angry

inhaling small gray feathers.

"We've hit a new low," Frederic muttered as a pigeon landed on his head.

"It's a hero's worst nightmare," Liam said. "People who don't want to be saved."

"The more I hear this song, the angrier I get," Gustav said. "Those people honestly think my father was secretly training their pet badgers to turn against them? And that he was going to outlaw meat?"

"While Rundark, on the other hand, promised free turkey jerky for every citizen," Rapunzel added. "It's so outlandish."

"And yet the people have no problem believing it," Liam said.

"I suppose Rundark was right," said Frederic, glumly shooing birds away with his feet. "You can't beat the bards."

"Dunky, didn't you and Gustav beat a bard once?" Snow asked. But Duncan was too busy naming pigeons.

"Willoughby Jones, Superbeak, Ralphie-Boy—"

Frederic had heard her question, though, and jumped with excitement—sending a flurry of pigeons flapping. "Snow, that's the answer!" he shouted.

"Thank you," said Snow. "What was the question?"

"Rundark said he'd kidnapped *all* the bards, but he couldn't have! Reynaldo, the bard who Gustav and Duncan assaulted last summer—he's still in Avondell," Frederic said giddily. Beneath all the dirty feathers stuck to his face, he was practically glowing. "We can get to him!"

"Why would we want to?" Gustav said, grimacing.

"Don't you get it?" Frederic beamed. "To *beat* the bards, we need to *use* a bard!"

"That's genius!" Liam cheered. "If we can get a bard to write truthful songs about the Darians, that could turn the people back to our side!"

"Looks like we're going back to Avondell after all," Rapunzel said without much excitement.

Duncan scooped up a handful of pigeon feathers and smooshed them under his overcrowded hatband. "I'm ready. Let's do it!"

34

AN OUTLAW CAN SAVE YOUR KINGDOM

The princes were arrested the moment they stepped foot into Avondell.

"Please, good sirs," Frederic pled as they marched along the slushy road to the palace, prodded by the pikes of a dozen earmuffed soldiers. "I know you have orders to take us in, but it's dreadfully important that we speak with Reynaldo, Duke of Rhyme. Could I possibly persuade you to take a message to him?"

"Whatever it is, you can tell the bard yourself," said a sergeant, tucking in his thermal ascot. "He's probably with Princess Briar right now."

"Briar?" Liam said. "Thank goodness. She'll get this mess sorted out for us."

"I doubt it," the sergeant said. "It was Her Majesty who ordered your arrest."

"What?!"

But the soldiers offered no more information; they silently marched the captives into the palace, up a shimmering, gold-plated staircase, and through two elegant, leaded-glass doors to the royal reception chamber, where they did indeed find Reynaldo. The bard sat on a velvet bench, blithely strumming his lute. And beside him, on her throne, sat Briar Rose. She was resplendent in a flowing, diamond-studded gown and matching tiara. Her signature tower of hair was back in all its glory, and she held a ruby-tipped scepter in her hand. But her face was utterly empty, eyes staring straight ahead with seemingly no thought behind them. Until she saw the League.

"Well, you took your sweet time getting here," Briar said, her expression quickly morphing into an annoyed sneer. Reynaldo's head whipped in her direction. The bard's handlebar mustache quivered as he dropped his instrument and began desperately rubbing at a gemstone clenched in his hand.

"Do you know how tired I am of pretending to be under this idiot's control?" Briar went on, pointing to the bard as he frantically rolled the jewel around between his palms. "It's been a week and a half, and he still hasn't realized his

Gem doesn't work anymore."

Reynaldo held the shard up to his lips and whispered, "Stop, stop, stop . . ."

Briar clubbed him over the head with her scepter, and he slumped to the floor. Briar then wagged her scepter at Liam. "I told you my father wasn't working with Dar," she said sharply. "This idiot bard is the traitor. And when I showed up back here, he tossed Daddy in jail and decided to start using me as his puppet instead. I've been playing along, hoping to overhear his conversations with Rundark. But he hasn't had any. He's terrified of the guy, now that Rundark knows he blew his big job and let the ladies escape." She turned to the perplexed soldiers who were standing by, trying to make sense of what they were hearing. "Sergeant, go get my parents out of jail immediately. Oh, and release Captain Euphustus Bailywimple, too. He never should have been locked up."

The sergeant ran off at once.

Briar looked back to Liam and tapped her foot impatiently. "Well? Do you have anything to say?"

"Um, thank you?" Liam said, red cheeked.

Briar shrugged. "I was hoping for, 'I'm so sorry I ever doubted you, Briar. I will never again underestimate your keen insight and profound intelligence.' But I'll take it. Now, would all you people stop gaping and get over here. We need to question Reynaldo and get whatever information we can out of him."

The Leaguers ran to her. Gustav lifted Reynaldo off the ground by his ankle and shook him upside down until he woke.

"Gah! Not again!" screamed the bard. "Don't hurt me! I'm a coward!"

"Tell us everything you know about the Darians," Liam demanded.

"They . . . um, come from a land east of Carpagia," Reynaldo stammered, still dangling. "They display a preference for black leather. Even in summer. And their bodily odors are not the most pleasant I've encountered. They—"

"How did you come to be allied with them?" Frederic stepped in to ask.

"Lord Rundark had a plan to frame the League of Princes for Princess Briar's murder," the bard said. "Since it all hinged on a bounty offered by the royal family of Avondell, he knew there would be a lot of attention on the kingdom, so he didn't want any Darians here. But he still wanted control. So he offered me the job of puppet master . . . and I accepted. Of course, I didn't tell Lord Rundark about the little jailbreak we had a few months back."

"Why?" Liam asked, not caring to hide the disgust in his voice.

"Because he wouldn't have been happy about that," Reynaldo said.

"I mean, why did you side with Rundark to begin with?" Liam groaned.

"Oh, why do you *think*?" Reynaldo said, seething. "I hate you guys! I used to love my job—until you had to go and make bard work into such a hassle with all your whining. 'Call me by my real name! I don't want to be Prince Charming!' Then you attacked me and destroyed half my lute collection. And just when I finally had my comeback hit—my song about the wedding of Prince Charming and Sleeping Beauty—you ruined it by ending the marriage."

"We also *saved your life* after Zaubera kidnapped you," Frederic said.

"What can I say? I'm not a nice person." The bard gave an upside-down shrug. "Plus, Rundark was going to get rid of all the other bards. No competition! No more high-on-himself boasts from Pennyfeather the Mellifluous. No more 'Watch me rhyme "ogre" with "booger"' nonsense from Lyrical Leif. Just me: Reynaldo, the only bard in the world!" He paused. "Can you please put me down now?"

"No," Gustav said flatly.

"Where are the other bards?" Liam asked. "Are they even alive?"

Reynaldo's face was nearly purple with all the blood that had rushed to his head. "They're alive," he said. "Lord Rundark thought he might have use for them in the future. They're at the Bandit King's original castle, the one he abandoned in Sturmhagen. The Warlord took it over merely as an added insult to the boy. Now, will you please let me go?"

"Done," said Gustav. And he dropped the bard on his head.

The doors to the reception chamber flew open and the sergeant strode back in with a very haggard-looking King Basil and Queen Petunia. They rushed to hug Briar, who returned the embrace—though she stopped when she noticed the Leaguers staring at her oddly. "What?" she snipped. "I'm human."

Another freed prisoner strode into the reception chamber.

"Captain Heffalump Barneygumble!" Snow cried with delight.

Captain Euphustus Bailywimple scowled when he saw her and Rapunzel. "Do you know the pains I've endured for letting you escape?" he said coldly. "I would have at least hoped you'd have the sense not to come back here."

"Calm yourself, Bailywimple. They're here as... friends," Briar said. "And so are you—don't worry, I know the whole story. You are hereby reinstated as Captain of the Guard."

The soldiers in the room applauded as the sergeant returned Bailywimple's sword and keys and pinned his badge onto his drab prison uniform.

King Basil, standing as tall and proud as he could in his shabby clothes, addressed the room. "I apparently owe thanks to many," he said. "For the return of my daughter and the recovery of my throne. And as this mess gets sorted out—"

The king's speech was cut short by screams and shouts that sounded from outside the palace. Calls for help overlapped with cries of rage and the sounds of clanging metal. Liam rushed to the nearest window and rapidly cranked it open. "It's the Darians!" he cried. "They're attacking! There must be nearly a hundred of them."

Everyone rushed to the windows.

"Jeez, they're trashing your guys," Gustav said, wincing.

"I don't understand," Queen Petunia said nervously. "We have an army of five thousand. Yet I see a mere dozen defending the palace. Where are our men?"

"Parallax Island," Reynaldo said, curling himself into a

ball like a frightened potato bug. "I sent most of Avondell's army across the sea on a quest to fetch the fabled Gossamer Strings of Parallax."

King Basil scowled. "You conniving knave," he said. "You set us up to be defenseless for this invasion."

"No, honestly, I didn't even know about this," said Reynaldo. "I just wanted pretty strings for my lute."

Gustav pulled away from the window. "They're through the gates!" he yelled. "Brace yourselves!"

"They're coming in the back way, too!" Captain Bailywimple cried. "We're trapped in here."

The sounds of battle echoed through the halls as the group in the reception chamber—the royal family, the League of Princes, two members of *ffff!*, and twenty loyal-but-scared Avondellian guards—gathered around the thrones and prepared themselves as best they could.

Five long minutes passed until, finally, Darians began to pour into the room from both sides. Leading the charge through the main entrance was Jezek, Lord Rundark's former bodyguard. Jezek carried no weapon. He didn't need any. The thick iron mail he wore, which covered him from head to toe in deadly spikes, turned his entire body into a weapon.

"Your services are no longer needed, bard," Jezek growled as he barged in. "Lord Rundark sent me to take over. That's what you get for lying to— What's this?" He paused, eyeing the princes with wicked delight. "I didn't know you had company. This is going to be even better than I thought. Get 'em, men!"

And thus began the Battle of Avondell Palace.

Years later, artists would depict the victory dinner—at which a lovely clam-and-tofu casserole was served—in colorful mosaics on the wall of Avondell's War Room, as was tradition. But as for the actual events of the battle, those would have to be passed on through story and song, from father to son and mother to daughter, from bartender to customer and horsekeeper to horse. And nearly every telling of the tale would be different, as there was such chaos and tumult in the royal reception chamber that day. But there are certain details that most would remember: Gustav fighting off six Darians at once—before even drawing his sword; Liam flashing his blade to slice through the bows of a whole team of enemy archers; Briar Rose defending her parents with mighty swings of her jeweled scepter; Snow White and Captain Bailywimple fighting side by side—he with his sword, she with a handful of expertly flung buttons. They would remember Rapunzel crying into her hands and flicking tears at anybody who looked hurt, and Frederic giving encouraging pats on the back to the Avondellian soldiers. And they'd most certainly recall that sneaky bard, Reynaldo, trying to slink out in the commotion, only to find Duncan tackling him to the floor and stealing the lovely pheasant feather from his cap.

But whichever details a storyteller would choose to include or dismiss, he would never forget the way the Battle of Avondell Palace ended. The League and their allies fought bravely that day, but they were gravely outnumbered. So Captain Euphustus Bailywimple took it upon himself to change the tide. Ducking behind the queen's throne with Snow White, he handed the petite princess his keys.

"I will carve you a path to the door," he said. "Head downstairs to the dungeon and release all the prisoners. Tell them that the true king is back and needs their help. Most of them are patriots. They will come."

Without waiting for Snow to respond, Bailywimple launched himself into the fray, bashing down every Darian in his path. But the foes were many, and even the Captain's skill could not keep him from being struck down. As he hit the ground, clutching the sword wound in his side, he saw Snow White race past him and duck out through the door. He closed his eyes and prayed she'd succeed in her mission.

She did.

Just when all hope seemed lost and the Darians had the heroes cornered between the two empty thrones, in swarmed hundreds of freshly released prisoners, all of whom now knew the truth about Dar and were eager for revenge. Overwhelmed, the Darian soldiers soon went down. All, that is, but one.

Jezek refused to give in.

"Dar shall rule all!" he hollered, knocking down one enemy after another. For a moment, it looked like the spiked thug might singlehandedly conquer Avondell. "You people are no match for me!"

And then one voice rose above the clamor: Duncan's. "Hey, I remember this guy! He's the crazy pineapple man I fought at the Bandit King's house. I know how to stop him. Things stick to him! See?" And then he threw a grapefruit at Jezek. Where he had gotten the grapefruit, no one knew, but it plunged straight onto a spike just over Jezek's brow and stuck there, dripping juice into his eye.

Everyone followed Duncan's lead, slamming the armored Darian with whatever

Fig. 28
DUNCAN, armed

items they could find around the room. Jezek howled and sputtered as fat books, planks of wood, cobs of corn, torn-down curtains, and padded footstools were plunked all over his body. He ended up with Reynaldo's broken lute on his backside and a throne cushion—slapped on by King Basil himself—covering his face. Unable to see, Jezek charged directly into a wall and knocked himself out.

Thus was Avondell liberated.

Rapunzel immediately began tending to the wounded. Captain Bailywimple opened his eyes and sat up, checking his side for a wound that was no longer there. "Opening that garden gate was the best decision I ever made," he said. "You have my deepest gratitude." Rapunzel, being Rapunzel, also fixed up a slew of battered Darians, but only after they were safely locked in prison cells.

As the mess began to be cleared, King Basil once again addressed the League. "You have saved our kingdom," he said.

"One down, twelve to go," said Gustav.

"Your Highness," Liam said, "we won a great victory today, but the war is far from over. Your further assistance would be a great boon to us."

"Avondell is in your debt," Basil said. "But I don't know what more we can—"

Briar stepped up beside him. "Don't worry, Daddy, I've got this." She turned to her sergeant, who was testing out a broken leg that had just been magically reconstructed. "Soldier, hurry down to the boatyard. Send our fastest ship to Parallax Island. Get the rest of our men back here immediately. Liam, you will have the full might of Avondell's army when you need it. Now stop being a good influence on me and get out of here."

"Where do we go next?" Gustav asked.

"Rundark's army is spread thin," Liam said. "He can't have more than a few hundred men in each of the conquered kingdoms."

"Yes, but we never would have won here without the assistance of the freed prisoners," Frederic said. "People who hadn't heard the bard songs and weren't under their spell."

"Yes," added Rapunzel. "And winning over the populaces of those other conquered kingdoms won't be as easy as turning a dungeon key."

"Oh, turning the key wasn't easy," Snow said. "It got stuck sometimes."

"I know what you mean," Duncan said sympathetically. "Keys have never been my friend either. Except for Mr. Key, the pirate. Although he did turn out to be a traitor. Hmm . . ." He thrust his finger in the air. "I am never locking anything again!"

"Anyway," said Liam. "It seems we're back to where we were: We need a bard."

"Or four," said Frederic.

"So I take it we're heading back to the Bandit Brat's old place," Gustav said.

"Huzzah!" cheered Duncan. "Off to rescue the bards again! Just like old times!"

PART V

On the Attack

35

AN OUTLAW IS SPEECHLESS

There was nothing special about Deeb Rauber's old castle. It was rather plain and blockish looking, as if its builders had simply piled up hundreds of bricks in a big square; more of a hideout than a fortress. The whole thing was very un-Rauber-like, really: unthreatening, unimposing, unexciting (which is why he abandoned it in the first place). Yet the heroes wisely approached it with caution. Well, most of them.

"Hey, remember the last time we were here, and we all piled on top of Frederic in the mud?" Duncan asked giddily.

"Shh!" Liam hissed as the group crouched among the shrubs on the eaves of the forest. He surveyed the grassy plains around the castle, which stood little more than a hundred yards away. "Only two guards out front," he whispered. "And my guess is there aren't too many inside either. It's not as if the bards are a high priority for Rundark."

"So let's take 'em out," said Gustav, cracking his knuckles.

"Not so fast," said Liam. "We don't want word of this mission getting back to Rundark. It would be ideal if we got in and out without being seen."

"Is there a rear entrance?" Rapunzel asked.

"Or a low window?" asked Frederic.

"Or an imaginary door?" tried Snow.

"No, no, and . . . I'm going to say no," replied Liam. "But that's why I brought this grappling hook. We're going up to the roof."

"Why don't Rapunzel and I stay here and watch the front-door guards?" Frederic suggested. "If they go inside, or if anybody new shows up, we'll sound some kind of signal to warn you."

"Good idea," said Liam. "What's the signal?"

Duncan drew a small wooden whistle from his pocket. "Use this," he said, handing it to Frederic. "It's a buffalo call. If we hear it inside, we'll know there's trouble. But if the bad guys hear it, they'll just assume it's a buffalo."

"What does a buffalo sound like?" asked Rapunzel.

"Like that whistle," Duncan replied.

He, Snow, Liam, and Gustav crept along the line of trees to the rear of the castle, where they left the safety of the forest and approached the castle. They were surprised to see a rope already dangling down the back wall, attached at the roof by a glinting steel grappling hook.

"That's odd," said Liam.

"That's *lucky*," corrected Duncan.

"Guess we don't need this," Gustav said, chucking their own rope into the woods.

After testing the mystery rope and finding it secure, they slowly climbed up.

"Hey," Duncan chirped. "Remember the last time we were here, when we all fell off this wall? That was awesome."

"Shh!" Liam hissed.

They reached the roof and, one by one, crawled up onto it, happy to find no sentries awaiting them.

"Hey," Duncan peeped. "Remember the last time we were here, when the Bandit King was going to duel with me and—"

"I have an idea," Liam interrupted. "Why don't Duncan and Snow wait up here and keep an eye on the rope?" The couple saluted in response.

Liam and Gustav opened a trap door in the roof (the

same one they'd once been pushed up out of when they were Rauber's prisoners) and stealthily climbed down the stairs into the castle. They tiptoed along stone corridors that had once been filled with the Bandit King's looted treasures but were now bald and featureless. Suddenly, Liam motioned for Gustav to stop. There were bodies in the hall—two Darians, both unconscious.

"That's odd," Liam muttered again.

Even more on the alert, the duo inched down the hallway. They remembered that in the next corridor they would come to a wooden door, behind which lay the castle's prison cells—the most likely place for the missing bards to be held. Gustav crept past Liam and poked his head around the corner to check it out. An ample fist smashed him right between the eyes, and Gustav stumbled to the floor.

"Oops," Val said as the big prince staggered back to his feet. Liam darted out of hiding.

"What are you doing here?" Ella snapped in an angry whisper. The door to the jail stood directly behind her.

"What are *you* doing here?" Liam snapped back.

"We came to rescue the bards," Ella said.

"Well, you can go now," said Liam. "Because *we* came to rescue the bards."

"No way," Ella barked. "We tracked Deeb for days until

we finally caught up with the brat and plied him for information. He's the one who told us the bards are here. This is my rescue!"

"Well, we just saved all of Avondell," Liam retorted. "This is *my* rescue!"

Ella, who had no desire to waste time or energy on a war of words with Liam, turned and reached for the door. Liam lunged forward and grabbed her from behind before she could get her hand on the knob.

"Hey!" Val said, grabbing Liam's shoulder. "Lay off my best friend!"

Gustav grabbed Val by the sleeve. "And you lay off *my* . . . cape-guy."

Ella swung her head back, smashing into Liam's nose. He had no choice but to let go of her. And as soon as he did, Val tugged away from Gustav, her sleeve ripping off at the seam. She lifted Liam from the ground and hurled him into the wooden door. The door burst open into the prison chamber, and Liam skidded across the floor, coming to a stop right in front of a cell full of startled bards. But the bards weren't the only ones in that prison chamber. Two Darian guards, who'd been playing cards at a small table, jumped to their feet and drew their swords.

Ella didn't give the guards so much as a glance as she

charged into the room, drew her sword, and took a swipe at Liam. He ducked, and Ella's sword clanged against the helmet of a dumbstruck Darian guard. The man dropped like a rotten apple from a tree. Completely ignoring the second guard, Liam whipped out his own sword and began trading blows with Ella. The Darian stood there in bewilderment until he was bowled over by Val and Gustav, who rolled, fists flailing, into the room like a human tumbleweed. The guard was knocked backward and crashed through the card table, out cold.

Two more Darians, having heard the commotion, barreled into the prison chamber, waving hefty axes above their tattooed heads. But when they saw the scene before them, they paused. There were four armed invaders, but they all seemed to be battling one another. "Which ones do we fight?" one guard puzzled, right before being knocked out by an off-target chair that Val had thrown at Gustav.

The remaining guard ran to the window and leaned out to shout for help. But his shout turned into a scream when Liam shoved Ella into him and he flopped out the window, landing on the two front-door guards. From somewhere outside the castle, a strange, low mooing sound could be heard. It was Frederic, desperately blowing his buffalo call. But as nobody knew what a buffalo sounded like, the noise was completely ignored.

Ella and Liam grunted and snarled, their swords locked together, as the bards looked on, hopping excitedly.

"Give up," said Liam.

"No, you," said Ella.

Each gave a final push, and both lost their weapons. They stumbled forward, falling into each other's arms as their swords flipped through the air. The two quickly stepped away from their accidental embrace. It was then that they first seemed to notice the unconscious Darians piled around them.

"We've made a mess of things, haven't we?" Ella said.

"Both literally and otherwise," Liam replied. Feeling suddenly very self-conscious, he grabbed the keys from the belt of an unconscious guard.

Gustav and Val, in the meantime, stood with their hands on their hips, catching their breaths. "You know, you're not a bad scrapper," Gustav said. "For a girl."

Val socked him in the jaw.

Liam opened the cell door, and the bards

Fig. 29
JAW, socked

flooded out gleefully. Pennyfeather the Mellifluous, royal bard of Harmonia, was there, clapping his dainty hands, as were Sturmhagen's Lyrical Leif, Erinthia's Tyrese the Tuneful, and Sylvaria's Wallace Fitzwallace. The four colorfully clad men doffed their floppy caps and bowed graciously. They were obviously very happy about their rescue, but something was off. They were quiet. And bards are never quiet.

"Pennyfeather," Ella said with concern, "I've never known you to go more than two minutes without giving some sort of long speech. What's wrong?"

All the bards began touching their mouths and shaking their heads.

"What? Have they all become mimes now?" Gustav asked. "Mimes are worse than bards."

"Can you not speak?" asked Liam.

They all shook their heads.

"What happened?" he asked.

The songsmiths each began gesturing and moving about as if competing in a game of charades. Arms waved, heads bobbed, men pirouetted.

"Even without speaking, these guys are too loud," griped Gustav.

"This is getting us nowhere," Liam said. "Follow me, everyone."

He led them down the hall and upstairs to the roof, where Duncan and Snow were waiting. Frederic and Rapunzel had joined them.

"I blew the whistle as loudly as I could," Frederic began. "But I had no idea if you'd heard. So we climbed up to— Oh, Ella and Val! How nice to find you here."

"The bards can't speak," Liam said, all business. "Duncan, give them a quill and some parchment."

Duncan pulled the requested supplies from his belt pouch and handed them off to Pennyfeather.

The bard sat on the castle ramparts and wrote:

'Tis a woeful situation we merry songsmiths find ourselves in. That foul and fury-filled tyrant, Lord Rundark—he of the woven whiskers and sinister, arched brow—hath stolen that which we of the bardly persuasion hold most dear. That vile criminal hath robbed us music makers of our most cherished gift. With an ignominious vo—

Gustav ripped the paper and pen away from him. "Someone who uses less words!" he called out. Wallace Fitzwallace raised his hand and took the paper. On it he wrote:

IT IS "FEWER WORDS." NOT "LESS WORDS."

Gustav yanked the bard's cap down over his face. He took the paper back and shoved it into the hands of Tyrese the Tuneful.

Tyrese wrote:

Rundark forced a potion down our throats. It took away our voices.

"I'm sorry," said Liam, trying to sound like he meant it. He was not a fan of Tyrese. "But with your help, we will be able to defeat Rundark and depose the Darians. We will avenge your lost voices."

"We need you to help us change the minds of the people," said Frederic. "We need you to write new songs, telling the truth about Rundark."

Tyrese began to write.

A good plan, for certain. Alas, we cannot help you.

"Why not?" Liam growled.

Tyrese raised an eyebrow at him and pointed to the part he had written about the bards losing their voices.

"So?" Ella said. "You don't have to sing the songs. Just write them. There are plenty of minstrels out there to perform them."

Tyrese scribbled furiously.

> This only shows how little you know about bards. A bard never puts his compositions on paper. The music of a bard is an aural art—meant to be heard, not read.

"I understand this is a tradition of yours," Frederic said. "But surely you can make an exception when we're talking about the fate of the world being at stake."

> Sorry. No.

The other bards stood behind him with their hands on their hips, looking quite determined. The Leaguers were stunned.

"Well, what do we do now?" Rapunzel asked.

Frederic's eyes brightened. "We'll just have to be our own bards," he said.

"I'm not singing," Gustav said.

"And I'm not exactly up on my songwriting," added Ella.

"I'm a writer. I'll do it!" Duncan said. He put one hand

on his chest, the other in the air, and began to croon. "Listen dear hearts to the tale I now sing, / of bad guys from Dar and something something!" He stopped and scratched his chin. "I should probably only use one 'something.'"

"We don't need to write songs," Frederic said. "We just need to be heard. We need to speak to the people of our kingdoms—convince them of the truth."

"I fear that you're right," said Liam.

"He is," Ella agreed.

"And as much as I hate to suggest this, I think we should split up," Liam continued. "Time is of the essence. Each of us princes should head to his own kingdom, to the people he knows best. We need to gather a crowd together, as many people as possible—and persuade them to rise up and fight for their freedom."

"How exactly are we going to do that?" Gustav asked. "We don't have the best track record when it comes to public speaking."

"And even if we split up and join you, you're only talking about two people for each of your kingdoms," said Ella. "How are just two people supposed to sneak into an enemy-occupied territory, avoid Darian soldiers, and gather a large enough crowd?"

"Who says we have to be alone?" Frederic said. "We have

allies out there—people who know us and who will believe us. Frank and the dwarves. The trolls. Smimf. The folks at the Boarhound. Maybe even the giants."

Liam swept his hair back and flourished his cape. "We can do this, people," he said. "We can—"

"Ooh, ooh!" Duncan bobbed up and down, raising his hand high. "Can I give the hero speech this time? I never get to give the hero speech."

Liam sighed and took a step back.

Duncan beamed. "We can do this, my friends!" he began. "We can save the day! And be heroes! Because heroes are awesome! And we are awesome! Don't be afraid. Being afraid is not for heroes, which we are. Being afraid is for . . . Well, I suppose if it's not for heroes, then it must be for villains. But who are the villains afraid of? Oh, I know! Us! The heroes! Um . . . Nothing can stop us, bring your A-game, a stitch in time saves nine, and don't count your chickens before they're hatched. Heroes rule!" He then ran in a circle, hooting and looking very proud of himself.

"What about the rest of the kingdoms?" Ella asked.

"Hey, if we can actually overthrow the Darians in these four kingdoms, we'll have taken down a third of Rundark's empire," Liam said. "That's a pretty good start."

"I'll go with you to Harmonia, Frederic," said Rapunzel.

"And Dunky and I will go home to Sylvaria, of course," Snow said.

"What about you?" Liam asked Ella.

"The League has fewer allies in Erinthia than anywhere else," she said. "I'll join you."

"Me, too," Val said.

"Are you sure?" Ella asked her gently. "Why don't you go with Gustav?"

"I don't like Gustav," she said bluntly.

"That's all right," Gustav said loudly. "I work better by myself anyway. Well, what are we waiting for? Let's go." He walked to the grappling hook and slid down the rope to the grass below. The rest of the League followed. Liam was the last to the rope. As he climbed over the edge, Tyrese ran up to him and waved a paper in his face. It read:

What about us? How will we get to safety?

Leaning the paper on the rampart wall, Liam took the quill from Tyrese's hand and quickly scrawled his answer:

SAVE YOURSELVES.

36

AN OUTLAW HANGS OUT WITH A BAD CROWD

While her brother and his friends set off to change the hearts and minds of their kingdoms, Lila was on a mission of her own. Wrapped tightly in her woolen cowl, hood up to shroud her face, she darted among the busy fishermen of Yondale Harbor (most of whom would be forced to turn over their entire hauls to the Darians in exchange for the promise of fancy bandannas at some point down the road). As she wended her way along the docks, she popped into every inn and tavern she saw, inquiring of sketchy bartenders, salty-tongued sailors, and grime-coated anglers for any news of Ruffian the Blue.

"He hasn't been seen for months," said the innkeeper at the Filthy Parrot. "Not since he tried to pilfer some goodies from that greedy tyrant, King Edwyn."

King Edwyn is a good man, Lila thought angrily. But she held her tongue.

A grizzle-bearded seafarer leaned over from his bar stool and added, "I heard Old Edwyn *and* Ruffian the Blue both ended up snacks for the snake."

"That big sand snake that the Darians brought with 'em?" asked another curious customer.

"Aye, that's the one," said the seafarer. "Swallowed them whole."

"But that's just rumor, right?" Lila said. Her voice sounded so high and young—and worried—she was afraid it would give her away. She cleared her throat and deepened her tone. "I mean, there's no evidence of that, right?"

"You sound pretty determined to get some news on Ruffian," the innkeeper said as he poured a mug of grog for a customer. "If that's the case, I suggest you try the Skewered Sea Horse at the west end of the pier. It's a big bounty hunter hangout. If there's news to be found, you'll find it there."

Lila nodded silently and headed back out to the wharf. Keeping her head down, she hurried to the far side of the docks, which dead-ended abruptly in the rocky wall of a sea cliff. There she found the Skewered Sea Horse, a true dive of a pub house. A squat building, it had only two windows, both of which had been shattered and covered up with planks of worm-eaten wood. Its weatherworn sign, barely attached above the door, flapped and banged in the wind. Even the dock itself was cracked and splintery outside the Sea Horse—and spattered with drops of red.

That's just from the fishermen gutting their catches, Lila told herself. *You've seen worse in your own dissection lab back home.* She paused for a moment. *Wow, I haven't thought of home in ages.*

Steeling herself, she opened the door and walked inside. The interior of the Skewered Sea Horse was dark but quiet. Mean-looking men sat at every table, each silently sipping grog or whispering cautiously to a companion.

Who do I ask? she thought, glancing around the room. *Most of these guys look like they'd— Oh, crud!* She quickly yanked her hood as far down over her face as possible. Yellow Tom and Wiley Whitehair were sitting at the bar. They hadn't seemed to notice her, so she hastened toward the back of the tavern, into its shadiest corner. Unfortunately, it was so shady that she bumped into a chair and tripped.

A customer at a nearby table reached out nimbly to grab her arm and prevent a fall. Lila looked at him and found herself staring eye-to-eye with an Avondellian elf.

"Uh, thanks for the save, buddy," she said, trying to sound casual.

But the elf reached up and pulled back Lila's hood, revealing her full face and coiled curls of chestnut hair. "I thought I recognized you," he said. "The young lady from the Wanted poster."

Lila pulled away from him and turned to flee. But her path was blocked by another bounty hunter—a pointy-nosed, small-eyed man holding two mugs of mead. "Yer right," the newcomer said. "She's

Fig. 30
LILA, cornered

the one we were looking for with Greenfang."

"You guys are with Greenfang?" Lila asked. Her breath quickened.

"We *were*," said the elf. "But I grew tired of his insults."

"Yeah, that and he left us to drown," the other added. "Lucky for us, my mongoose can swim. Anyways, Greenfang's not what you'd call a team player. So we broke off from him. I'm Erik the Mauve. That there's Periwinkle Pete."

Lila slumped. "So I escaped from Greenfang only to be caught by you two."

"No one has *caught* you, young lady," said Pete. "Leave whenever you'd like." Erik sat down across from Pete, leaving an open path to the exit. "Though if you'd like to have a seat and tell us how you escaped from Greenfang, we would love to hear it. Was it thoroughly embarrassing for him?"

Lila's first instinct was to run. But it was overridden by her swelling curiosity. "I don't understand. You don't want to collect the bounty yourselves?"

"Bounty's been called off," Erik said. "Apparently that Briar lady ain't really dead, so, you know, no one's gonna pay us to find her killers. We've got no beef with you personally. We were just after the money. Now there's no money."

Lila stood still and silent for a long moment, considering

her situation. She pulled up a chair and sat down with the bounty hunters. "So you guys are out of work?" she asked.

"We all are," said Pete. "A tavern full of bounty hunters with no one to hunt."

"I think I can remedy that situation," Lila said. She stood up on her chair and yelled, "Attention, bounty hunters!" Heads turned. "Hi there, Wiley. No hard feelings, eh? So . . . I'm assuming most of you recognize me. But for those who don't—I'm a very rich princess. And I'm looking for an army to invade that old castle up on the hill and find some people inside. Who wants in?"

Every customer in the place stood up. Even Wiley Whitehair.

"Sweet," Lila said. She turned to Erik. "You said you had a mongoose. Big one?"

"'Bout the length of two warhorses, end to end," said Erik.

"Good," said Lila. "I've got a special job for you two."

37

AN OUTLAW IS NOT SPEECHLESS

It was early March, and while the air was still crisp and chilly, the massive snowdrifts, which for months had blocked the streets of Harmonia, had melted to nothing more than gutter puddles. And the citizens of that formerly fair kingdom—when they weren't working themselves to the bone in Lord Rundark's leather pants factories—had returned to their favorite pastime: strolling. One couple, trying to walk as elegantly as they could despite their aching shoulders and sore backs, were startled by the sudden approach of a tall stranger in a long coat. The man had his collar turned up to hide his face, and at first, the couple assumed he was a Darian overseer, showing up to order them back to work early. But they soon saw that the stranger was no Darian—he carried himself with far too much poise and sophistication.

"Sorry to startle you," said Reginald. "I only meant to ask if you'd heard about the ball."

"Ball?" the woman asked, her eyes lighting up at the mention of the word.

"Yes, seven o'clock tonight at Von Torkleton's Silver Spoon Factory," said Reginald. "Wear your best."

"But what about the overlords?" the man asked, uncertainty in his voice.

"Oh, I wouldn't mention it to them," said Reginald.

"Oh, please, let's go," said the woman. "We haven't been to a ball in ages."

"I don't know . . . ," the man muttered.

"I'm sure everyone else is going," said Reginald. "Tell your friends. All of your friends." And he darted across the street to approach another strolling couple.

"Do you think they'll show?" Rapunzel asked, tapping her foot anxiously as she glanced up at the clock.

"Oh, they'll show," said Frederic. "If there's one thing the people of Harmonia won't pass up, it's a chance to dance."

There was a rush of wind as the doors of the spoon factory blew open and Smimf appeared. "I whispered about the ball in the ears of as many people as I could, sir, Your Highness, sir."

The doors opened again, and Reginald entered. "Ah, I see you've succeeded in clearing the factory floor," he said as he unbuttoned his long coat.

"Yes, they did," snapped an old man who was tied to a chair in the corner. "Where are all my spoon-making machines anyway? And when are you going to release me?"

"Your machines are fine, Mr. von Torkleton," Frederic said. "And I'm terribly sorry we had to . . . detain you in such a way. Your factory was the only space outside the palace large enough to host a gala like this. I hoped you would cooperate, but—"

"But you wanted me to turn against Lord Rundark, and I won't," the spoon maker griped. "The man promised me endless vats of silver as long as I keep providing his men with new daggers."

"Lord Rundark isn't the most truthful man in the world," Rapunzel added.

There was a knock at the factory door. Reginald, in his regal finery, answered it. And in they strode, one couple after another dressed in splendid, sparkling evening wear. It was far from the entire populace of the city—many were too afraid of disobeying the Darians—but it was still a crowd of several hundred. Frederic began to sweat.

"You can do this," Rapunzel said, giving him a quick squeeze.

Frederic stepped up onto a platform, which, only a few hours earlier, had served as the base of a clinking, clanking spoon-shining device. "Hello, everyone," he said. "You all know me, Prince Frederic. I'm sorry to say there is not going to be a ball tonight. In fact, there won't be another ball again ever." Gripes and grumbles arose from the well-dressed crowd. Many people immediately turned and headed for the exit. "I'm sorry, but it's true," Frederic continued. "No royal balls. No parties, no galas, no dances, no cotillions, no shindigs, no hootenannies, nothing. Not if Lord Rundark remains in charge."

The factory door remained shut.

"Ah," said Frederic. "I see I've gotten your attention."

"Look out!"

"Run!"

"Oh, my heavens! There are two of them!"

Cries of terror echoed across the Erinthian countryside as two towering giants, each over a hundred feet tall, stomped through the kingdom's northern towns. One mother in the well-to-do community of Near-Farthing ran to her window, pushed aside the curtains, and peered out.

"They're coming," she cried. "Dearest, we have to leave. I don't care if it means breaking the Darian curfew. I'm not going to sit here and let my family be smashed to bits." Her husband nodded. They grabbed their two young sons by the hands and dashed outside. But trying to outrun a giant is useless. The family screamed as they were scooped up into an enormous hand.

"Aw, please don't cry now," the giant said in a deep baritone, holding the family up before his surprisingly gentle-looking face. "Sorry for scaring you folks, but it's all for a good cause, I promise."

"You're taking too much time, Reese," said the second giant, who happened to be Reese's mother. With massive, stony teeth and haphazard hair that looked like a smoky explosion, Maude was a more imposing sight than her son. "If you stop to apologize to everyone you snatch up, we'll never gather enough of 'em in time."

"You're right, Mum," Reese said. "Once again, you know best. I should— Hey, stop that, Mum! You're not supposed to crush anything."

"It was just a shed," Maude said, creating a gust of wind as she waved her huge hand dismissively. "I'm sure you've crunched a few houses along the way, too. It's not like you'd be able to tell with those ridiculous shoes on."

"I was tired of getting stabbed in the foot," Reese said. He looked down, admiring the titanic shoes that adorned his feet. "I think they're rather fashionable."

Maude shook her head. "A giant in shoes. It's just not natural." She stooped to pluck a stuck cow from between her own bare toes, while Reese carefully placed the family he held in one of his spacious pockets. The abductees were shocked to find many of their neighbors already crowded inside.

"Interesting way to spend an evening, eh?" said Davy Wilkins from down the block. He offered an open box to the newcomers. "Fish cracker?"

The giants continued their human-plucking spree across eight more villages until they finally reached a great bald hill, where they stopped and emptied their pockets, depositing close to four hundred disoriented and confused Erinthians onto the grass.

"Hey, it's the traitor, Prince Liam!" shouted Davy Wilkins, pointing up to the crest of the hill. "He's probably the one who sent those giant to attack us."

"I am," said Liam. "I mean, I didn't send them to *attack* you. I sent them after you. Not *after* you. I *asked* the giants to get you."

Cursing and rolling up their sleeves, the crowd began to march up the hill toward Liam and the giants. Maude cleared her throat, and everybody stopped in their tracks.

"Listen," said Liam. "I know you all hate me. But that's because you don't really know me. Just like you don't really know these giants. You run from them, assuming them to be horrible monsters bent on destruction, when, really, these giants are good people. They are heroes."

"The lady one stepped on my house," a man yelled.

"That, uh, was an accident," said Maude. She looked away and started scraping dirt from under her nails.

"Well, okay," said Liam. "Accidents happen. I will, um . . . I will pay to have your house rebuilt."

"And my barn?" a woman called out.

Liam sighed. "Yes, and your barn, too."

"And my golden carousel?" shouted another man. "Will you pay for that?"

Liam raised an eyebrow. "The giant smashed your golden carousel?"

"No," said the man. "I'd just like to have a golden carousel."

"Ooh!" a woman called out. "And I'd like to have a coach with enormous platinum wheels. And I want it to be pulled by a team of centaurs."

"I want a fountain that spurts chocolate milk," cried Davy Wilkins.

"People," Liam said, trying not to get exasperated, "we're not here to ply you with gifts."

"Why not?" asked Davy Wilkins. "Lord Rundark is going to let us all trade in our shrimpy little houses for golden temples."

"Ah," said Liam. "And here is the real problem. You see, Lord Rundark is *not* going to do that. You people don't know Lord Rundark like I do. I've *met* Lord Rundark. Would you like to hear about the *real* Lord Rundark?"

And the people of Erinthia, always hungry for gossip, leaned in.

In a pleasant little cabin on the outskirts of Sturmhagen's pine forests, Rosilda Stiffenkrauss had just gotten home from another backbreaking day of planting Lord Rundark's crops and was about to start dinner when she heard her oldest son calling from outside.

"Mom! Trolls are taking our veggies!"

"Not again," grumbled the farmer woman. She wiped her hands on her apron, grabbed a shovel, and marched outside. There were three trolls in her yard—each one at least eight feet tall, with leafy green fur, curving horns, long yellow claws, and a mouth full of sharp fangs. And each had its long, hairy arms full of stolen carrots, beets, and parsnips. As soon as the creatures saw Rosilda emerge from her home, they turned and fled with their nutritious loot.

Rosilda could have let it end there, accepting her losses and turning back for a peaceful meal with her loved ones. But like so many other farmers of Sturmhagen, she had long since grown tired of troll vegetable raids. There was no way she was letting those shambling towers of kale make off with her hard-earned produce.

"After 'em, kids!" Rosilda shouted, her frizzy orange hair whipping wildly. She and her eleven children (armed with sticks, buckets, rakes, and whatever else they could grab) chased after the trolls.

"Wait for me!" yelled her pint-size husband, angrily wielding a nail clipper.

They ran and ran, pursuing the trolls across meadows and through forests, until they finally caught up to the beasts at the

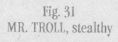

Fig. 31
MR. TROLL, stealthy

borders of Troll Place, Sturmhagen's self-governing troll enclave. There, they were surprised to see dozens of other farm families emerge from the woods, chasing dozens of other trolls. Rosilda stopped running and held her arms out to the sides, bringing her family to a halt. It was clear that they—and all the other farmers—had been purposely lured there.

"What's going on here?" she wondered aloud.

"I'm what's going on," said Prince Gustav, stepping out of a troll fort (which was really just two upright logs with a rock balanced between them).

Mr. Troll, the one-horned "mayor" of Troll Place, loped over to him and said in a gravelly voice, "Trolls did what Prince Angry Man asked. Brought all farmers to Troll Place. Well, all farmers that not too busy plowing crops for Ugly Beard Man."

"Nice job, Superfuzz," Gustav said, patting the shaggy beast on the back.

"Ach! Why am I not surprised to find our lovely Prince Charming involved in this," Rosilda said, and dozens of her fellow farmers grunted in agreement. "You were supposed to stop the trolls from raiding our veggies, and here you are commanding 'em to rob us!"

"Hey, calm your freckles, lady," Gustav said. "I just

needed a way to get you here. You'll all get your crops back."

"Uh-oh," Mister Troll said, releasing a distinctly parsnip-scented belch. "Angry Man not mention give veggies back."

"We've had enough of this," yelled one farmer. "After twenty hours of pulling up beets for Rundark, we shouldn't have to come home and find these walking piles of mulch stealing what little we grow for ourselves."

"Yeah!" cried another. "I don't care how big those trolls are! Let's get 'em!"

"We're ready for war!" shouted a third.

"All right!" whooped Gustav. "That's the Sturmhagen spirit I'm looking for! War is what we need. But not against the trolls. We've got to take the battle to the people who are really causing all your problems."

"Keep talkin', Prince," Rosilda said. "'Cause I'm angry. Somebody's gettin' hit with this shovel, and you've got five minutes to convince me it shouldn't be you."

CLANG! CLANG!

Flik the dwarf, seated on the driver's bench of an open-backed wagon, rang a bell as he traveled through the Sylvarian village of Whistleton.

"Come one, come all!" called Frank, the dwarf at the reins. "Come see Daring Duncan, the renegade prince, captured at last! Follow us to the old fairgrounds and watch Duncan get a dunking!"

Villagers by the dozens ran from their cottages to join the long parade of Sylvarians already marching behind the wagon—the wagon in which Duncan and Snow sat, tied up.

"Stop smiling, you idiot," Flik whispered to Duncan. "You're supposed to be our captive."

"But it's working so well," Duncan replied. "I knew that if anything could get Sylvarians to break Lord Rundark's curfew, it would be a chance to see me humiliated."

"That's right, everybody," Frank continued shouting. "Beetle-brain Duncan, the Prince of All Losers, is going to get a pie in the face and a dip in the dunk tank! Maybe a good bath will finally wash the stink of failure off of him!"

"Frank," Snow scolded, "you don't need to be so harsh."

"You want people to come or not?" Frank retorted.

"It's okay, Snowy," said Duncan. "All part of the act. I know my good friend Frank doesn't mean a word of it."

Frank said nothing.

Flik continued to sound his bell while eleven other dwarfs on ponies helped corral the jolly revelers into one long line. A short time later, they reached the abandoned site of the Sylvarian Royal Fair, a ghost town of empty game stalls and unused rides. It had been years since an actual fair was held in the kingdom—people stopped coming after King King insisted that every visitor through the gates had to pose for a take-home souvenir portrait painted by the king himself.

As soon as all the parade followers had filtered into the fairgrounds, Duncan popped up from his seat in the back of the wagon and flicked off his fake bindings. "Ta-da!" he shouted, taking a bow. "I was never captured! It was all a trick! We tricked you!"

People started throwing trash at him.

"Dunky, I don't think that's the best way to get them on our side," Snow said gently. Frank rolled his eyes.

"Citizens, you need to hear the important things I have to say," Duncan tried. "I'm very important. Hear my words, and they will make you important, like me!" He ducked a flying wad of used handkerchiefs.

"Still not working," said Snow. People started leaving the fairgrounds.

"Don't go," Duncan called. "How can you turn away from someone with a hat like this?"

The crowd got steadily smaller.

"Okay, okay!" Duncan yelled. "If you stay and listen to me, I'll still get in the dunk tank."

The people stopped and listened.

* * *

And so it was that the four princes, in four different kingdoms, each began the most important speech of his life.

"I know you've heard bard songs recently that claim my father to be a hard-hearted and duplicitous ruler," Frederic told his people in Harmonia. "Those same songs speak of Lord Rundark as a kind and generous man. Neither could be further from the truth. But these are bard songs, you say. How can we not trust the word of our bards? Well, have you ever really thought about some of the things you've supposedly learned from bard songs?" He stood tall and proud as he spoke.

"You all loved 'The Tale of Cinderella,' right?" he continued. "That song ended with Ella and me getting married and living happily ever after. But where is Ella now? Not married to me, that's for sure. In fact, I'm in love with someone else." He said it without even realizing it. But Rapunzel heard it.

"So there you go," Frederic went on. "A blatant falsehood, right there in a bard song. And her name isn't even Cinderella! It's Ella! You all know that! And mine isn't Prince Charming—even if I've grown to somewhat like that name. But let's see how many more lies we can find in bard songs."

* * *

"'The Tale of the Sleeping Beauty' claimed that I was Briar Rose's one true love," Liam said to his people in Erinthia. "But how does that match up with the story in 'The League of Princes Fails Again'—the one about me trying to *escape* my wedding? I don't understand how you can listen to those two contradictory songs and believe that both are completely true."

"So are you saying that Princess Briar isn't really sweet and beautiful?" asked a woman in the crowd. "That she is awful and terrible and ugly."

"Well, no. Briar is . . ." He looked over at Ella but couldn't quite read the expression on her face. "She's just . . . Look, she and I have come to be . . . non-enemies. But, uh . . . maybe that wasn't the best example." He wiped sweat from his forehead.

Ella stepped up. "But, hey, what about 'The Bandit King Rides Again'?" she said to the crowd. "That song by Tyrese mentions the Bandit King tying the bones of his enemies in his beard. But Deeb hasn't even hit puberty yet!"

The crowd began to murmur. The message was sinking in. Ella stepped off to the side, letting Liam take center stage once more. "Go get 'em, champ," she whispered.

"See what I mean?" Liam said, loud and sure. "You can't automatically trust everything you hear in a song."

* * *

"Yes, that's right," Duncan said to the crowd at the fairgrounds. "I had no magical ring of flight. I just fell off the Bandit King's roof. And when I defeated the evil witch, I didn't use an enchanted power sword. I just chucked a stinky steak at her."

"You know, that's a lot more believable," one man said to his wife.

"And don't even get me started on the witch," Duncan said, gesticulating wildly. "The songs call her the Nameless Witch. But she *had* a name! Wendy! Or something! And she didn't have three heads! Only one!"

"The song never said she had three heads," remarked a man in the crowd.

"That doesn't matter," said Duncan. "My point is . . ."

"Bards. Pah! You can't trust those puffy-pantsed song-sellers," Gustav spat. "Everything they say is wrong."

"Angry Man right!" Mr. Troll howled in agreement. "Tiny Guitar Men always sing about trolls be monsters."

"You *are* monsters," said Rosilda, impatiently flexing her fingers around her shovel. "That's your evidence? Good thing you're not a lawyer, Prince Charming."

"Ha! No, *there's* your evidence!" Gustav said, grinning. "Prince Charming! There's no such guy! I'm the one in the

Rapunzel story. Which is full of lies."

"Like what?" someone asked.

"Like . . ." There were plenty of mistakes in that song for Gustav to mention, but they involved details he didn't exactly want to publicize. He clenched and unclenched his fists, breathing heavily. "Like how long I fought the witch for," he finally said. "The song has me battling her for hours. It really took about three seconds. She threw me out the window the moment she saw me."

Jaws dropped.

"And in the part after I was blinded, when the song says I used my sense of smell to track down bears and kill them for food—that's all wrong, too," he said with his head down and his long blond hair hanging in his face. "I just lay in a ball and cried. I was starving and nearly dead when Rapunzel found me."

"Wow," a man said. "The song made you sound like an average loser, but in reality you were a horribly pathetic loser."

"I believe you," Rosilda said. "No one would admit to such things if they weren't true."

Gustav looked up. He sniffled. "Well, then let's start talking about this Rundark guy."

* * *

"The song tells you Rundark will make you happy," Frederic said. "Are you happy?"

The people in the factory looked down at the fancy clothes they wore, the same outfits Rundark had forbidden them to wear, saying tassels and lace would get in the way of their machinery work. Many muttered unkind words about their Darian overseers.

"The songs say Rundark is generous," said Liam. "But what has he given you so far?"

"Nothing," said one person.

"A sore back and tired fingers," said another.

"Low self-esteem," said a third.

"The songs say Rundark has the cheeks of an angel," said Duncan. "But have you seen the man? His cheeks are filthy."

"Come on, people," Gustav said, raising a sly eyebrow. "Rundark ain't gonna make your gardens grow any faster. The only way that guy's ever used a spade is bashing it over someone's head. Which, while admittedly pretty cool, still ain't gonna make your gardens grow any faster. Believe me, I know. The trolls and I have tried it."

* * *

"We Harmonians are smart people," said Frederic. "What makes more sense? Believing what we're told in a song? Or believing what we see with our own eyes? Were your lives better before Dar took over? Or since? My father may have been a tad strict, but at least he didn't force you to ruin your manicures by sewing leather pants all day. Let's take Harmonia back!"

The people raised their frilly sleeves and chanted a dignified-but-forceful "Huzzah!"

"Come on, I know you Erinthians like your cozy, cushy lives," said Liam. "But how cozy do you feel digging in a silver mine with Darians cracking whips over your heads? I'll be the first to admit that my parents aren't perfect—but you can't say they didn't know how to pamper their people. And if you ever want the chance to be lazy again, you're going to have to work for it!"

"I don't wanna work!" one man yelled. "I just wanna be rich!"

"Then let's fight to be rich!" Davy Wilkins called out. And he was greeted with cheers of approval.

Liam looked to Ella. "Not what I was going for," he said. "But I'll take it."

* * *

"What it basically comes down to is this," Gustav said. "You people are wimps."

"What?"

"How dare you!"

"Of all the nerve!"

Scores of angry farmers started rolling up their sleeves, ready for a brawl.

"You heard me: *wimps,*" Gustav continued. He stood with his hands on his hips, staring down his nose at the people surrounding him. "You think you're all big, tough Sturmhageners. You wrestle bulls for fun and split logs with your teeth. Nothing can stop you, right? But then a guy with a fossil on his head comes along and starts telling you what to do—and you all shut up and do it. All I'm saying is that real Sturmhageners would've tossed Ol' Bonehead out on his backside."

The crowd grew agitated, a fury welling up inside of them. But for once it wasn't directed at Gustav.

"You're more of a sly one than I gave you credit for, Prince Gustav," Rosilda said. "We're all true Sturmhageners here. Each of us—down to my littlest wee one. And if you wanna take Castle Sturmhagen back, you've got yourself an army."

The farmers all raised their makeshift weapons, hooting and howling.

* * *

"So as you can see, Lord Rundark is actually an evil tyrant who's turning your country into a prison and you into his captive workforce," Duncan explained with remarkable clarity.

"That may be," said a man in the crowd. "But he's still better than your father."

"Now, hold on a minute!" Duncan barked, his cheeks red and his nostrils flaring. Snow flinched, never before having seen such a look on her husband's face. In fact, she'd never seen Duncan exhibit any expression more negative than a mildly knotted brow. "My father is a good man!" he snapped. "He may be a terrible king, but he is a good man, and he does not deserve your scorn. None of my family does. It doesn't matter that the shoes my sisters invented are really just blankets you tie around your feet, or that my mother refers to grass as 'dirt hair'—they're good people who only want the best for this country. They've tried so hard for so long to make this kingdom a better place. But you all are so embarrassed by them that you've abandoned them in that quest. Not a single one of you will give them any help. And they need the help—because they have no idea what they're doing! But that is not—I repeat *not*—worse than what Rundark is doing! Forcing you to work for his glory?

Taking away your rights? You should be ashamed of yourselves for thinking it. Because right now, I am ashamed to be Sylvarian."

The crowd was stunned into silence. Several people began tugging at their collars or shuffling their feet. Many stared self-consciously off into the sky.

"Jeez, man," one villager finally said. "I feel terrible about myself right now."

Duncan's eyes were lively. "Does that mean you'll fight the Darians with me?"

"Yeah, I guess so," one woman mumbled. "Since you're making us feel so guilty about it."

"Woo-hoo!" Duncan cheered. "It's revolution time!"

38

AN OUTLAW STORMS THE CASTLE

In later years, future scribes would write books referring to that day as "The Warriest Day in the History of the Thirteen Kingdoms"—because those scribes were terrible at naming things. But on that day, those lands did indeed see more war than they ever had before. Simultaneous battles raged in five separate kingdoms. Prince Frederic and his squadron of impeccably dressed rebels charged Harmonia's royal palace, wielding the only weapons available to them: big spoons from von Torkleton's factory. Liam's greed-fueled mob cut a quick path through the gates of the Palace of Erinthia (it didn't hurt that they had a couple of giants flicking enemies out of their way). Lila and her platoon of bounty hunters busted down the doors of Yondale Castle and ambushed the startled Darians inside. Gustav's army of furious farmers fought ferociously—as did their troll allies—turning the thatch-roofed village that surrounded Castle Sturmhagen into a raucous free-for-all. And Duncan inspired his Sylvarian revolutionaries with rousing chants and war cries—while the ax-wielding dwarfs went toe-to-toe with the bad guys (dwarfs are *expert* warriors, after all).

Yes, the Warriest Day was a pivotal point in the history of the Thirteen Kingdoms. And since *scribes* would recount its battles, as opposed to bards, people would actually get to hear about the best parts.

THE BATTLE OF HARMONIA

Frederic's elegant militia was in high spirits as they marched on the Harmonian palace sounding cries of "For etiquette!" and "For decorum!" But spoons-versus-battle-axes isn't exactly a fair fight, and things quickly turned grim. Frederic feared he'd made a terrible mistake, until a certain speedy messenger turned the tide. Thanks to the fast footwork of Smimf, many a Darian soldier was left standing baffled, wondering why the sword he was about to swing had suddenly vanished from his hand in a gust of wind.

Smimf's barrage of invisible attacks presented the

perfect opportunity for Frederic and Rapunzel to sneak inside the palace and search for King Wilberforce (but not before promising to give the messenger a very nice tip). Racing up to the king's chambers, carrying a sword he prayed he wouldn't have to use, Frederic found his father being dragged down a marble-tiled hall, unconscious. A purplish bruise ringed Wilberforce's left eye, and his normally buoyant mustache hung limply over his lip.

The Darian who held him had a curving, pointed beard and hair that jutted from the sides of his head like wings. He pulled the king over to an open window. "Do not come any closer or we'll see if the king can fly," the man warned.

"Ah," said Frederic, keeping his distance. "I see you are a coward."

The Darian laughed. "You'll regret those words."

"I regret no words," Frederic said. "I love words. And the words I just spoke were the truth. You are a coward, because only a coward would rather defenestrate a helpless old man than face me in a fair fight."

"I wasn't gonna defenish—"

"Defenestrate."

"Yeah, I wasn't gonna defenestrate him," the wing-haired man said. "I was gonna throw him out the window."

"That's what 'defenestrate' means," said Frederic.

"Then why didn't you just say 'throw him out the window'?"

"Because I love words," Frederic said with a smoldering intensity. "But my point still stands: You are afraid to duel me."

The Darian released King Wilberforce and took a shaky step back. He'd never before faced a foe who seemed so utterly sure of himself. *This guy must be some sort of master duelist*, the villain said to himself. *He'll take me down in a second.* He raised his hands in surrender.

And then the king woke up. "Frederic!" he called out, struggling to his feet. "What are you doing here? You'll be killed!"

"Father, be quiet!" Frederic whispered. Behind him, Rapunzel shook her head adamantly.

Wilberforce didn't back down. "Stop playing hero, Son! Run while you can!"

"Oh, so you're Prince Frederic, eh?" the Darian asked, dropping his hands. "You're the talker, I hear. They say not to let you start talking, 'cause you use your words to confuse people and foul them up, and that's how you beat 'em."

"Really? They say that about me? That's so neat." Frederic beamed.

"They also say you're a terrible swordsman." The Darian drew his blade and launched himself at Frederic. The prince deflected the blow, surprising even himself.

"Well," said Frederic. "I suppose this is what it has come to, Mr. . . . ?"

"They call me Princeslayer," the villain sneered. "And today I finally get to live up to that name."

CLANG! CLACK! CLANG! Their blades clashed together. Rapunzel ran to King Wilberforce and helped him off the floor.

"You know, Mr. Slayer," Frederic said, panting between words. "I can"—*CLACK!*—"still use my words against you"—*CLANK!*—"even while we fight."

"Ha!" Princeslayer spat. "There's nothin' you could say to throw me off"—*SWISH*—"now that I know who you are."

"Not even"—*WHOOSH! CLASH!*—"that you just let my father escape?"

Princeslayer gasped and spun around. "Come back here, you old— Huh? No, he's right where I left 'im."

And Frederic clubbed him over the head with the hilt of his sword. Princeslayer landed on his face. End of fight.

"Oh dear," muttered Rapunzel as she tried to sop up

the tears of relief that streamed down her cheeks. "Can't waste these."

King Wilberforce had fallen to his knees, but Frederic helped him back up. The old man looked into the prince's eyes.

"I'm sorry," he said. "And thank you."

THE BATTLE OF ERINTHIA

The Darian forces in Erinthiopolis didn't stand much of a chance against Liam's revolutionaries, especially when two of those revolutionaries were over a hundred feet tall. While Liam, Ella, and Val took the fight straight to the palace guards, Reese and Maude took care of the rest of Vero's troops. The giants dropped boulders on pikemen, kicked archers into neighboring counties, and stomped on cannons with ease.

"This is wonderful," Reese crooned as he crushed a catapult under his heel. "Not even the teensiest bit of foot pain. I should've started wearing shoes ages ago."

Of course, those who are new to wearing shoes may not be the best at tying them. Ten minutes into the battle, the giant's shoelaces flopped loose. And he tripped. "Oh, fudge," Reese blurted as he toppled onto his face. Happily, he managed to take out most of the Darian army in doing so. Less happily, he also managed to crash his battleship-size head through the palace's eastern wall. Wide cracks shot like lightning across the sides of the building. Heavy chunks of debris rained down, and one entire tower snapped off, shattering like an egg on the courtyard below.

Maude shook her head. "Shoes," she muttered.

That was when Liam began to panic. "My parents are in there!" he cried as a portion of the roof collapsed. He, Val, and Ella quickly disarmed the Darians they were battling and dashed to a door at the base of the palace's easternmost tower. As Liam threw the portal open, gray bricks tumbled to the ground, the entire arched doorway about to cave in. But Val thrust herself in under the arch, bracing it with her strong arms and back. "Go quick!" she groaned. "I'll hold it as long as I can."

"Are you sure you—" Ella began to ask, but Val didn't let her finish.

"Go!"

Ella and Liam squeezed past Val into the slowly crumbling palace. They raced upstairs toward the royal couple's bedchamber as walls cracked all around them and clouds of white dust filled the air. They barely sidestepped a chandelier that crashed onto the steps between them. As they darted out of the stairwell on the third floor, they nearly crashed into Vero, who was racing in the opposite direction. The dapper swordsman skidded to a stop, flicked his long ponytail over his shoulder, and drew his rapier.

"Now this is an unexpected conundrum for me," he said. "Here I was, fleeing for my life, when I find myself face-to-face again with the man I have been waiting so long to duel. Which do I choose? Personal safety? Or the chance to test my sword against that of the famous Prince Liam? It is, as we say in my country, *a tough one*, no? Hmm . . . I choose to fight." He leapt into a fencing stance.

Liam immediately jumped into a counterstance, sword held high. "Find my parents," he said to Ella.

"Why don't *you* find your parents? I don't know where they are," Ella urgently suggested, while ducking a falling ceiling tile.

"Good point," Liam said. "Sorry, Vero." And he sped off.

Vero sighed. "Disappointed again," he said, his blade still at the ready. "But not a total loss, yes? I still long to fight the legendary Prince Liam, but this is not so bad, eh? To settle for a duel with the second best?"

Ella glared at him with eyes like flaming meteorites. "Oh, you just said the wrong thing, mister." She flew at him as if she had been shot from a cannon.

Liam, in the meantime, found King Gareth and Queen Gertrude chained to their four-poster bed. "Mother, Father," he began, "I know you're probably not happy to see me, but—"

"Of course we're happy to see you, you fool," the queen snapped. "The palace is collapsing. Get us out of here!"

Which he did. On their way back to the stairwell, dodging falling bricks and leaping over growing chasms in the floor, they saw no sign of either Ella or Vero. But they never slowed. Liam and his parents hurtled down the steps and ran for the exit.

"Hurry!" Val yelled when she saw them. "I can't hold it much longer!" Liam, Gareth, and Gertrude squeezed out past her, right before Val herself tumbled into the shattered courtyard and the doorway completely caved in.

Liam turned back toward the smoking pile of rubble that had been his palace's eastern wing. "Ella! Ella!"

"What?" Ella replied.

He spun to see her dragging a woozy Vero by his ponytail.

"Oh, yeah," said Val. "She got down way before you did."

The battered swordsman looked groggily up at the prince. "I still wish to duel you someday," he wheezed.

"But honestly, I do not see how you could be, as we say in my country, *better than her*."

THE BATTLE OF YONDALE

Thirty-seven bounty hunters burst into the dining hall of Yondale Castle, taking the Darians by surprise and starting a massive food fight. Axes chopped into shields, and potpies were shoved into faces; war hammers were swung into helmeted heads, and chains of sausage links were wrapped around throats. And while all this went on, Lila, astride a giant mongoose, searched the dusty, gray corridors of the castle, looking for any sign of its missing resident.

"King Edwyn?" Lila shouted.

"Your Highness!" called Periwinkle Pete, who sat behind her with his bow drawn. "If you can hear us, make a noise!"

A muffled shout rose from somewhere along a cold, dim passage that sloped downward into the lower levels below the surface of the cliff. Erik the Mauve, sitting just behind the animal's pointy ears, steered the mongoose in the direction of the sound. The great, furry creature sniffed, caught a scent, and began galloping. It slid to a halt before a cobweb-coated door, the entrance to the royal catacombs, the resting places of the kings of Yondale's past.

Another moan sounded from behind it.

"Everybody off," said Erik. "The mongoose won't fit through there." They dismounted, and Erik tugged open the ancient door. "Funny," he said. "The cobwebs only cover one half of the—"

Madu kicked the door open from the inside and slammed a heavy club over Erik's head. "Boo!" the tattooed Darian cackled as Erik slumped to the stony floor. "Ha! Weren't you easy to lure in here?"

"You!" Lila sneered, drawing her quarterstaff.

Pete stepped in front of her protectively and raised his bow. "I've got this," he said. *THWIP! THWIP! THWIP! THWIP!* With arrows through his vest and kilt, Madu was pinned to the wall. Pete strode into the catacombs to face him. "Now, tell us where the king is."

"Um, Pete," Lila said, running in after the elf and tugging at his sleeve. "He's not as trapped as you think. He—"

But Madu had already changed. He was now a thirty-foot-long, writhing sand snake that had no problem at all wriggling out of some clothing stuck to a wall. Pete shot off another volley of arrows, all of which hit the snake, but none of which seemed to slow it down. The thing lashed its sinewy tail at the elven archer and sent him hurtling into the dusty grave of a long-forgotten king.

Lila stared down the snake. "Come and get me," she said, and ran back out into the corridor. The snake followed her through the doorway and stopped when it saw her standing there, scratching behind the ears of a very large mammal. The snake's face contorted into something like a grin.

"Ssssso, you brought a big weassssssel," Madu hissed. "I eat weasssssselsssss for breakfasssssst."

"One problem," Lila said. "This isn't a weasel. It's a mongoose. And you know what a mongoose's favorite prey is?"

The sand snake's tear-shaped eyes went suddenly round with horror. Madu tried to slither away but never had a chance. In a flash, the mongoose lunged at the snake, pinned it down, and sank its long, sharp teeth into its scaly, reptilian neck.

Lila didn't stick around to see what happened next. She darted back into the catacombs. A quick look at Erik and Pete revealed that they were both still breathing. She called out for the king again, and this time she was met with a weak voice in response. Following the sound, Lila stumbled into a musty chamber that was lined with the bones of ages-old Yondale royalty. King Edwyn was there, too. For once he was the youngest in the room. But he was sound asleep, curled adorably around a small cameo portrait of Snow White.

She heard the faint voice again, from behind her, in another chamber across the way. She ran. Squinting into the darkness, Lila saw a figure huddled on the floor.

"Ruffian," she breathed.

"Lila, is it really you?" the old bounty hunter asked weakly. He pulled back his hood to get a better look at her.

"You're alive," she said, trying not to cry.

"Yes, somehow," Ruffian said. "My resistance to snake venoms must be even stronger than I realized. Normally, it's enough to keep me going for several days after a bite. A few weeks at most. But months have passed, haven't they? I kept expecting to die, but I didn't. I thought I'd never see you again, but here you are."

"Thank you, genie," Lila whispered.

From out in the hall they heard the loud, satisfied belch of a mongoose.

THE BATTLE OF SYLVARIA

While Frank and the dwarfs were busy carving their way through the Darian opposition outside the salmon-pink walls of Castlevaria, Duncan was busy doing something he'd never done before: leading his people. He might only have been leading them in a series of rousing chants—"We are Sylvaria! We will take care o' ya!" "Duncan, Duncan, he'll do somethin'!" "Let's go dwarfs! You'll win, of courfs!"—but everybody was cheering along with him. In fact, most of his subjects seemed to be enjoying themselves. Most had not quite absorbed the idea that they were in a war zone—unarmed (since Duncan had forgotten to bring any weapons).

Eventually, Snow tapped Duncan's shoulder. "Frank and the boys have almost beaten all the bad guys," she said. "Shouldn't we go check on your family?"

He gave a vigorous nod, the feathers on his cap wagging like an excited sea anemone, and turned to the crowd. "You people have done a great job with the chanting. But it is now time to storm the castle. And seeing as none of us is armed—well, except Snow; she has hazelnuts—I couldn't possibly ask you to go in with me. Don't be offended! I'm not saying you'd all definitely be defeated in there, but . . . I wouldn't want to leave it to chants."

And with that, he and Snow ran past the battling dwarfs and into the castle, where they discovered Duncan's entire family tied together and dangling by a rope over a large, bubbling cauldron.

"Oh, Duncan!" King King called down when he saw his son. "You're just in time. Our captors are making soup!"

"I think you're the soup, Dad," Duncan said.

"Is that how you kids are complimenting one another these days?" Queen Apricotta asked. "Well, we think you're 'the soup,' too, honey!"

"Thanks," Duncan replied. "We should try to get you down."

Just then a door opened, and Falco rushed in, looking panicked. (He'd been in the bathroom when the battle started—every villain's worst nightmare.) He dashed in front of the boiling cauldron, unsheathed a wavy-bladed dagger, and gnashed his sharpened teeth at Duncan and Snow.

"I remember you!" Snow said. "You chased me and Lila in my wagon that one time. You were quite rude."

Duncan eyed the pasty-skinned, baldheaded Darian strangely. "Are you like a werewolf?" Duncan asked. "Only instead of a wolf, you turn into a naked mole rat?"

Falco growled.

"Ooh, yes, ask him more questions," King King said from up above. "He likes to play charades, this one."

Sneering, Falco pointed up at the suspended family.

Then, slowly and with malice, he drew his finger across his throat.

"You met a bird who gave you a necktie?" Duncan asked.

Falco snarled and repeated the same gestures.

"Moon-men can see down your throat?" Snow guessed.

"There's a cough drop stuck on the ceiling?" Duncan tried.

The fanged Darian threw back his head and howled in fury.

"I must be right," Duncan whispered to Snow. "See how mad he is?"

"Maybe now's a good time to strike," Snow suggested.

"Oh, yes," said Duncan. "Please do."

As Falco reached for a dagger, Snow whipped a handful of hazelnuts at his head. The tiny missiles stung his face. He staggered backward, dropping his knife, spilling over the huge cauldron, and setting his pants on fire.

"He must be a liar," Mavis said.

"I never believed a word that came out of his mouth," added Marvella.

While Falco writhed on the floor trying to pat out his flaming legs, Duncan threw a heavy tapestry over the fire to smother it, and Snow threw the dropped dagger up at the dangling rope, slicing loose the royal family.

"Hooray for Duncan and Snow!" The queen beamed. "Our heroes again!"

"The important thing is that it's all over," said the king. "Our kingdom is safe once again. Which reminds me, Duncan, I've made a decision—"

With a hiss and a snarl—and very blackened pants—Falco reappeared. He snatched Duncan from behind, crawled out the window, and, beastlike, began scaling the wall of the castle.

"Where are they going?" Queen Apricotta asked.

They scrambled out to the front walk, where the dwarfs had finished off the last of the Darians.

"Frank! Frank!" Snow called. "The toothy man stole Duncan! He's climbing the big tower! You've got to go up there and rescue him!"

The dwarfs glanced upward to see the hunched figure of Falco scuttling to the tip-top of Castlevaria's tallest tower with Duncan flopping over his shoulder. "Aw, jeez, Snow," Frank said. "I, um . . . We can't . . ." He sighed.

"What do you mean, *you can't*?" Snow barked. "Go get him!"

Frank hung his head, and in a voice barely above a whisper, he muttered, "Dwarves are *not* expert climbers."

Snow looked to the crowd of Sylvarian bystanders. "Well, somebody's got to help Duncan! Somebody do something!"

The crowd began chanting: "That's Prince Charming! Please don't harm 'im!"

It did not help. Duncan was completely at the mercy of the rabid Falco. "I think I can see my old house from here," he said to his captor.

Standing balanced on the conical roof of the tower, Falco lifted Duncan over his head. But when he did, a long, dangling feather from Duncan's cap jutted down into the Darian's eyes. Falco blinked and shifted his head, but that only made more of the feathers get in his way. They poked his eyes and tickled his nose. Falco squinched up his face, trying to hold back the sneeze he felt coming. But it was a sneeze that would not be denied. And as Falco let loose with that massive, head-whipping nose-blast, his feet slipped. He dropped Duncan and tried to catch himself. But the Darian's clawed hands couldn't find a grip. He plummeted two hundred feet to the rocky ground below.

High above the cheering crowd, Duncan clung to the tower's spire, his arms and legs wrapped around it. He took off his hat, kissed it gently, and said, "Your job here is done. Return now to your own kind."

He released the hat into a gust of chill March wind and watched it soar high up into the clouds, where it was eventually adopted by a flock of passing geese.

THE BATTLE OF STURMHAGEN

Lord Rundark had underestimated the people of Harmonia, Erinthia, Yondale, and Sylvaria, assuming them too timid, too self-interested, or too dumb to revolt. But he never had any such illusions about Sturmhageners, who he knew to be stubborn, prideful, and easy to anger. Which is why Sturmhagen was teeming with hundreds upon hundreds of Darian warriors. (That and it was also really close to Dar, so they didn't have to walk very far.)

When the rabid, vengeance-hungry farmers clashed with their Darian oppressors in the cobblestone alleys and courtyards outside Castle Sturmhagen, it was all-out war. The Darians might have had better weapons—massive swords, spiked maces, and double-bladed pikes as opposed to pitchforks, shovels, and big sticks—but the farmers had heart. They also had trolls, which helped even more.

As roaring trolls hurled soldiers through brick walls and rebels used picnic tables as battering rams, Gustav was glowing. *I'm doing it,* he thought as he ripped a lamppost from the ground and used it to bat down a trio of Darians.

I rallied these people together. I'm their leader. And I'm going to win this. Nothing can stop me!

And then a voice. "There you are."

She stood on the castle steps in her tall, brown boots and long, flashy coat. Her captain's hat was tipped back, and her long black hair tumbled over her shoulders. A gleaming cutlass shone in her hand.

Gustav stomped his foot when he saw her. His nostrils flared. "Fine!" he shouted. "Come on, then! You and me! Right now! Final battle!"

"I didn't come here to fight you, Goldilocks," Jerica said. "I came to help."

"I don't believe you," Gustav said quickly. The rebellion raged on all around them, swords and shovels clashing mere feet away. But the two stood staring each other down.

"I swear I didn't know what Rundark had planned," Jerica said.

"Likely story," Gustav snipped. But he made no move—either to fight Jerica or to walk away.

"It was a job," she said with a shrug that was either apologetic or impatient—Gustav couldn't tell. "Rundark paid good money for me to drop you guys on the island, so I did it. I didn't ask questions. I never do. That's the way it always is. But this time . . ."

"This time *what?*" Gustav asked. He felt his sword hand trembling and wasn't sure why. "This time you found such a big sap that you decided it would be fun to hit him with a double whammy? This time you thought it would be hilarious to break some big goon's heart *before* you marooned him on an island? This time—"

"I didn't expect to fall for you, okay?" she barked back at him. "That *doesn't* usually happen. And you know what else doesn't usually happen? I don't usually go back for the people I strand at sea."

"Except that didn't happen," Gustav scoffed, lifting his elbow to smash the face of a Darian who charged him from behind.

"It did," Jerica insisted, ducking a raving warrior who leapt at her. "When I returned to port and heard what Rundark had been doing on the mainland, I headed straight back out to sea to find you again."

"It's true!" It was Roderick Key, exchanging blows with a Darian guard a few yards away. "It's because of you that the captain made us all skip shore leave! I missed sing-along night at the Salty Parrot! Not that I'm complaining."

Gustav looked around. A few feet away, Tauro was clotheslining Darians with his tree-like arms. Just past him, Mr. Flint was slamming an anchor over the head of an unlucky thug—and Sadie Squawkins was pecking at the bandanna of another. Even Scotty the cabin boy was there, whipping around two flopping mackerels like a pair of nunchackus.

"Wow, is the whole crew here?" Gustav asked.

"Well, I left Gabberman and his buddies on the *Dreadwind*," Jerica said (while forcing a struggling Darian into a headlock). "My ship is probably sinking as we speak."

Gustav hunched his shoulders and furrowed his brow. "I still don't know what to think," he grumbled.

"Look, Gustav, I'm *here*," Jerica said, sidekicking a Darian who tried to sneak up on her. "I came straight to Sturmhagen looking for you. I didn't know I would walk in on a revolution. But now that I'm here, just accept my help."

"Let me ask you one thing," Gustav said soberly. "Did you keep the money?"

"Of course I kept the money," Jerica half laughed. "It was a *lot* of money."

Gustav shrugged. "Yeah, I woulda kept it, too," he said. "Welcome to the team—nice to have you on board. Or *off* board, I guess. Look out!"

The castle's heavy oaken doors burst open, and a seemingly endless stream of Darians poured out—howling thugs who were armed to the teeth (that is, they held daggers not just in their hands but also between their teeth). The pirates rallied to defend themselves, but were quickly overwhelmed.

"There are too many of them!" Jerica cried, parrying two sword thrusts at once.

"I know where we can get reinforcements," Gustav said. "Follow me!" He grabbed Jerica's arm and tried to pull her away from the fray.

She yanked her arm back. "I can't leave my crew!"

Gustav glared at her. She glared right back.

"Starf it all," he grumbled, and ran off without her.

He dashed around the corner of the castle, where he wrapped his fingers around a rusty iron grate and ripped it from the stone wall. He raced down a dark, muck-filled tunnel, through another dented grate, and along a series of chilly, gray-walled passages, until he reached a long, very crowded cellblock. Behind nearly every barred door in the prison was one of Gustav's greatest enemies—his brothers. All sixteen were there: Henrik, Björn, Alvar, Ulrik, Osvald, Torvald, Sigfrid, Harald, Hans, Frans, Jorgen, Lars, Knute, Gunnar, Sven, and Viktor. They leapt to their feet.

"Little brother," said Henrik, the eldest. "Thank goodness!"

"Quick! Let us out!" said Jorgen. "We can hear the battle out there."

"Hurry!" shouted Torvald.

"We've been in here for months," pled Viktor. "Please, open the cells!"

"Free us, Gustav!" cried Sigfrid. He pointed to a hook on a nearby wall, where a ring of keys hung mockingly just out of reach.

Gustav grabbed the key ring and stared it at. He wanted so badly to milk this moment, to use it as the perfect way to get his brothers back for every name they'd ever called him, every prank they'd ever played on him, every bit of credit they'd ever stolen from him. He wanted to force an apology out of them. Or make them promise to do his laundry for a year. Or tell them he wouldn't release them unless they admitted to the world that it was really *he* who had saved the bards from Zaubera.

But Jerica was in trouble. So, with his jaw set and his eyes narrowed, he simply unlocked each cell door.

His brothers emptied out into the cellblock, stretching their stiff muscles and cracking their knuckles. Then they shoved him out of the way and ran off to join the battle, hooting, "Out of the way, loser!"

Gustav lay on his face in cobwebs and grime as his

siblings' footsteps vanished down the corridor. He closed his eyes. "I really am an idiot." But then he heard more footsteps, a solitary pair or boots, heading his way.

"Let me assist you." A hand wrapped around his and pulled him to his feet. And then *off* his feet. Gustav looked up and flinched. Wrathgar—shoulders heaving and mustache swaying—was holding him up by the wrist, dangling him in the air.

"I may have just lost sixteen princes," the enormous masked Darian rumbled. "But I got back the only one I really wanted. You and I have unfinished business."

"Oh, yeah?" said Gustav. "Well, finish *this*!" He thrust his free fist into Wrathgar's chest. And then he bit his lip, trying not to yelp in pain.

"I have to admit, I'd been hoping for a rebellion just so I would have the chance to quash it," the former dungeon master intoned, casually strolling toward the exit. "All the sweeter that, in doing so, I finally get to finish what I started last summer. By which I mean *killing you*."

Wrathgar held Gustav out at a full arm's length so that the prince's flailing legs couldn't reach him. He stepped outside onto Castle Sturmhagen's grand white stone steps and surveyed the epic battle going on all around them. Escaped princes were pummeling his Darian guards, farmers were clobbering his soldiers with shovels, pirates were hacking the bows of his archers, trolls were slamming his spearmen through picnic tables. "This won't do at all," he mumbled.

He flipped Gustav upside down and grabbed him by the ankles, then marched down the steps, swinging the prince like a big human flyswatter. Friend or foe, Wrathgar didn't seem to care who he attacked. Gustav's increasingly sore body was smacked into one fighter after another—and bodies went flying. Sigfrid was sent stumbling head-on into a tree, Osvald hurtling into a well. A Darian bodyguard was plowed into a trio of stunned trolls. Mr. Flint was launched up onto a roof. Gunnar was batted into Harald, who stumbled into Tauro, and the three bowled over a squad of Darian archers.

Cutting a swath through the mob, Wrathgar soon reached the open cobblestone plaza at the rear of Castle Sturmhagen, the area known as Celebration Courtyard, where, a year and a half earlier, the League of Princes had mounted a stone stage to be honored with their very first victory statue. The platform still stood at the center of the plaza, but the only thing on it now was a wide pinewood pedestal bearing one of Zaubera's elephant-size Mega-orbs.

"Hey, Rope Face!" Jerica shouted, chasing after the

Darian behemoth. Wrathgar spun to face her. She grabbed a battered helmet off the ground and threw it at him. It missed by several yards.

"Your aim is laughable," Wrathgar said (with no hint of laughter).

"Oh, yeah?" she taunted. "Let's see yours."

Nostrils flaring, Wrathgar brought his arm back and hurled Gustav at the pirate captain. He flew through the air like a burly, blond javelin and slammed hard into Jerica. The two of them crashed backward through a wooden bench.

"Oh, no. You okay, Pirate Lady?" Gustav slurred groggily. Jerica lay groaning amid splintered planks of wood, cradling her left knee.

"I got you away from him, didn't I?" she said, wincing. "Can you walk?"

"Of course," he said, standing up. Then he immediately fell over.

"Try again," she said, pulling herself to her feet. Gustav stood up. He wobbled but managed to stay upright. "Good," Jerica continued. "Now let's go stop that . . . that . . . What is he, half hippo?"

Gustav looked over his shoulder at Wrathgar. Having lost Gustav as his "weapon," the gigantic Darian was now beating people with Mr. Troll.

"Okay," Gustav said woozily. He lowered his head and got ready to charge. "Stuuuurm—"

Jerica grabbed him. "Not like that," she said. "We need to distract him."

"With what?" Gustav asked, cringing at a sound that might have been crunching bone. "The only thing I've seen him stop for is his boss."

"Then let's get his boss," Jerica said. She pointed to the Mega-orb up on the stage. "I know how to use those things, remember?"

While Wrathgar continued to decimate his opponents—roaring with delight the entire time—Gustav and Jerica limped up onto the stage and stood behind the colossal crystal ball. Jerica put her hands on the orb and waved them in a series of jerky gestures while she muttered words in a language Gustav didn't understand. The Mega-orb began to glow. The otherworldly mists inside the globe swirled, and Lord Rundark's scowling face appeared.

"Wrathgar! What is going on over there?" the Warlord barked. The former dungeon keeper froze at the sound of that dark baritone voice. He dropped Mr. Troll into the pile of unconscious bodies around him and ran to the lip of the stage.

"A revolt, Lord Rundark," Wrathgar said, looking up into the enormous crystal. "But as you can see, I put an end to it."

"Are you the only one left?" the Warlord asked sharply.

"I don't see how that makes a difference," Wrathgar said. "The rebellion has been quashed."

Behind the orb, Jerica whispered to Gustav. "Now." With a grunt, they leaned their shoulders hard into the tremendous glass globe. It tipped forward off of its pedestal.

"Wrathgar, I'm going to send some people over there to investigate the situation," Rundark said.

"No!" Wrathgar barked back. "I have everything under con— Why is your face moving down like that?"

And the Mega-orb flattened him.

Gustav and Jerica plopped themselves on the edge of the platform, as haggard princes, pirates, farmers, and trolls began dusting themselves off and tying up dazed Darians.

"Parts of me hurt that I didn't even know I had," Gustav said. "But, hey, I just saved my kingdom."

"Actually," said Jerica. "I think *I* saved your kingdom."

Gustav bristled. "You never would have been able to push that—"

"Shut up, Goldilocks," Jerica said. And she kissed him.

39

AN OUTLAW CATCHES UP WITH OLD FRIENDS

Smimf had a very busy day. The young messenger crisscrossed kingdoms at supersonic speeds, delivering messages between the Princes Charming and their allies. As villagers and nobles alike worked to pull injured rebels from the rubble of the Erinthian palace, Liam and Ella read through their stack of letters. Val, holding herself up on crutches, stood by to listen.

Dear Friends,

Harmonia has been liberated! And astonishingly, I had something to do with it. But here is the REAL miracle: My father sent the entire Harmonian guard across the border to assist the people of Jangleheim! He said he couldn't sit idly by while other nations suffered under the yoke of Darian oppression. MY FATHER did that; I had to check to make sure he was not still mesmerized. But I guess this experience has made him look at the world a bit differently. I hope you are all faring well.

Sincerely,
Frederic

Hey guys,

RUFFIAN IS ALIVE! Oh, and did you know that Yondale has a totally wicked navy? It's just that nobody's been using these guys for years, so they've just been fishing and giving tours and stuff. What a waste, right? I told sweet old King Edwyn to send a few ships over to Hithershire and a bunch more up to Svenlandia. And I'm going with them! I figured if I kicked the Darians out of Yondale with only a handful of bounty hunters, overthrowing them again with a few ships full of tough navy guys should be a piece of cake.

Later!
Lila

HERE'S THE DEAL. STURMHAGEN IS FREE. JERICA IS A GOOD GUY. WRATHGAR IS UNDER A GIANT MARBLE. AND MY BROTHERS ARE STILL JERKS. BUT HALF OF THEM TOOK AN ARMY UP NORTH TO FIGHT IN FROSTHEIM. AND THE OTHER HALF ARE DOING THE SAME DOWN IN CARPAGIA. SO I GUESS THAT'S OKAY.

—GUSTAV

Fellow Heroes,

You have to see this funny caterpillar I found! It looks like it has whiskers!

Yours truly,
Duncan

"Amazing," Liam said, looking up from the paper.

"You think so?" Val said skeptically. "I've seen the kind of caterpillar he's talking about. They're pretty common."

"No, I feel like we've entered a new age," Liam said. "People helping people . . . from *other* kingdoms. I still can't believe I convinced my parents to send Erinthia's troops down to Valerium."

"Excuse me, sir, Your Highness, sir," Smimf said, reaching into his messenger's bag. "I've got one more letter here. It's not technically addressed to you, but I think you should read it. You see, on the way here, I passed a . . . well, a creature of some sort. He was fuzzy, with big pointy ears, sort of like my grandmother after she got bitten by that werewolf. Anyway, at first I thought this creature was dead—he was lying on the side of the road under a tree. But it turned out he was just sleeping. When I woke him, he said his name was . . . Hardrot, I believe. He said he was supposed to deliver a letter, but that he was just too tired to go on. Seeing that I was a messenger, he asked me if I could take it the rest of the way for him. But before I could ask him where it was going, he'd passed out again—just like my grandmother after she lost that poker game with the slumber fairies."

"Let me see the note, Smimf," Liam said. The boy handed it to him, and Liam scanned it. "It's from Gabberman," he said. "And it is not good news. Smimf, I need you to take a message back to all the other League members. Tell them to meet at the tunnel entrance at the foot of Mount Batwing as soon as possible. Rundark is about to make his biggest move yet, and if we don't stop him, all our victories thus far will be meaningless."

Even around Mount Batwing, winter was shuffling off, making room for spring. It was green grass now, rather than snow, that filled the cracks in the rocky rises at the foot of the mountain. Birds twittered among the branches of the pines as Liam and Ella rode up to the small clearing and dismounted to greet their friends. They were surprised to see only Frederic, Gustav, and Duncan waiting for them.

Rapunzel, it turned out, had remained in Harmonia to administer medical aid to all the wounded fancy people. Jerica had quite a few injuries among her crew as well, and—with regrets—told Gustav that she had to see them taken care of before she could head off on another adventure. Lila was busy with the siege of Svenlandia's royal castle. And Snow remained in Sylvaria, trying to coax King King down from a flagpole (he claimed to have a fear of charades now and had climbed the pole in terror after seeing someone make a hand gesture). Val was perhaps the sorriest to stay behind, but her broken leg hampered travel quite a bit.

"Well, then I guess it's just the five of us." Liam said.

"What's the emergency?" Frederic asked. And so Liam pulled out Gabberman's letter.

"'To Any o' Ye Princes,'" he read aloud. "''Tis a sorry thing to be the bearer o' bad news, but I've gleaned some information that ye princes need be hearing. Dire tidings it is, quite urgent. Arrrrr!'"

"Did he actually write 'Arrrrr'?" Frederic asked.

"Yes," said Liam. He continued reading: "'We been ported off the coast o' Yondale for a spell, and tonight we seen a suspicious vessel come into the harbor. So we snooped around a bit, and we seen that her crew was Dar folk. They was unloading some o' the strangest cargo this old pirate's ever set eyes on. Cannonballs, they looked like—'bout the size o' witches' cauldrons. And glowin' with a fierce light, like somethin' inside of 'em was fixin' to explode. We heard 'em talkin' 'bout these doohickeys like they was bombs. "Just one of these puppies'll take down an entire castle," says one. "With his mega-cannon, the Warlord can launch 'em from New Dar all the way to Frostheim," says another. "I hates it when a dragonfly lands in me grog," says a third (though I don't think that was relevant). Anyways, there's thirteen o' them glowin' bomb thingies on a wagon headed for New Dar as we speak. Or as we write, rather. Or as I write and you read. Aye, that's it. Good luck stoppin' the bombs! Yers Saltily, Cap'n Horatio Gabberman.'"

"I can't believe it," Frederic said.

"I know," said Duncan, equally wide-eyed. "Horatio? That's a ridiculous name!"

Gustav raised an eyebrow. "What am I missing here?" he said.

"Don't you see?" Frederic said. "Those glowing

cannonballs Gabberman saw? They're the magical bombs that Zaubera had planned to destroy our island with. The Darians must have dug them up and are bringing them back to Rundark."

"Who apparently has a cannon capable of launching those bombs anywhere he wants," Ella added. "If he can't control our kingdoms, he's going to destroy them."

"We need to stop that shipment of bombs before it gets to Rundark," Liam said. "Ella and I rode through the night, using Ruffian's mountain shortcut, which only took two days. Since the Darians are carting a big, heavy wagon, we can assume they'll need to take the main shipping road down from Yondale, which requires at least four days' travel. So the bomb wagon should most likely arrive here the day after tomorrow. We should have plenty of time to head along the mountains to the north of Rauberia and set up an ambush."

"I have a question," Duncan said, raising his hand. "If it takes four days to get here from Yondale, why are the Darians not arriving until the day after tomorrow? Do you think they'll stop at Woolly Wally's Alpaca Farm? I know *I* would."

"What are you talking about, Duncan?" Liam asked.

"The alpaca farm in southern Yondale. They let you feed the alpacas. And pet them. You're technically not supposed to ride them, but I kind of did once, which is why I'm not allowed back."

"No, Duncan—why are you questioning the time frame?" Liam said brusquely.

"Oh. Because of the date on here." He handed the letter back over to Liam, pointing to some numbers scrawled on the reverse side.

"It's dated four days ago," Liam breathed urgently.

"Let's move!" Ella barked. She was already on her horse. "Those bombs are arriving today!"

They mounted up and galloped out along the edge of the vast meadow that surrounded Rundark's castle. Keeping close to the eaves of the forest, they moved westward, trying to stay out of view of the guards who patrolled the ramparts of the eighty-foot-tall Wall of Secrecy. In five minutes, there it was—the huge iron gate of the fortress. And the heroes were able to catch the briefest glimpse of a bomb-filled wagon rolling inside. And the gate slammed shut.

"Quick, everyone!" Liam ordered. "Back to the secret tunnel!" He turned his horse around, but Frederic held up his hands to stop him.

"No tunnel—we already checked," Frederic said. "It's completely sealed up, packed full with rocks and dirt. Rundark must have discovered it after our last encounter."

Liam flopped forward, burying his face in Thunderbreaker's mane and muttering, "Why, Gabberman? Why did you send the narcoleptic half-ogre to deliver your urgent message?"

The others sat there on their horses, staring out at the foreboding fortress. Its dark-gray stone and sharp silhouette were in stark contrast to the lush green meadow that filled the valley and the luminous pink, blue, and yellow blooms that sprouted in bunches all around it.

"Is it just me," asked Duncan, "or is this place a lot prettier than last time?"

"It's spring," Ella said with a shrug.

"No, Duncan's right," said Frederic. "It's more than just the change of seasons. When we raided this castle last year, the land around it was dry and barren. This place used to be called the Orphaned Wastes, remember? We haven't seen this valley lush and vibrant like this since . . . well, since Zaubera lived here."

"I'd completely forgotten," said Ella, leaning down to pluck a small white flower. "But, yes, when she died, all the plants and grass died with her."

"This valley is a wasteland by nature," said Frederic. "Her spells were what brought it to life the first time, and they must be what has revived it again now. Interesting that, even in her weakened state, she felt the need to . . ." He stared, as if mesmerized, at the flowing waves of greenery.

"What is it, Frederic?" Ella asked.

Frederic shook his head. "Probably nothing," he said. "We've got a bigger question to deal with right now—and a familiar one. How do we get past that wall?"

Liam scanned the battlements. "Well, first we can . . . No, maybe we . . . Perhaps . . . Ugh. I don't even know how we *reach* the wall, let alone get past it. There are five times as many guards up there as there were last time. A couple of giants would help. Too bad Maude dragged Reese away to ground him. She said we humans and our covered feet were bad influences."

"What if we had an army?" Ella asked.

"Sure, that would be nice, too." Liam sighed. "Too bad every single one of us sent our nation's soldiers off to fight other battles."

"Not *every* one of us," Ella said, grinning. She pointed westward, toward the mountains. Pin-striped soldiers were marching into the meadow by the hundreds, followed by cavalry on silver-armored horses. And cannons—gorgeously painted, rainbow-swirl cannons—were towed alongside them on sturdy war carts. At the head of the charge was a golden coach emblazoned with the flag of Avondell.

"Briar!" Liam said, hopping to his feet. They spurred their horses and raced to meet the Avondellian army. They caught up with the coach when it was about two miles from the Wall of Secrecy and waved down the driver. The man pulled up on the reins and brought his horses to a stop. The entire army came to a halt as Briar stepped out of her coach.

"What's going on here?" Briar snipped. She was clad in a red-and-black dress, with sharp-angled shoulder pads and reinforced leather sleeves. "Are you losers late for the invasion, or have you started without me?"

"We were late," said Duncan. "Because Liam doesn't know how dates work."

Liam shot him an exasperated look, then turned back to Briar. "How did you know to come here?" he asked.

"That messenger boy told me. He said you'd sent him. Did you not?"

Fig. 32
BRIAR, combat ready

Liam grinned and shook his head. "I told him to give the message to the other members of the League."

"And he thought that included me—how cute," Briar said. "Well, I'm here. And I'm wearing my combat gown. So what do you need?"

"Rundark's got a wagonload of magical bombs in there," Liam said. "Apparently he's constructed some sort of mega-cannon. Based on its assumed size and the angle of trajectory needed to fire it, the weapon is most likely located on the roof. So—"

"You need to get inside, Liam—just say that. I swear, nobody on Earth wastes more time talking than you do," Briar said with a snort. "But you're in luck, because I brought an army." She turned around, cupped her hands around her mouth, and shouted, "General Kuffin! Tear down that wall!"

With elegance and precision, the nattily dressed Avondellian warriors advanced on Rundark's castle. As soon as they got within range, the Darian archers began unloading scores of arrows upon them. The Avondellian cannons fired in return, blowing huge hunks of stone from the upper edges of the wall and crumbling the ramparts on which the archers stood. With a creak, the huge iron gate swung open, and platoons of snarling Darians flooded out into the meadow. They met the Avondellians head-on, and soon the entire field echoed with the clashing of blades and the clattering of armor.

The heroes stood, watching the chaos from afar. "Okay," Briar called as she stepped back into her coach. "Say ta-ta to your horsies for now and get inside."

"In there?" Liam asked.

"With you?" added Gustav.

"Well, if you'd rather ride openly across the battlefield—" Briar began.

"Slide over, sister," Ella said, climbing in. The princes squeezed in after her.

Frederic, who was squished against the far door next to Gustav, cleared his throat. "So, um, Briar . . . are you sure this coach can make it through—"

"I brought Worthingham," Briar said, nodding slyly. "He's the driver I used to send through treacherous obstacle courses for fun. You know, back when I was cruel and awful. Hit it, Worthingham!"

The driver cracked the reins, and the coach took off with a jolt. It whipped left and right, narrowly avoiding dueling warriors and wild, riderless horses. A squad of Darian spearmen tried to block the coach, but it pivoted, kicking dirt up into their faces. Everybody inside held on for dear life except

Briar, who hummed cheerily.

The coach barreled through the gateway and across the drawbridge, and skidded to a stop at the front doors of the castle.

"Last stop," Briar said. "Everybody out."

Gustav threw open the door and stepped directly into the castle's entry chamber, where he clobbered two bewildered sentries. Frederic, Duncan, Ella, and Liam filed out after him.

"Hey, losers," Briar called as they rushed down the hall. "Do me a favor?"

They paused briefly to turn back to her. "What?" asked Liam.

"Try to win for a change, okay?"

Liam nodded as Briar closed the door and screamed something at Worthingham. The coach took off again.

"To the roof, people," Liam said to his team. "Let's end this."

40

AN OUTLAW CAN BE A HERO

And so it was that the League of Princes faced off against their two greatest foes in a climactic battle that would forever cement their places in history. But rather than dwell on that horrible, violent conflict, let me instead recount to you an interesting conversation that occurred between Reginald the valet and Frank the dwarf.

"Sir Dwarf," said Reginald. "I hear you will be petitioning the Inter-Kingdom Dictionary Guild to have 'dwarves' recognized as the official plural of 'dwarf.'"

"That's right," grunted Frank. "What of it?"

"I happen to have some connections on the Guild Board," said the valet, straightening his tie. "You may not know this, but it was through my influence that we no longer need to pronounce the *B* at the end of 'comb.'"

Aw, who am I kidding? Let's get to the battle.

After leaving Briar's coach, the League crawled into the first dumbwaiter shaft they found and climbed straight to the castle's roof, where they immediately noticed that Rundark had made significant changes. All of Rauber's candy kiosks and ringtoss booths were gone. The rooftop was now one big rectangle of flatness—except for the dome (stolen from a Svenlandian cathedral) that still rose up from its center.

"Where is he?" Gustav asked. "Where are the bombs? And the big cannon?"

"Maybe Gabberman was wrong?" Frederic suggested. "Maybe that cart was just bringing in a load of melons?"

Liam grunted. "I hate melons."

Then a loud noise rose from beneath their feet, like the grinding of a thousand metal gears. A cracking sound followed, along with a hurried hiss of air, as the huge dome split down the middle and its halves began to separate.

"Ooh, I hope it hatches a giant chick." Duncan beamed.

Inside the open dome they could see a complicated weave

of moving mechanical parts. With a chorus of screeches and crunches, a circular platform appeared: a gleaming steel disk two feet thick and fifty feet across that rose up into the air on a tall, rotating column. Rundark stood on the platform, along with six brutish bodyguards. Beside the Warlord was a vision orb, sitting on a pedestal of carved bone. But what caught the heroes' eyes most of all was the cannon—thirty feet-long, bloodred, and wide enough to load a cow into (if, for any reason, you'd ever want to load a cow into a cannon). And right next to it sat a large wooden bin piled high with glowing, cauldron-size bombs.

Rundark caught sight of the stunned princes and let out a bemused huff. "It takes a special type of fly to revisit the web of the spider it was lucky enough to escape," he said.

"Heroic flies," Liam said proudly.

"I was thinking stupid," the Warlord replied.

"Yeah, that's us," said Gustav. And with that, he leapt up onto the slowly rising platform, grabbed one of the bodyguards by the ankle, and tossed him off. Ella and Liam jumped for the edge of the disk and pulled themselves up. But Frederic and Duncan were too late; they couldn't quite reach the lip of the platform. While Ella drew her sword and fended off bodyguards, Liam leaned down and grabbed the outstretched hands of his fellow princes.

As the disk continued to rise, Frederic and Duncan felt their feet leave the floor—but Liam didn't have the strength or leverage to haul them both up at once. Gustav did, though. He head-butted a guard off the edge of the platform and then pulled all three men up.

"Everybody good?" Gustav asked. "Okay, let's fight."

He and Liam drew their swords and joined Ella in battling the remaining four guards. Liam quickly disarmed one enemy and kicked him down to the roof. Ella tricked a pair into tackling each other and tumbling off the side. Gustav picked the last one up by the collar and simply dropped him over the edge.

The five heroes faced Lord Rundark. He still stood by the vision orb with his arms folded across his chest. He'd made no move to join the fight, nor did he seem to care that his men were rolling and groaning on the roof below.

And the platform rose still. It passed flying birds. It appeared to pass clouds. It passed what might have been a flying hat. Duncan peeked over the edge and watched the men on the roof become mere specks. Frederic tried to mentally calculate how high up they were but started hyperventilating once he'd counted past three hundred feet. Then, suddenly, with a loud, metallic screech, the disk came to a halt. Ella and Liam grabbed the others and formed a human

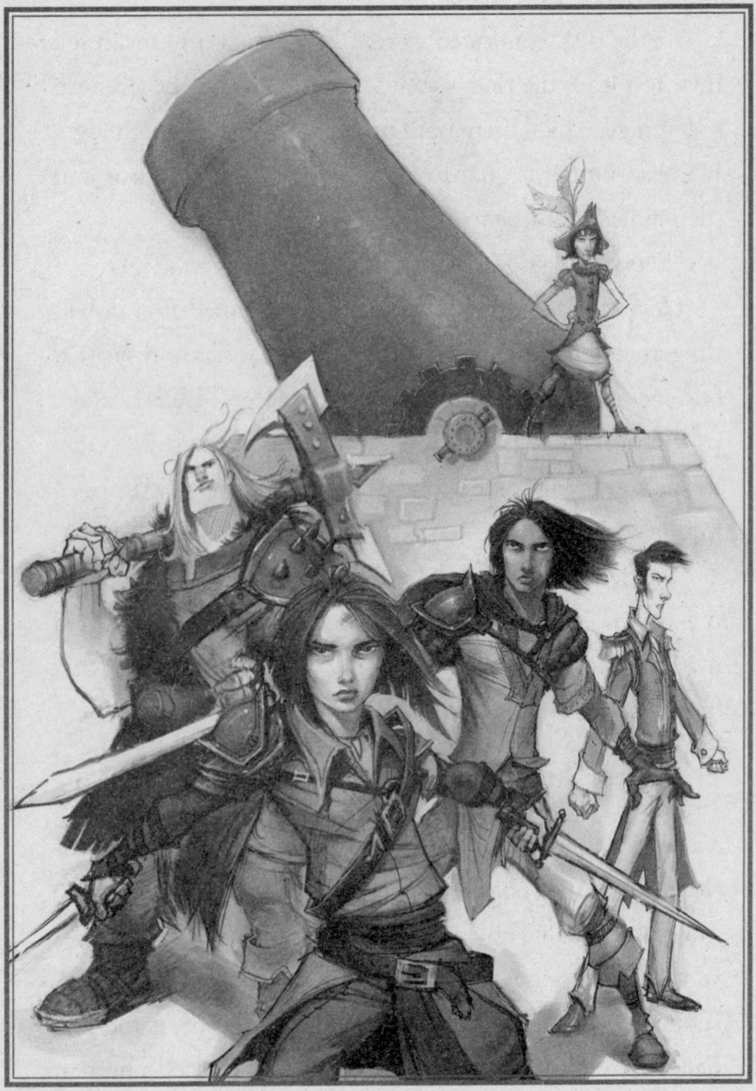

wall between the Warlord and his mega-weapon.

"What's the matter, Rundark?" Liam said to their silent, smirking foe. "Afraid to take on all of us?"

"No," the Warlord said. "I was just waiting until we were high enough to guarantee that the fall would kill you." His lips curled. In the bright light of day, his glowing green aura had not been so easy to see. He raised his hands and shot forth five bolts of blue lightning. Everybody went down. The heroes rolled and skidded across the platform, moaning as smoke wafted up from their singed clothing. Duncan slid perilously close to the edge, but Ella caught him by the neck ruff.

"And that's right—Zaubera's here, too!" cackled the ghostly witch as her spectral form separated itself from the Warlord's body and flew gleeful loops in the air. "I never get tired of zapping you guys," she clucked.

"Yes, but you failed to knock them off the platform, witch," Rundark said.

"That would be too easy," Zaubera replied. "We need to have some fun with them first."

"Bah!" Rundark barked. "It's time to destroy the world." Ignoring the smoldering heroes, he ran his hands over the vision orb to activate it. In each of the Thirteen Kingdoms, citizens outside their royal palaces jumped, startled to see the giant Mega-orbs crackle to life. Most people had practically forgotten about the enormous crystal balls, thinking of them as nothing more than oversize public art displays. But everybody's attention was drawn to the orbs now. Mists swirled within them, and an image appeared—the Warlord of Dar standing by an enormous cannon with the clear blue sky as his backdrop and five writhing people at his feet. Slowly but surely, crowds began to gather.

In Sylvaria, Snow White and the royal family huddled close, horrified to recognize Duncan amid those writhing figures. In Harmonia, Rapunzel gripped Reginald's hand as she spotted Frederic in the orb's image. Val pounded her fists against the giant sphere in Erinthia, as if doing so would help her reach Ella. Lila, who had just chased a Darian general from Svenlandia's royal palace, started cursing herself for not being there to help her brother. And in Sturmhagen, Jerica saw Gustav's prone form within the orb and stomped on Wrathgar's hand (which was still sticking out from under it).

By the hundreds, people came together around the orbs, watching with bated breath. And back on the sky-high platform in New Dar, Rundark looked out upon thirteen different crowds at once. Thousands of faces flickered within the mists of his orb—the faces of people he was about to obliterate.

"People of the Thirteen Kingdoms," the Warlord said. "I offered you paradise in a world under my rule. But you have refused my benevolence. And now you will reap the consequences. I thank you in advance for so cooperatively gathering around my targets."

He strode over to the bin and hoisted out a bomb. It sizzled and glowed with a throbbing light. He loaded the bomb into the cannon and turned a crank to raise the barrel to a steep angle. He drew a tall match from his pocket, struck it across his leg to light it, and brought it near the cannon's long fuse. Before the match made contact, though, its tiny flame went out.

Rundark turned and glared at ghostly Zaubera, who was hovering over his shoulder with her lips still puckered from blowing out the match. "What do you think you're doing?" he snapped.

"You don't kill the audience before the show," the witch said. "We didn't plan on it, but we've got those loathsome princes right here. And snivelly Cinderella, too. We can't let this golden opportunity slip by! We destroy them first. In front of the whole world, just like we planned before."

"Like *you* planned before," Rundark said. "I neither need nor desire your brand of theatricality. I crave only destruction. Besides, it's not as if these people are going to have long to ruminate on the deaths of their heroes. In a matter of moments, they'll all be dead themselves."

"And where's the art in simply surprising them with their own obliteration," Zaubera scoffed. "You're always so practical. Let's toy with their emotions first!"

As the villains bickered, Frederic dragged himself to Rundark's skeletal pedestal and pulled his head up to stare into the vision orb. "Everybody, listen!" he shouted to the far-off crowds. "Rundark has super-powerful magical bombs. And they will be headed straight toward those giant vision orbs you're watching. You need to get as far away from those orbs as possible!"

And all around the Thirteen Kingdoms, seven people turned away from the orbs and fled. Yes, that's right: seven. The thousands of others stayed glued to the action. They'd discovered a new form of moving-picture entertainment, and nothing was going to tear them away.

"Seriously, leave!" Frederic tried again. But he was quickly cut off by Zaubera's phantom form swishing by and startling him back onto the floor.

"Nuh-uh-uh," the witched cooed. "No interfering with my spectacle." She hovered before the orb and addressed the audience. "Ladies and gentlemen, we now present for your viewing pleasure: the Death of the League of Princes."

"Bah! Enough nonsense," Rundark spat as he lit another match.

Duncan crawled over to Gustav. "Throw me at him!" Duncan said.

"Didn't that go badly once before?" Gustav asked warily.

"Yes," Duncan replied. "But nothing can fail *that* horribly twice"

Gustav shrugged. "Can't argue that logic." He stood up, grabbed Duncan, and hurled him headlong at the Warlord. Rundark dropped the match to catch him.

"Aha! See?" Duncan crowed, lying cradled like a baby in the Warlord's arms.

Then Rundark hurled Duncan, spear-like, back at Gustav. The collision sent both princes hurtling dangerously close to the platform's edge. Ella and Liam ran to pull them to safety.

"Guys," Ella barked, "we can't keep saying it's five against one and then attacking him individually!"

"She's right," Liam said. "We do this together. On the count of three . . ."

"Let's finish them off now!" Zaubera hissed. "Open yourself up to me! We'll fry them slowly while their loved ones watch!"

She wafted toward Rundark, but he raised his big, calloused hands and waved her away like a foul odor. "No!" he barked. "I shut my mind to you. I'm tired of giving power to a petty old spirit. I am Warlord of Dar! Not the stoolie of some dead hag."

"Three!" Liam shouted. He, Ella, Gustav, and Duncan leapt as one at Rundark. Frederic, who was on the other side of the platform, took a deep breath and ran to join them. Or, rather, he tried to. On his first step, he slipped in a puddle of his own sweat. Viewers in far-off cities screamed as he tumbled off the platform—and gasped as he gripped his fingers around the rim of the disk.

While his friends struggled to take down the Warlord, Frederic dangled hundreds of feet in the air, his legs flailing wildly, hoping to find a foothold that simply wasn't there. He glanced down and bit his lower lip, wondering if he could perhaps use his coat like a parachute and glide gently to the soft grass.

The soft grass! The soft, lush, vibrant grass. That just might be the key to saving them all.

"Zaubera!" he called. The witch's ghostly face appeared over the edge of the platform, grinning wickedly.

"Well, look what we have here," she said. "I don't even need Rundark to finish *you* off. I'll just blow on your fingers until you get so ooked out by my ghost breath that you let go."

She began puffing on his fingertips. And the cold dampness of her breath felt so icky that her plan almost worked. But Frederic was determined.

"No," he said, straining to hold on. "Zaubera, listen to me: I know you're not a hundred percent evil. There's goodness in you."

"Where?" the ghost-witch said, looking down through her transparent torso. "I certainly don't see any."

"The grass down there, the flowers," Frederic said. "You did that. Why? You must have wanted to bring a little beauty into the world."

"What?" she spat. "A wicked sorceress isn't allowed to have a garden? I like to have an attractive backdrop when I slay my enemies."

"You don't really want to kill us," Frederic said.

"Yes, I do," she said plainly. "And I will. And thanks to all the eyewitnesses watching through my vision orbs, I'll finally get the fame I deserve."

Frederic could hear the battle raging on the platform above him, his friends shouting and crying amid the crash and clamor of combat.

"Liam, no!" *BAM!*

"Look out, Ella! He's about to—" *CRACK!*

"Duncan, what happened to your pants?" *KA-KRAM!*

With all his might, Frederic pulled himself up just high enough to glance over the edge of the platform. He saw his friends on the floor. And he watched as Rundark, with another match in hand, finally lit the cannon's fuse.

Frederic's strength wavered, and he dropped back down, hanging once again only by his fingertips. "Don't let him do it, Zaubera," Frederic pleaded wearily. "Think about your grand vision. Don't let him rob you of that."

The ghost-witch furrowed her misty brow. "And what am I supposed to do to stop him? Huff and puff on him until he catches pneumonia?"

Frederic's right hand slipped off. And his left didn't feel like it could take much more. "Use me," he said. "I open my mind and body to you. Use me."

"Really?" Zaubera asked giddily. "Well, you don't need to tell me twice!" She whooshed down to Frederic. At first he felt an odd rush of chill air, but a second later, he felt invigorated—stronger than he ever had before. With only the fingertips of his left hand, he pulled himself nimbly up onto the platform.

I have Zaubera's magical strength, he thought. And then he realized that he had more than just that. He had access to her mind, her thoughts and memories. A parade of images marched through his head. He felt Zaubera's terror as the dragon's gaping jaws came at her. He felt her anger as he and the other princes escaped from her after their first encounter two summers ago. He felt her petulance as she threw a tantrum, flash-frying a trio of pitiful henchmen who had let one of her prisoners escape. But he also saw much older images and felt much more distant emotions—ones that the witch herself had nearly forgotten. Frederic saw a woman who loved nature, who wanted nothing more than to tend her garden and share its treasures with her neighbors. He saw a woman who was hurt, intensely, by the jeers and barbs of vicious bullies who tormented her. He saw a woman who wanted to be a hero, who sacrificed her beloved garden in order to save the lives of three children in a fiery inferno—a misinterpreted act for which she received no thanks and was instead branded a dangerous villain.

"I understand now," Frederic said aloud.

"It is about time," said Rundark. "You finally understand that fighting me is pointless. Your world is over. And I will rule the wastes that remain."

But Frederic ignored him. Instead, he directed his words to Zaubera. "What they did to you was unfair," he said. "It was wrong. But you didn't have to become what they assumed you to be. You could have worked to prove them wrong."

"Hey, Tassels," Gustav said gently as he struggled to sit upright. "Who are you talking to?"

"Zaubera," Frederic said. "She's in my head."

"What?" Rundark snapped. For the first time ever, they noticed a hint of fear in his eyes. He raced toward Frederic, who found his hands suddenly moving of their own volition. His arms stretched out before him, and his fingers began to twitch as a ball of crackling blue energy appeared between his palms. He whipped the magic missile at Rundark, and it exploded against his broad chest, knocking him off his feet.

"Way to go, Magic Tassels!" Gustav crowed.

Liam and Ella raised their heads off the ground. "What's going on?" Liam muttered.

"Zaubera's not totally evil," Frederic said. "I think I convinced her to switch sides." And then his arms went wild. He was sending energy bolts everywhere. One crashed into the base of the cannon, another came dangerously close to igniting the entire crate of bombs. One blue blast would have sizzled Duncan if Liam and Ella hadn't each grabbed one of his feet and yanked him out of the way.

"Come on, Duncan! Wake up and move!" Liam urged.

Duncan's eyelids fluttered. "Papa Scoots, is that you?"

"Hey, Tassels, you wanna watch where you're shooting

those things?" Gustav called, ducking as a bolt sailed over his head.

"I'm not exactly in control here," Frederic said, his eyes wide with horror.

"You fool!" Rundark barked, ducking behind the cannon to avoid the magic missiles headed his way. "Do you realize what you've done? She'll kill us all! I've seen inside that witch's mind, too! She's a cruel and sadistic beast. She thrives on bringing pain to others. That's why I knew I could use her!"

"Don't listen to him, Zaubera," Frederic said as his arms continued to whip about, spraying fire across the platform. "He only sees in you what he wants to see. There's more to you than that! The world is watching, Zaubera. If you do the right thing now, do you think they'll care about anything you've done in the past? You'll be a hero—the hero you were always meant to be. You can write your own destiny!"

With a fizzle, the magic bolts stopped flying. Frederic stood, panting, unsure of whether Zaubera was still in control. All was quiet except for the faint pop and crackle of the fuse that was a mere inch from unleashing massive destruction.

"Go for the fuse," Ella whispered to Liam. "Now."

Liam darted for the cannon. But Rundark leapt out from

behind the great gun. He stood there under its massive, up-tilted barrel, blocking Liam's way. "The end of your world begins now," the Warlord said.

Then Frederic raised his hand and loosed an energy bolt that slammed into the base of the cannon. The crank spun wildly, and thirty feet of iron cannon barrel came down on Rundark's head. The Warlord's skull helmet cracked in half as the man fell. But he wasn't down for long. Dizzied, and angrier than ever, he crawled out from under the giant weapon—which was only seconds away from firing.

Zaubera's spectral form whooshed out of Frederic's body.

"What are you doing?" Frederic blurted. "He's still coming!"

"Do you think those people out there are going to give *me* credit if they see skinny Prince Charming shooting down the big bad guy?" the witch said. "No, I'll finish this myself."

Blinded by rage, Rundark roared and ran at the ghost. Zaubera, glowing bright and fierce, flew straight back at him. And instead of passing through him, she knocked him backward. Rundark staggered in confusion. And the phantom witch pounded into him again. He stumbled up against the open mouth of the cannon, his eyes wide with shock. One final jolt from Zaubera, and the Warlord tumbled into the cannon barrel. Then the hand crank started spinning and the barrel began rising, and with an ear-shattering boom, the cannon fired. The otherworldly bomb—with Warlord of Dar draped over it—hurtled into the sky. With a gleeful grin on her phantom face, Zaubera zoomed up at tremendous speeds to follow it. And when her ghostly form reached the bomb, it exploded. The blast could be seen from every one of the Thirteen Kingdoms—not just through the vision orbs, but up in the sky among distant clouds.

Frederic, feeling comfortably un-strong again, walked over to the vision orb on the platform. "Ladies and gentlemen," he said. "That . . . spirit you saw was that of a . . . magic-user named Zaubera. She just stopped a madman from destroying the world. Remember her name: Zaubera. Because she just saved your kingdom."

With a soft crackle, the orb—and all the other orbs around the world—went black.

"Are you okay?" Ella asked Frederic.

"Yes," he replied. "What about you guys?"

"I've never felt better," said Duncan. "Except for most other times in my life."

"What do you think happened to Zaubera?" Liam said. "Can a magical blast like that *kill* a ghost?"

"No, I'm still here," the witch said, startling everyone. "And I just want you to know that this doesn't mean I like you guys now or anything. In fact, I— Huh? Where are my ghostly fingers going? And my whole body? Ooh, does this mean I get to stop—" They never heard the end of her question, because she vanished completely, faded away into nothingness.

The friends stared at one another in silence for a moment. "You know, she'd said something before about not having done enough good deeds to get into the afterlife," Frederic said. "I didn't know whether she meant it literally, but maybe . . ."

They all heard a high-pitched tinkling sound.

Duncan's face lit up. "You know what they say about bells, right?" he asked. "Whenever a bell rings . . ."

"Shut up, Pipsqueak," said Gustav. "It's just the sprites."

Blink and Deedle appeared over the edge of the platform. As soon as they saw the princes, the tiny blue fliers zipped over to them.

"Zel knew you be here!" Blink said cheerily.

"Holdety tight," Deedle said. "We found big crankety wheel in castle. Strongety man going to turn it and bring you down."

The platform jolted and then slowly began descending.

"Oh, and war is over," Blink said. "We winnety!"

The exhausted heroes cheered, but their celebration was

cut short as soon as the platform reached the bottom and they learned the identity of the "strongety man" who had cranked them down.

"Looks like the rat has finally caught its prey," said Greenfang.

"Does that make us the cheese?" Duncan asked wearily.

The bounty hunter drew his scimitar and flashed his crooked yellow teeth. The Leaguers braced themselves, but as worn-out as they were, none was ready for a fight. And they'd all lost their weapons.

"What do you want?" Liam asked.

"I told you months ago," Greenfang replied. "I never give up."

"But there's no more bounty for us," Frederic said. He wanted to collapse.

"I don't care." Greenfang flared his nostrils. "I. Never. Give. Up." He raised his sword and stomped up toward them. Ella hunkered down. Gustav balled his fists. Duncan stood on one leg.

But Liam just raised his hands in the air. "Fine, you never give up. We get it," he said with fatigue in his voice. "So *we* give up."

Greenfang stopped in his tracks. "What?"

"We surrender," Liam said. "You win. You've caught us."

Greenfang paused, pressing his lips together in thought. "Um, okay then," he said. "Mission accomplished. Since there's nowhere to take you, um, I guess . . . have a nice day." He sheathed his sword, and walked away.

41

THE VILLAIN WINS

And so the Thirteen Kingdoms were liberated from Darian rule. Well, all except Eïsborg, which people always tend to forget about. It's very far north. And barely anybody lives there, anyway. We even forget to put it on the map in the first book. The fifteen Darians stationed there would end up sitting around for two and half years wondering why their vision orb never turned on anymore.

None of the vision orbs ever turned on again, actually. They'd been powered by Zaubera's magic, and when the witch died her second death, the orbs all went kaput. Despite people's best efforts at kicking them and attempting to attach antennas to them, they remained dull and opaque forever. The thrilling prospect of moving-picture entertainment would have to wait.

Zaubera's mystical bombs fizzled out as well and became nothing more than oversize bowling balls. On a sadder note, the lovely lawns and flowering gardens that surrounded the castle all shriveled and turned to dust again, returning the valley to its former dry, gray ugliness. Not that Deeb Rauber cared. He was never much into posies and petunias anyway.

As soon as the last of the Avondellian soldiers had filed out with the last of the Darian prisoners and the enormous castle was empty once again, the Bandit King scurried out of the hollow boulder he'd been hiding in and ducked back inside his former home. The place was a wreck—the candy rooms had been trashed, all the naughty fingerpaintings had been torn down, and he was going to have to build himself a new bandit army from scratch. But the kingdom was all his again. He strode directly into his old throne room.

"I have returned!" he shouted to the empty chamber. "Deeb Rauber, the Bandit King, the one true ruler of Rauberia! Once again, I have the power!" Feeling quite proud of himself, he strutted up to his throne and sat down.

"Eeeeeeyowww!" he screamed, jumping up and holding his stinging backside, having completely forgotten about the tack he'd placed there.

EPILOGUE

A HERO CAN LIVE HAPPILY EVER AFTER . . . OR NOT

Three months later . . .

The small fishing boat was sinking fast. Its frantic three-man crew huddled on the disappearing bow as rough waves crashed into them and the dorsal fins of hungry sharks circled mere feet away. But despite the dangers in front and below, the men couldn't help but stare up at the awe-inspiring bulk of the *Dreadwind*—and the man on the rope hanging from its bow. "Grab on, Rub-a-Dub-Dubbers," Gustav said as he scooped all three into his arms. After being hoisted back up onto the deck of the great ship, he set down the fishermen.

"You saved us," one said, quivering with gratitude (or perhaps hypothermia). "Thank you!"

"You're welcome," said Jerica. She handed the drenched fisherman a piece of paper. "And here's your bill."

The man looked at the invoice in his hand and said, "Um, thanks again?"

While Mr. Flint trotted out some fresh clothes for the refugees, Jerica tossed Gustav a towel, and the two walked down the deck together. "I've got to admit it, Gustav. You were right," she said. "With so many idiots trying to sail ships these days, we're making even more money as a rescue ship than we used to rake in with piracy."

"I told ya," Gustav replied, yawning. "I just wish I wasn't so darn tired."

"I've been telling you—you can't spend this long at sea living on nothing but hardtack," Jerica scolded. "We've got to get some protein into you."

"Then catch me a cow," Gustav said.

Jerica touched her finger to his chin and cooed, "I think you're just afraid that all those ugly blotches are going to mar your gorgeous face."

Gustav turned bright red. "That is not what I think!" he snapped.

Jerica laughed loudly. "Oh, you are such an easy mark," she chuckled. She called up to the wheelhouse. "Mr. Key, take us into port. Gustav needs a steak."

The *Dreadwind* pulled into Yondale Harbor the next day. As the boarding plank was lowered to the dock and the crew was about to disembark, there was a sudden rush of wind, and Smimf appeared on board. He rushed straight to Gustav.

"Sorry for the interruption, sir, Your Highness, sir," the messenger said. "But I have an urgent message for you." He handed a note to the prince and vanished just as quickly as he'd come.

"What is it?" Jerica asked, peering over Gustav's shoulder at the letter.

Gustav's expression became serious. "It says to go to the Boarhound . . . poz-thah-stee?"

"Posthaste," Jerica said. "It means fast. So what are you going to do?"

"Apparently, I'm not going to eat a steak."

Duncan sat on his throne in Castlevaria with Snow White in hers beside him. A long line of waiting citizens filled the polka-dot carpet before them, each person waiting for his or her chance for an audience with the royal couple. It was tiring business, but Duncan and Snow didn't mind. They enjoyed chatting with their people. It was what they had done every day since becoming king and queen of Sylvaria.

King King and Queen Apricotta had decided that ruling a kingdom was far too dangerous of a career for them, so they retired and handed the reins of the kingdom over to their son and daughter-in-law. The former monarchs left the castle and moved to Duncan and Snow's old estate in the country—which, as you can probably guess, did not make the dwarfs very happy.

"Hello, Sylvarian," Duncan said to the woman at the head of the receiving line. "Or should I just call you Sylvie?"

"My name's Agatha," said the woman.

"I'm so sorry to hear that," said Duncan. He thrust his chin high and loudly declared, "Your name is now Sylvie! Next!"

"But . . ." the woman began to say, but she was quickly ushered out by Mavis and Marvella, the "royal helpers."

"Come this way, Sylvie," said Mavis.

An old man approached the throne. "King Duncan," he said. "I lost one of my shoes while fighting in the rebellion. I've had one bare foot for three months now. I was hoping you might find it in your heart to provide me with a replacement."

Duncan thought about this for a moment. "Which side did you fight on?"

"Yours," the man said, rolling his eyes.

"Well, okay then," the new king said.

"I can crochet him a new shoe," Snow offered.

"Ooh, you're a lucky man," Duncan said. "Snowy—I mean, Queen Snowy—is a wiz with the needles. She even knit our crowns. Have no fear, sir; your feet will be in good hands."

The man was led away. But before the next person in line could speak, there was a burst of wind, and Smimf appeared. "Sorry to cut in line, sir, Your Highness, sir, but I have an urgent message for you."

Duncan and Snow read the letter as Smimf took off.

"I suppose we should go to the Boarhound," Snow said.

Duncan furrowed his brow. "But I'm a king now," he said. "I'm needed here, aren't I?"

"No!" shouted the people in line.

"Well, I guess it's settled then," Duncan said. He and Snow stood up and began to walk out. "Mavis and Marvella, you're in charge while we're gone!"

The twins clapped their hands and hopped into the thrones.

"Who's next?" asked Marvella. "No, wait. Who's fifteenth?"

"All requests must be made in song," Mavis announced.

"They'll do fine," Duncan said, nodding, as he and Snow left the castle.

In his cozy log cabin in the northern hills of Avondell, Ruffian the Blue was propped up in bed with a book. He was relaxed. So relaxed, in fact, that he had his hood down. And then Lila burst in, carrying a tray of food. She pulled the book from his hands—losing his place in the process, which made the old bounty hunter frown—and plopped the tray onto his lap.

"Here you go, Ruff," she said. "Eat up! You've got to get your strength back."

Ruffian squinted skeptically at the array before him. There were two blocks of cheese, a mug of well water, a roughly torn hunk of bread, four apples, a bowl of radishes, and a large onion.

"What?" said Lila. "I don't cook."

Ruffian put the tray aside. "Lila, I appreciate your desire to speed my recovery, but eating scads of raw radishes is not going to help," he said. "Now, you may have provided a magical shot to my immune system, but I was probably no more than a few breaths from death by the time it kicked in. It is going to take a very long time for my body to overcome the effects of that venom. I may never get back to the shape I was in. In fact, my bounty hunting days may be over."

"Impossible!" Lila snapped. "You're the best bounty hunter in the land!"

"I was," Ruffian said. "But now I think somebody else is."

Lila shuddered. "Ugh. Don't tell me it's Wiley Whitehair," she said with disgust. "He can't even sneak up on people because his skin crinkles so loudly."

"No, Lila," Ruffian said in a monotone. "Not Whitehair."

Lila cocked her head. "Orangebeard, then? Yellow Tom? Beige Barney? Marvin the Maroon?"

Ruffian gave her a deadpan stare. "Sometimes, young lady, I cannot even understand how you—"

Lila cracked up laughing. "I'm just joshing with you, Ruff," she said. "It's me, right? I'm the best?"

Ruffian let out a long, slow sigh. "Yes, Lila. It is you."

"Yes!" Lila crowed. She ran to the door of the cabin, threw her bag over her shoulder, and grabbed her quarterstaff. "So this means I get to go on missions by myself, right?" she called in to her bedridden mentor.

"Yes, but—"

"Great! First thing I'm going to do is—"

"You are *not* going to try to find my daughter," Ruffian said sternly.

Lila walked back to his side. "But, Ruff," she said, "if I can find her for you, you'd have somebody to love and to be proud of, somebody who could love you back and take care of you."

Ruffian said nothing in reply; he simply picked up the breakfast tray and placed it back on his lap.

There was as knock on the door, and Lila answered it.

"An urgent letter, Miss, Your Highness, Miss," said Smimf.

Lila opened the letter and read it. "Hey, Ruff," she said. "I think I have my first assignment."

"Belly hurt," Mr. Troll moaned. He lay on a long table under the shade of Rapunzel's porch roof. He patted his long, green claws against his shaggy tummy.

"Go ahead, Frederic," said Rapunzel, who was standing nearby. "The patient's a friend of yours; you can take the lead on this one."

"Um, well, yes, let's see," Frederic stammered as he strapped on an apron and pulled long gloves over his hands. "Have you eaten anything unusual today?"

"Only carrots," said the troll.

"How many?" asked Deedle. He and Blink were

hovering across the table from Frederic, waggling their antennae.

"'Bout six hundred," said the troll.

"Well, I think we've gotten to the *root* of the problem," Frederic said. He and Rapunzel chuckled. The sprites rolled their eyes.

"Well, Mr. Troll," Frederic continued, "I think you've simply eaten too much. If you—"

Trumpets blared as ten armored soldiers approached on horseback, escorting a very ornate carriage. When the coach stopped, Frederic was surprised to see Reginald step out—but he was even more shocked to see who exited after the valet. "Father? You . . . you've left the palace?"

"This is something I could not leave to a mere messenger," King Wilberforce said as he approached and placed his hands on Frederic's shoulders. "I am proud of you, Son. And I want you to know that all is forgiven . . . at least from my end." There was a sadness and humility in his downcast eyes that Frederic had never seen before. "I want our family to be back together again."

"I forgive you, too, Father," Frederic said. "And believe me, there is a *huuuuuge* part of me that misses life at the palace. But . . . well, hold on." He turned to Rapunzel. "I don't suppose there's any chance you'd come back to Harmonia with me."

"Oh, Frederic," she said, her voice heavy with regret. "But my calling . . ."

Frederic's eyes lit up. "What if you could practice your healing arts in Harmonia? We have plenty of resources, you know. What if we promised to build you the biggest, most advanced clinic in the Thirteen Kingdoms? It could have all the latest medical technology: toadstool grinders, ointment spatulas, leeches—you name it. Really. I'm a prince—I might as well start taking advantage of it."

Rapunzel was stunned by the possibilities. "Well, that would certainly change things," she said. "I could care for so many more people. And so much more effectively! And you and I could still be together! Oh, thank you, Frederic!"

"Well, um, speaking of you and we— I mean *me,* we and me . . . No! *Us,*" Frederic stammered. Rapunzel raised an eyebrow. "Sorry, um, what I'm trying to say is . . . um, you make me happy. And happiness is good. So I was wondering if, maybe, it would be at all possible that, in addition to coming back to Harmonia with me and, you know, opening the clinic, if, well, maybe you'd like to marry me as well."

Rapunzel couldn't hold back her laughter. "Now I see why they call you Prince Charming," she said, her face aglow. "But, yes. Yes, of course I will, Frederic."

Frederic beamed. "I'm sorry I don't have a ring," he said. Mr. Troll grabbed Deedle and yanked off the sprite's belt. He handed it to Frederic, who slipped it on Rapunzel's finger.

"Wait one moment," King Wilberforce said, stepping up to the couple with a jingling of unearned medals. "Frederic, might I remind you of your position? You are of noble blood. Any bride you choose must be of the proper ilk."

"And . . . ?" Frederic said sternly, holding Rapunzel's hand tightly as he stared directly into his father's eyes.

"And . . . ," said King Wilberforce. He swallowed loudly. "And that is why I want to say: Welcome to the family, Miss Rapunzel."

Everyone present, including the soldiers, cheered. They hadn't even noticed the sudden whipping wind as Smimf appeared.

"Congratulations on your impending nuptials, sir, Your Highness, sir! I have an urgent message for you. Good-bye!"

"What is it?" Rapunzel asked as Frederic read the letter that had been thrust into his hand.

"Any chance you'd like to honeymoon at the Stumpy Boarhound?"

The thief slowly crept out of the window of the village hall, the solid gold town seal tucked neatly under his arm. He was completely unaware that Ella, Mistress of the Sword, was watching him from the roof of the house next door. As the thief made his way down the alley between the two buildings, she pounced.

Unfortunately, Liam, who had been waiting in ambush just around the building's corner, leapt out in his own attempt to intercept the thief. Ella's boot connected with Liam's jaw. He hit the wall, and she landed, ungracefully, on her back.

"What are you doing here?" she snapped at Liam as she sat up.

"What are *you* doing here?" Liam snapped back, holding his aching jaw.

They both laughed.

"How long are we going to keep doing this?" Ella asked, standing up.

"I don't know. It is kind of silly, isn't it?"

"Do you think it's time . . ."

"Time we gave our partnership another try?"

They shook hands. And their hands stayed clasped together a bit longer than most people's do when they're just shaking hands.

"Oh, no," Ella said with sudden urgency. "The thief!"

The man who'd stolen the town seal was almost two blocks away already. They took off after him. "He's heading toward the old mill," Liam said as they ran.

"Keep him moving in that direction," Ella said. "I know a quick way around." Liam nodded, and they split up.

Running at top speed, Liam gained ground on the crook and chased him along the side of a creaky old watermill. At the corner of the mill, Ella jumped out and surprised him. He was trapped. Ella bopped him on the head.

"That worked rather nicely," she said.

"Indeed it did," Liam replied. "Partner."

They were halfway finished tying up the thief when—*WHOOSH!* Smimf.

"This place looks amazing," Jerica said as she stood outside the Stumpy Boarhound. "Why didn't you take me here sooner?"

Gustav chuckled and reached for the door as Frederic and Rapunzel came up the block.

"Gustav!" Frederic called. "We're getting married!"

"Tassels! That's awesome!"

"Hello, friends of King Duncan!" came a cry from down the alleyway. Duncan and Snow ran up to join them. Ella and Liam were not far behind.

"Ho, there, brother!" Lila chirped, leaping down from a nearby rooftop.

"Um, hey," said Liam. "Nice to see you all, but what's the emergency?"

"We don't know," said Frederic. "None of us has been inside yet."

Gustav opened the door, and they all stepped into the tavern.

Something was wrong. There were no shouted curses, no sounds of plates shattering over someone's head. It was quiet. And virtually empty.

Liam looked to Ripsnard, who was spit-shining wine glasses behind the bar. The tavern keeper smiled at him warmly. "Hey, League o' Princes," he said.

"Where is everybody?" Liam asked.

"I kicked 'em all out," Ripsnard replied.

"Why?" Frederic asked.

"Because I paid him to" came the reply from across the room. All heads turned toward the Official League Founding Table in the far corner, where Briar Rose sat in candlelight, tenting her fingers deviously. "It's not like this place has a private room, so I decided to make the whole tavern private. Come, sit down. And pull up some extra chairs—there are more of you than I expected."

The whole gang moved toward the back table. Some sat down immediately, while others, like Lila and Gustav, did so a bit more cautiously. Ella remained standing.

"Come, come, now," Briar said. "I don't bite. Much." She flashed a sly grin.

"It's okay, Ella," said another voice. Val stepped out of a shadowy corner to stand behind Briar.

"Val," Ella said, shocked. "How did you get involved with all this . . . whatever this is?"

"I have a new job," Val said with pride. "I'm the princess's bodyguard."

"Princess." Rapunzel repeated the word to herself. "Wow, I guess I'm going to be a princess now, too. That's going to take a lot of getting used to."

"You'll fit right in at the palace," said Frederic. "Everybody there likes turnips."

"Maybe I can cook up a big pot of soup as a peace offering to your dad when I move in," Rapunzel added.

"I'm a queen," said Snow. "I can move in any direction I want."

"And I'm a king," said Duncan, "But I'm still King King's son, so does that means I'm also a prince? Maybe I'm a pring. Or a—"

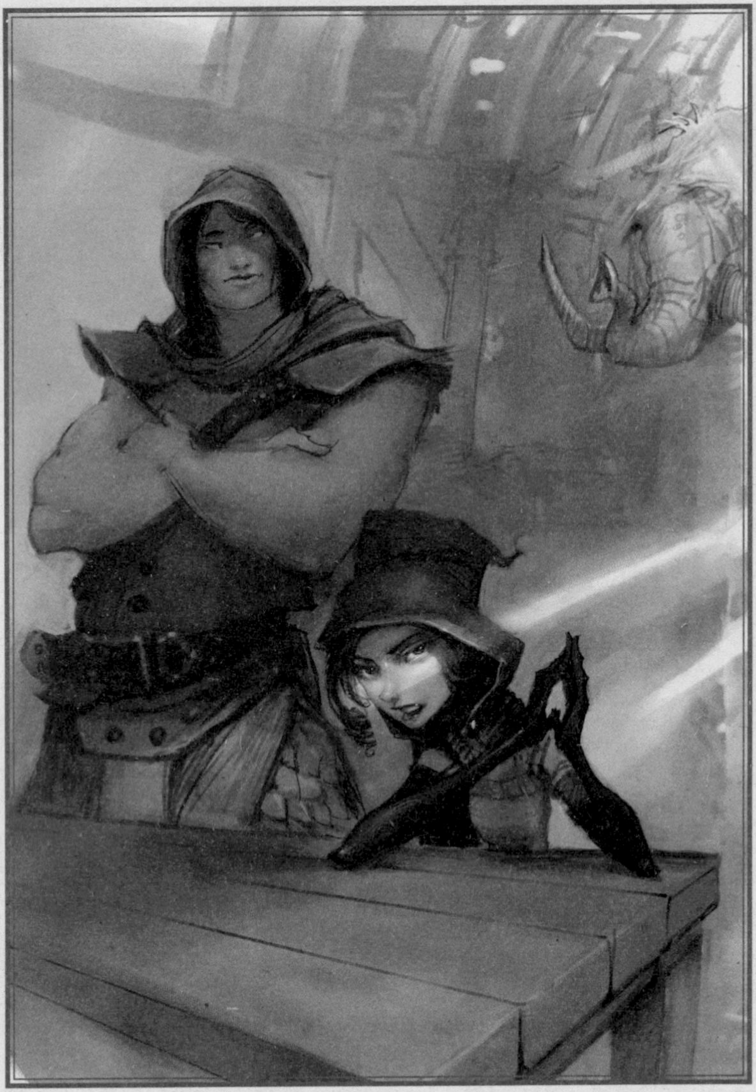

"Quiet," Liam said—and everybody instantly stopped talking. "In retrospect, I am so happy I made that wish. Now, Briar, why did you summon us all here? What's so urgent?"

"Well," said Briar, tapping her gloved fingers on the table. "I suppose it's not all *that* urgent. But, hey, it's me—I like drama."

"So this was all some sort of joke?" Gustav grunted.

"Oh, no, darling. I am always serious. Deadly serious," Briar said. And then she laughed. "Just shut up and listen. I've learned of this beast—a colossal, hairy brute—who's been kidnapping people and dragging them off to some old castle in Carpagia. He claims to be some sort of 'cursed prince' looking to retake his rightful place on the throne, but I'm not buying it. "

"And why exactly are you telling us this story?" Liam asked.

"Ha! And you call yourselves heroes," she scoffed. "Someone needs to stop the beast. And it sounds like a job for us."

"Us?" ten voices asked at once.

"Yes, us. The League," Briar said. She sat back in her chair and crossed her arms. "So are you in?"

Glances were exchanged around the table. There were

some uneasy winces, a couple of ambivalent shrugs, a few determined nods, and one delighted giggle (but only because Duncan had spotted another funny caterpillar).

"Well?" Briar asked impatiently.

I think you can guess the response.

THE END

ACKNOWLEDGMENTS

Thank you to Noelle, my greatest source of support in both life and art. Thank you to Bryn (a.k.a. the real Lila), the strongest, bravest girl I know. Thanks to Dash, whose own talents continue to stun and awe me every day. Thanks to my ever-present, ever-ready, and ever-helpful agent, Cheryl Pientka, and the whole crew at the Jill Grinberg Literary Agency. Thanks to my awesomely skilled editor, Jordan Brown, for trusting me, nurturing my vision, and helping me bring the Thirteen Kingdoms to life. Thanks to Kellie Celia and Debbie Kovacs at Walden Media, my guides through this crazy world of authorship since the very beginning. Thanks to Casey McIntyre and Caroline Sun at Harper-Collins for getting the word out. Thanks to Amy Ryan and her crew for helping me present my stories to the world in such a beautiful package. And on that note, I must also once again thank Todd Harris for the incredible illustrations—Todd, your imagination knows no bounds.

Thanks to the trusted friends whose early input was crucial to honing this manuscript (you know who you are). Thanks to all the bloggers, booksellers, teachers, and librarians who continue to support me and my work. Thanks to all the wonderful readers who have posted online about the Hero's Guides, recommended the series to their friends, asked their school libraries to stock the books, and even hosted Hero's Guide–themed birthday parties (Hi, Lilly!). And a ginormous thank-you to the many friends, family members, neighbors, colleagues, and kindhearted strangers who came to our aid during a time of personal crisis—you are all heroes to me.